I0674932

THE KING
OF SAINT FRANCIS

BLUE BOX BOOKS

THE KING OF SAINT FRANCIS

RETURN OF THE WICK CHRONICLES
BOOK FOUR

All Rights Reserved
©2019 K.A. Thompson

No part of this book may be reproduced or transmitted in any form or by any means without permission in writing from the publisher.

Published by Blue Box Books
www.blueboxbooks.com

ISBN 978-1-932461-67-1

Printed in the United States of America

THE KING

OF SAINT FRANCIS

MAX THOMPSON
WITH K.A. THOMPSON

THE KING
OF SAINT FRANCIS

RETURN OF
THE WICK CHRONICLES
BOOK FOUR

THE KING OF SAINT FRANCIS

PART ONE

1

Jackson Blackshear, King of Pacifica, Midlam, and Florida—the United Kingdom of Pacifica—set his coffee mug on the table, turned on his tablet to check his email and the news, leaned back in his chair, and set his feet on the table. His heels touched and his feet fell to either side, shoelaces clicking against silverware on one side and a plate on the other. He was either oblivious to Hyrum's sharp intake of breath or he simply didn't care, and when his daughter wandered past on her way to the kitchen and mumbled, "Really classy, Dad," he didn't react.

In fact, he hadn't blinked since his dirty, sweat-encrusted running shoes landed on top of the wood table, and from where I sat on the breakfast bar, I wasn't sure he was even breathing. He focused on the tablet, that long, thousand-yard stare that said his brain was elsewhere, and it stayed there until Hyrum could no longer bear it.

"Aubrey's gonna yell at you," he hissed.

Jax blinked and sucked in a deep breath, but he didn't move his feet.

"Jax, she's gonna be really mad."

"Eh. Fuck it," Jax grumbled.

Oz stopped at the edge of the breakfast bar, unsure she'd

heard him correctly, but Hyrum stood up, reached across the table, and shoved Jax's feet off it.

"What the hell, Hyrum?" Jax said, sitting up, surprised at the anger he saw in his brother-in-law's eyes.

"What if one of the babies saw that? They'd think it was okay and they would get in a lot of trouble."

"Saw what?"

Hyrum stomped into the kitchen to grab a cloth and bottle of cleaner and grunted "You know," under his breath as he sprayed where Jax's dirty shoes had been.

Jax set the tablet down. "Hy, I'm tired. It's four thirty in the damned morning, and I was in meetings until after ten last night. Whatever I did, I apologize. But no, I don't know."

"What if Aubrey came out?" Hyrum asked. "She works really hard, Jax. She has lots to do every day and she keeps the house nice and clean, and—"

"What?"

Oz stepped over to the table and nudged Hyrum away. "He's half asleep, Hyrum. I don't think he knows what he did. Go get ready for work. Drew's driving in today, and he'd like the company."

Drew—and Hyrum knew it—didn't want to be the one driving the car. If Hyrum went with him, Hyrum could drive, and he wouldn't spend the ten-minute commute terrified that he was about to slam the front end of the car into a mass of nuns out for an early morning jog along the marina, or a group of early-rising tourists headed for the Golden Gate Bridge to view the city as the sun rose.

Hyrum did as Oz asked and went to his room to get ready for work, and she sat in his vacated chair.

"What?" Jax grunted.

"He's right, and you know it. If Mom had come out and seen you with your feet on the table, she would have had a stroke."

"My feet weren't on the fucking table."

"Dad." She sucked in a deep breath. "Fine. You're tired, I can see that. Why are you up so early?"

Jax was up almost every morning by four thirty, so he

could spend some quiet time with Hyrum before going out to run with Will. Late nights usually meant sleeping in the next day, though, and he skipped the run around Union Square. Hyrum understood that and didn't mind.

"Habit," Jax answered.

"Go back to bed," Oz said as she got up. "Snuggle up to mom, go back to sleep. I'll tell Will you're not running today."

"I'm still running. Why are you up?"

She patted her belly. "This one is taking tap dance lessons and using my bladder as a practice floor. I might as well get some work done, too."

He watched her leave, reaching for his coffee. "So, what of it, Wick?" he said, not looking at me. "What the hell did I do? Did I stick my feet on the table or not?"

You should go back to bed like Oz suggested.

"That's not helpful, cat."

I could have told Will and he could have relayed the message, but it was just a brain fart. He was half asleep and had no idea he'd made himself a little too comfortable at the dining room table; if Aubrey had seen it, she would have made him sit upright and probably sprayed him with the cleaner, wagged her pointy finger and grunted, "Bad boy," but she wouldn't have been that upset by it.

It didn't seem worth mentioning.

Maybe I should have.

Jax exited the elevator with an unknown teenage male and stopped at the apartment entry in time to see his two-year-old nephew Charlie bolt across the living room and down the hall, giggling joyfully, without a stitch of clothing on. Three-year-old Rhys was stretched out on the sofa with the video monitor remote in hand, jabbing at the volume as he tried to drown out the sound of his two-year-old sister's piercing wail.

Alex, Charlie's twin, was one and a half minutes into a royal temper tantrum, a wad of blue cloth clenched in her fist, and she shook it in her tiny rage.

Jax stepped into the living room, leaving his still-unknown companion standing just past the entryway, watching slack-jawed as his King took the remote from Rhys and turned down the sound on the cartoon he was watching, warning it was far too loud.

"But I can't hear it. Alex is screaming."

"She'll stop soon."

"You don't know her very well, do you?"

The Queen sat in her chair, feet up, very much undisturbed by the chaos, though she did have a sharp eye tuned to the naked toddler knocking on a door near the end of the hallway. She barely noticed as Jax stepped over to Alex, hands on hips. "What's your problem, Princess?"

"The t-shirt—" Queen Aubrey gestured to the wad of blue clenched in Alex's fist "—is the wrong shade of blue. It's not a *pretty* shade of blue, and it doesn't have a unicorn on the front.

We won't bring up the fact that she doesn't *have* a t-shirt with a unicorn on it. I doubled checked with her mother to be sure."

Jax bent at the waist, hands on his knees. "Alex. There are no unicorns. They're extinct. Grandpa Eli ate the last one thirty-five years ago."

She stopped screaming and sniffed, "Nuh-uh."

"He did. It was disturbing. Did you know they had rainbow blood? He bit down, and it spurted everywhere. He was covered in sticky rainbow-glitter for a week. But the good news is that he scraped it all up, and then sold it online."

"Weally?"

"That's how they make rainbow cotton candy."

She sat up. "You silly, Unca Jax."

"Want to know where chocolate milk comes from?"

She nodded.

In a stage whisper, he said, "Brown cows."

"Dear," Aubrey sighed. "Really."

I jumped onto the coffee table. Rhys sat up, snickering, because he'd heard the same tired joke from his Uncle Jax before, though the image of the old King, Eli, munching on colorful unicorn flesh was new. And he was about to ask about the boy who waited silently, but heard Hyrum in the hall, telling Charlie—for the hundredth time, most likely—that no one wanted to see his wiener and he wasn't bringing his blocks out unless Charlie put some pants on.

Charlie turned and ran back into the living room, yelling, "Aun' Aubwey, I need pants!" He skittered to a stop when he realized Jax was there and looked up. "No one wants to see my wiener."

Jax caught the diaper Aubrey tossed to him and gestured for Charlie to lie down. "Mr. McAllister," he said, glancing up, "come on in. They're partly feral, but they don't bite."

Mr. McAllister hesitated, leaning forward to look first, and as he stepped in Aubrey popped up and nearly growled at Jax. "You should have said you weren't alone." She rushed over to the confused teenager and reached for his hand. "I'm so sorry. I had no idea you were waiting there."

He tried to bow as she shook his hand, and sputtered, "Mrs. Your Majesty."

That made her laugh. "Just Mrs. Blackshear for now. You're in our home. We leave the titles at the front desk."

"Yes, ma'am."

She stepped back and took a closer look. "I know you, don't I?" Before he could answer, she lit up. "Sean McAllister! You were my student ten years ago. Third row behind Katie Sontag. Carla Woodman spent the year trying to pass notes to you."

"Is it a good thing or bad thing you remember him?" Jax asked as he got off the floor, Charlie now freshly diapered.

"He was a wonderful student," Aubrey assured him.

"Thank you," Sean said, now three degrees more timid than he'd been a minute earlier.

"Mr. McAllister is a reporter with the university newspaper. He asked for an interview, and I have time."

"You just want one more journalist on your side," Aubrey teased.

"To be truthful, I've barely started with the newspaper," Sean said. "The journalism sponsor swore that anyone who could get a short interview with the King would get an A for the semester." He shrugged. "I honestly don't know what I'm supposed to do. I've never interviewed anyone before."

"And yet you had the balls to walk up to the front door and ask the guard for an appointment." Jax turned to Aubrey. "Fortuitous timing. Will and I had just ended a soul-crushing, slumber-inducing video conference with the Consortium and we were headed for the door. I figured, why the hell not? It beats going to city hall and dealing with all the department heads who want just a little bit more."

"Having a day?" she asked.

"It's been a day for the last month," he sighed. "I want to play hooky in the worst way. Find a beach, line up a bunch of umbrella-topped fruity drinks served in pineapples, and then not come back."

Hyrum came down the hall carrying a bucket filled with his favorite colorful plastic snapping blocks and paused to say hello before pouring them out onto the living room floor. Charlie and Alex scooted closer and Rhys slid off the sofa; Hyrum, who was forty-seven going on eight, was their favorite playmate, and as long as they shared nicely, he allowed them to play with his toys, even his favorite ones.

Aubrey gave Hyrum a quick kiss on his cheek. "Sweetheart, this is Sean. We'll be over at the table with him."

"Okay." He wiggled the bucket. "You can play, too, if you want. It's loads more fun."

"Maybe after we're done talking," Jax said, sparing Sean the decision between playing with the King's brother-in-law or interviewing the King himself.

"Relax," Aubrey said to Sean when he stiffened by the table, confused by protocol, not knowing if he needed to wait until they were both seated before he sat down, or if he only needed to wait for the King. "Honestly, we don't follow any strict royal rules at home. Whatever you would do in someone else's home, do here."

He still waited until she was seated before pulling his chair out.

"I'm sorry," he said. "I just—when I was little, I knew my teacher was the Queen, but she also wasn't. You know?"

"And that's how I wanted it. At school, I was just Mrs. Blackshear."

"But she's also your Queen." Jax's reminder was laced with warning: she's open and friendly, but don't get too familiar. "All right. Your first interview. Fair to say, it's not mine. Any idea what kind of story you're planning?"

"Honestly, sir, I hadn't expected to get two words out to your guard."

"The guard who shoots everyone wasn't here today," Hyrum called out.

"Hy," Aubrey sighed.

"Bang!" Charlie barked, slapping a block down before asking Rhys what a *bang* was.

Sean snickered, and visibly relaxed.

Jax turned from the kids. "All right. Might I suggest we just talk? Learn a little bit about our lives here, see where it takes you. Most interviews I grant are with seasoned journalists who are angling for a sound bite or who are looking for the things I don't say, hoping to get a hint of something lurking that might be newsworthy."

I have a million things to tell him that you never say.

"Try to find something most people don't know," Aubrey offered. "Tell a story using the truth. But remember, that truth should be something your readers want to know, something they'll find interesting."

He glanced into the living room. "Well, I don't think most people know that the inside of the royal house has nothing palatial about it. I know I'm not the only one who would be surprised by that." He turned to Jax. "You don't even have a door. Someone getting off the elevator is basically inside your home."

"There used to be a door," Jax said. "Big, wide thing with obnoxiously large knobs. But it was always open, and when my father abdicated Aubrey suggested that the wall be opened a bit. There was no point to a door that hadn't been closed in a decade."

"Every person who lives in this building is family," Aubrey added. "This is their home as much as it is ours. There's no door because we want everyone to feel free to come and go as they please, no matter what time it is."

"Funny how they all show up at dinner time," Jax snorted.

"How much of your family lives here, then? Or is that like a secret?"

"Not a secret," Jax said. "It's public record. Our daughter, Oz, lives here with her husband, Drew. Our son, Zed, and his wife, Sophia, along with their boys, Marco and Jonathan, live in an apartment downstairs. My father, Eli, also has an apartment downstairs."

"His brother, William—most people refer to him as the Emperor—lives upstairs with his wife, Aisha, and those three rugrats," Aubrey said, pointing to the kids. "My brother, Hyrum—" she pointed again "—lives with us. Aisha's son, Jay, lives across the hall from Eli with his fiancée. Did I forget anyone?"

I jumped from the coffee table and ran to the dining room, scrambling to get on a chair where she would see me.

"Oh, yes. And this is Wick. He lives everywhere in this building."

"He runs the damned building," Jax said.

I'm in charge. You finally admit it.

"I've seen the Emperor around town with the cat on his shoulder," Sean said. "Prince Andrew, too."

"Wick is especially close to them," Aubrey said. "It's rare that they can get out the door without him. But when they do, he keeps me company and helps watch the children."

What she didn't tell him—wouldn't tell him—was that Will and Drew understood me. Not on a spiritual level; everyone here *got* me, but they literally understood every word that came out of my mouth. They could hear the words behind each meow; Drew thought I sounded like a young teenaged boy, which fit my small stature. I was no more than six pounds, but sometimes weighed less, which worked in my favor when there were dead and delicious things to eat for dinner.

Aubrey also wouldn't tell him that I was probably four hundred years old, nor that Oz and Jax could see sound and used that to determine when people were lying. Nor that Zed could smell feelings and hear the voices of the newly dead, that she was an empath, that Hyrum could shoot electricity from his fingertips, and especially not that Will could touch a person and hear everything they were thinking. He could take a memory away or plant a thought that felt like one's own, he was freakishly strong...and he wouldn't be born for nearly two hundred years.

The royal family, the House of Blackshear, could travel through time.

Sean McAllister was here to learn about us, but there was so much he should never know.

3

"There was a time when the monarchy embraced some of the traditional trappings of European royalty," Jax explained. He remained at the table with Sean, while Aubrey stepped over to the kitchen to start dinner. "When the old Hilton near the Bay Bridge served as the royal house, it was redesigned and decorated to impress visiting dignitaries, and there were servants on every floor. The King and Queen had personal valets and secretaries, cooks, housekeepers—name it, they had it. The children had nannies and private teachers and were insulated from the world. King Norval railed against it all as being unnecessarily ostentatious, but it wasn't until the reign of Queen Wyatt that normalcy was brought home."

Queen Wyatt did not want her children to grow up with a sense of entitlement; the idea of an American-borne monarchy was, she stressed, to be equal to the people, not above them. Her children would learn to clean their own rooms, scrub their own toilets, wash their own clothes, and they would attend public school. "Our educational system is exemplary," she claimed. "We hold our children to the highest standards, and my own are not exempt from the level of excellence we expect. My children will enter school with their peers and will continue as we expect for everyone."

Her firstborn began preschool at four along with a hundred other little boys and girls in San Francisco, and her other offspring followed until they had each completed a university education.

"Now, granted," Jax explained, "the servants weren't just fired on a whim. She needed help. She admitted that she had no clue how to go about cleaning and cooking and required as much instruction as her children. But she damn well did it. The servants became the teachers, and by the time she abdicated they were no longer needed and were retired with generous pensions."

Sean seemed as puzzled by that as he was by the unpretentious apartment, and the sight of the Queen peeling her own potatoes befuddled him. "There aren't many people who would argue against you having at least a housekeeper and cook. I mean, look at England. They have a dozen castles and hundreds of servants, from drivers to valets that *literally* put the clothes on their bodies."

"And that works for England," Jax said. "Their monarchy goes back over a millennium and is steeped in tradition. Ours is barely a toddler by comparison, and it took time to understand that our traditions needed to be more like the America we'd left behind. We needed to shed the oligarchical trappings that were the downfall of the United States. There's nothing wrong with a head of state living like the man down the street. There's everything wrong with him thinking he's owed more."

The insanely rich were few and far between in Pacifica; privately, the royal family had their investments which gave them a wide measure of comfort. Will, at the very least, was one of the insane, though you'd never know by his spending habits. Publicly, the King's wages were modest and more of a stipend than a salary.

"Your income is public record," Sean ventured. "You haven't had a raise, ever. The council offers you one every year, and you decline. I'm not the only one who wonders why."

Jax held lifted his hands, palms up. "Because of everything here," he said. "We have a comfortable place to live, with room enough for everyone and room within the building to expand as our family grows. We have guards, so our kids and grandkids are protected. I have a personal driver, so I don't need a car of my own. In terms of living expenses, we pay for our food, entertainment, and personal clothing. I get a modest stipend, yes, but with that comes a pension should I retire. There are public investment funds that covered my kids' college educations and their weddings. Our medical is covered."

He took a deep breath. "Besides, if I accepted a raise, I'd have to admit this isn't a temporary gig. To be honest, one of the few things that makes it palatable is the idea that I'm not stuck doing it. So I remind myself of everything we have, and that I can walk away—that makes it a touch easier. Money has a way of tying a person down."

"May I ask, do you receive the basic income entitlement?"

"I don't," Jax answered. "By law, I'm not eligible because my income is guaranteed, and while the Queen is, she doesn't accept it. Neither do our children."

"I don't think Will does, either," Aubrey mused. "I've never asked, but that seems like something he would refuse."

"No, Will takes it," Jax said. "It all goes to the shelter system, though. That was kind of a 'screw you' to my father when he refused to allow Will to accept a job with the shelter when he was seventeen." Jax chuckled. "My dad had other ideas for Will's employment, so Will volunteered instead and set his BIE to pay out to the shelter's children's program."

"The Emperor's playground," Sean said, mostly to himself.

"That's part of it," Aubrey said.

"No, I mean, that's what everyone calls it. The kids who are in it. That playground probably saved my life, Mrs. Blackshear. Before I was your student, my mom and I had to run from my father, with nothing but the clothes we were wearing. My mom had an ID card on her, but that was it. We never spent a night on the street, because the shelter was there and open, and the playground gave me a place to go while she went back to school and then looked for work. I had school, food, playtime, friends… toys. I had to leave everything behind, but they made sure I had things to play with in the apartment they gave us. We never had to stay in the shelter because that same night my mom took me there, we were given an apartment we could call home, rent-free for at least a year until my mom could get onto her feet. We still live there. My mom will die there because it means so much to her."

Oh, she's gonna start crying.

She did.

Just a tear or two, but still. She stopped peeling potatoes and dried her hands with the dishtowel she kept draped over the oven door handle and leaned against the breakfast bar. "How old were you?"

"Four, I think. I saw the Emperor there a few times. I was scared to death of him, too, but there was one time when another kid ran up to him...he was one of the big kids, so he was probably all of six. We'd just finished lunch, and he was still hungry, but the rules were one plate per kid. He saw his shot, someone other than one of the playground staff to complain to, and he took it. He told the Emperor he was still hungry and was *always* hungry, and the Emperor turned to the supervisor and told her, loud enough for us to all hear, that there was plenty, so if we wanted more food, then give us more food. And after that, there was always a big box of fruit and one with cheese and crackers that we could get snacks from all the time. Little cartons of milk and juice. I mean, at first we were like little pigs, and most of us took home as much as we could stuff in our pockets."

"I remember that," Jax said. "They tracked how much was eaten at the shelter and how much was taken home. It led to doubling the food vouchers given to the parents."

Sean nodded. "Those vouchers kept my mom sane. She got a job a couple of weeks after she graduated, but she was always worried about feeding me and was terrified she'd have to leave me at home alone while she worked. But the playground was open day and night, and never turned me away, even after she was drawing a paycheck. Paying for daycare would have destroyed her, you know?"

"Would you like to meet him?" Aubrey asked.

He was spared having to answer when Drew leaped into the living room from near the staircase, startling everyone with a loud "Ta-da!" He was clad in a skin-tight shirt and leggings that showed off more than his muscles.

Charlie jumped up and ran to him, wrapping his arms around Drew's legs. "Unca Dwew!"

The adults, however, were stunned into temporary silence.

"No one wants to see your wiener," Hyrum finally said.

"Stylin,' eh?" Drew said, turning his leg.

"What the hell, Drew," Jax finally said. "Are those ballet tights?"

"Something like that." He plucked the dark blue fabric away from his thigh. "I had an idea—" He stopped when his brain engaged and realized Sean was there. "Oh. Hello."

"This is Sean," Aubrey said. "He was a student of mine, and now reports for the university paper."

Jax turned to him. "There's your story. The arguably brilliant mind of Prince Andrew. Also, no, we really don't want to see his wiener."

4

Leaping into the living room was meant to make the kids giggle, but Drew apologized for embarrassing Jax and Aubrey in front of their guest. They shrugged it off—it was a shame there were no pictures for Sean's article—and Oz suggested he model it again later.

"Not at dinner," Aubrey sighed. "Please. Family-friendly talk only."

Rhys, Charlie, and Alex were lined up on one side of the table. Rhys was in a booster seat, because high chairs are for babies and he hadn't been one in *forever*—which was approximately six months, or a decade in toddler time—and was wedged between his siblings, who didn't care about high chairs and were eating bites of chicken and potato dropped onto their plates by Jax and Aubrey. Other nights, when Will and Aisha were there for dinner, or Zed and Sophia, or even Jay and Navi, the toddlers ate first and then played in the living room where someone could keep an eye on them.

Hyrum and Drew bumped elbows, prompting Jax to muse for the hundredth time that they needed a bigger table.

"That would require shopping," Aubrey said. "I don't have time. Between Hyrum's appointments and his education, furniture shopping seems like a luxury I shouldn't take."

Take Hyrum with you. He'd like that.

Jax looked at Oz and Drew. "Fine. You two do it. Find one like this, but twice as long."

Oz patted her expanding belly. "I'm busy growing another person."

"Yeah, well, take him with you. This family isn't getting any smaller, and we'll wind up sitting on each other's laps on holidays. Make the time."

Aisha knows a great place to buy furniture. Will made her spend a million dollars there, and then they had babies that throw up on everything.

"They did not spend a million dollars on furniture," Drew said.

Well, she complained about how much it cost.

Will stepped into the living room then, and after a chorus of "Daddy!" and giving kisses to his kids, he asked, "Who's complaining?"

"We are," Oz said. "Dad's forcing us to shop for the table *he* wants."

Charlie tilted his head back so he could see his father. "Daddy, Unca Dwew showed us his—"

"I did not!" Drew sputtered.

"Yeah, you kinda did," Hyrum snorted. "And no one wants to see it."

"Ah," Will said. "Do I want to know?"

"Prince Andrew in ballet tights," Jax said. "No, we still don't know why."

"I had an awesome idea about incorporating—" he started, but Will held up his hand to stop him.

"We'll discuss it later," Will said. "If the idea is viable, once you have something to show—"

"I know," Drew sighed. "Father-in-law or King."

"Which one of us will want to know?" Jax asked.

"Both. It's pretty cool. Like, on a scale of one to ten, it's a twelve."

"Sometimes," Jax grumbled, "I kind of hate you both."

Rhys got to his knees and turned to see Will. "I'm trapped here."

"Did you have someplace you needed to be?"

"Yeah."

"Are you done eating?"

"Yeah."

"And where is it you need to be?"

"I gotta pee."

Will lifted him from the booster seat and over the back of the chair. "A more direct way of getting your point across would have simply been to tell me you needed to get up."

Rhys shrugged as he headed for the hall. "It worked."

"That boy is not just three years old," Aubrey said.

"It's worse," Jax said. "He's Will at three. Sarcastic little shit with a big vocabulary."

"Thank you," Will said. "I appreciate the compliment. How'd the interview go?"

"Less an interview, more a discussion." By the time Sean left, he had everything he needed to secure the promised grade from his journalism instructor—a photo of him with the King, taken by the Queen—and a basic knowledge of the royal family, but nothing much that would serve as a basis for an article. Jax suggested he go home and think about it, decide what he most wanted to know, and they would meet again. "I get the feeling he wants to talk to you more than me, though."

"He benefited from the Emperor's Playground," Aubrey explained. "He also seems a bit fearful of meeting you."

"Which means it must happen," Jax chuckled.

"I must admit, I was surprised that you granted him an interview on the spot, and more so that you brought him upstairs to do it. Inviting a reporter, even a student, is not like you."

"I was just as surprised," Aubrey said.

"I caved to an impulse," Jax said.

"Yes, but—" Will stopped when Charlie's arm cocked back.

Jax went on. "He seemed like a good kid, not a gossip-sniffing tabloid wannabe."

Charlie tossed the last bite of his chicken onto the table. "I done. Want down."

"That was rude," Will said to him, though he pulled the highchair away from the table anyway. "Play in the living room while we give Alex time to finish."

"I done," she said, though she shoved her last bite into her mouth instead of throwing it, and around the clump of chicken she asked to get down. After Will let them both out of their chairs, Aubrey told him to sit, and she'd get him a plate.

"Thank you, but I'll wait for Aisha," he said.

"Is it my turn to do dishes?" Hyrum asked, watching Alex toddle after Charlie.

"Mine," Drew said. "Go. I know they want you to play with them."

"Storytime?" Hyrum asked Will. "It's almost their bedtime, and you don't want them excited too much."

Will nodded as he pulled the highchairs out of the way so that he could sit. "Storytime would be helpful, thank you. Though perhaps not one in which things get eaten this time?"

Hyrum laughed under his breath as he headed for the pile of toddlers wrestling in the living room.

"Rhys loves the story about Lazybones and the space monster," Will explained as he sat down. "The other two? The last time he told it, they slept in our bed until we were sure we could move them without waking. And then we worried Rhys would wake them and repeat the story."

"Are you ever giving them their own rooms?" Drew asked. "Control the damage before it starts."

Rhys did not want a room of his own. There were rooms available; Jay had moved to Drew's old apartment downstairs, leaving two vacant bedrooms. For now, all three tiny tots slept in the nursery, and Jay's bedroom had become their playroom. They seemed content to share a room, and Aisha was glad to have a separate place for their toys.

"They'll get their own rooms when they ask," Will said. "So far it hasn't occurred to them, and Rhys declines when offered."

There was a soft knock at the entryway. Rhys popped up from his spot at Hyrum's side and ran to the table, yelling, as if he wasn't two feet away, "Mr. Dalton is here, Uncle Jax!"

Felix Dalton, one of Jax's guards, one of the few who had been in his service since his teen years, stepped into the living room without waiting for further invitation. The knock was a courtesy; any of the guard were free to enter at any time but other than an emergency they each took a moment to warn that they were there.

"Sir," he said, with a nod toward Aubrey, "His Royal

Highness, King Eli, is on your secure line and wishes to speak with you."

Jax got up with a grunt. "What now? Any gossip I should know about, Will?"

"None that has been passed on to me."

"Lovely. He wouldn't call my office this late unless it was important."

Go with.

"No, Wick," Will said as Jax disappeared into the hallway. "If I'm needed, he'll either call me or send a guard."

I can go snoop if you want.

"That's not necessary."

Maybe not, but it might be fun.

Will pointed to Hyrum. "Go listen to the story. Report back if he's telling them about Lazybones and the space monster. That would be more helpful than spying on Jax."

I didn't say I wanted to be helpful.

I went over there, anyway and climbed onto Rhys's lap as he snuggled against Hyrum. Drew finished the dishes and disappeared into the bedroom with Oz, though the door was left open, so I was pretty sure they were only watching a video or reading. Drew might be working; he did more of that in the evenings than he should, but she didn't seem to mind, which meant I didn't need to lecture and remind him of Will's advice to focus on her more than his job.

Hyrum regaled the kids with stories from the Bible. They interrupted frequently to ask questions—why did Delilah cut Sampson's hair? That seems mean. Why did the whale eat Jonah? That's mean, too—but he never lost his place and answered every question he could, and when he thought they were tired of those stories, he promised them a true story, one about a boy who walked across the country with nothing but bread and peanut butter in his backpack, who met angels along the way who kept him safe.

This was their favorite story, and they asked him at least once a week to repeat it. Sometimes, the boy was the hero of his story, the one who never gave up, but most of the time the angels were the heroes because without them he didn't think the boy would have survived.

When Jax came back almost an hour later, the angels had just spent a hard winter with the boy in a cabin, making sure he was warm enough and had food. They came and went, but they left him with a tiny cat who danced with him and listened to his stories every night until he fell asleep. Will glanced up a few times as Hyrum told the story, but when Jax returned, Will was deep into conversation with Aubrey and missed the part when the angels had to leave the boy so he could finish his journey, alone.

They'll know it's true, someday.

Jax sat at the table, quietly, not wanting to interrupt whatever Will and Aubrey found to be so important. They stopped talking, though, and Aubrey asked Jax if everything was all right.

"You first. What's up?"

I jumped off Rhys's lap and went back to the kitchen, in case someone was about to get upset.

Will sucked in a deep breath, which meant he was trying not to lie, because Jax would see the colors around him change if he did. "I have concerns," he said after a moment. "Regarding the young reporter. While I had no issue with giving him a short interview to satisfy his instructor, I'm not sure giving him continued access to the royal family is a good idea."

"In case he sees something," Jax guessed. "Hyrum has his gifts well under control now."

"Rhys," Will started. He was interrupted by his children springing up from their spots by Hyrum, all squealing, "Mommy!" in unison.

"It's a shame they hate it when you two come home," Jax snorted.

"Their joy is brief and easily forgotten." Will gestured to Hyrum; after hugging Aisha's legs, their children abandoned her and returned to snuggle up to him, waiting for the rest of the story. He stood as she approached—he almost always did, unless he had a small child on his lap—and kissed her, and as always, asked about her day.

"Remind me never to volunteer to teach an introductory algebra class again," she sighed. "And heads up," she said to Jax, "one of the communications professors felt it fair to warn me that he offered up a high grade to the first entry-level student to land an interview with you. He doesn't think any of them will try it, but there might be one or two brave souls in his first-year Journalism class."

"There's one brave one." Jax told her about Sean; he'd gotten all he needed for the easy A but wasn't satisfied with that. "He intends to get a story out of this. All he needs is an angle."

"You're setting a precedent," Will warned him.

Jax nodded. "And I'm all right with that. If this goes well, I'm not opposed to an arrangement with the professor. The future caveat is that the grade will require more than simple access to me with a photo as proof. I want the little bastards to earn that grade."

"Set limits," Aubrey said. "Decide now if he's only to speak with you, or if he can interview the rest of us as well."

"That's up to you. Just be judicious. Don't let him see you use a portal, and especially don't let him see you use Will's jump tech. That's information I don't want the world to have. Ever." He looked at Will. "Is it a mistake? I could cut the kid off now without making waves. I think he would understand. Might even be relieved."

Everyone else had escaped to their bedrooms or upstairs. Toddlers needed baths, and Oz thought that sounded like a great idea so she wandered off to soak in water as hot as she could stand; Drew had work to get done and Hyrum had a new box of colored pencils he wanted to use without the help of small children. Aubrey went with Aisha to help bathe kids so that Will could sit and relax for a bit, which was really just an excuse for her and Aisha to eat chocolate and drink wine.

I warned Will that they might get into his very expensive bottle of Chambrizi, brought home from his birth When. He thought it would be worth the price of the bottle because then Aisha's kisses would taste like raspberries.

"Good lord, spare me," Jax uttered. "You don't always have to be so...sweet."

"But I do. Given my certainty that I am not as adept at certain things as I'd like to be, occasionally being sweet makes up for that."

"Yeah, no, being a drippy dork doesn't make up for sucking in bed."

They'd gone out onto the balcony, even though it was cold, and they sipped at hot chocolate instead of scotch. Will used his mug to keep his hands warm and stared down into it.

"While I worry it sets precedence, as long as everyone is careful, it's not a mistake. You've got a strong record of advocating for education in Pacifica, and this will be viewed as the King taking an active role in it. Putting your money where your mouth is, so to speak."

"Damn, what I wouldn't give to just teach again," Jax sighed.

"If not for your travel demands—"

"I know. If I could stay in one place for a semester or two, it would be possible. I don't think there's a school in Pacifica that would want me, though. The security nightmares, the number of kids who would sign up for the class, the media clustering around campus..."

"Private venue," Will suggested.

"Tell me how we could make that happen. You know we can't. I come with too much baggage for anything close to that. Every hoop I'd need to jump through would suck the fun out of it." He set his mug aside. "I hate this job, Will. I fucking hate it."

"And yet, you're so good at it."

"I'm good at a lot of things. That doesn't mean I want to do them for my entire damned life."

You can't quit. Oz is having a baby. She can't be Queen right now.

"Go inside if you're cold," Will said to me.

That's not what I said, and you know it.

"I had a video meeting with Oliphant yesterday," Jax said. "Ever want to reach through a video monitor and just punch the hell out of someone's face? It was everything I could do to keep from going off on that smug bastard."

"He's smug but quite popular in the UK," Will said. "He gets the job done."

"That fucker is compensating for something. Or hiding something. He reminds me of Levi before he attacked Chicago. That smarmy, self-serving—"

"He's nothing like Levi," Will said. "Levi was in Russia's back pocket and overly confident because of it. Oliphant is merely a product of his upbringing combined with knowing he's on point most of the time."

"I'd still like to sucker punch the arrogant son of a bitch." Jax grunted as he got up. "Back in a minute."

He's fun tonight.

"I noticed."

Wanting to punch someone isn't normal.

"We all have those moments. Jax is not immune."

I'm not buying it.

"I'm not selling anything. He's entitled to days like this."

He's not even drinking.

"He's had a long day, Wick. Pacifica is on the precipice of expansion, and what he sees is more work."

Expansion?

"New England." If he was going to explain further, he was stopped by the opening of the door and Aubrey's presence.

Hey. We're talking here.

She stepped out, rubbing her arms against the sudden cold. "Did Jax give up already?"

"A liter of hot chocolate versus a sixteen-ounce bladder," Will said. "I'm sure he'll be back in a minute to regale me with his desire to inflict pain upon Britain's Prime Minister. He wants to punch Cyrus Oliphant."

She sat in Jax's chair. "Punch."

"He's quite irritated at the moment. Irrationally, it seems."

"Will," she breathed.

What?

"He also wants to abdicate and become a teacher again."

"He always wants that. If he could ask Santa to make it happen, he would. Was this spurred on by Sean's interview or... something else?"

"I believe it was the reporter." He sighed. "Largely, the reporter. I have an idea that might ease his frustrations a bit."

He wanted to invite Sean to the upcoming reception for Florida's new Prime Minister. It was a low-key affair, meant mainly to introduce her to people she would encounter often in her work, and it was a wealth of observation material for a budding young journalist and his student colleagues. Jax would enjoy the idea that he was helping Sean learn how to interview publicly, and if possible, guide a camera crew into covering the whole thing.

The presence of student-reporters and cameras would, Will thought, prevent the reception from becoming too political. It would give Jax the opportunity to flex his teaching muscles and might offer him clarity on the aspects of his job that he enjoyed. "It would appeal to his ego, as well."

"He doesn't mind receptions," Aubrey mused. "But that doesn't change the root problem. Will, we both know—"

"Give it time," he said gently.

"How much time, Will? When do we say something?"

Tell me.

"When the time is right," he said, ignoring me. "I'm hoping he'll see it for himself. Give him time for that."

Tell me.

"Wick is freezing," Will said. "Could you take him inside when you go back? He's too stubborn to go on his own."

I'm going to pee on everything you love.

She promised to take me in a minute. "Any idea what Eli needed? I know I shouldn't ask him directly."

Will snorted. "It was a personal matter he felt worthy of a secure channel. The representative from Canada has been flirting with him, and he has no idea how to discourage her. Jax believes he should not."

"When will he move on?" she asked, not expecting an answer.

Eli was never moving on. He didn't want to.

She scooped me up. "Don't let Jax linger out here too long," she said. "If he's not in bed in an hour—"

"Stop worrying," Will sighed.

"You can't make me." She bent down to kiss his cheek. "I'm a lot like Eli, Will. I will never move on."

5

The reception for Florida's newly elected Prime Minister was held at the old Hilton. She'd served in the position following Florida's surrender to Pacifica, appointed by Red Munson in his final act as First Minister as a giant, throbbing middle finger to the former quorum leadership of the Church of Florida.

Florida remained a bastion of old men and repressed ideology, despite Red's efforts to bring equality to their table. They grumbled at the changes he had made while serving as First Minister, wailing that women in the workforce would bring civilization to its knees, and not to mention, who the hell would make dinner every night? Clean the houses? Bathe the children? When Florida fell, surrendering to Pacifica, when Red championed the appointment of a female interim Prime Minister, men revolted. There were riots, violent protests threatening to burn Florida down to its roots. Hot spots erupted from the Carolinas to the Keys. Men marched in the streets, thrusting grammatically-challenged and ill-considered signs in the faces of amused reporters sent to cover the protests for their media outlets. While they threw temper tantrums, women quietly registered to vote, enlisted in Pacifica's military, enrolled in schools, and applied for employment.

On her first visit to Florida since running away at fourteen, Queen Aubrey granted a short interview with a jaded, disinterested local news jockey. He was intent upon using her to prove the point that women belonged at home—after all, it wasn't news that she stayed home to care for her adult brother, so clearly that was an admission that she knew her place.

Weary, Aubrey sighed, and then calmly reminded him of the truth. "I worked as a teacher for over twenty years, came home every day and cooked for my family as well as the guard staff, cleaned house and cared for our children, and did it while also managing my royal duties. The fact that I've now retired from teaching has little bearing on my abilities."

"But you *did* take your place and made sure you followed through with your duties as a wife and mother. And your employment teaching small children was well suited for a woman."

"My duties," she scoffed. "Would it pain you to know that the King of Pacifica was a teacher before he took the throne? Or that he changed as many diapers as I did? That he has no trouble getting on his knees to scrub the kitchen floor or to clean up after a sick child? That he comes home, sees what still needs to be done, and does it without being asked? We are all capable, and I guarantee, the day our daughter becomes Queen she will be an incredibly strong ruler, one of whom you wouldn't dare ask these questions."

She went on to praise the interim Prime Minister for her no-nonsense approach to settling Florida following the short war with Pacifica, making sure the transition was as painless as possible, keeping the Church close but without any say in government function. Her praise was as close to the endorsement of an individual candidate as she dared get, and in the final days of campaigning before the election, when asked her opinion of the candidates, Aubrey declined to answer but thought her praise of Acting Prime Minister Sandra Warren should stand.

Warren felt honored by the announcement of the reception, though privately she'd told Red that the formality of the occasion was something she wasn't looking forward to. She preferred to meet heads of state one on one, saving the massive crush of a governmental occasion for later, when they were all more assured of her abilities and less dismissive of her position as being temporary.

He promised her that Pacifica's receptions were rarely formal and were often more like a cocktail party; this time, the

King had promised a young reporter unprecedented access and would conduct a recorded interview on site. It would be a reception of distractions, ideal for engaging in small talk and then moving on.

"Think of this as more of a practice reception. This is something you can take your kids to. There will be food, desserts, music, and unless they're too tired by new parenthood, the royal offspring will have half the room dancing before the night is over."

Two hours in, there was music playing, but it was soft, and no one was dancing. Jay and Navi stayed home to babysit the sticky people, except for Rhys and Marco, but there was still the chance for the others to shed their parental garb and head to the middle of the floor to goad the old people into doing something other than drinking as much alcohol as humanly possible.

They were waiting, too, because it seemed inconsiderate to disrupt Jax's interview with loud music. He was seated with Sean McAllister near the windows that overlooked the pavilion, doing more prompting of questions than he was answering them. His voice seeped from speakers around the room, and there were teenaged camera operators spread throughout, recording the amused reactions of a dozen leaders of the free world.

"Does that kid realize he's not in control?" Oz asked Drew, not expecting an answer. "Every time he gets close to a serious topic, Dad nudges him away, and I don't think he notices."

Will nodded. He had Rhys on his hip and me on his shoulder, and as he spoke, we both wound up placed gently on the floor. "He won't risk saying anything to offend the people in this room. Mr. McAllister might aspire to find a major story here, but in truth, this is just practice."

He bent over to speak to Rhys. "I'm going to rescue Mommy from the British Prime Minister's wife. You stay here with Drew for a few minutes."

"I can help save her."

"Little man, if you go over there, she'll want to pick you up and hug you, she'll probably kiss you, and we'll spend half an hour hearing stories about her grandchildren. Do you want to listen to stories about kids you've never met?"

He shook his head, vigorously.

"I'll be back in a minute or two."

Rhys looked up at Drew. "That means twenty minutes. He's on Daddy time."

"Maybe you're on toddler time," Drew said.

"I can't even tell time," he said earnestly. He pointed at Oz's belly. "Does that one know when it's time to come out? Mommy says Alex and Charlie came early."

Oz's hands went to her tiny bump. "I hope he knows. He's supposed to be here in time for your Daddy's birthday."

"That's not a very good birthday present."

"I'll get your dad some underwear, too." She patted Drew's arm. "I'll be right back. I see food. I want food."

You should offer to get it for her.

"I know better, Wick. If I'd offered, she'd give me that *look* and then remind me she's perfectly capable of getting her own stuff."

That's when you give her a look of your own and remind her that you're trying to be a gentleman and an example to the munchkin.

"Does Wick want something?" Rhys asked, pointing to the buffet table. "I can go sneak some meat for him. Marco's already eating all the grapes."

Marco was sitting on the floor by the buffet table, a bowl of red grapes in his lap, and he was biting them in half before popping them in his mouth. Zed had noticed, but it was keeping Marco quiet, and he wasn't bothering anyone except for the few who might want grapes that had not been molested by a two-year-old.

"Are you hungry?" Drew asked him. "We can go over and get food, too."

He screwed his face up as he considered it. "I'm not really hungry, but there's strawberries and I haven't had one in years."

Three weeks. He had strawberries three weeks ago. Eli brought them back from his trip to Chile.

"I don't remember the last time I had strawberries," Drew said. "Come on. Let's go grab some before they're gone."

Drew turned and started for the buffet, assuming that Rhys and I would be on his heels. He was halfway across the floor before Rhys realized he was supposed to follow, and as he took the first step toward Drew, a stream of dignitaries and their spouses cut ahead of him, leaving a wall of legs between Drew and us.

"Oh no."

It's all right. He'll come back for you.

"Drew, come back!"

He will. You're safe here. I'll bite anyone who bothers you.

"But I was gonna tell him I needed to—" He sucked in a deep breath. "Oh no. Oh no. Where's Daddy?"

Drew will come back. So will your dad.

"Daddy?" He lifted onto his toes, scanning what little of the room he could see, his breath quickening. "Daddy? *Daddy!*"

A dozen people turned to look at him, but no one moved.

"Where's my daddy?" Rhys cried, his eyes filling. "I need my daddy!"

I promise— Rhys's hand went to his belt buckle, and he dropped to his knees. *Oh. I see the problem. I can lead you there. It's just across the hall.*

"*Daddy!* I need help!"

Big hands slipped under his armpits and lifted him, and before I could look up, Rhys had been slung onto someone's hip and they were heading for the door. I scrambled to catch up, and then climbed Jax's leg and back, settling on his shoulder as he pushed the restroom door open with his foot. "I've got you, kiddo," he said. "Your daddy was all the way across the room. I didn't think you wanted to wait."

Rhys started tugging at his belt before his feet were on the floor. "I need help, Uncle Jax. It's stuck."

Jax set me on the bathroom counter and bent over to help Rhys unbuckle. When his pants were around his ankles, Rhys scowled and decided his suit coat was in the way, so Jax took that and set it next to me and waited quietly while Rhys chose the urinal he wanted and then while he peed.

"That was close," Rhys sighed. Then, "Oh. Uh oh. I gotta sit, Uncle Jax."

Jax gestured to the stall to their right, while Rhys unbuttoned his shirt. "Son, are you planning on stripping for this?"

"Don't want to get anything on my shirt." He looked up. "It's a long shirt."

Jax took it and set it on the jacket and helped Rhys up. "You okay? This is pretty tall."

"I dunno. I might fall in. That happened once at home. Jay laughed, but he fished me out. Then Daddy got a new potty, one I can get on by myself. But not the kind the babies use. Except just Alex uses it now. Charlie doesn't wanna. But one time he peed into the litter box."

Jax started to kneel, to give Rhys something to hold onto.

"No, you're gonna get your pants dirty, Uncle Jax! Daddy puts paper on the floor."

He pulled toilet paper off the roll and set it down to kneel on, telling Rhys to hold onto his shoulders. "I haven't done this in a long, long time," Jax said. "Not since Zed was your age."

"Does Uncle Zed hold onto Aunt Sophia's shoulders now?"

"I'm pretty sure he can manage by himself," Jax said.

"Oh. Yeah. His feet go all the way to the floor. Did you ever fall in?"

"Once or twice," Jax snorted. "I was probably drunk."

Rhys's eyes widened. "When you were *my* age?"

"No, when I was in my twenties. Before I was King. *Someone* had scrubbed the toilet and left the seat up."

"You were twenty?"

"I was probably around Oz's age."

"Wow. That was in the olden days."

"Yes, thank you for that."

"I'm done. I need help or I'll make a big mess. Daddy says it's okay to need help because I'm only three."

"You'll be able to do this by yourself soon enough," Jax promised.

"I'm sorry."

"For what? I don't mind wiping butts, cowboy. And one day when I'm really, really old, you can return the favor."

"Hyrum lets me hold his legs when he helps me."

"Then, by all means, hold my legs." Rhys bent over and latched onto Jax. "Those are my ankles, by the way."

"They're stuck to your legs."

"Point made. All right, let's wash our hands and then we'll get you dressed again."

Rhys sighed, and let Jax lift him so he could reach the sink. When they had finished and Jax was tucking Rhys's shirt in, he asked, "Are you having fun tonight?"

"No."

"Bored?"

"Yeah. Marco doesn't want to play, and Hyrum is talking to a lady who said he was cute, so I don't have anything to do. We didn't bring any toys, anyway. Are you having fun?"

"I am."

"But it's *boring*. You like doing boring things with your friends?"

"Kind of. I don't get to see these people every day, so it's nice when we have casual receptions. We get to talk and have a few drinks together, and we don't worry about anything important."

"Grownups are weird. How come Bree isn't here? Red's here."

"She's busy being a fifth grader, I suppose."

"She's in sixth grade," Rhys said. "She's almost a grownup."

"Does that mean she's weird, too?"

"No. She still likes to play with us. I wish she was here. She makes up games, and they're fun. And sometimes she and Hyrum tell a story together and he laughs so hard they snort. It's funny."

"Ready to go back?"

"Do we have to?" He pointed to the small room near the door, where there were chairs and a sofa. "Can we go in there for a minute? It's for feeding babies, but we won't get in trouble."

Jax led him to the sofa, and once he was seated, Rhys climbed into his lap and rested his head on Jax's chest.

"Tired?"

"I think it's almost bedtime. When are we going home? I bet Charlie and Alex are having their snack right now, and then they get to take a bath and go to bed, and Jay reads really good stories at bedtime. He does voices."

"This will go on for a couple more hours, Rhys."

"Hours?" he asked with a tiny twist of a whine. "But I'm tired now."

Jax gave him a tight squeeze. "We'll sit here for a bit longer. Maybe a little rest will help."

Rest wouldn't stop the tears. Rhys blinked, and they rolled down his cheeks. He pressed his face into Jax's chest, oblivious to the tiny sparks that danced at his fingertips when he clutched his uncle's shirt.

"Okay. You're long past tired." Jax cupped his hand around Rhys's and pulled it up for a quick kiss on his fingers. "Maybe Oz or Hyrum is ready to call it a night, too. I'll find someone to take you home, all right?"

"Does Marco have to stay?"

"He can go home, too, if he wants."

"He's eating all the grapes. He probably wants to go home and throw up."

"If he eats all the grapes, I don't think vomiting is what he needs to worry about."

Rhys snorted a laugh. "He's gonna poop a lot tomorrow."

"Explosively."

"That's a Daddy word. He uses a lot of big words. Oz says he sounds like a history teacher."

"You use a lot of big words, too, cowboy. Did you know I used to be a history teacher? I taught teenagers."

Rhys looked up. "Did you like it? Mommy likes being a teacher."

"I did. I miss it."

"Do you like being a king? Is it fun?"

Jax hesitated. "I liked being a teacher. I had more time for things like playing on the floor with little boys and their blocks and cars than I do now. I miss that, too."

"Daddy says being a king is hard work."

"It can be."

"I don't have to be one, do I?"

"Nope, you get to be a prince and whatever else you want to be." When Rhys yawned, he got up, holding his nephew close.

"Come on, let's find you a ride home. You know, you've been very good for a little boy who's bored out of his mind."

"Mommy said I need to learn to suffer through your crap because there's more of it when I'm older."

"Did she?" Jax laughed. "You're doing good, kiddo. You've been more patient tonight than I think we expected."

"Thank you for helping me poop, Uncle Jax." He tugged at Jax's lapel. "What's that?"

Jax craned his neck to see. "It's a microphone. Mr. McAllister was asking me—goddammit, it's still on."

He yanked the door open and waiting on the other side were Will and Aubrey, amused smiles on their faces. Jax thrust Rhys at Will and reached for the small pack that his microphone was clipped into and yanked the wire out, then grumbled, "How the hell long have you been standing out here?"

"Long enough to enjoy the audio proof of how sweet you are," Aubrey said, rewarding him with a kiss.

Jax had something to say, but Hyrum strolled up and reached for Rhys. "I asked the cat lady to take us home. Is that okay? She said she would make sure that Rhys and Marco and me get inside okay. I'll make sure they get stories and brush our teeth."

"Can I have a snack first?" Rhys asked.

"There are apples and yogurt in the fridge," Aubrey told Hyrum. "A vegetable tray in the drawer, if the boys would prefer that."

"Don't let Marco have grapes," Rhys said. "He ate all the ones here."

"That's his parents' problem," Jax snorted.

"It will be your problem if Marco falls asleep in your apartment," Will said. He looked up; Aisha was headed this way, her shoes dangling from her fingertips. "I told you those shoes were ripe with regret."

"Oh, hush. No, I had an epiphany when Hyrum said he was taking the kids home. I haven't nursed in weeks."

"And?"

"Oh, hon. When this thing is over, we're heading for Fuzzy's and the first booze I've had in close to four years."

= = =

Sean declined the invitation to accompany them to the bar. That felt private, and he'd gotten enough material to start a rough outline of the article he wanted to write. He wasn't done; if the King was still willing, he wanted to interview—or simply observe—him further, but at the close of the reception he was eager to get home and begin scratching out notes.

"The opening to his article will be 'The King of Poop,'" Will said. "Or possibly a paragraph explaining the level of boredom experienced by the King's nephew at a reception for Florida's Prime Minister."

"No," Jax said, "it'll be something about Drew nearly exposing himself to several young children in the Queen's living room."

Drew sighed and leaned back in the booth. "Everything that needed to be covered was covered."

"We could damn near tell your religion, son."

"Oh my god," Drew groaned.

"Did you show them what the tights can do?" Oz asked him.

Drew gave a light shrug. "Will won't let me. He's afraid the King will get super excited and tackle my father-in-law to the floor in order to be the first to get his hands on it."

Oz looked at Will. "The King's going to eventually get it, anyway. It's only got military and law enforcement applications. You want him backing this."

Jax promised to set the crown aside and listen as Drew's father-in-law instead. "Damn near everything you come up with has the government's interest. I've managed to look the other way a few times."

Drew looked at Will, who gave a slight nod.

"Okay, well, you know the exoskeleton my dad created?"

"Standard issue for elite combat troops," Jax said.

"It's amazing tech. Like, super lightweight and damn near impenetrable. Makes you faster, stronger, and you can jump like a damned lion. But it has some major flaws. For starters, there are too many exposed areas."

Drew once shot a soldier wearing the exo-suit in the face. He would know.

"If you're proposing he creates armor as additional cover, it's been done. Test combatants thought it made the suit dangerously uncomfortable and added weight that rendered it top heavy."

Drew nodded. "Yeah, that's the problem. And it still doesn't address exposed skin at the neck and face, not to mention junctures along the abdomen and ribs. But what if we could cover a soldier from head to toe in a material that would make them bullet-proof? And I mean that literally. A suit that can't be penetrated by bullets, lasers, knives—essentially any projectile."

Jax and Will both sat up straighter.

"The tights I had on were made from the base layer that goes under the exoskeleton. What if we could make *that* impenetrable? Make it work in tandem with a transponder, so that with a quick thought, it could expand to cover the head, including the face, and still allow the soldier a complete visual field?"

"That would be a game-changer, Drew."

"It wouldn't be completely impervious, but damn near close."

"And how do you propose altering the base suit to be able to do this?" Will asked.

"Nanobots. I've figured out how to layer and interlock them. They nestle in the fibers of the tights and activate when needed."

"It would mean launching transponder technology," Will mused. "Those transponders won't exist for another forty years."

"But basic transponders *do* exist. They have for centuries."

"The ability to create a cyber-integrated neural network with one does not."

"How big a hurdle is it?" Oz asked.

"Moderate."

"You haven't tested this on yourself yet, have you?" Aubrey asked Drew.

He shook his head. "That would require re-programming my

transponder, and I refuse to risk not being able to communicate with Wick. I would need a second one, I think."

"There's still the issue of its existence," Will said.

"So drag the inventor through a portal and inspire him to invent it a little early," Aisha said.

"No need," Will said, sipping at his scotch. "He's sitting across the table from me. Figure out how it works, Andrew. Create one. If you can do that, we'll proceed. And I remind you, the entire thing needs to be smaller than a grain of rice, and able to connect to one's brain no matter where in the body it's placed. My father initially embedded his in his chest."

Finn picked the center of his breast bone to implant one in himself, then broke it when another version of himself jabbed at it and crushed it. The mistake left him stranded two hundred years from home, which was less a problem than it could have been. Finn from the future had already sent Will to live in this When, and he was on hand to help his father find his way home, though Finn had no idea who he was or that they were from the same century.

To be fair, none of us knew who Will really was. He was the Emperor, a touch-phobic enigma that we alternately adored and were befuddled by.

To be equally fair, I was Will's cat when he was a boy, but my memory was as shot as Finn's, and I didn't remember that fact for a long time, not until Finn activated a program in my transponder that opened the memory floodgates—right before he was going to send me through a portal and to my probable end.

Will went through the portal in my place. When he didn't come back, I followed. And then we both got stuck…time travel is tricky when the world is ending.

And to throw a weird little wrench into all this, I'm probably somewhere around 400 years old.

Yeah…there was a whole lot we weren't telling Sean McCallister.

Not on purpose, anyway.

6

The top to the exoskeletal base layer was stretched out on a wobbly desk in a near-empty room in Ozoo Enterprise's new base at the fringe of the Presidio. On the wall next to the door was an engraved plate that said Research & Development, but most of the work the company was invested in occurred at the warehouse in the Wastelands. Moving was a long process, hindered by sensitive equipment and humidity; there was an unusual excess of moisture in Nevada's air this year, and Will was reluctant to take anything outside of the climate-controlled building until it had abated.

Slap a transporter unit on stuff and jump it over.

"If we still haven't moved it by the end of February," Will allowed. "I'm not confident about jumping objects as large and as sensitive as the computers and cooling tanks."

That means you didn't even think to consider it.

You're welcome.

Drew clipped wires to the hem of the shirt and plugged those into a hand-held control panel. "This will function in place of a transponder. It's voice activated, and the nanobots should respond to whatever I say. I hope."

Half under his breath and full of hope, Drew uttered, "Engage." When a dark blue metallic sheen spread across the material, he grinned and then picked it up and tested its weight. "Super lightweight. This is only about half the nanobot coverage I expect in the final product, but it won't weigh much more."

Will took it from him. "Add the weight of the cowl and

the pants…I don't imagine the entire thing will feel like much different than an under-garment. Which I assume is your intention?"

"Only under the exoskeleton."

"Make it a bit more modest and it could be a uniform unto itself," Jax mused.

"Modesty issues can be overcome with the use of a dance belt." Will handed the top back to Drew. "Do you have a completed set?"

"Sort of. It's cobbled together with basting stitches. I don't think it will hold together if a person puts it on, but I managed to get it onto a drone." He gestured toward a door behind them. "I didn't want to bring it out in case the kid reporter was with you."

The drone, a nonfunctional android—it was an early working model, decommissioned when it became obsolete, its functions insufficient for deployment to the space station Elysium—had been perched on a rolling pallet and looked like an oversized toy. It had never been given the humanoid face its descendants received, and only had an oval, smooth faceplate. The head was the right size, though, and it had arms, legs, and a torso, so for demonstration purposes, it was adequate.

Drew clipped the controller to the waistband of the pants and let it dangle. He stepped back, uttered "Engage," and the suit came to life; in barely a blink it was covered in a dark blue metallic sheen, and a slip of fabric enveloped the drone's head. Nothing of the drone remained visible.

"That part works. I'd like it to be a silent command, initiated by a thought."

"You'd have to have wicked control of your thought processes," Jax mused. "Some poor kid is going to think 'Yeah, I'd like to get engaged to this totally hot woman' and that thing will kick on and ruin the moment."

"Why would anyone wear this in an intimate endeavor?" Will asked.

"Why would a soldier take it off?" Jax countered. "This would be for the elite units, right? The men and women who are always on call?"

"We can change the activation commands," Drew sighed. He reached under the wobbling table for a small box and opened it. "Let's try ballistics."

The drone was returned to the small room it had been stored in, placed where it was visible from and centered in the open door. Drew held the box out to Will, and he reached in for the handgun that had been stored in pieces, and we waited while Will assembled it, inspected it, and then loaded one bullet into the chamber.

"Why does he get all the fun?" Jax sighed melodramatically.

"He's the only one of us who's ever fired one of these," Drew said. "I've seen them in movies, but this is my first up-close encounter with an antique gun."

"Why not use a laser pistol?"

"Because," Will answered, aiming, "the idea is to test explosive impact. We could throw rocks at it, but that wouldn't tell us enough about speed and impact."

Drew and Jax stepped back, and Will pulled the trigger. There was a bright flash at impact, and after Will set the gun down, Drew ran into the room to check the drone.

"Not a freaking dent." He slid his fingers over the slightly discolored spot the bullet had bounced off and then slipped his hand under the top. "I don't feel any damage to the drone's surface."

He didn't want to remove the top to check, in case the stitches fell apart.

Will told him to have the suit disengage; he wanted to test the sensors. He loaded another round and then fired at the drone again; a millisecond before impact, the nanobots activated and the bullet fell to the ground.

"Please tell me you have a laser pistol here," Jax said.

"You're kinda hoping the droid will explode, aren't you?" Drew snorted.

"Maybe."

"Sorry, but no. I don't think it would hold up to that just yet. It needs a tighter weave and another layer, I think."

"Also," Will said as he took the gun apart, "Drew has a soft spot for that particular drone. He's already laid claim to it for display in his office."

"Is it a lady drone?" Jax teased. "What's her name?"

Drew's face flushed. "Hypatia."

"Named for someone who is believed to be one of the first female mathematicians," Will said before Jax could poke harder.

It didn't stop him. "And does she have a middle name?"

"Aisha," Will said. "Go on. Try to make fun of that."

"You're kidding, right?"

"He's kidding," Drew said. "And before you get all 'Oh no, AI is the devil,' this is the only drone I've named, and not until it was removed from service."

"Good. Now explain why the nanobots aren't continuously activated. The material is light enough. Why not make the whole thing an armored uniform without the need for the transponder?"

"Heat dispersion," Drew answered. "When the nanobots are interlocked, the suit will retain a fair amount of body heat. When they're not locked—" he moved his hands from a flat position to palms facing an inch apart "—they allow for air movement. Without that, it would feel a lot like wearing a plastic suit. You'd sweat like crazy, and eventually pass out."

"You make a habit of wearing plastic clothing?" Jax asked. "Do I want to know what kind of kinky things—" Jax would have kept poking, but the door opened and Vicat came in, Rhys trailing a few steps behind.

"Apologies," she said. "The Queen asked me to bring Rhys. His brother and sister aren't feeling well, and she thought he would be better off out of the house until his mother gets home."

Will held his arms out, an invitation for Rhys to run and jump up. "What's up with Charlie and Alex?"

"They have stuffy noses, and Aunt Aubrey says they're whiny, and Charlie said he was gonna rub snot on me."

"Yeah, that's going around," Drew said. "It's just a head cold. How's Hyrum? He would have played with you in his room away from the cooties."

Rhys shrugged.

"Hyrum has a therapy appointment today," Jax said. "Where's Oz?"

"Wastelands," Drew said. "Just for an hour or so."

The Wastelands were Oz's pet project. It covered more than half of Nevada, land scorched by overuse of an old solar farm, a place where little grew and if dust could be harvested and sold, it would be a cash crop. She'd had an idea to build an old west theme park there, something that sprung from Jax's childhood notion that the Wastelands were the perfect image of a town from the 1800s, with saloons and dirt streets, where horses were tied to posts outside, and men swaggered with pistols strapped to their hips.

She wanted to turn his image into reality and was three years deep into execution. The town center had been built; it was a two-mile stretch of newly constructed history, with hotels and theaters hidden behind pseudo-crumbling facades. Past the northern end of the street, construction was underway to build an amusement park, one intended to give patrons a taste of the fun they could find just an hour and 320 miles away in Disneyland.

"The Wastelands, Vegas, and Disneyland," she'd said. "The Pacifica Triangle. Done right, it will be a tourism magnet."

Investors agreed and plunged their resources into a ten-year project.

"I brought a book with me, so I won't be in the way," Rhys told Will.

"You're never in the way. What are we reading today?"

"Drew gave me a big book. Harry Potter. He says it's really, really old but lots of fun."

"Was I right?" Drew asked.

Rhys nodded enthusiastically. "Are wizards real?"

"There are none that I'm familiar with," Will said.

Drew snorted. "Well..."

"Simulated wizards don't count."

"Is magic real?" Rhys asked.

"Science is real," Will told him. "Sometimes it seems like magic." He turned and pointed to the drone still in the office. "See that? Do you know what it is?"

"It's a robot."

Drew pushed it out of the office and to the middle of the floor where Rhys could get a better look.

"What's it wearing?" Will asked.

"Tights like Alex likes. Only hers are red. Charlie likes them, too, but only the pants."

Will set Rhys down and told him to touch the tights to see what they felt like, and then come back. While Rhys ran a finger over the drone's knee, unimpressed, Will pulled his shoe off.

"Now, throw this at it."

Rhys looked at the shoe but didn't take it. "That's mean."

"I promise, you won't hurt it."

With a sigh, he took the shoe and lobbed it at the drone. Just before contact, the suit engaged, and Rhys squealed. "How did it do that?"

"You decide. Was it magic or science?"

Rhys didn't answer. Drew uttered, "Disengage" and the suit reverted, which prompted Rhys to pull his own shoe off to chuck at the drone. When the suit engaged again, Rhys skipped over and ran his hands over the shiny surface. "How does it do that?"

"Well, you know the nanoglobe you have in your room?" Drew asked. "The one with all the shiny things inside that move to music? That's what's on this suit. It reacts to impact the same way your globe reacts to music."

"What's that mean?"

"It means," Will said, "that these tights are made to protect the person wearing them. To help them not get hurt. Have you decided? Is it magic or science?"

Rhys looked up. "Why not both?"

"Indeed. Why not?"

"Did you make this?" Rhys asked Drew.

He nodded.

"Was it fun?"

"Sure. I have fun all the time when I work. I get to take things apart and see how they work, then I get to make something better."

"Daddy, can I do science like Drew does?"

Will started to answer, but Drew snorted and said, "Kiddo,

you're so far ahead of the curve already that when you're my age, you'll be doing science that really will feel like magic. You're probably smarter than I am, and at least as smart as your dad."

"Andrew—"

"I know. Being smart isn't the most important thing in the world. But Rhys has an amazing brain." He squatted so that he was eye level with Rhys. "Do you know why I keep giving you big books like Harry Potter?"

"They're fun."

"Lots of fun. But they're also important. They're big books with big ideas, and you understand them. That's where the magic is." He tapped Rhys's forehead. "It's all in here. You're going to have a lot of magical ideas, and if you keep reading and learning, you'll be able to make them happen."

A flash of worry crossed Rhys's face. "But I like comics and little books, too."

"So do I. That's all part of the magic. Little books can give you ideas, too. Comics can help you see the idea build right in front of your eyes."

Rhys looked up at Will.

"Andrew is right, Rhys. It doesn't matter what you read, but it matters that you keep reading. In fact—" he reached down to pick Rhys up again "—how would you like to have a later bedtime? If you promise to read for twenty minutes, you can stay up half an hour later."

"Promise?" He squished Will's cheeks together, the same way Hyrum did when he sat on Jax's lap and was being serious. "A whole half hour?"

"I promise."

Rhys touched his forehead to Will's. "I have witnesses, you know."

"I am aware." He set Rhys back down. "Help Drew put the drone away, and we'll go to the bakery."

"You are so screwed," Jax chuckled.

"Aisha and I have already discussed it."

"No, I mean overall. He's *three*, Will. By the time he's a teenager, you won't know which way to turn."

Will watched as Rhys patted the drone's knee and told it goodbye. "No worries there. He may be, as Drew says, ahead of the curve, but he's innately sweet, and I don't think he'll lose that."

Even Vicat laughed.

7

Sean McCallister stood with his hands clasped behind his ramrod-straight back and apologized profusely for allowing Jax to get even three feet from the interview chair with his microphone still on. It was something he hadn't given any consideration to, not until he realized that everyone at the reception could hear the King taking care of his nephew in the restroom. "If it caused a lot of embarrassment...I am really sorry."

"I was not embarrassed," Jax assured him. He looked at Rhys, who sat opposite him at the table outside the bakery and who was breaking his cinnamon roll into long strips. "He needed a little help. Nearly every adult who was in that room is a parent and has done the exact same thing."

"Absent an audience," Will chortled.

"Everyone poops," Rhys said as he shoved a long, icing-coated strip into his mouth.

"Sit down, Mr. McAllister," Jax said, gesturing to an empty chair next to Rhys. "I assume that because the interview was interrupted, you still need more information?"

Sean did as he was told and sat down, glancing nervously at Drew who clearly found it all amusing.

You used to be afraid of Jax, too, you know.

"I have enough to write an article," Sean said.

"But?"

"But...I admit, I'm insanely curious about your life and what day-to-day things are like for the royal family. You're all a hell of a lot more normal than I expected."

At that, Drew barked out a laugh.

"What's so funny?" Rhys asked.

"He thinks we're normal," Drew said, gesturing to Sean.

"Oh. No. We're magicians." Rhys picked up a strip of his cinnamon roll and held it toward Sean. "You want a bite?"

As Sean declined—politely—Will told him that was probably a wise choice, given that Rhys had licked the entire roll before disassembling it.

"Only some of the frosting," Rhys said.

"People generally prefer their food absent of little-boy spit," Will said.

"But you've had a bite when I've licked something." He broke a piece off and leaned toward his father. "You want some?"

Will generally avoided junk food, but he took the small bite and popped it into his mouth. "Thank you. And yes, I don't mind a little of your spit. Other people do."

"You didn't want Charlie's spit before."

"That's because Charlie had sucked on that cookie for ten minutes. It was soaked."

"How come you don't like cookies?"

"Because," Will said, "I prefer fruit when I want something sweet."

"I was supposed to get strawberries last night," Rhys said, squinting at Drew.

"He hasn't had them in *years*," Drew told Will.

"Do you ever get to have strawberries?" Rhys asked Sean.

The question caught him by surprise. "Well…no. I had a few once, when I was little. Mostly we had apples and bananas for fruit. Sometimes grapes, when they were in season. I thought they were pretty rare."

"Were," Jax said. "The climate in the southern part of California has stabilized enough in the last decade to re-incentivize its growth. And we now have a strong trade agreement with Chile for off-season fruit imports."

"What do they get in exchange?" Sean asked.

"Tech. We import their fruit and export our vehicles and computer parts. Midlam exports grain and industrial equipment.

In another twenty years, I expect we'll be able to farm most of our own fruits in season."

"And hydro-farm offseason," Will said. "Though it may still be more cost effective to import."

"What's import mean?" Rhys asked.

Will gave him a brief explanation; I watched Sean more than Rhys because he seemed fascinated by Rhys's genuine interest. Will told Rhys just enough to give him a mental image of one country buying things from other countries, enough that he assumed it was like picking out a toy online and having it delivered. He took issue with the notion that it was necessary.

"But I know where we can buy strawberries right here, Daddy," Rhys said, earnestly.

"And where's that?"

"On the pier near the seals, from the man with the little outside fruit store. Hyrum and me got some plums a few weeks ago. Can we go there today and see what he has? Maybe he has strawberries."

"We can. But we're walking. Even uphill."

Rhys nodded. "I can walk that far."

You're carrying him in a mile, you know that.

Jax lifted a hand as if he were scratching his chin, twitching his thumb just so, and one by one a dozen men and women across the Square began moving. "I think we could all use a walk today," he said, getting up. "Mr. McAllister, you're curious about our family life, then take the chance to see it up close. We're going to Pier Thirty Nine to buy fruit and then do whatever else the young prince would like."

"Within reason," Will said.

"Don't be a killjoy," Jax said.

"Fine. The last time I took him there, he wanted to get on that ride with all the elastic bands that propel a person thirty feet in the air, and if he gets his way, we're all riding on it."

PART II

8

We were more than halfway across the Square when Royal Guard Vicat popped up from her bench, head cocked as she listened, her fingers twitching to signal the guard closest to Jax. She was still listening carefully as she sprinted toward us, and as the shadow fell over the far edge of the Square she called out an order for the guards to scatter. She yelled at Will to grab Rhys, who yelled at Drew to grab me, and as Drew scooped me up and latched onto Sean's wrist, Vicat tackled the King and sent him through the portal.

"Don't ask, just move!" Drew shouted at Sean.

I could have gotten through on my own, you know.

As we tumbled out the other side, Jax had rolled onto his knees, and Vicat was on her back, exhaling hard through pursed lips. Will set Rhys down and knelt beside him, making sure he was all right, and Drew let go of Sean, who was muttering "Oh my god" on repeat.

I think he's gonna wet himself.

"He won't wet himself, Wick," Drew sighed. "You all right there, McAllister?"

"Oh my god." He pointed at people zipping by overhead, jet packs harnessed to their backs. "Oh my god!"

"What the hell happened?" Jax asked Vicat. "What did you hear?"

"Air car, sir." She peeled herself off the ground, moving gingerly. "The last time I heard a whine like that, a six-passenger tourist van had lost its thrusters and power shut down. Its landing was not pretty. When I saw the shadow?"

"The trajectory placed it crashing close to where we were," Will said.

"How many people were on the Square?" Jax asked.

"Aside from the guards, fewer than a dozen," Vicat said. "Most of them were on the far side."

Drew took a deep, shuddering breath. "Jesus. The guards."

"I gave the signal to scatter," Vicat said. "They heard."

"You hope."

"It might not have crashed," she said.

Will knew better. "As quickly as that shadow loomed? That car was considerably distant from the sky lane and losing altitude quickly. What we need to know is intent."

Jax didn't care about intent. "I am not your assignment," he reminded Vicat, voice a tick away from being a growl. "Rhys is your assignment. You're *his* personal guard now."

She didn't flinch. "Monarch above all," she said. "Save the King, then worry about others. In this situation, he comes second."

"And I understand that," Will said. "She made sure I had him. She fulfilled her duty."

"If you ever have to make that decision again, he comes first. Understand?"

"No, sir. He will not."

"You know better, Jax," Will said. He got up from the ground, lifting Rhys. "He's not in line for the throne. The only person you can direct her to save before you is Oz. And even then, she would face repercussions from the council and the head of the guard."

"I don't care. He's just—" Jax sighed. "Fine."

"I'm okay, Daddy," Rhys said.

Sean still hadn't moved, though he'd stopped muttering and now looked like he was about to cry.

Jax stepped over to him. "Something you may not have covered in your classes yet. When someone requests that the information you're given, either directly or by example, is off the record, you're under no legal obligation to honor that, other than by your own ethical code. The law protects the truth."

He nodded.

"However, if *I* tell you something is off the record, *that* is legally binding. My word is law."

"I get it."

Oh, yay. He has his King hat on.

"From the moment we left the table at the bakery until I tell you otherwise, everything you see, and everything you hear is off the record."

Sean nodded again.

"Your personal fallout for violating this is more than an annoying legal issue that you can pay a fine for and be done with. There is no hearing, no trial, no chance to defend yourself. My judgment will be swift, it will be harsh, and without appeal. And I'm sorry, but there's no turning around and changing your mind about all of this. You're stuck with it."

Jax knows he has no authority here, right?

"But stuck with what, sir? What happened? Where are we?"

"Where we were three minutes ago, Mr. McAllister. Standing on Union Square in downtown San Francisco...although we are now two hundred years in the future."

The sigh Sean let out was laced with a lot of *yeah, right* and a little bit of *just go fuck the hell off.* He might have been about to say something—he took one of those *I'm about to say something* breaths—but stopped when everyone turned at the sound of footsteps and the sight of movement.

Rhys squirmed to get out of Will's arms and ran at the older man coming toward us. He squealed, "Pop-Pop!" and threw his arms around the old man's legs, then stepped back so that Will could give him a quick hug.

Grinning, Other-When Finn took a few more steps, tilted his head as he looked at Jax, and said, "Long time, Jax. Nice to see you not...old."

Sean turned to Drew. "No, really. What the hell is going on?"

"You wanted to see how we live? Here it is. We took a serious jump into the future, and it's not even close to being the first time. And yeah, that's who you think it is. Finnegan Blackshear, the Emperor's father. We jumped two hundred years, and he's still alive."

= = =

Sean needed to sit down. While Rhys bounced on his toes, pointing at a man hovering nearby, begging for his own chance to fly, Sean paled and wobbled. Drew caught him before he fell, and Finn offered the apartment as a place to rest for a bit before going home. "And you," he said to Rhys, "are hungry, right?"

"Daddy was taking me to get strawberries."

"You're in luck. I have a big bowlful in the fridge."

Rhys held his arms out so that Finn would pick him up. "Is JoJo here?"

"She's at home, in our other When. I'm only here to check on some work. I can go get her if you need her."

Rhys shook his head. "No. I just need strawberries."

"You want them," Will corrected. "Your life would go on just fine without them."

"Daddy doesn't get it," Finn said to Rhys. "He's never understood that sometimes a want is the same as a need."

"Dad," Will sighed.

"Eh, go home and lecture the younger me. Maybe he'll listen, and in thirty-five years we won't have this conversation."

"Thirty-five or two hundred?" Sean asked Drew. "If you're going to bullshit me, can we at least get it straight?"

"This Finn is from thirty-five years in our future," Drew explained, ignoring the flare of temper in Sean's voice. "But we're two hundred from the day we went through the portal. Somewhere around here, there's another Finn, and he's pushing three hundred years old. Hell, there might even be an older one. There was this whole thing with the world ending, but—" he shrugged "—it didn't, so all the Finns kind of...congregate."

Sweat popped out on Sean's upper lip. He didn't believe Drew, but with people flying overhead, he didn't disbelieve him, either.

When Rhys was seated at the table with his strawberries and Sean was on the sofa—he hadn't noticed how threadbare this apartment was compared to the one of his King, nor the piles of tattered books scattered among computer parts and odd bits of lab equipment—Will gave Finn a kiss on his cheek. "How's Mom doing? Any signs of illness yet?"

"That's years away, Will. Stop worrying."

"I'll worry until she lives past the age she was when she died," he said, quietly so Rhys wouldn't hear.

"Well, if you don't bring the kids to see her soon, she'll swear she's about to die of a broken heart."

"It hasn't been that long."

"A month, at least. Just after Christmas. In grandmother terms, that's more than a year."

Will was about to refute that, but Jax came in and asked Finn for something with sugar, it didn't matter what. "It seems Mr. McAllister has issues with his blood sugar. He needs to eat."

"I'll share my strawberries," Rhys said. "Mommy says they have their own kind of sugar and that's why I like them."

Finn spared him the loss of a single strawberry and pulled a box of graham crackers from the pantry. He offered one to Rhys, but he scrunched up his nose and said that was too much like cookies, and he only liked cookies once a week.

"That's oddly specific," Will said.

"Aunt Aubrey makes cookies on Sunday. If we eat at least three bites of everything at dinner, we can have a cookie. If we eat all our vegebatles, we can have three."

"Vegetables," Will corrected.

"That's what I said."

You like her cookies, too.

"Indeed, Wick, every now and then I appreciate her cookies."

"Does Wick like strawberries?" Rhys leaned across the table to talk to me. "You want a bite?"

I've never had one.

"They're not toxic to cats, Wick. Give it a try."

I jumped up, and Rhys rolled a berry across the table. He warned me that the green part didn't taste good, but the red part was sweet. I bit down, chewed a bit, then reluctantly swallowed. *It tastes like nothing. I can feel it in my mouth, but that's it.*

"You don't have many sweet receptors," Will said.

I enjoy how they smell, though. Tell him I said thank you for letting me try it. But from now on, I'll just sniff them.

Sean brought his crackers to the table and sat down. He was even paler than he'd been on the Square, with the beads of sweat on his upper lip accompanied by sweat dripping from his scalp.

"Is this more than low blood sugar?" Drew asked, following him in. "Could it be a quick reaction to going through the portal? Some kind of time wedgie?"

"We'll know in a few minutes." Will grabbed a water bottle from the fridge and set it in front of Sean. "Eat. We need to be sure you're all right."

"I'm fine. I just…this happens when I freak out. I'll try to freak out a little less."

Rhys got to his knees. "You should have a strawberry. They make everyone feel better. Except Wick."

Everyone sat down and passed the box of graham crackers around. Sean accepted the offer of a strawberry and then nibbled on his cracker, eyes darting as he followed the conversation. Jax wanted to know if either Will or Vicat thought the aircar coming into downtown San Francisco truly was intentional; the nearest permitted access point was miles away. How could it be possible that someone got that far by mistake?

Vicat erred on the side of caution and suggested he presume it was intentional until proven otherwise. Will offered the explanation that it could have been a taxi or delivery car, which would be permitted downtown, and believed the focus of their concern needed to be timing their return to avoid any detritus, while not appearing out of order.

"No way of knowing how far spread out the wreckage is," Drew said. "Technically, we could all be pinned under half the car."

"Eh." Finn got up. "Sit tight. There's a portal upstairs. I'll pop through and peek out a window. No one will even know I'm there."

"Unless Oz is working out up there. She might be home by now."

"Then she'll be surprised."

"Don't startle her intentionally, Dad," Will said. "She's pregnant. Scare her, and she might wet herself, and if that happens—"

"Your junk will wind up hanging out your nose," Drew snorted.

Vicat got up. "I'll go with him. I'd like a look at the vehicle and any other details that might be important."

"Translation," Drew said when they were in the elevator, "she's uncomfortable having to spend this much time this close to us."

"She's a guard," Will said. "Not a friend. Of course, she's uncomfortable."

"I like her," Rhys said around a mouthful of berry. "She's nice. The other guards don't talk to me."

"They're not supposed to," Jax said.

"Vicat has been given leeway," Will said. "Rhys seems more comfortable with having a moderate social connection to the person watching him."

"He's not supposed to be aware of his guards at all," Jax said.

"And yet, without being told who they were, by the time he was two and a half he could pick them out."

"How old are you now?" Jax asked him, teasing.

Rhys shoved another strawberry in his mouth and then held up three fingers.

"And how old were you when you developed an obsession with strawberries?"

He folded his index finger down, but before he could bend his ring finger, Will warned, "Don't," and Rhys giggled.

"Are we going home after we're done eating?" Rhys asked. "Can we go outside and watch the people fly first?"

"No hurry," Jax told Will. "We can take an hour or two if you'd like."

"We should take Sean to a bunch of Whens," Rhys said. "Maybe we can make him throw up."

Sean's eyes went wide, and the look that shot between Will and Drew was the answer Rhys didn't hear.

Oh, we are so doing this.

9

There was a wrecked air car on Union Square. Vicat reported that it appeared to be mostly intact and was surrounded by guards and police officers and standing nearby were two men with an officer on either side. Neither had been cuffed, but one was bouncing nervously on his toes and appeared to be talking fast, as if offering an explanation he thought no one would believe. The police officers didn't have the stance or countenance of those guarding terrorists, though at the distance she observed from, she allowed for the possibility that she was mistaken.

Finn had no opinion. His concern was with the placement of the wreckage in proximity to the portal. "You could have stayed on the Square and been fine, I think. But either way, the elevator door to the lab opened two to three seconds before the wreck, so as far as perceptions go, you could all be safe in the lab."

"Then there's no need for tight timing on our return," Jax said.

"The important details are in the odds of whether someone attempted to land a car on you," Will said.

Heaving a sigh, Jax nodded. "Yeah, but if they had, I'd have an excuse for staying indoors and avoiding the world for a few days. I could cancel meetings, sleep in, play with the kids…hell, dust the entire place from top to bottom and save Aubrey the trouble. Mop a few floors. Cleaning the damned apartment sounds a hell of a lot better than another intractable negotiation between two political opposites with their heads up their asses. If that car had wrecked on purpose—?"

"You don't need an excuse to take a day off," Drew said.

"Kinda do."

Will gave a tight nod to Drew and then glanced at the closest bedroom door.

"Come on, squirt," Drew said to Rhys. "This is boring. Let's go into the bedroom and watch people with jetpacks. We might even get to see someone who's just learning how to fly, and they might smash into something."

"That's mean." Rhys laughed anyway and bolted for Oz's old bedroom.

"You might enjoy the spectacle, too," Will said to Sean. "As will Vicat."

"Something to say?" Jax asked when they were out of the room.

"This feels like more than a wish to have a few days off. You're a bit disappointed that someone didn't try to kill you."

"I just want some time off, Will. That's all."

"Then take time off. I can send Drew for Aubrey, and you can stay here as long as you like."

"Hyrum."

"Is self-sufficient for long periods of time. Regardless, Aisha and I can keep an eye on him, as can Oz and Drew."

"Or bring him, too," Finn said. "Bring everyone. Have a family vacation. If you want to travel, you already have ID and bank cards here. Use them. I have a car parked nearby. Use that, too."

He was tempted. "Oz won't come, not now. And Aubrey won't risk coming here in case something happens at home. Our priority right now is Oz and that baby. To get Aubrey here before he's born would mean dragging her, and honestly, I don't have the stones for that."

"But you admit, you need time off."

"Want, not need."

"As my son so recently illustrated, sometimes a need is couched within a want. We'll stay here a few days and torture Mr. McAllister with the future. You can sleep the entire time if you choose or help us make him vomit. Your choice."

He couldn't stay without telling Aubrey. With a soft grunt,

he got up and said he would be back in a minute; he'd try to convince her to come with him but knew better. He offered to take Rhys home, but Will wanted to give him time here, to see where his father had grown up.

"Ask Aubrey to tell Aisha where we are. If she wants to join us, give her a time roughly five minutes after you come back." If she wasn't here within ten minutes, he wouldn't worry about taking Rhys out of the house and leaving her behind.

You kinda don't want her to come, do you?

"I would be thrilled if she did," he said. "But yes, I would like some time alone with Rhys, without his brother and sister interrupting constantly. He doesn't get enough solo attention."

You could have asked Jax to tell her to leave them at home. Jay would babysit.

"I could have."

But you didn't think of it.

"I did, but Rhys is with us now because they don't feel well. Regardless, I'm not sure I would ask that of her. I get plenty of time with all the kids, while she gets less than she would like."

You know you'd only be gone about ten minutes, tops.

"I am aware. Personal perception matters in this."

Now you get why she felt like she was abandoning Jay when we were stuck in the simulator helping the elves fight the Shedu.

"I get it now."

Are we ever going back? I worry about Fluffy and Jeff.

"They're fine." He checked on the program from time to time, watching the lives of the creatures I'd created speed by in little blips of data. But he couldn't tell me specifics: had Jeff grown? Did Fluffy eat anyone else? Were Shivan and Krisf and Kilfin happy? And most important, was the evil wizard Tobias still trapped in the alternate simulator universe?

"What's he going on about?" Jax asked as he came back into the apartment with Hyrum. "Aubrey will deliver your message to Aisha and says we can take all the time we want."

"And Oz?"

"She thought about it. Then the baby kicked, and she said to tell Drew he wasn't allowed to have too much fun."

"Wick wants to go back into the simulator and check on his offspring."

"Can we do that?"

Will nodded. "It's a failsafe destination, but my father made sure we could get back to it."

"Where are we going?" Hyrum asked. "I didn't bring extra clothes."

Jax pointed toward the bedroom where Rhys and Drew were still watching people on the Square. "Don't worry about that now. Go watch the flyers. Drew is pulling for someone to wreck."

"Take tonight to decide," Will said. "We can go in the morning."

Jax nodded, and then followed Hyrum.

"He's drained," Finn mused.

"It's more than that. Think of the timing, Dad. In your past, what year was it that Jax seriously began contemplating retirement?"

"He stepped down when baby Eli was a year old. I imagine he was chewing on it for a while before that, likely from the end of the war onward. You think he's headed in that direction again?"

"Was there a breaking point?" Will asked.

"Aside from your death? He broke then, Dash. It was a long slide from there. He was torn between his grief and Aubrey's grief, and the war...it made everything so much worse."

Will knew the story. He'd died in the last loop of time; his loss nearly broke his best friends, and it ripped his parents apart. When the war with Florida ended—there was only one in that When—Jax kept the throne just long enough for Oz to find her footing and for Eli to start crawling. When baby Eli was a year old, Jax abdicated, and it wasn't until he was just the Queen's father that his grief began to lift.

Maybe he's just having a bad day. Or week. He's allowed to be tired.

"My gut suggests otherwise," Will said. "And it's more than that, Wick."

"You think time is trying to right itself?" Finn asked, avoiding the other question that would follow: *will it take you while it does?*

Will didn't know. But if Jax needed a few days off, he was getting them.

10

Rhys was secured in a pack on Will's back, and he draped his arms over Will's shoulders. He'd complained once—he didn't like having his father's head taking up so much of what he could see—but he knew better than to complain again. Will didn't need to find a portal to use to take a whiny little boy home; he had his personal transporter wrapped around his wrist and could have Rhys home quicker than the three-year-old could say he was sorry.

I rode on Jax's shoulder; it was a bit awkward because he was no longer used to carting me around, but Drew was keeping an eye on Hyrum and Sean as we walked toward the Ferry Building and he didn't need to worry about me, too. A block down Market Street Hyrum reached for Drew's hand, eliciting a quiet snort from Sean, which prompted Jax to turn his head and glare.

Hyrum was as excited as he was nervous. One of his favorite pastimes was riding his bike to the Ferry Building to watch the boats as passengers boarded, and he especially enjoyed the sight of a ferry streaming across the bay. It was one of the first places he'd felt comfortable going on his own. That he went by himself at all was a milestone moment; during his first three years living with his sister and brother-in-law he'd always asked someone to go with him. Usually, it was Drew, often Will, but one morning when no one was available to go with him, Aubrey shocked everyone by suggesting he go by himself.

She wanted to wrap him in cotton, layer after protective layer, but he'd proven he was capable of doing things on his own. He'd walked out of Florida and then across the entirety of Midlam just to deliver a message to his sister, and though he got lost a few times he never quit trying to get to her. When he asked during breakfast if someone would go with him and no one could, she popped his bubble of disappointment. "Ride your bike there, Hy. Stay in the green bike lane and be careful crossing the Embarcadero. And be sure you use both of your locks when you get to the storage rack. But you can go if you'd like."

He was as wide-eyed as Jax. "Alone?"

"You can even get lunch at the Ferry Building." She deliberately, painfully for her, ignored his sudden worry. "You'll be fine."

Hyrum knew he had guards; that factoid had been withheld from him for the first three years to avoid upsetting him, but when he heard Jax discussing Rhys's personal guard assignment with Vicat, he asked why he didn't have one.

"Because you have four," Jax said, as if it were a matter of course. "You're a member of the royal family, Hyrum. We all have guards, even Eli. Don't worry, they won't tell on you if you get into a little mischief. They're only there to make sure no one hurts you."

That morning, he wanted to know if his guards could keep up with him if he rode his bike too fast.

"They will if they want to keep their jobs," Jax mused.

He'd spent the morning waving at passengers on incoming ferries and talking to tourists who wandered down the pier, unafraid. At lunchtime he went inside and bought a cheeseburger and fries, but not, he reported, a root beer, because that seemed like too much sugar. Instead, he bought a milkshake, because that had milk and milk is healthy.

Aubrey overlooked his mental gymnastics and praised his efforts. After that, he was happy to ride his bike to the pier alone and began riding to his therapy appointments by himself, always stopping for lunch. Aubrey hated the amount of junk food he was getting but said nothing to him about it.

Her baby brother, who had never been expected to mature or be more intelligent than the average five-year-old, six if they were lucky, was reaching for independence and no matter how much it frightened her, she wasn't taking that away from him.

In the When of Will's birth, however, he was nervous and wouldn't have gone to the Ferry building alone even with the promise of a root beer with his cheeseburger. There was traffic here, cars zipping down the street where his bike path should be, and cars zipping overhead. The noise of it all pricked at him, but he still bounced on his toes as he walked, because at the end there were boats.

Jax glanced over his shoulder. "You've been here before, haven't you, Hy?"

"Nuh. I've been to the doctor here, but that's all. I didn't get to see anything. Dr. Brian was too busy fixing my arm, and then I had to go home on account of it was dinner time, and Aubrey wanted to make pork chops. I like her pork chops."

Brian Massimo, Mass to everyone else, was the family physician and was also from this When. Hyrum tripped over a toy car in the living room and landed on his shoulder, breaking it and his arm. Mass looked at the images of his broken bones and told Hyrum he could fix it there, at home, and it would hurt for a month or two, or he could take Hyrum to this When and he wouldn't feel anything. A few hours of treatment that he would sleep through, and he'd be good as new.

"We can explore a bit more if you like," Will told him.

"I dunno. It's loud here."

He stopped caring about the noise and the traffic when we crossed the Embarcadero to the pier. There was a ferry gliding under the Bay Bridge, twice the size of the boats he was used to. It was long and sleek, slicing through the water with no apparent effort, no rocking from the waves that rolled behind it.

Hyrum let go of Drew's hand and ran down the pier. Sean stopped, watching as the massive boat neared, and croaked, "*That's* a ferry?"

"Tourist ferry," Will said as he peeled the pack from his back to let Rhys out. "Hold someone's hand, Rhys. There are too many people here for you to run around."

Rhys latched onto Drew's hand and tugged because he knew Drew would run with him to catch up to Hyrum.

"That looks like a damned space ship," Sean said.

"Hey, he's talking now," Jax said to Will. "I thought we'd shocked him into a life of silence and contemplation."

Sean found his temper along with his voice.

"A car nearly landed on us. Then the next thing I know I'm jerked along and wind up, what, a couple hundred years in the future? With no warning? And then fuck it all, there's a familiar face, but *he's* from a completely different spot in time, and oh, by the way, he's the Emperor's father but not *really,* yet the Emperor treats him like he is, and the *toddler* understands it all. I'm the only one surprised by *any* of this. So yeah, I shut up. Because *what the hell?*"

"What the hell," Jax said. "And when we go home the worst of it will be that you can't tell a soul."

"Who would believe me?"

"It doesn't matter. You still can't tell anyone. If you even hint about it, eventually someone will start paying attention to us. We can't have that."

"Perhaps the greatest story of a reporter's life," Will said as he slipped the empty toddler-pack back on, "and you can't write about it. You will be tempted, eventually."

"I don't think so." He stepped past them to go watch the ferry come in with Hyrum and Drew.

"He'll write about it someday," Jax mused.

"Undoubtedly."

"What do you already know?"

"His journalism career will end with his graduation. His flirtation with news is simply a means to satisfy a credit requirement. He'll go on to open a small bookstore specializing in rare printings, where he'll spend quiet hours writing fiction. He'll enjoy moderate success in both endeavors."

"So. He will write about this."

"Possibly. It's not likely that this happened to him in the previous timeline. But if that part of his life remains true, then he'll eventually write about this."

Then give him something to write about. Or throw up. Rhys wants to make him throw up.

Rhys and Hyrum were waving to the ferry, jumping up and down as it neared.

When we were close, Rhys let go of Drew's hand and wrapped his arms around Jax's leg. "Uncle Jax, do you have a boat?"

"Nope."

"Why not? Kings should have boats."

"Even if I could afford one, no one would let me play with it," Jax said. "I don't even get to drive a car. And your Daddy's motorcycle? No one will let me on that, either."

"Why not?"

Jax bent over to whisper loudly to him. "I don't think they want me to have any fun."

"Uncle Jax can't risk his life for hobbies," Will told Rhys. "Besides, the one time someone let him near a bicycle, he didn't follow the rules and almost got hurt."

Rhys poked at Jax's nose. "You have to follow the rules. Why didn't you?"

"Because I was having fun," Jax said. "And then your daddy made me stop and threatened to tell my mom on me."

"I didn't make you stop. You reached the end of the street. I merely prevented you from repeating the ride."

"Where'd you ride?" Sean asked.

"Down California," Jax snickered. "Seriously, don't ever do that. It was as terrifying as it was fun and if I'd hit a bump?"

"I ride down California," Hyrum said, puzzled. "That's the way to Dr. Cheshire."

"But I didn't slow down. At all."

"Oh. I slow down before I get to the flat places. Otherwise, I might hit someone else on a bike."

There were more bicycle riders in the city than there had been just three years before; bike taxis had always been popular on the Embarcadero, but it could be years between sightings of casual or commuting riders. Then Hyrum got his bike for Christmas, along with Oz , Drew, Zed, and Sophia, and popularity followed in their wake. In the years since they'd gotten the bikes, hundreds of people began riding them, and at least three sales and repair shops had opened downtown.

"When we were kids, there were cars on the streets," Jax said. "So it was really stupid of me."

"How old were you?" Sean asked.

"Sixteen. Old enough to know better. And no, that's not off the record. The world can get a glimpse into how stupid I was."

"I'm not a fan of exposing anyone's teenage years," Sean said. "Nothing's fair game before you're a bona fide adult."

"And regarding the King, I agree," Will said. "Let sleeping dogs lie, Jax."

"We got a dog?" Rhys asked. "He won't eat Wick, will he?"

"It's an expression, Rhys. It means to leave things alone. We didn't get a dog."

At the same time, Rhys and Hyrum sighed. "A dog wouldn't be fair to Wick," Will went on. "He's old and might not be able to run fast enough to get away from it."

I have a hover cart. If you want to get them a dog, go ahead. It'll get used to me.

"You have always been fundamentally opposed to the idea of puppies, Wick."

That was before you had kids. Maybe they want a pet. I'm not really a pet.

Drew started to say something, but Will shook his head.

"Well, now I'm intrigued about Prince Jackson," Sean said. "What'd you do that the Emperor wants covered up?"

"Nothing," Will said at the same time Jax said, "What didn't I do?"

"It's all off the record. Aside from the one thing, you haven't told me that the record can resume."

Drew tousled Rhys's hair. "Maybe we should just watch the boats and then go get some lunch. How about it, Rhys? Your daddy told me about a place with awesome fajitas and grown-up drinks as big as his head. One time, Aunt Aubrey drank *two* of them."

"Did she throw up?" Rhys asked Jax.

"That'd be telling, son," Jax snorted.

"That means yes." Rhys giggled and turned back to face

the water. "Daddy, can we ride a boat soon? Back home with Mommy?"

"We can. I'm sure she would enjoy a ferry ride."

"Take him to Sausalito," Drew said. "Maybe you'll find cupcakes there."

Sean wanted to ask what that meant because Jax and Will laughed, but Hyrum latched onto the idea. "Cupcakes! I know how to make them. If we go to the store and get everything, I'll make some for us. Finn won't mind if I bake in his kitchen, will he? I'll clean up."

Will told him to just watch the boats for now, and when he and Rhys had seen enough, we walked to the Mexican restaurant where Aubrey had once ingested enough alcohol for four people. We sat on the patio near the floor heaters and watched traffic fly past, including one teenager pushing the limits of his flight pack by doing taut loops, which prompted Rhys to ask when he would be old enough to try that, and when he was old enough, could he have one?

"We can't take one home," Will said. "It doesn't exist in our When."

"Then can we move here?"

Jax pointed skyward, in the direction of Elysium. "I thought you wanted to go live there. In space."

"I can live here until I'm twelve, and then I can go to space."

"What changes at twelve?" Will asked him.

"Mommy says when I'm twelve I might become a suffer kind of idiot, so that would be a good time. I can go before she gets mad at me."

"Insufferable," Will chuckled. "And she was teasing. Boys tend to become mouthy little things at puberty."

Rhys frowned. "How does she know?"

"Jay was once a twelve-year-old boy," Will said. "She went through it with him."

Rhys went back to eating his lunch, but his brain was obviously turning, so no one was upset when he interrupted their conversation by blurting out, "How come you're not Jay's daddy?"

"Because James is."

"But you're married to mommy."

"When Jay was born," Will said, carefully, "Mommy was married to James. They divorced when he was—"

"What's that mean?"

"It means they stopped being married to each other."

"Are you and Mommy gonna do that?"

"Divorce? No. We waited too many years to be together for that to ever be an option."

Jax leaned toward his nephew. "They're not allowed to, Rhys. They're not just married, they're *super* married. It's called a King's Decree, and it can't be undone unless I say so, and I won't say so. They're going to be married forever. Okay?"

"Promise?"

"Promise."

"It's more complicated than that, though, isn't it?" Sean asked. "Doesn't overturning a decree also require additional judgment by the Supreme Court?"

"Only if I deny a request to break the decree. The couple can petition the court to examine my reasons, and the court can recommend I amend my decision, but it hasn't happened yet. Neither have I agreed to dissolve a decree. Getting me to agree to perform one in the first place is terribly complicated, and I won't do it lightly."

"He wouldn't even do it for his own daughter," Drew said.

"Seriously?" Sean frowned. "If anyone has a reason to stay together—"

"It wasn't for lack of faith in their decision to get married," Jax said. "I have no doubts about their relationship. The world needed to see that this marriage was their choice and that they wed in the venue of their choosing. If I'd performed a decree, it would have suggested their marriage was arranged for the benefit of the crown."

"And made acquiring Midlam questionable?" Sean wondered.

"That was a secondary concern. My daughter is not chattel. I don't want anyone presuming I traded her for land. The world needs to see her as independent as she truly is."

"And she was independent enough to arrange her own marriage," Will said, amused.

"The presumption is that you made the purchase offer of Midlam to protect it from Florida," Sean said. "I've never heard anything else. Midlam's defense was weak and becoming part of Pacifica was meant to make Levi Munson turn tail and run."

"Partly," Jax said.

"How did a freak like that get control over Florida in the first place? He was a monster like—"

"Stop," Will ordered. "We're fully aware of his proclivities."

"But—"

"It's not something we need to discuss right now," Will said.

"He was my daddy," Hyrum said, voice thin. "He was a bad, bad man, and I don't like to hear about him." His eyes went red. "I don't want to be like him."

"You aren't," Jax said.

"Not even a tiny, tiny bit," Drew added. He turned to Will. "Hey, is Rhys big enough to go to Bounce? I bet he and Hyrum would both like that."

Nice. Make him worry about barfing instead of Levi.

Will nodded. "If you go into the chamber with them. Jax and I will not." He gestured to the head-sized margaritas on the table. His was still more than half filled, but Jax had drained his.

Bounce was an anti-gravity chamber designed entirely for play. There were games to be played inside but time spent floating and rolling around was just as much fun. The walls were heavily padded to prevent injury, and the level of gravity could be controlled outside the chamber.

Drew went inside with a very apprehensive Hyrum and excited Rhys, and before Will closed the door, he reached out and grabbed Sean by the wrist and pulled him inside. Will ignored the protest Sean blurted out and sealed the lock, then sat back on the little sofa with Jax and flipped the switch to turn it on.

"You know they just ate," Jax said as they rose from the floor. Rhys giggled and reached for Drew's hand, and Hyrum grinned, but Sean was truly pissed off. "They're coming out coated in half-digested fajitas and refried beans."

"We can hope."

"I miss being able to do shit like that, Will. I miss tearing around town without worrying about what the hell might happen to me. I miss taking a skiff out on the bay and jumping breakers. I miss ice sliding in Dolores Park..."

"And stealing your father's beer? Drinking far too much and then vomiting a literal fountain of booze?"

"That, too. We had fun when we were kids."

Will chose to not remind him that he had not been present for most of Jax's teenaged years. He was a periodic interloper, giving Jax time to age ahead of him. It wasn't until Will turned seventeen that he decided to stay, and by then Jax was only a few months from turning eighteen.

"You didn't leave it all behind, Jax. You traded that insanity for a life with Aubrey and raising a family with her."

"We still had fun after we got married, even after the kids were born. Things didn't start to suck until my dad abdicated."

"You're just tired, Jax. It didn't suck then."

"It wasn't the choice I would have made for myself."

"I beg to differ. You looked forward to becoming King. It happened two decades sooner than you expected, but you had no issue with assuming the throne."

"Fine. But I wanted more time to just be a husband and father. And teacher."

"None of which requires the risky behavior of your youth."

"Buzzkill," Jax huffed.

"Do you really want to revisit those days? There's no one here to stop you. I'll get you a flight pack, slap it on you, disable the safety nets, and set it to maximum."

The idea amused him. "I'd zip through the air with my ass over my head."

Will set me on Jax's lap and got up. "Fine. I have a better idea. Give them half an hour and then meet me outside." He tapped the bracelet on his wrist and vanished.

Sean McAllister's mouth dropped open, but he couldn't stop spinning long enough to ask Drew what had happened to Will, and by the time he'd righted himself, Rhys rocketed head first into Sean's stomach. Jax couldn't get to the controls fast enough to stop the inevitable, but at least the vomit only spread out on Sean's face and not the rest of them.

11

Will returned with two more jump bracelets and his meticulously restored early twenty-first-century Triumph Bonneville motorcycle. There was no safe space in the city to ride, not at his intended speed, so Drew grabbed Sean's wrist, Jax held Hyrum's hand while carrying Rhys on his back, and we jumped to the last long unbroken stretch of imitation asphalt highway in the United States of Pacifica. It cut through the old salt flats in Utah, a two-hundred-mile sweep that had been maintained as a tourist attraction. Visitors could take a short course on the safe operation of mid-twentieth to early twenty-first century automobiles, and then rent a car—usually a convertible—for a day, which was spent riding to one end and back at speeds considered pathetically slow by the day's standards.

Late January was an unpopular time to rent a restored convertible. Utah was cold and often blanketed in snow, which was less than ideal for the average consumer looking for a pleasant way to spend an afternoon. Will had chosen a bright and sunny, warm spring-like day, perfect for a King displaced in time to take a ride on the coveted yet forbidden motorcycle.

"Everyone gets a ride," Will said. "Jax first. You can work out amongst yourselves who's next."

"Even me?" Rhys asked as Drew peeled him off Jax's back.

"Even you."

"Mommy will be mad."

"Don't tell Mommy," Drew suggested.

Will crouched so that he was face level with Rhys. "We

won't lie to her. You get to take a ride, but I'll go very slow with you, all right? She won't be upset. Everyone else will ride on the back of the bike, but you'll ride up front so I can hold onto you."

I will not be riding but thank you anyway.

"I can go slow with you, too."

Give Rhys or Hyrum my ride. I prefer to spectate.

Drew mocked me for my use of "spectate" and set me on his shoulder. His mockery was followed by gentle fingers stroking my furs, particularly under my chin, so I didn't feel pressed to bite him for it.

Will cut a line in the ground with the heel of his shoe and told us to stay behind it until he'd stopped the motorcycle and dismounted. Rhys and Hyrum promised they would sit down and wait, but Drew snorted and said, "He's talking to me, guys. We all know I'm kind of immature."

Maybe he was talking to Sean. You're not an idiot.

"We know who he meant."

Hyrum and Rhys.

"Yep. Come on, he knows I've wanted to ride that thing for, like, six or seven years."

Didn't he say he'd teach you to ride it by yourself?

"That feels like a lifetime ago. When we were in the safe house. Somewhere near there he's got a couple of bikes stored away. If things there had ended differently...yeah, maybe we would have had time then."

Jax knows how to ride. Why is he on the back?

Will told Jax to get on the back of the bike before he slung his own leg over. Rhys startled when the engine roared, but he and Hyrum lifted their arms, fists pumping, when Will took off in a hard, fast start.

"Probably because it's been thirty years since he's been on one. Besides, just because this is kind of like his vacation from being King, that doesn't mean Will is going to let him take risks that are too big. Aubrey would hurt him."

"She runs everything, doesn't she?" Sean asked.

"He certainly consults her about anything to do with family and home," Drew answered. "There's an equality that kind of tilts to unequal because of his time constraints."

"Aubrey is the rule maker at home," Hyrum said, laughing. "If I ask him if I can go for a bike ride, he always says, 'I don't see why not, but check with your sister first.' Our mom says that's wrong, but I think she secretly likes it that Aubrey can tell Jax what to do and he doesn't get mad."

"Is it true that men basically own women in Florida?" Sean asked.

"Husbands kinda own wives," Hyrum said. "Dads own daughters."

"Not so much anymore," Drew said. "There was a definite theocratical patriarchy in play before they surrendered to Pacifica, but they've made huge leaps in the last couple of years."

"Kinda," Hyrum said. "My brother Joe says that old women still do what their husbands say and ladies his wife's age are afraid of what they can do. Mom and her friends think the things Jax is doing are wrong. She says women belong at home and shouldn't have ambition."

"And yet your mom voted for a female Prime Minister," Drew said. "She was fairly vocal about her excitement when she did."

Come on. That woman flops back and forth like a rubber pancake.

"I voted for her, too," Hyrum beamed. "Will took me back so I could vote because I'm allowed to vote there, even though my daddy said people like me shouldn't get to. It was my first time voting! I voted for her, and I voted for scholarships for girls, and I voted for sports things for girls so that they can have fun, too. I didn't understand some of the other stuff, though. Will said it was okay to skip those because I didn't understand even after he explained it all, and he said he couldn't tell me how to vote. That wouldn't be right."

"You're still a Florida resident?" Sean asked.

Hyrum shrugged.

"Hy didn't give up his citizenship when he came here," Drew explained. "He's a ward of the King and has everything that entitles him to, but renouncing his citizenship wasn't a requirement. And moving forward, the only thing that will be required is proof of residence. As long as he keeps his Florida ID, he can vote there."

"But I'm not gonna," Hyrum said. "Will said I need to get a driver's license here before I get a ticket because if I get one, Jax won't make it go away and it would take all my money to fix. And I'm never gonna live back there again anyway. I want to vote here, and maybe you can explain the voting things to me."

Maybe after someone explains them to Drew.

"Did you see your mommy when you went?" Rhys asked.

"Nuh. I saw Red and Bree, but only for a few minutes."

That surprised Sean. "How can you go home and not see your mother?"

Both Hyrum and Drew opened their mouths to speak—it was complicated, Florida was no longer home, and Hyrum was painfully aware that his mother no longer wanted him with her—but Rhys beat them to it. "She's a bitch."

"Rhys! That's not nice," Drew said, even though Hyrum laughed.

"But I heard Hyrum's brother Joe say so," Rhys said. "Hyrum says Joe doesn't lie."

"It's still not nice. And that's on Aunt Aubrey's bad word list."

Rhys sucked in a tiny, sharp breath. "Are you gonna tell on me?"

"No, of course not. None of us will."

"There's a list?" Sean asked.

The List was born not long after Aubrey and Jax started dating, when she became fed up with his vocabulary. The worst offender then, though, was Will. He used the words that eventually populated the list as coveted adjectives until she asked them both to knock it off around her. Aisha jumped on that; she didn't mind their language as much but thought that at the very least, it was a habit to be broken given how much time they spent around King Eli and Queen Donna.

"They actually wrote out a list," Drew said. "On paper, even. It's faded as hell, but it's in her desk, and I have been told more than once to consult the list about my choices."

"I said a bad word, but I didn't have to look at it," Hyrum said. "Aubrey just sighed and told me to stop repeating things Jay says."

"Jay has a mouth," Drew snorted. "No one drops an f-bomb the way he does."

Rhys started bouncing where he sat and pointed to the encroaching rumbling dot in the distance. "There they are! Look!"

Will was leaned over the tank, and Jax held on tight; they zoomed past in the opposite direction, the engine screaming.

"Holy shit, that's fast," Sean muttered.

"Eighty, ninety, maybe," Drew said. "No worries. Will's never wrecked."

"Still. I think I'm going to pass on the ride offer. That just looks dangerous."

"Suit yourself. Who's next?" Drew asked. "Hy? Rhys?"

"You go!" Rhys yelled. "Go fast!"

"I don't mind waiting until you've taken turns," Drew told them.

"I wanna see you go zoom," Hyrum said.

As Will brought the bike to a stop, they all got up. Hyrum and Rhys jumped up and down, cheering, but they did as they were told and stayed behind the line. Drew handed me to Jax as he came near and then trotted over to Will, trying to look less excited than I know he was. He'd been waiting for this since his 20th birthday, and if not for Levi Munson's men grabbing Oz, he would have learned to ride back then.

After some directions, Drew got on, tapped Will on the shoulder, and then grabbed onto his waist just before Will cracked the throttle open.

"Was it fun, Uncle Jax?" Rhys asked. "Did you go super-fast?"

"It felt like we were going faster than I ever have riding on Zed's air bike," Jax said. "It was *lots* of fun."

"More fun than riding your bike on California?" Hyrum asked with a snicker.

"It felt a hell of a lot safer."

"Either bike goes down, and you're in a world of hurt," Sean said. "Or dead. Most likely dead."

"Nuh," Hyrum grunted. "Don't say that."

"Come on. He's pushing a hundred miles an hour. If he wrecks, it's over."

Rhys balled his hands into fists and clenched them to his chest. "Daddy might die?" His eyes filled, and he wailed, "I don't want Daddy to die."

Hyrum snatched him up before Jax could, but Jax still reached out to rub his back. "No, your daddy won't die on that bike today," Jax said. "Sean didn't mean that."

"Well, I—"

"Shut up," Hyrum seethed. He gave Rhys a kiss on his cheek. "Your daddy is the best bike rider, okay? Jax wouldn't let me get on it if he wasn't. Right, Jax?"

"Absolutely. When he gets back with Drew, Hyrum will take you over to him, and you can ask your dad about the bike and how safe he knows how to be, okay?"

"Okay." He sniffed and set his head on Hyrum's shoulder. I watched Hyrum rock him back and forth, and there was still fear brimming in his eyes.

I'll show him.

When Will brought the bike to a stop and Drew jumped off, grinning wildly, I stepped over the line and followed Hyrum. Before he could tell Will the problem, I hopped onto the back seat.

Take me for a ride. Rhys needs to see you're a safe rider.

Will shut the engine off. "What happened?"

"Sean told Rhys if you wreck the bike you might die," Hyrum said. "But you're a good rider and you can explain it to him, right?"

Show him. Go slow. I won't fall off, and he'll see. You wouldn't let me on the bike if you weren't positive that I'd be okay. Me more than the others since I'm so small.

"You sure about this, Wick?"

I hate it more than I hate pigeons, but I'll do it. Rhys thinks you're going to die.

Drew led them back to the line, and Will fired up the bike. I couldn't hear anything going on over there, but I was pretty sure Drew was letting Sean know what a douchebag thing he'd just done. He pulled Sean away from the others, jabbing his pointy finger as he spoke.

I couldn't keep watching him. Will shouted that he was going to go very slow, in a wide circle, so if I needed to jump off, he'd have plenty of time to stop and not run me over. "Lean when I lean," he said. When the bike began to move, I dug my claws in, and as he started to turn, I leaned a little bit, but I didn't have enough weight for it to matter either way. His saying so was just habit; he wanted Jax and Drew to lean, to help him keep the bike balanced.

He rode the circle three times, making sure Rhys saw how comfortable I was.

Still, when the bike stopped and I jumped off, Rhys wanted to watch Hyrum ride first. Drew reminded Hyrum that he had to keep his arms around Will's waist and to hold on tight. "You'll want to do this—" he pumped his fists in the air "—but you can't. Okay?"

Hyrum nodded enthusiastically and ran over to the bike.

See? I said to Rhys, counting on Drew to tell him what I was saying. *He's not going to let anything happen. He loves us and wants to keep us safe.*

Sean stared at his feet, not as contrite as he should be.

Jax stepped next to him. "Consider the company you're in, Mr. McAllister," he said, half under his breath.

"I know who you are," he said, defiant.

"I'm not speaking as your King," Jax said. "I'm speaking as that little boy's uncle. Understand, we're fiercely protective of our family members, especially the children."

"I wasn't—"

"Stop. I don't care about the blunt truth or your intentions. You spoke to the worst fears a three-year-old can have. It will not happen again. Understand?"

Sean nodded, but I didn't think he really got it.

"Uncle Jax! Look!" Rhys pointed to Will. He'd slowed down

and was weaving back and forth in wide curves, dipping the bike from side to side to make Hyrum laugh. "Hy isn't falling off!"

"Daddy needs to try harder," Jax said, lightly. "Your turn is next. Do you want to ride?"

Rhys dropped into a deep squat, and then jumped as high as he could, shouting "Yes!"

Will scooted back on the seat and placed Rhys close to the tank, and he wrapped one arm tightly around the little boy's waist. For the next ten minutes they rode in wide circles and long, slow lines; Will kept his feet on the ground and never changed gears, and barely used the throttle.

"Tell me what you see," Jax said to Drew when they inched past.

"One hell of a happy little boy. Why? What is it you're seeing?"

"Everything I ever wanted for Will. Everything I want for myself. One day, I want that to be me with your kids. Zed's kids."

"It will be."

"Not as long as I have the crown," Jax said with a sigh.

Drew wanted to tell him he was wrong; he could have that now, with Zed's oldest. He didn't, though, because they both knew that for Jax to have the life he'd begun to long for, it meant handing the crown to Oz, and that was something neither of them wanted.

= = =

Sean hid in the bedroom he'd been given for the night. He'd retreated into silence, unwilling to risk ticking Jax off any more than he already had. He uttered a single "thank you" when Will bought dinner at *Sof y Z's* for everyone, and after the bedroom was pointed out to him, he slipped into it when he thought no one was looking.

Rhys fell asleep on the sofa, watching TV with Drew and Hyrum. His head was buried against an old throw pillow, his feet were across Hyrum's lap, and Drew had his hand on Rhys's chest, feeling the slow, gentle rise and fall of his breathing. He promised Will that he would move Rhys to a bed when he was certain he wouldn't wake up; Jax had twitched in the direction of the balcony and Drew gave a slight nod toward it, telling Will to go.

"The bike today was fun." Hyrum kept his voice soft. "Will went really fast, and when he turned, the feet things on the motorcycle rubbed on the ground. Don't tell my mom."

No one ever told his mother anything, but his asking had become habit. Valerie Munson had long stopped voicing an opinion on the things Hyrum did, whether from disinterest or acceptance that she no longer had a vote. I don't think he cared if the things he did would upset her. Aubrey had become his surrogate mother, and he looked to her for guidance. Jax was his surrogate father and head of the family, though it hadn't taken long for him to grasp that life in Pacifica, with his sister and her family, was not as rigid as life had been under his father's roof.

No one here was going to yell at him for being a step behind. No one would ever tell him he was stupid, and no one would ever hit him.

Or worse.

"The real worry," Drew told him, "is if Oz will get mad."

"Oz likes fast things."

"But Oz is also going to have a baby in a few months and might not want me taking chances."

Oz is only going to be mad she couldn't play, too.

"She's not like that," Hyrum said. "Are you gonna have a lot of babies?"

"I don't know. I keep telling Oz we're having them until we have a daughter. I'd like to have a little girl."

Hyrum snorted. "That means you're gonna have a bunch of boys."

"What about you, Hy? Don't you ever want to meet someone and have a baby of your own?"

Hyrum scrunched his nose. He'd told Drew a long time ago that he wasn't interested in having a girlfriend; women only liked men with jobs and who liked grown up things. He didn't want to stop playing. He wanted to keep his blocks and cars, to stretch out on the floor and draw pictures for an hour or two, and just wanted everyone else to have kids so he would have someone to play with.

This time, he hesitated. After scrunching his nose, he gave the idea weight. "I'd be a really good daddy," he said. "But only for babies and little kids. After that, they'd be embarrassed by me."

"No, they wouldn't. Look at Bree. You're still her favorite uncle."

"But I'm not her daddy. It's true, you know it. If your daddy had been like me when you were thirteen, you wouldn't want your friends to know."

"My dad was never home," Drew said. "And when he was, he was busy helping my mom. I have a feeling if he'd been like you, he would have paid more attention to his kids and played with us more. If he'd done that when I was Rhys's age, by the time I was a teenager I would have loved him so much that nothing he did would embarrass me."

"But your dad is nice."

Drew nodded. "I know. But my parents were never there, Hyrum. You would be."

"Your parents are smart."

"So are you. Stop telling me you're not."

"I can't even do fractions, Drew."

"You don't *want* to do fractions. That has nothing to do with how smart you are." He turned on the sofa to look at Hyrum. "I'm going to tell you a secret, okay?"

Hyrum nodded.

"My mom can barely read. I mean, she can, but the words kind of swim in front of her and it's *really* hard. When she was Midlam's Queen, my dad had to read out loud to her every night so she could memorize things."

"Nuh."

"It's the truth. But you know what? I didn't even realize how hard reading is for her until I was almost twenty years old. Kids see in their parents what they want to see. If you had a kid, he'd see a dad that loves him. Nothing else."

"Maybe. I'd have to do kissing things to be a daddy, though."

"It certainly helps."

"I'm too old, anyway. No lady is going to want to do kissing things with me. That's okay. I can just be a good uncle."

"You're the best uncle. Can I ask you something really personal?"

"About kissing things?"

"Kind of. But it's private, so you don't have to answer." When Hyrum nodded, Drew asked, "Have you been able to, you know, do things by yourself?"

After a lifetime of abuse from his father and the heavy-handed teachings of his church, Hyrum had been terrified of even thinking about touching himself. It hadn't mattered that Zed promised him it was normal; it hadn't mattered that his therapist assured him that he was entitled to privacy in the matter. It was wrong, it was only for daddies, and—the worst part of it—it was for punishing bad boys.

"Red said God wouldn't be mad about it," Hyrum answered in a near whisper. "He said Daddy lied to me."

"What did Red say?"

Red, when told the things Levi Munson had drilled into Hyrum's head, took a sharp left turn away from his religion and told Hyrum that Zed and Dr. Cheshire were right; there was nothing wrong with it. "God made our bodies so that we could do that if we wanted. He said it's to stop us from doing kissing things before we're old enough or have wives and husbands. If God hadn't done that, we'd be like animals and would go into heat when it was time to make babies."

Good job, Red.

"I think your brother is pretty smart," Drew said.

Hyrum leaned a little bit closer. "Drew, he said *girls* do it, too. How does he know?"

"He's got a wife, Hy. She probably told him."

Hyrum scrunched his nose again. "I can't figure out how. But Red also said that any man who says he never has is lying. Even church men."

"Probably."

"Even married men?"

Drew nodded. "Just because you're married, that doesn't mean you have sex whenever you want. Hell, I'm not waking Oz at three in the morning just because I'm horny. I go into the bathroom and take care of it myself."

"Aubrey said as long as I'm in private at home and I wash my hands after and don't talk about it during dinner, Red is right. But she said I could ask her questions if I needed to and she doesn't get embarrassed even though I think she lied about that."

"Lock your door," Drew chuckled. "It's super awkward when someone walks in on you."

"That happened?" Hyrum was both horrified and amused.

"Once when I was around fifteen. My mom walked in. It wasn't a huge deal. She just said, 'Sorry, I should have knocked,' then turned around and left. And Oz has walked in a few times."

"Was she mad?" Hyrum whispered.

"No. I think she thinks it's funny."

Hyrum glanced over the back of the sofa, making sure no one else was there. "How *do* girls do it?"

I made a quiet, polite exit because Drew was surely going to tell him, and I didn't need a refresher of that information. I headed for the balcony where Will and Jax were sipping Finn's most expensive scotch. I jumped onto the little table that was between them, careful to not knock over the bottle.

My allowance was not enough to pay for it if I broke it.

"Movie over?" Jax asked me.

No. But they're not watching it, either. They're talking about bouncy things.

"Hyrum is willingly discussing sex?" Will asked.

Of the solo variety. He has questions. Drew is answering. I didn't need to hear more.

"Good for Hyrum," Jax said. "Though Aubrey might have a nervous breakdown if he ever gets a girlfriend."

No worries there. He's not interested.

"Boyfriend?" Jax asked.

I don't think he realizes that's an option.

"He's aware of same-gender relationships," Will said.

But not for himself. He might not understand that's an option for himself.

"He'll figure it out if that's the case," Jax said. "Let's just be glad he's happy and comfortable now. If he turns fifty and decides then he wants to find someone, we'll deal with it then. And then let's hope whomever he's interested in is at least in the same ballpark age-wise."

He can't have a younger partner?

"How young is the issue," Will said. "It would be better, publicity-wise, if he didn't start dating someone thirty years younger."

"Or thirty years older," Jax snorted. "I don't think he would care about rocking a senior citizen. I'd be amused as hell, but I have a feeling that would lead to some serious heartbreak."

"Truth?" Will asked. "Have you always been so content to have him living with you? You've always welcomed him, but—"

"Will, I loved that boy from the moment I laid eyes on his filthy, gritty self. I wanted him the second I saw Aubrey's eyes light up. I think I knew in that moment she would fight anyone who wanted him to go home. Even me. But damn, I wanted him. If he ever moves out, I'll be just as upset as Aubrey."

"That boy," Will chuckled. "He's two years younger than you."

"And will always be her baby brother." He reached for the bottle. "We need to take him to Fuzzy's with us the next time we go. Not on a boys' night out with Drew and Zed and Jay. Just the three of us."

"Don't shoot pool with him. Aisha's been teaching him about the angles of the game. Where he falters with basic math, he excels at the visual aspects of geometry."

"Eh. I'll play a few games. Let him win some cash off me."

"You're witness to that, Wick."

Jax is toasted.

"He's not drunk yet. Just pleasantly warm."

"Don't let me get drunk," Jax said. "Drunk is only fun when Aubrey's around."

I dunno. I bet we'd find it pretty freaking funny.

"A few years ago, you said you wanted to keep coming here with her. It was the only way you thought you'd have the strength to hold onto the crown."

"I know. But you kept knocking Aisha up, and what's the fun in it if we can't get her drunk, too?"

She can drink now. Will can't knock her up again.

"Twice does not imply that I kept doing it. But Wick is right, she's not having another baby, and she'd be more than happy to come here and drink shamefully-sized margaritas with you. If Jay will babysit, we'll come."

"Babysit," Jax scoffed. "We'll be gone for a minute. Hell, when we go home from this, Union Square will be in turmoil and we'll have to be careful to not cross our own path."

Finn said to use the lab as a diversion. You can go back later.

"How long do you want to stay here?" Will asked.

"Not too long. I know Aubrey won't have time to miss me, but I'd rather be here with her. Nothing personal."

"Not taken personally," Will said. "I think you still need a diversion."

"At least one." Jax sighed. "I have an odd request. I've been having dreams about being stuck on the bridge. I can see the crowd forming below and everyone shouting at me, no one helping. I should be terrified, yet I'm not. I feel like I could fly. Why wasn't I scared?"

"I presumed you were."

"In the dreams? Eerily calm. I'm barely holding on, but I look up, away from the people screaming at me to get down and waiting for me to fall, and I watch as you run toward me. It's a full-on sprint, cranking your way up the on-ramp, all skinny arms and legs and that mop of hair flapping behind you. You stop to talk to someone for just a moment, and it's...I know. You'll save me."

"Who is it I speak to?"

"Just some guy," he said, shrugging. "I can't really see his face. I want to go, Will. My stupidity started there. I need to know if surviving that flipped a switch and started the risky behavior, or if I was always an idiot."

Will didn't take the shot. "Why now?"

Jax took his time. The chair creaked as he bent forward to look down at the Square, and the ice clinked against the side of his glass. I heard it swish around once and settle at the same time his thoughts did. "I'm not just tired and irritable. I feel like running, Will. I feel like grabbing Aubrey and running away, finding that beach in Hawaii or New Zealand, and leaving the world behind. And this doesn't feel like me. It feels like a scared little boy hanging off a bridge, waiting for someone, anyone, to stop staring and just get up and help."

"Then we'll go," Will said. "Give me time to make sure Rhys is in bed and to ask Drew to keep an eye on him, and we can go."

"In the morning." He slugged back the rest of his drink. "I've decided I'm getting drunk."

He probably would have, too, if Drew hadn't skittered onto the balcony, followed by the sound of Rhys crying out for Will.

= = =

I made it back to the living room before Will did. Rhys was sitting up on the sofa, and Hyrum kneeled on the floor, pleading with Rhys to look at him. Sean ran down the hall, and he slid in his socks across the floor before he stopped, then stood there with his mouth hung open.

Rhys's hands were on his thighs, palms up, sparks swirling above his fingertips. His breath came in great gulps, and when he saw Will, he sobbed, "Daddy, I can't stop it."

Hyrum was still begging Rhys to listen to him. Will sat carefully and scooted close to Rhys, his hand sliding across his son's back. "It's all right," he said, gently. "Does it hurt?"

"No, but it won't stop. Make it stop, Daddy."

"Not this time. Listen to Hyrum, little man." He brushed tears from Rhys's cheeks. "He knows what to do."

"But you can stop it! You stopped it before!"

"Hyrum can help *you* learn to stop it."

The sparks flew higher, dancing on thin tendrils of white and blue light. With a sob, Rhys nodded and looked at Hyrum.

"Think up a picture in your head, Rhys," Hyrum urged. "Look at your hands and pretend all the sparks are falling back inside your fingers. Tell them to go away. Say it out loud. Say 'Stop it! Go away!' and think up a picture about them sucking back into the tips on your fingers."

"Like pretending?"

Hyrum nodded.

Rhys closed his eyes and muttered to himself. "Stop it. Stop it. Go away."

"Pretend in your head you can see them going away."

The thin tendrils faded, and the sparks fell to his fingers and disappeared.

"See?" Hyrum said. "They do what you want them to. Someday you won't even have to pretend. They'll just stop when you want."

"How did you know?" Rhys rubbed the back of his hand across his nose. "Did you see me do it before?"

Hyrum looked to Will, who nodded, and then he scooted back to sit on the coffee table. Holding his hands a few inches apart, he sent sparks and light dancing between his outstretched fingers and let them dance around his hands. When he'd worked up enough light to make Rhys squint, he formed a small ball of energy. He let it linger, pulling his hands apart so that the ball floated above his palm, while Rhys watched with wide eyes. When he was sure Rhys was fascinated and not terrified, he closed his fingers around it, and it disappeared.

"It's a secret, okay?" he said to Rhys. "I was scared the first few times, too. No one knew what was happening and they thought I was a freak."

"What is it?"

Hyrum shrugged. "I dunno. But before I learned how to make it stop, I set a tree on fire."

Rhys's mouth dropped open.

"And one time?" Hyrum leaned forward and said, conspiring, "I set my daddy's hair on fire."

"No way!"

"I was mad at him. He was being mean to my sister, and I

wanted to stop him, but I didn't mean to throw sparks at him. Try not to set anyone on fire. It makes them mad."

"I won't." He looked up at Will. "I tried to stop it, Daddy, I really did."

"I know you did." He kissed the top of Rhys's head. "You'll get control over it as you get older."

"I can help you," Hyrum said. "We can practice together."

Will nodded. "That would be helpful, Hyrum, thank you. We need to tread carefully with this. There may be things of which you're capable that he isn't. He might not be a sparky sponge."

Hyrum, we'd learned, could not only expel energy, but he could also absorb it.

"When does it happen?" Hyrum asked. "When you're mad?"

Rhys shrugged. "Dunno."

"Typically, when he's tired," Will said. "Most of the time he doesn't notice. We've controlled it by placing our hands over his, but I don't think that will work much longer."

"What about the babies?" Hyrum asked.

"So far I've seen no indication that they have this gift. Rhys is displaying this at roughly the same age my abilities became apparent. If Charlie and Alex have a gift, as well, those haven't presented yet."

"Gift?" Sean sputtered. "It's a *gift?*"

"How else would you describe it?" Will's voice was laced with warning, and I don't think Sean noticed. "He can do something unusual, yes—"

"It's a goddamned superpower, that's what. It's fucking *amazing.*" He zoned in on Hyrum. "How? How do you do that?"

Hyrum shrugged. "It just happened. Maybe he got it from me."

"It's contagious?"

"Genetic," Will said. "And enough for now." He picked Rhys up. "Bedtime. Do you think you can go back to sleep?"

"I don't have my pajamas. Or my bear. And Charlie and Alex are at home and I don't want to be alone."

Will assured him that he could sleep in his underwear, and he wouldn't be alone. "I'll be with you. If you need something to hug, you can grab onto me. And I think it's time for *all* of us to go to bed."

Jax put the scotch bottle back into the cabinet and grumbled that he wasn't drunk enough, but Sean turned around and headed back into his room, in case he'd stepped over the line again.

"You two can stay up," Jax said to Hyrum as he turned toward the hall. "Will just didn't want Rhys to fight going to bed."

I went into the room with Will and Rhys and curled up on the window seat to keep an eye on them, but Will stayed awake all night, making sure that a stray spark didn't burn the house down.

12

On the day that six-year-old Jax decided to run away from home in search of the old west town he was certain covered the Wastelands, Union Square was crowded. Cars parked along the street and others floated close to the center line; air bikes zipped between them, weaving in and out of traffic, sometimes sliding onto the sidewalk to get by.

There were enough people walking past and cutting across the Square that we were able to sit on the steps and watch the door without appearing to creepily loiter, waiting for a little boy carrying a backpack with contents that wiggled. He stepped out at ten past nine in the morning, looked both ways, and then headed down the street, in no apparent hurry to get where he was going.

"The question I've always had," Will said as they got up. "Where were your guards?"

We crossed the street, cutting in front of an idling delivery van. "There was only one," Jax answered. "He thought I was still in the apartment. That was back when I was supposed to wait at the front desk and have the guard on duty call him to take me to school. I waited until the desk guard was distracted and slipped out."

"How fired was he?"

"Very. He was stripped of rank and reassigned to the army, where I imagine he spent the rest of his enlistment cleaning toilets on Mare Island. My personal guard is the one who suggested someone always be on me, following, no matter what.

He was gutted that I'd slipped out and he hadn't been aware. I'm not sure he ever accepted that it wasn't his fault."

Once we were across the street and hidden between two parked cars, Will patted the pocket on his sweatshirt to make sure I was still there, and we jumped. We made one stop near the ball park to see if little Jax was being followed, and when it was certain he wasn't, we jumped again, popping up at a spot half a block from the pedestrian entryway to the upper level of the Bay Bridge.

The bridge was closed to most traffic; bicycles and air bikes were allowed, as well as foot traffic. On this morning there was a steady stream of people heading into Oakland and beyond, and a smaller stream of people on bikes coming into the city. No one paid attention to the determined small boy heading up the ramp. They should have noticed; he was alone, on foot, with no adult in sight. He was their Prince, yet no one looked at him closely enough to see that.

Once he'd made it onto the bridge and a few hundred feet past, he stopped, peering between metal support slats to get a bearing on his destination.

"I'd assumed the Wastelands were just on the other side of the bridge," Jax explained. "When I looked and they weren't, it made sense that if I got up a little higher, I'd be able to see them from here."

"You'd never been to Oakland?"

"I was six," Jax said. "Logical thinking was not my strong suit."

"So. You'd been to Oakland. Directly across the bridge. Where cars fly above the sky lane, and the infrastructure is decidedly contemporary compared to San Francisco."

"Shut up," Jax said, chuckling.

Little Jax grabbed onto the railing and pulled himself up.

"And there he goes," Will murmured.

With every foot he scaled, more people stopped to watch, yet none of them tried to grab him before he was out of their reach. We stayed out of the way, on the opposite side of the bridge, trying to keep the crowd between the prince and us.

When he was ten feet up, Will turned to look at the ramp and spotted the fifteen-year-old version of himself running toward us.

It was just as Jax had dreamed; young William sprinted, his arms and legs pumping as hard as he could manage, trying to get there before it was too late.

He stopped short of the crowd, mouth open. People had realized who Jax was and were yelling, ordering him to get down, and get down *right now*; he made it twenty feet up when his foot slipped, and the strap on his backpack caught on a bracket. He pulled his arm out of one side of the pack, thinking, Jax said, that he could hold it with the other while he climbed down, but it was stuck, and he'd made the mistake of looking down.

"From up there, it looked a hell of a lot higher," he said.

"That *was* high," Will said. "It *is* high. Too high."

Now people were yelling for him to just throw the backpack into the bay and get down. Only one person that we could see had fished a phone from their pocket to call for help, and young William stood there, frozen.

"Why is he not moving?" Will whispered to himself.

He knows he's not supposed to be here. He's waiting for the Emperor.

"What made me go?" he wondered out loud.

Little Jax was screaming for help now. William took a half step but hesitated; the Emperor was coming, this was the Emperor's job.

Someone spoke to him.

"No. Not possible," Will muttered. He waited only a few seconds more and then went over, standing behind him. "*You* are the Emperor," he whispered. "No one else will rescue him. Go. Before it's too late."

The teenager turned, and his eyes lit up as he recognized himself.

"When they ask who you are, your name, tell them 'Emperor.' The King will believe you. Get him safely to his mother, then go home and explain this to Finn."

Young Will took off, leaping at the railing and then the

tower, ignoring the people who were now screaming for him to wait, let the police handle it. Sirens blared in the distance, but he continued climbing until he had little Jax in a firm grip and had freed the backpack from the bracket it had hung up on.

The first police car came to a loud, siren-squealing stop a few feet from the entry to the bridge and Queen Donna raced out the back door. By then, William was on the ground with the prince clinging to him, and he pushed through the crowd, shoving at more than one person with his shoulder when they tried to reach for the prince. Once clear, William set Jax down, and he raced to his mother, leaving the backpack with his rescuer.

William felt the wiggling and heard the voice coming from inside; he unzipped the pack and whispered into it before handing it over. I was still at home, in his When, curled up on his bed, yet also in the backpack, demanding to know what was going on.

Queen Donna stood on the bridge in bare feet, dressed in a sweatshirt and jogging shorts, her usually meticulously coiffed hair tied in a loose ponytail. Typically reserved, she was crying hard, tears coating her face as she scooped her son up and held him tight.

King Eli arrived in the next police car. He didn't run, but he walked swiftly to his wife and son, and once he was sure the boy was okay, he strode purposefully toward William.

"And thusly did you become the Emperor," Jax said.

"And thusly in ten seconds did I run from His Majesty like a stupid, scared boy and am still genuinely surprised I didn't wet myself."

He was only off by five seconds. He handed the bag with me inside over, and when the King asked, he said his name was "Emperor," and then dashed off in a spurt of panic.

"We were both scared shitless," Jax mused. "But this isn't it. Whatever flipped my switch didn't start here. I was six and stupid, that's all."

If anyone's life changed here, it was Will's.

"Indeed."

And we've been noticed.

King Eli, his arm around his still-sobbing wife, was watching us. When he realized we'd comprehended his recognition, a slight grin crept onto his face and he winked.

There was no pretending we weren't who he knew we were. Jax grinned in response and Will gave him a short, two-fingered salute. Then while the world was fixated on the wayward little prince and his crying mother, even knowing Eli was watching, we jumped back.

= = =

Rhys was right where Will had left him, at the kitchen table with Drew, eating a waffle with too much syrup, half of it coating his chin and cheeks. He hadn't been told we were leaving; as far as he was concerned, we'd been in another room and were finally ready for breakfast.

"Drew makes good waffles, Daddy," Rhys said. "He puts cibbanom in them. No. Wait. Cimmanum. Cinnamon."

Will glanced at his plate. "And how much butter is on that?"

"Lots."

Drew shrugged. "He wanted all the little divots filled with butter. The kid is skinny as a rail, so I decided it didn't matter."

"It's not his weight I'm concerned about."

"Fine. I'll give him some fruit when he's done. Sit down, I've got a bunch of waffles ready."

Jax had no problem with waffles drenched in butter with far too much syrup. Will took a waffle, but he broke it into pieces and bit into it plain, which made Rhys groan.

"Waffles have to have butter and syrup. That's the rule."

"Did you try it without first?" Will asked. "The cinnamon Drew put in it makes it very tasty all by itself. I might even have two. Or three."

"Really?" He shoved the last bite of his in his mouth, ignoring the river of syrup that ran down his chin. "I like this. It's not squishy like Mommy's waffles."

That's because your mommy's waffles have been drowned in the tears of everyone who has to eat them.

Will speared a piece with his fork. "Would you like to try a bite and taste the cinnamon?"

"Can I?"

Will told him to take a swig of his water to get the syrup taste out of his mouth and then handed his fork over. "Well?" he asked as Rhys chewed.

"That's like a cookie! It tastes like Aunt Aubrey's dickerdoobles."

"Snickerdoodles," Will said, amused. "Do you want another waffle?"

"I'm full. Can I go wake Hyrum up? He's still sleeping."

"He was up late," Drew said. "Let him sleep."

"But he'll miss waffles and he likes them lots."

"I'll make more when he gets up," Drew promised. "But he needs to sleep, so we're leaving him alone, and his door closed, all right?"

Rhys sighed. "Okay. Can I watch TV?"

"Wash your hands and face first," Will said. When Rhys was down the hall, he turned to Drew. "All right, why don't you want him to get Hyrum? He wouldn't mind if Rhys woke him."

"Yeah, well, I suspect Hyrum is plastered across the bed, bare-assed naked. He was weirdly excited to be told that sleeping without clothes on isn't a sin."

"Do we want to know?" Jax asked.

"Probably not." He peered over the breakfast bar. "Wick, have you eaten?"

I ate before we left. I'm good, thanks.

"He's turning down food. Is he all right? Did something happen?"

"We both fed him," Jax said. "He's stuffed. Why the hell were you discussing nude sleeping with Hyrum?"

"He asked, Jax. I told him we're all born naked, so it clearly wasn't God's problem, just something that weirds out old, uptight people."

You should warn Aubrey. Sometimes she checks on him at night if he had a bad day.

"Or not," Drew snorted. "Surprise, Aubrey."

"He doesn't have a problem with her seeing him naked," Jax said.

"It's not the nudity she'd be shocked by," Drew said. "Let's just say that after some assurances from Red about his eternal soul, adolescence seems to have finally caught up with him."

"What? Oh. Good for him. Tell him to lock his door, then."

"Were it Zed, you'd rush down the hall to throw his door open and bellow, 'Breakfast, you little pervert!'" Will said.

"Of course I would."

They all turned at the sound of a bedroom door opening, but it was Sean, and Rhys stopped him before he could get two steps out of the room. In his little boy loud voice, he informed Sean that we weren't waking Hyrum up even though there were waffles with cinnamon in them, and Hyrum likes waffles as much as he likes cookies. Sean inhaled, catching the aroma of warm cinnamon and maple syrup, and told Rhys that he liked waffles, too. When Rhys latched onto his hand to lead him to the kitchen, Sean grinned and let himself be dragged through the living room to the table, and he sat where Rhys told him to.

"Don't let Daddy tell you no syrup and butter. You have to have lots of butter. It's a rule."

"Well, then," Sean said. "I won't let you down."

I'm gonna get Hyrum. He'll feel bad if he misses waffles.

Hyrum was hanging hallway off the bed, his head only a few inches from the floor. One hand rested on his chin and the other gripped at his blanket, and the only thing he had on was his left sock. Even as flexible as I was, I didn't see how that was comfortable.

I sniffed his eyelids and then his nose, and when he didn't stir, I moved to his ear, licking the spot where it met his face.

Wake up, dude. It's time to eat.

He took a deep breath, but his eyes remained closed.

I stuck my mouth right at his ear and shouted *Waffles!*

His eyes fluttered. "Waffles?"

Dude.

I backed up a few steps.

You heard me? Old Hyrum understands me. Do you now?

"You're upside down, Wick," he said, voice thick with sleep.

No, you are. Now tell me if you understand me.

He blinked a few times, and then pulled himself back onto the bed. The bright light in the room made him squint, and then frown. "I slept late, didn't I? It's light already."

You were up late. Put some clothes on. It's breakfast time.

I didn't wait to see if he would follow. I bolted through the cat flap and down the hall, calling for Will and then Drew. When I leaped for the table, Will reached out to grab me, lest I wind up in the syrup.

"What the hell, Wick?"

Hyrum understood me. It was only one word, I think, but he heard it. Waffles. I said there were waffles and he said it back. 'Waffles?' Just like that.

"Not to burst your bubble," Drew said, "but he might have smelled them, and it was a question. Like, 'do I smell waffles?'"

Oh.

"I'm sorry. Would it make you feel better if I got you a piece of bacon? There's some in the fridge."

Bacon would not make me feel better; I wanted Hyrum to understand me. He spent long, sleepless nights telling me his deepest secrets, and I wanted to be able to tell him I was truly listening. I wanted to have a conversation with him that didn't involve Will or Drew interpreting, mostly because he would never say in front of them some of the things he told me in private.

Still, I wasn't about to refuse a slice of bacon.

Hyrum was still trying to wake up as he shuffled down the hall. He dropped into his chair with an audible thud and asked why no one had woken him up. "I almost missed breakfast."

"I would have made fresh waffles when you got up," Drew said as he broke the bacon up into Wick-sized pieces.

"Did Wick tell you what we were having?" Will asked.

Hyrum grunted. "Someone did."

The room fell quiet, until Rhys reached for a waffle and tossed it onto Hyrum's plate. Will and Drew stared at each other and Jax stared at me, leaving Sean to glance at everyone, trying to figure out why there was a sudden lull.

It was only one word. More will come later.

As I munched on my bacon, they started talking again, trying to decide what to do for the day. What was left unsaid was the reality of letting Drew and Sean wander freely with Hyrum and Rhys: it couldn't happen. Drew was a little too computer savvy and might be tempted to look himself up, and Sean shouldn't see too much of anything.

"How's the beach here?" Jax asked Will. "I wanted time off and sitting on a beach watching Rhys and Hyrum play sounds pretty damned good."

They looked up at hearing their names. "Could we?" Hyrum asked.

Will didn't want to take Rhys to Ocean Beach, where the currents were strong enough to suck a little boy under too fast to save. He opted for the beach at Crissy Field. It was small but rarely crowded, and they could splash in the water if they wanted.

"No swimming," he warned them. "It's too cold. You can go in ankle deep, and that's it."

They didn't care. Will pulled his old sand toys out of the storage locker downstairs, and we took a taxi to the marina. While Jax and Will sat on a bench, the others went onto the beach to build sand castles, which would end—as it usually did at home—with Rhys the Giant stomping them back into the ground.

"It's January," Jax mused. "Why the hell is it so warm?"

"Because it's January. Clearly, you haven't been here often. If you want cold, come in July."

Jax chuckled. "What's that old saying? The coldest winter I ever spent was a summer in San Francisco."

"Usually attributed to Mark Twain, however erroneously."

"That doesn't make it less true." Jax turned to look behind us. "How long do you think it'll take Drew to realize the Ozoo complex is still there and at least four times its current size?"

He saw. He's trying to not make a big deal about it.

"You don't have a problem with him seeing it?" Jax asked.

"I should. But part of me wants him to understand he's doing more than tinkering with ideas. He's building a legacy."

"What about Oz? Did she open the Wastelands in this timeline?"

"If she'd wanted to, there was no time. She finished school, became a mother, then Queen. That Drew was able to build that—" Will nodded to the buildings across the street "—while also functioning as King of Midlam is a testament to how well they worked together. He couldn't have done it without her. And before you ask, no, I know nothing about the Wastelands as a tourist attraction. I'm as eager as you are to see where it takes her."

I want to go and ride a horse. And go to a saloon. She said there would be saloons, right?

"I have to admit, there's a part of me that hates the idea that she and Drew have set aside the idea of ending the monarchy. I know they sought advice from their elder selves, and those people regret it, but it did eventually work out. Didn't it?"

What about brothels? Like, above the saloon.

"In time. Yet even now, a large part of the population wishes they hadn't. They romanticize the notion of an American monarchy and fall back on the truth of how well it worked."

There's gonna be brothels. She wants everything accurate. You can go hire yourself a hooker.

"Wick, stop," Will sighed. "There will not be hookers in the Wastelands."

Yeah, there will, whether you want them there or not.

Jax chuckled but went right on with their conversation. "You would be King now."

"Finn is alive. He would likely be King. And had he been King?"

The world would have ended.

Will nodded. "No one else was doing the work at the same depth as he. The world would have ended."

Drew ducked as Rhys chucked a handful of sand at him.

"Then it needs to end," Jax mused. "The monarchy, not the world."

"Not necessarily. We have the Old Mint. If its preservation remains a part of the duties of the monarch, the information contained within is protected. Eli could choose another heir. Or if Finn becomes King, the work will still be done. He would be in the position to facilitate all of it."

"How? He won't have time, and even if the information is there, the tasks need to be followed through with. And if he's busy running the country, will he even meet your mother? Will you be born? And holy hell, if you're not born..."

"Stop."

Tell him who would really be King.

"Wick?"

Finn wouldn't be King right now. Tell him.

"What's he going on about?" Jax asked.

"A fact of life that I had set aside. Finn would not be King, not unless his father abdicated."

Jax let that sink in. He got to his feet and stared at Drew, opened his mouth to say something that wouldn't work its way out, and then sat back down. "My grandson is still alive?" he finally managed.

"Alive and well and living in the Marina district. My mother had a home there and left it to him."

Tell him the whole truth. The truth you didn't know until Finn and Jo came to live in our When.

"It's unnecessary," Will said.

He's going to ask why Finn never talks about him. And if you don't tell him, he'll probably come here on his own sometime and go find him.

"He will not. Jax is not that immature."

"Yes, I am," Jax said. "Whatever he's talking about, I'm probably that immature. Is it something to do with your grandfather?"

With a sigh, Will nodded. "A request. Don't ask Finn about his father. They don't speak, and it would hurt him deeply to be reminded of that."

"What happened?"

"I did," Will sighed. "He was not forgiving when Dad let me leave. He understood it meant that he would never see me again—even after seeing proof that I'd lived, he wouldn't bend. He'll see me but refuses to speak with his own son."

He's kind of a hypocrite. Drew let him leave when he was nineteen to move to another When.

"Drew let him leave because my mother needed him, Wick."

Rhys caught Drew unaware and dumped a bucket of sand down the back of his pants.

"Does he know about Rhys?" Jax asked, laughing at Drew's discomfort. "Or the twins?"

"He knows but hasn't met any of the kids. Not yet."

They watched as Drew chased after a squealing Rhys, and as Sean handed Hyrum another bucket filled with sand, nodding in Drew's direction.

After a long stretch of quiet that was filled with the sounds of laughter coming from the beach, Jax sat back and grunted. "Eli wouldn't have been King. He left his birth When to take your mother forward. And he stayed there. Oz and Drew would have chosen someone else as the crown prince. Or princess?"

Will argued that they would have chosen him in his youth and held the ceremony when he was sixteen. Even knowing what was coming, if that Oz had chosen to hold onto the crown, he would have had time to go off and live his life, then return to take the throne. "Presuming she didn't abdicate," Will said.

"How is it possible that he's still alive?"

"He's beating the average," Will said. "But remember, he cheated time somewhat. His visits home were few, and there are many, many years between his birth and my father's that he essentially skipped."

"You're making my head hurt."

"Only because you're overthinking things. Who would have been King doesn't matter. The fact of this When is that Oz gave up the throne to a shaky democracy, and she had significant regrets."

"Oh, god. Are they still alive?" His voice was tightly bound with hope. "If their son is…"

"Jax."

"Come on. I know I'm not. Aubrey's not. We'd be, what, over two hundred fifty? It's possible, isn't it? Eli will only be twenty-five years younger than his father. He's here, he's—"

"He cheated time, Jax."

Stop holding onto secrets, Will. Things will change. They're different people.

"I know, Wick." To Jax's unasked question, he added, "He points out that our lives are not the same. The Oz and Drew of my history are not the same Oz and Drew of my present. Their lives took a new trajectory six years ago."

"Come on, Will."

He still didn't want to tell Jax anything. His adult life had been bound by secrets, all the things he could never tell anyone about their own lives. The only reason he spoke about his grandfather Eli was because Oz and Drew had already named him. He was four months away from being born, but he wasn't a secret.

"I don't want to break your heart," Will finally said.

"Then they're not. It's fine. I just had this sudden hope that they'd known you when you were small."

"Well." Drew was now on his back, and they were covering him with sand. "Once Eli left, they began to live their lives in multiple Whens, for a time anyway. I have memories of them, though they're faint and I'm not sure if what I remember is truth or wishes. They saw me frequently, until my third birthday. After that, I think they came to see me from a distance."

"Why did they stop?"

Oz and Drew knew who their great-grandson would become. They understood where his life would take him, and they didn't want to influence the choices he and Finn would have to make. "They'd had the chance to know me as an adult. They wanted the next version of themselves to have that chance as well."

They knew your brain would hold onto them too well if they kept coming.

"I was three, Wick. I don't think how my brain functioned was all that apparent."

"Bullshit." Jax jutted his chin in Rhys's direction. "He's three. He's brilliant. We can already tell. Surely Oz and Drew recognized that in you."

Will grinned. "Are you finally admitting I'm smarter than you?"

"Shut up. I'd never admit that." He laughed, not just at himself but at Drew's discomfort. "You're intelligent. I'll give you that."

"Hyrum," Will called out. "Dig Drew out. If you dump much more sand on him, he might not be able to breathe."

Remember when he and Oz buried Zed here? You yelled at the guards.

"I remember both versions of bringing them here," Will said.

He reminded Jax of a day when Drew was twelve and Oz was just ten. He'd brought them to the beach so that they could play in the sand, much like Rhys and Hyrum were doing now. While the guards kept an eye on them, he crept along the backside of the tiny building that housed the restroom and broke the neck of a man who had a gun sighted on young Andrew.

When you change things in your timeline, he learned along the way, the memories stick with you. He'd changed Oz's timeline by saving her from drowning and remembered them both. He remembered the before and after of changing Jax's timeline when he kept him from dying on his bike ride down California Street. But because it was an older version of himself who changed Drew's path, Will remembered because he'd met up with himself on Ghirardelli Square after the kids were in a car on the way home with their guards, and the older Will transferred the memory to him with a touch.

He swore he only ever changed things that veered from the history he knew, the timelines written out in the Old Mint, but I knew better.

He changed things to keep his own heart from breaking.

"I'm grateful for that," Jax said. "Still annoyed you didn't tell me when it happened, but I get it."

There were things he hadn't changed, things that happened after he didn't die three months before his 43rd birthday. In Will's history, the information he knew and had cross-checked at the Old Mint, Levi Munson had not captured Oz at the start of his war with Midlam. She'd remained at home and hadn't been whisked away to a safe house in Denver along with Drew and her brother, Zed.

On Jax's request, Levi came to Pacifica to—ostensibly—negotiate peace. He had no intention of giving up, and every intention of killing Andrew to bring the Queen of Midlam, his mother, to her knees. Levi had been positive Drew's death would cause her to fold and hand over her country. He hadn't counted on the intense level of support Midlam enjoyed from Pacifica, and he hadn't counted on his eldest son warning them that Drew was in danger.

Jax hated Levi before the war erupted; he hated him even more when he saw his daughter's broken body, the deep, black bruises and puncture wounds he'd inflicted on her. His rage was white hot, seeing the proof of her broken bones and the myriad of cuts that would scar like fine lace over her body. He wanted Levi Munson dead, though he didn't gloat or celebrate when his father-in-law was murdered in a jail cell in Leavenworth, Kansas, just days following his conviction of war crimes and offenses against the King.

"Everything he did to Aubrey when she was a girl," Jax said, voice soft. "Everything he did to Hyrum. Look at him, Will. How is he still such a sweet, wonderful person?"

"How is Aubrey still that?" Will countered.

"I should have had him killed the day after I took the throne," Jax said.

"She asked you not to."

"But if I had, everything he did to Oz—" He stopped abruptly, his eyes on Drew, who was stomping across the sand, fingers splayed, threatening to attack Rhys with the Giant Tickle Monster. "That was it, Will. That was when the switch flipped. It had nothing to do with being a wild little kid. I started resenting this life the day you grabbed my kids and ran to Denver. You could take them to safety when I couldn't. You could protect them. I began hating it the day I saw them again, and how broken my baby girl was." He bit back the tears that threatened. "If I had killed Levi—"

"Aubrey would have never looked at you the same way, Jax. And if you jump back and do it now?"

"I know," he said, barely a whisper.

"Given a life with her over revenge on him?"

"I know."

Take him to the simulator. We were going to go check on Jeff and Fluffy anyway, weren't we?

"What are you suggesting, Wick?"

You told Jax once that you could arrange it, him against Levi in the simulator.

"You think we should pull Tobias out of the alternate program just so Jax can have at him?"

He could beat the snot out of a man who looks like Tobias, and no harm would really be done.

"A great deal of harm could be done," Will said.

But it's an option.

"It is."

He explained to Jax what I proposed, expecting him to give it a moment of consideration and then brush it off. Instead, Jax stood up, told everyone to gather their toys, because we were heading back to the apartment to clean up, and then going on an adventure.

"Are you sure about this?" Will asked.

"That goddamned computer-generated freak used Levi's face to torment my daughter. Damn right, I'm sure. He hurt her. He's a dead man."

PART THREE

13

Saint Francis—Finn's simulated vision of the city a thousand years in the future—looked a lot like it had when we left it five years earlier. Buildings were faded monuments to the San Francisco it had once been, with a forest sprouting around and through it. The air was crisp, and fog marked the morning in cloudy clusters. The bakery was long gone, replaced by a crumbling hut that had once served as a traveler's rest stop, and the Square was covered in patchy layers of dirt, the concrete cracked and marred by divots.

The lab entry was right where we'd left it, down the stairs in the center of a shabby shack.

It was quiet, the sounds of breath hiding behind beating hearts; Will and Drew's hearts beat with excitement, but Hyrum, Jax, and Sean's galloped with fear. Only Rhys seemed unaffected. He rode through the portal on his father's hip and stayed there as he looked around, curious to see if this matched the stories told in hushed tones with the lights dim and his brother and sister asleep across the room.

Before we left the San Francisco of Will's youth, he spoke with Rod, a tech in Finn's lab, telling him where we were going, and requested someone remind Finn that the last time we were there, it was days of chicken and eggs and little else. With a subtle nod toward Rhys, he asked Rod to make sure there was something more. Fruit. Sandwiches. But not, for Hyrum's sake, peanut butter.

Hyrum had lived on peanut butter for two years. He'd been promised he never had to have it again, and he went out of his way to neither see nor smell it.

"What do you think, Rhys?" Will asked his son, breaking the silence. "Does this look like you expected?"

Rhys nodded. "It's creepy. I like it."

"Where are we?" Sean asked, voice thin.

"One thousand years in the future," Will said, omitting that we were, in truth, in a When only thirty-five years ahead of our own. Telling him about the simulator might come later; other than the one time in Bounce, he hadn't thrown up, but his pallor suggested it was a strong possibility. "This is Saint Francis, home to elves and Shedu warriors."

"And Jeff and Fluffy!" Rhys beamed. "When do we get to meet them?"

Drew grinned and looked past Will's shoulder. "You should meet him first."

Strolling across the Square was a man with tousled black hair; he wore loose linen pants and a shirt a size too large, belted at the waist by a sword he rested his hand upon. The closer he got, the quicker his pace and the brighter his smile became. A few feet away, he blurted, "Emperor! Prince Andrew! And friends!"

Will shook his hand but Drew lifted him in a giant hug. "Shivan, man, how's life? You look good. Hell, you look older. How old are you?"

"Life is amazing. And I'm thirty-five."

"How the hell? It's only been around five years since we were here, I think."

"Time flies." Shivan turned to Will. "You spawned. With the lady Aisha?"

"Indeed."

Shivan stepped closer. "You have her eyes," he said to Rhys.

"You know my mommy?"

"I do. Your mommy is a brave and noble warrior," Shivan said. "Where is she?"

"At work. But Charlie and Alex are sick so she might come home to take care of them. They have colds."

"Our other children," Will explained.

If Will had more to say about them, Shivan's interest evaporated as soon as he got a good look at Jax.

"The King Jackson," he breathed. "They weren't lying. You really do look like my father. If you had a beard and more gray hair, I'm not sure I could tell you apart."

"Is that a good thing?" Jax asked Will.

"Yeosef was modeled after you. You'll note faces that seem vaguely familiar throughout." He introduced Shivan to Hyrum and Sean, who was now visibly shaking and so pale he was no longer pink.

Are Jeff and Fluffy still here?

Shivan looked down. "Wick! I've missed you. Fluffy is a wonderful companion, but he doesn't fit on my shoulder."

We can get you a pint-sized kitty. Are they still here?

"They're still in Krisf's care," Shivan said after Will passed the question along. "Jeff has grown a bit and is experimenting with new skins. Fluffy is leaner, but otherwise, he's the same. They're both beloved here, so no taking them home with you, all right?"

I would do it if I could, and he knew that.

"Jeff is experimenting with skin?" Drew asked, confused.

"He learned that he can think new things for himself. He's turned blue, green, yellow, and is currently red. It's a very pretty red. I think I like it more than the black."

"Jeff is real?" Hyrum bounced on his toes, holding his hands to his chest the way he did when he was excited. "He's not just a story?"

"Here, he's real," Will said. "Would you like to meet him?"

Both Hyrum and Rhys nodded.

"Lead the way," Will said to Shivan. "None of them will be happy until they see for themselves that Fluffy and Jeff are fine, especially Wick."

I climbed Drew's leg to get to his shoulder and warned him to keep an eye on Sean. He hadn't thrown up yet, but he was starting to sweat, and the shaking hadn't eased up. *He also isn't very observant for a reporter.*

"How's that?"

You're talking to the cat. Will has spoken for me, like a hundred times. So have you. Sean hasn't even noticed.

"Give him some time. He's processing a lot right now."

He needs a better processor. Like, one of those nanobot-filled dual octuple-core thingies you're always talking about. Jam one of those in his brain before the sight of Jeff makes his head explode.

= = =

There were no hills to contend with. Saint Francis was mostly flat; Finn hadn't altered that part of the program after listening to Will's feedback, and no one was complaining about it. Rhys and Hyrum scrambled ahead of us, stopping when Will or Shivan warned them they were getting too far ahead or heading in the wrong direction, but their excitement wouldn't allow for a leisurely stroll from downtown to Ghirardelli Square. We moved at a pace comfortable for Will and Drew; Jax kept up well, but Sean was huffing and close to breaking out into a jog.

I thought it was a bit mean of them, but when I turned to look at him for the fifth time, Drew whispered, "If he's hurrying to keep up, he's not thinking about how afraid he is. We won't go so fast that he just can't do it."

It was close. He scrambled for just over two miles, saved only by the lack of hills. If this had been at home, a block of Powell Street probably would have killed him.

We approached Ghirardelli from behind; the last time we'd been there the ocean lapped onto dirt where a long stretch of land and then the aquatic park should have been, but Will wasn't sure what we'd find and asking Shivan might hint to the simulator's always-listening computer what he expected. If he expected something, it would probably be there.

Hyrum and Rhys skittered to a stop at the end of the street. For several feet ahead there was a cobblestone path, and beyond it, a beach. Fluffy was in the sand, running, and sailing twenty feet above him was a thirty-foot-long bright red dragon with dark blue eyes, and right where I'd planned them, handles at the base of his long neck.

I'd wondered if he'd keep them; I'd thought them into his creation so he could carry Oz and Drew easily, but I wasn't sure at all that Krisf would risk taking him for a ride. He'd promised to care for Jeff, but no more than that, and I hadn't thought to ask.

He headed out over the bay to make a leisurely turn, and when he did Fluffy spotted us and began galloping in our direction. Shivan was right; he was still a massive thing, as tall as a Clydesdale horse and then some, but he was lean like a tiger and no longer the kitten I'd created. He squealed, and it pierced the air, making Rhys giggle as he covered his ears. Hyrum bounced on his toes and his hands twitched at his chest as he called out, "Here, kitty, kitty, kitty!"

Fluffy came to a stop in front of Rhys and Hyrum, and Jeff landed right behind him, stretching his wings before folding them slowly. He was showing off, letting us see how much he had grown. I wanted him to lower his head so I could sniff him, but before I could ask, we were distracted by the sick thud that Sean's body made when he passed out cold and hit the ground.

14

Fluffy sniffed at Jax the way I sniff the air when something dead and delicious is in the oven. He started at Jax's head and worked his way down, and when Jax held his hands out, palms up, for further inspection, Fluffy touched the tip on his tongue to Jax's left hand, and then set his massive chin in the other.

"You're a love bug, aren't you?" Jax murmured. He did what Fluffy wanted, and scratched under his chin, leaning in to reach the side of his neck. The resulting purr caused the ground to vibrate, which made Rhys and Hyrum squeal again.

"Curious that he went to Jax first," Drew whispered to Will. "I assumed he'd go to Rhys."

Rhys doesn't need him.

"Is he all right?"

"Tired," Will said.

Sean, who was now awake and mostly coherent, sat on the ground behind us, leaning against the brick foundation of Ghirardelli. "That's a cat," he muttered. "A goddamned cat."

There's a dragon, too, Mr. Observation.

"He's a nice cat," Drew said. "He's only eaten one or two people that I know of."

That got Sean to his feet. "No. No way."

"I'd worry more about him." Drew gestured toward Jeff, who waited patiently behind Fluffy for his turn to sniff the new people. "He's friendly, too, but I've seen him torch an entire platoon of soldiers. If Wick wants him to erupt, he'll erupt."

"'If Wick wants.'" He visibly relaxed. "Fine. Mess with me. I don't care."

"Wick's right, you're not very observant." Drew turned away, and Jeff squatted down, stretching his long neck so that someone could pet him between his nostrils. Drew beckoned Rhys to come over, but he froze, suddenly not so sure he wanted to get that close to the smoky end of the friendly dragon.

"It's not personal," Will said to Jeff. "He's very small, and you're very large."

He'll wait. He knows Rhys needs a minute.

Hyrum did not. He skipped over to Jeff and asked him—not Drew or Will—if he could touch his snout, too. "My name is Hyrum. I'm really happy to meet you." He stroked Jeff gently, his hand gliding over Jeff's skin. "You're as soft as Drew said. He said you were pretty, but he didn't say you were the most beautiful dragon in the world."

A new rumbling began alongside the one Fluffy had created.

I had no idea he could purr.

New weapon. Jeff-purr-induced earthquake.

Jax moved from Fluffy to Jeff, asking, as Hyrum did, if it was all right to touch him. "You're magnificent," he breathed. "If I'd met you when I was young, I might have decided to live here."

"A boy and his dragon," Will said, amused. "I imagine your life would have been vastly different if you'd had Jeff following you around like a puppy."

He had me. Wasn't that enough?

"You were unable to tag along to help him avoid some of the decisions he made while away from home," Will said.

"I needed a chaperone from thirteen to seventeen," Jax said. "But you've always been fantastic, Wick. You know that."

Sometimes I need to hear it. You never tell me I'm pretty, either. Tell me I'm pretty and that you love me.

"You need affirmations?" Will asked.

No, but hearing Jax say that out loud would be really funny.

Rhys finally stepped away from Will and went over to Fluffy, reaching out hesitantly. He touched one of Fluffy's massive paws first, fingers brushing over fur. "Daddy, he's soft. Is he like Wick? Can I talk to him?"

"He would enjoy it if you spoke to him. Keep in mind he'll

understand you, but he can't speak to us. Wick has a sense of what Fluffy wants, but as far as we know, he's nonverbal."

"I like your stripes," Rhys told Fluffy. "Orange kitties are pretty. You're the orangest kitty I've ever seen."

Fluffy lowered his head so that his nose was at Rhys's face level. He stuck his tongue out just a bit and touched it to Rhys's cheek, which made him squeal.

"Daddy, he kissed me!" He stretched on his toes to plant a kiss just above Fluffy's nose. "Hy, come see! He's soft and really nice."

It took half an hour before they were ready to push on. Shivan waited patiently, his hand resting on the hilt of the sword that had once been too heavy for him to wield. He was soaking up every detail, the sight of the spawn of the Emperor and Lady Aisha, the King Jackson, and his good friends.

He glanced at Sean once or twice, but what he saw didn't make him happy.

When we finally moved on, heading for the elfin village, Drew fell into step next to Shivan. "How are you thirty-five now?" Drew asked. "I was twenty when we left here, and you were fifteen. Now I'm twenty-five."

"Time's a tricky thing," Shivan said with a grin. "Maybe it's magic."

"I thought the magic ended with Hagar and Tobias."

"There's always a little magic, Andrew. Call it science, if you will. The whims of a man sitting somewhere in your reality, tinkering with the code that gives us life. Our days are shorter than yours, and our years speed by."

From behind us, Rhys piped up, "Do you teach history, too?"

"He's mocking your speech patterns," Drew said. "You sound a lot like Will now, and we keep telling him that his daddy sounds like a history teacher."

"Ah." He spun around, walking backward. "I'm trying to find my voice. It's been a long time since I've spoken to a human. Usually, when I'm conversing with my wife or children, I use somewhat of a...code. Small, clipped words. Does that make sense to you?"

"You talk like my little brother and sister?"

"Could be," he chuckled. "I have a little boy about your age. I hope that you get to meet him before you go home."

"What's his name?"

"Quinn."

"How many little monsters do you have?" Drew asked.

"Just three. Two boys and a girl. Darville is twelve, Therese is eight, and Quinn is almost four."

"And your wife?"

"Thirty-four."

That made Drew laugh. "No, I meant her name."

"Ah. That makes more sense. Her name is Lani. We met in the school that the Emperor created before you left. She threw chalk at me and told me to stop grumbling about learning math, then I asked her to help me understand it."

"Smart man."

"She's an elf," Shivan added. "The day we crossed the meadow, when the tornado struck and Jeff protected us, she had been battling the Shedu. She grabbed a tree and held on. When we left, she tended to her own wounds and then continued the fight." He slowed, then stopped, and turned to face Will and Jax. "She bears battle scars, much like Oz. She carries that same strength. I'm grateful for having met Oz because I might not have appreciated the beauty of her fierceness and the marks she carries if I hadn't." He looked right at Jax. "She honors the Blackshear name, Your Majesty. If anyone is worthy of it, it's Lani."

"I look forward to meeting her," Jax said.

Shivan turned to walk forward and Will asked, "What about the Adomondai name?"

"We only use it because of familiarity. We embrace the House, Emperor. My children are descended from Kings and Queens, and I don't wish for them to hide from it."

The rest of the way to the village, Will and Drew shared stories of their battles against Tobias and the Shedu, mostly for Sean's benefit, but to also amuse Hyrum. They omitted the bloodier details for Rhys's benefit, but there was no mistaking the danger they'd been in, even after they realized where they were. Will pointed toward the sky, where Jeff glided above; he was not the only dragon in St. Francis, and the others were just as likely to eat a man as they were to breathe fire.

"You can die here," he said simply. "So be careful."

"And the things you think about count." Drew turned to Jax when he spoke. "A wish could become a reality. So can a nightmare."

Jax nodded as if he understood, but really, all he wanted was to find the man who looked like Levi Munson. And then he wanted to destroy him.

15

The first time I saw the elfin village, five and twenty years ago, it was filled with old people and a few small children. They did not, to Drew's chagrin, live in hollowed out trees. They lived in long rows of townhouses built in the woods of the Presidio, each door painted a different bright color. The row houses were still there, but instead of the odd blanket of quiet that had bothered Oz, the town swelled with children's laughter and the chatter of conversation. In the center, the town square, there was a large circle set off by heavy rocks, and a few feet outside of that were split logs to serve as seating.

There was a fire crackling in the center of the circle. The flames were less than three feet high; Shivan pointed it out and said that it was kept going day and night, a tribute to the freedom enjoyed from the skull-splitting rain they had feared under Tobias's tyranny. At night, more wood was added, the flames shot up, and it was a popular place to gather.

"Fluffy is not allowed in the heart of the village once the fire is stoked," Shivan said. "While I think he would keep clear of it, not everyone is convinced. He tends to stay back there—" he pointed to a well-worn spot in the ground near the path we'd entered from "—and watches. Children flock to him, and Krisf has difficulty getting everyone to stop feeding him."

What if it rains?

"He has access to the back door of an empty home," Shivan said, pointing to a red door near the end of one row of houses.

"He can sleep there any time he chooses. We'd never make him live uncomfortably, I promise you."

"What about Jeff?" Hyrum asked, looking over his shoulder.

"Jeff has a lair near the bridge of gold. He took over an ancient military fortress and keeps watch over the bay."

"Fort Point," Drew said absently.

Shivan shrugged. "It's now the Lair of Jeff. He's often seen perched on the wall or at the top of the bridge, looking out over Saint Francis. Aradyn thinks he's waiting for the Shedu to rise up again."

No one wanted to know what he would do if that happened. Krisf believed he would enjoy a buffet of toasted Shedu snacks, but Aradyn feared Saint Francis would end in ashes.

"He lived, then," Drew mused. "I mean, I know Will reset things so the lost ones in the fight would be home when the elves left the Square, but part of me wasn't sure."

"Neither was I," Will admitted.

"Jesf, too?" Drew asked.

Shivan nodded. "He's well, though he still can't speak. No one really understands how Oz restored Krisf's tongue. We've tried, but...no luck."

Tobias knew the danger of two elves well-versed in history and the tales the elves passed down through generations. He had the teachers' tongues cut out, believing he would silence them.

Once Oz understood how the simulator worked, how I was able to create Jeff and Fluffy from wishes—but after Jesf and Aradyn had died in a bloody battle with the Shedu—she grabbed Krisf by the head, imagined the stub of his tongue growing and finally made whole, and gave him back his voice. She never saw the others after Will restored their code to the program, and she never explained to Shivan exactly how she'd done it.

"My daughter did that?" Jax asked, pleased.

"That and more," Shivan said. "I owe her much of what I've become."

Will was about to ask exactly what he'd become when Aradyn bolted from his home and headed for us. "Mayor! You brought them back!"

"Stop calling me that," Shivan grumbled.

Aradyn threw himself at Drew and hugged him hard, and then did the same for Will. He was puzzled by Jax, tilting his head, uncertain. "Yeosef? What happened? You sneezed, and your beard fell off?"

Jax opened his mouth to answer, but Shivan laughed and said, "King Jackson, Aradyn. Father of the Princess Oz."

He introduced Rhys and Hyrum, and as an afterthought tacked Sean onto it.

Damn, he really doesn't like Sean.

"You didn't come here to defeat the wizard again," Aradyn said, now serious. "Yet I feel as if this isn't a casual visit."

Will asked about Kilfin and wanted Krisf and Jesf present when he told them why we were there. If Hagar had not gone into the alternate simulator with Tobias, he would have wanted him, as well.

Aradyn's eyes swept over the lot of us. "Your Trident is incomplete. Whatever you need to do, can it be done without the Princess and the lady Aisha?"

"New trident," Drew said. "Will, Jax, and me. It's enough."

Aradyn tilted his head as he considered Drew. "And the shaft? The lady Aisha was necessary, Prince Andrew. Without the shaft, the trident is no more than a heavy cluster of sharp things, useful only to a point."

He stopped a young boy who was running past and asked him to fetch Jesf and Krisf. We would meet at the mayor's house, in the small courtyard out front.

"My children will be there," Shivan said. "Rhys will have someone to play with while we talk."

Hyrum shifted uneasily.

"Hyrum is disinterested in heavy discussions," Jax said. "If he could—"

Shivan didn't ask why. He told Hyrum he would welcome an adult eye on the children; his wife typically went to check on her parents before dinner time and would appreciate the chance to visit them on her own for once.

"Bet the grandparents won't be as happy," Drew snickered.

"Not at first. But an hour or two alone with Lani? They'll enjoy it."

He led the way to his home at the fringe of the town square. The mayor's house was not vastly different than the others; it was in the middle of a long row of homes, but there was a yard of sorts. A waist-high fence bordered the edge of a small lawn, and there were toys scattered about.

"Sorry," Shivan said as he gestured to the wooden chairs clustered on the right side of the lawn, inviting everyone to sit. "I consider it a victory when the toys aren't piled up on the stairs."

He opened the door and called to his wife, telling her they had guests.

"If we're imposing, we can talk elsewhere," Will said. "I don't imagine—"

His train of thought completely derailed when Lani stepped outside. She was tall, quite a bit more than Shivan, and her dark brown hair was tied in a loose ponytail, wild strands brushing across her forehead. She was not nearly as pink as he was; dark freckles splattered across her nose and cheeks, and her smile radiated. They all fell quiet, staring at her, until Rhys squealed, "Daddy, she looks like Mommy!"

"Does she?" Shivan asked. He introduced her to everyone, save Sean, and explained that Hyrum would play inside with the children if she wanted to take the rest of the afternoon to visit her parents. She propped the door open with a rock left on the porch for just that reason and then led Rhys and Hyrum inside to meet Shivan's children.

"All right," Drew said as they sat down, "just before you met her, did you wish for a girlfriend like Will's *really* hard?"

"Stop it. She doesn't look that much like Aisha."

"She could be Aisha's younger sister," Drew said. "So. Were you?"

It was Will Shivan looked at. "Perhaps not so much a wish as someone adept at interfering in my world placing her there?"

"I did not," Will insisted. "If she was in the meadow fighting the Shedu, she existed before you met her. Coincidence, I'm sure."

Drew snorted, hard. He knew as well as Will did that Shivan's deepest wish could change the appearance of someone else in his world. Jeff did it for himself, trying on new colors as his skin. Fluffy had made himself leaner. If Shivan had wished for a woman like Aisha, the computer in control of the program easily could have given him his heart's desire.

He was spared further needling when Krisf and Jesf ran up, and half out of breath.

"Emperor! Andrew!" Krisf shouted. "And friends."

Jesf waved, almost shyly.

When we'd last seen Krisf, his voice was weak and raspy; now it was clear and strong. He bounced on his toes the way Hyrum did when he was excited. Even when he sat down, his knees went up and down as he bounced on his toes. After a minute, Jesf reached over and slapped the leg closest to him and shook his head disapprovingly.

They spent the next ten minutes getting caught up. Shivan had been mayor for ten years; it was a figurehead position, he claimed, given that the elves were largely self-policing and decisions were made together, usually around the fire. Disputes were unusual, but when they occurred, his word was the final say. He consulted with the elders, but his decisions were the binding ones.

"Sounds a bit like being King," Jax said.

"King of a tiny, tiny spot in the middle of the world," Shivan said.

"Saint Francis is the world, here," Will pointed out.

They preferred to pretend there was more beyond the farthest explored fringes. Shivan imagined the world he'd read about in school, and in the stories he'd been told as a child. Somewhere out there was a vast continent to explore and beyond that an ocean to cross. He dreamed about Paris, seeing the Eiffel Tower, and exploring England, hopefully meeting the Queen.

"Currently, England's monarch is a king," Will said. "Is there a particular queen you'd like to meet?"

"Elizabeth the second," he answered. "She's made so many changes and added modern touches to her rule. I admire that."

"That was also several hundred years ago," Will said.

"In your world, maybe. In mine, she reigns over the United Kingdom. I think that if I were to find England, she would be on its throne."

"You're sitting with a real, live king," Drew pointed out. "That's not impressive enough?"

"He looks like my father," Shivan chuckled. "So, no."

Lani stepped from the house, trailed by a skinny pre-teen with wild black hair. She kissed Shivan and said she'd be back by dinner time and gave a little wave as she left the courtyard.

Darville, Shivan's oldest, stood next to his father and waited until he was asked what he needed.

"Hyrum," he said. "He's...youngish? How do I treat him? As an adult watching us, or as a playmate? I'm not sure—"

Jax interrupted. "At heart, Hyrum is a child. Treat him as an equal, and he'll be fine."

"And the boy? Rhys? Is Hyrum in charge of him?"

Will nodded. "Rhys will look to him before he looks to anyone else in the house. If there's any question, just send them outside."

Shivan looked up. "Thank you for checking, Darville."

He started back inside but hesitated at the door. "Mom left fruit out, but Rhys says he can't have anything without asking."

"We have fruit?" Shivan asked. "And you're actually willing to touch it?"

"Shut up," Darville snorted. "She bought strawberries this morning."

"Those are Rhys's favorite," Will told him. "He can have some but limit him or he'll stuff himself."

Finn must have gotten the message about food.

"Indeed."

Aradyn leaned back in his chair, folding his arms at his chest. "All right, we're all here, the children are taken care of, and Lani is off. Surely you're here for a reason, Emperor."

"We are. And you won't like it."

"You're not turning our program off," Shivan snapped. "You swore, Emperor. As long as your computer exists, we live."

That's an odd conclusion to jump to.

"And I will keep that promise," Will said. "What I'm about to tell you might be worse."

"Worse than ending our lives?" Aradyn asked.

"Possibly. I'm opening the entrance to the world to which Tobias was banished, and I'm bringing him back."

Aradyn exploded to his feet, face flushed, hands in fists. The loudest objection, though, was the strangled squeal that erupted from Jesf, just before he leaped over the courtyard gate and ran.

"Absolutely not!" Aradyn bellowed. "We forbid it!"

"I'm not asking permission," Will said evenly. "I'm giving you warning."

Krisf's hands went to his throat, pressing in as he felt himself swallow. "You can't."

Only Shivan remained calm, and he listened to Aradyn yell at Will for several more minutes before telling him to stop. "We exist at the Emperor's whim and by his generosity. Hear him out."

"We *exist* because his father created us," Aradyn reminded him. "We survived because Oz dared to face him. The Emperor is merely a tine on the trident."

"He has the power to go back to his world and flip a switch, Aradyn. That's all it would take to end us. Not only has he not done that, he created a new world for Tobias and Hagar. Hear him out. He wouldn't open that door without reason."

"You'll entertain the notion because you miss Hagar," Aradyn hissed. "The old wizard made his choice to leave here with Tobias. He knew he could never come home."

Will sat back and let them argue. Drew was uncomfortable and slouched in his chair, trying to not look at anyone, but Jax watched defiantly. When it seemed that they were done and the anger had shifted to stubbornness, he cleared his throat. When they turned to him, he said, "He's doing this for me. I'm the one who wants Tobias back here."

"You're insane," Aradyn growled.

"Why?" Shivan asked.

Jax looked Shivan in the eyes and didn't break his gaze. "You saw what he did to my daughter. He tormented and tortured her. He used her deepest secrets against her. He purposely made himself to look like the man who systematically tortured her, tortured my wife, and tortured Hyrum. Will is bringing him back. Period."

"To what end?" Shivan asked.

"So I can kill him."

16

The idea that Tobias, arbiter of the worst decades in the elves' history, might finally meet the end he was surely owed was not enough to sway Aradyn. He kicked his chair away from the circle and didn't flinch when it cracked against the fence, a slat from the seat bouncing back and into his legs. His face remained red with anger, and when he spoke, tiny bits of spit leaped from his lips.

"You will not open that door."

"His magic is gone," Shivan said. "There's no harm, other than the offense of seeing him again."

"That offense is enough. Consider how many of us he killed, Shivan. How *ruinous* our lives were under his rule."

"I remember."

"You were a boy," Aradyn spat. "And you're not an elf. You have no idea—"

The light in Shivan's eyes hardened. "I was willing to die to save you. My life was wholly about freeing the elves. Don't tell me I have no idea. I have every idea. I fought next to you, Aradyn. I was there when you died, and I mourned you. I wanted to avenge you. I never needed to be an elf for that."

Sean scowled, and Will saw the look that was there and quickly gone.

"Elves are men," he told Sean. "Not tiny tree dwellers."

"I'm just trying to figure out why it matters what he is. He's their mayor."

"For now." Aradyn's voice was cold. He turned to leave, and

at the gate added, "Allow this, and I'll make sure you lose your station."

"Feel free. I would be thrilled if my life were finally my own."

Aradyn slammed the gate behind him but didn't get five feet away when Will said, "It's not up to Shivan, Aradyn. I control the code that will open the door. I didn't come here to ask your permission nor to soothe your feelings on the matter. I came here to open that door, and how you feel about it is irrelevant."

He stormed off without acknowledging that he'd heard Will.

"That was a little bitchy," Drew said as Aradyn skirted the fire. "You, not him. What he feels isn't irrelevant, Will. We're turning his world into a hunting ground. He has a right to be upset about it."

"But not to forbid it. I understand the idea of Tobias is unpleasant, but Jax has a right to confront him."

"I'm not disputing that."

"And neither am I," Shivan said. "This isn't a bad thing, Emperor. I think once Tobias is here, Aradyn will find that he has his own demons to exorcise. We all do. There was no closure when he stepped through that opening to a new world. He was here, he tortured every living thing in Saint Francis, and was gone. We deserve the chance to see him to his rightful end." Shivan turned to Krisf. "Well? You've been silent the whole time."

He nodded. "Sometimes it's better to hold one's tongue and hear all the things unsaid."

"And what aren't we saying?"

"This isn't about what Tobias is due. It's about revenge. It's cold-blooded and has nothing to do with justice."

"Noted," Jax said.

"That said, count me in. I have no problem with revenge where the dark wizard is concerned. Oz gave me back my voice. Wick gave me the responsibility of Jeff and Fluffy, which gave me purpose. Confidence. For that, I'll gladly stand beside you, and when the moment comes, I'll step back. The final blow is yours, King Jackson."

= = =

At sunset, the elves began gathering near the fire, and Aradyn was still fuming. He complained to anyone who would give him more than a few seconds of their time, seething over the Emperor's plans to invite Tobias back into their realm. He loudly proclaimed Shivan to be incapable of fulfilling his duties as mayor. He boasted about the men and women who had already died at the dark wizard's hands, and in the Emperor's battle to best him. He pointed at children and warned their parents that bringing the wizard back would mean their end.

That was when Shivan stood and ordered the older elf to stop talking. He could be as angry as he wanted, but wrapping parents in fear was not fair, and he wouldn't stand for it.

"Then sit down," Aradyn hissed.

The boy we'd first met at water's edge five years earlier would have backed off and sat down. The man he'd grown into stood toe to toe with Aradyn, hands on his hips, and warned him again of saying anything that would scare the children and their parents.

"Ask them!" Aradyn spat. "Ask them what they would have the Emperor do. Give them a voice in the turn of their own lives. Vote."

"This isn't a democracy," Will said. "Discuss as you will, but I am opening that door."

Aradyn spun on his heel, turning from Shivan. "Tell him. Tell them."

"Tell him what?" Krisf asked. "The Emperor's father is our creator. The Emperor himself is a large part of why we're free now. He risked his life, risked the lives of his friend, his niece, and his *mate* to fight a battle we were too afraid to step into on our own. We've lived in peace, without want of anything, for twenty years because *he* allowed us autonomy. You'd really deny him this?"

"We never asked him for anything," Aradyn said.

"No, we simply prayed that the prophecy would be fulfilled. Instead of acting on our own, we waited for the Trident, and for the Lord of Prophecy to claim his place and end the dark magic that held us captive. We were frightened and cowardly. We could have done for ourselves what he and Oz and Andrew did, yet we did *nothing*."

"We were held captive, Krisf. The rain—"

"Yes, the rain that could peel the meat from a man's bones. Yet did anyone have the nerve to test that until the Emperor did? Don't answer. We already know."

A buzz of voices rose from those seated around the fire. A few feet behind Aradyn, an older elf stood, clearing his voice to be heard.

"You told us that Tobias's magic was stripped from him. Was that true?"

"It was," Shivan said. "His medallion was melted into the Square, along with Hagar's. The medallions were the driving force in their magic. They may have a bit of it left, but not enough to wreak havoc."

"Then what's the harm?" the elf asked.

"The harm?" Aradyn turned red again. "The Shedu still roam Saint Francis. We don't know their loyalties. If he returns—"

"Most of them were filler," another elf said. "Are filler. There aren't many, and without his magic, Tobias won't be able to recreate them."

Still another said, "Tobias never saw justice. Maybe it's time."

Krisf held his hand up. "Make no mistake, this isn't justice, it's revenge."

"Semantics," the elf said with a shrug.

Jax finally spoke. "He might not even be alive *to* return. If time there moves differently than here, he could be long dead. But I want the chance to face the man who tormented my daughter. And yes, make no mistake, I intend to kill him."

On the other side of the fire, Jesf rose from his seat and made his way over. He hesitated next to Aradyn, patted him on the chest, and then went to stand next to Will.

"Jesf, no," Aradyn pleaded.

He gave a slight nod of his head and then tapped a spot just above his heart. He turned to Will and tapped the same spot on his chest and nodded.

"You never found your voice," Will said gently. When Jesf shook his head, Will asked, "Would you like to?"

Eyes wide, Jesf looked to Krisf, who urged him to do it. "We've tried, Jesf. I don't understand how Oz did it, but the Emperor might."

"I know how she did it," Will said.

Jesf placed three fingers against his chest and tapped rapidly, tilting his head a tiny bit to the right.

"To speak again," Krisf murmured. "To eat and not choke on every bite, enjoy something other than mush. To smile and not worry that spittle will run down your chin. To sing. To laugh. To whisper late at night. To tell Reed how much you love him."

Oh good. He found someone.

"Wick," Drew hissed.

"It will only take a minute," Will said. "Nod yes, and I'll do it."

"It doesn't hurt," Krisf said. "It's an odd sensation, like the unfurling of a towel. And the fullness in your mouth will feel foreign for some time. You'll find yourself absently touching it. And you'll welcome every odd thing about it."

Aradyn sat down, hard, knowing he'd lost support.

When Jesf nodded, Will placed his hands on either side of his head, the heels of his palms on his cheeks. He was listening for the clicks of switches to be flipped, imagining the code, and picturing in his own head the growth of a tongue from a long-scarred stub. Like Krisf, Jesf's eyes went wide as his tongue began to grow, and he repeatedly swallowed as his mouth filled.

He nearly hyperventilated when Will dropped his hands away from his face. He didn't know what to do, other than continue swallowing at the feeling of an overly full mouth.

"Come on," Krisf said. "Let's see it."

Instead of sticking out his tongue, Jesf clapped a hand over his mouth and shook his head.

Will reached out and touched his fingers to Jesf's throat, something Oz hadn't done to Krisf. A moment later, he pulled back and said, "You can speak, Jesf. Krisf was raspy at first, but you should have considerably more clarity."

Again, he shook his head.

There was a collective groan.

"On his own time." Will was still looking at Jesf. "Perhaps your first words should be reserved for the ones you love. Reed is your husband?"

Jesf nodded.

"Were I in your shoes, I think the first time I spoke it would be for Aisha. Those words I know she longed to hear, and the things I longed to say."

"I'll walk home with you," Krisf offered. "He should be told what happened. But I'll leave before you speak, all right?"

"And I'll see you to your home for the duration," Shivan said to Will. "It's yours for as long as you like."

"We have the lab—"

Shivan nodded to his yard, where Rhys and Hyrum were playing with Quinn and Therese. "They're safe here, Emperor. Lani will watch them while we're gone. And if the worst happens, we'll care for them until someone comes for them."

= = =

"How much of the elves agreement did you influence?" Drew asked Will once we were settled into the guest hut. It was sparse in the way Hagar's hut had been: there were beds and a tiny kitchen, with bales of hay as furniture. The only modern thing about it was the bathroom—to the left as always—and this time there was a litter box.

"I couldn't reach Aradyn," Will said. "It was easier to reach those who weren't guarding against the intrusion."

"You can do that?" Jax asked.

"To a point. It's something Wick discovered before. He thought about Shivan walking ahead of us and the tripping, and a moment later..."

Mad skills. I have them.

"No creating creatures this time, Wick," Will said. "Jeff and Fluffy can accompany us, and you need to be happy with that."

We'll see.

"Do you have any idea what's going on?" Drew asked Sean. "You've been seriously quiet."

"Observing. And I've got part of it, I think. We're in a computer program. The elves aren't real, but whatever has His Majesty pissed off is. You've been here before, you fought off some evil...huh, wizard, I guess, and then locked him away, and now you want to bring him back. To hunt him."

"Do you have a problem with that?" Jax asked.

"Sir, I've erased so many computer programs, it would be hypocritical if I did. He's not real. It's like...it's like tracking down an error in your code and deleting it. You're not hunting a real person."

"But it will feel very real," Will warned him. "The danger is real. If you're wounded here, you're truly wounded. If you die here, you're dead."

"Seriously," Drew said. "I got shot in the hip last time. It hurt like a mother."

"To that end," Will said to Sean, "you aren't expected to participate. You never agreed to this. You can remain in the village with Rhys and Hyrum if you choose."

"Are you kidding? I might be useless, but I won't miss any of it." He thought about it a bit more and added, "Unless you need me to babysit. Hyrum seems to have it under control, and he probably knows more about taking care of a kid than I do, but I don't mind being his backup."

"I trust Hyrum with my son's life," Will said. "Then you're coming?"

Sean nodded. "Like I said, I might be useless. But I want to be there. And I want to figure out why Shivan hates me so much."

I noticed that, too. It doesn't make sense.

"You're not Aisha, and you're not Oz," Will said. "Hyrum and Rhys are family, and he can sense that. You don't have a transponder connected to the computer, so he has no idea what to make of you. Give him time. He may come to merely dislike you."

"I'm not exactly worried about what a piece of data thinks about me. I mean, I get it, he's an alternate kind of reality and should be treated like he's real, but if he hates me, I'll get over it."

And that's what Shivan senses. He doesn't think Sean will have his back.

"Stupid question?" Sean asked.

Will nodded.

"Dinner tonight. What we had was real food, at least it smelled and tasted real, and I'm sure as hell not hungry now."

"It was real."

"Then what about Shivan and his family? What happens to the food they eat? It's not like it fell through to the floor. And it's not like theirs was computer generated. They took food from the same plates as we did."

Oh. This should be good. What about it, Will?

"They ate the same things we did," he answered. "It will process differently, but their bodies aren't simple projections. They're complex and created from solid but malleable materials." He shot Drew a warning look: don't explain any further. "Pay attention. You'll note that the residents of the simulator often don't eat when we do, or they choose from other foods. Those foods are, likely, a simulation as well. But when needed, they can consume what we do."

"That's a warning, too," Drew said. "There are dragons here. You look like food. Don't forget that."

17

On the walk back to the Square, Sean asked Jax, as if the notion had just occurred to him, how he planned on killing Tobias. "Unless you have some kind of funky, jewel-encrusted royal dagger strapped to your leg or plan on taking Shivan's sword, we're unarmed. So how will you kill him?"

"With my bare hands if I have to." Jax wasn't kidding. He said it casually, as if this were an everyday kind of thing for him. Get up, kiss the wife, have a cup of coffee, go outside and kill a wizard, come home and play with the kids. "And before you ask, no, I don't have some well thought out plan of attack. I'm playing it by ear."

Chasing Tobias unarmed was not an issue. Will opened the lab and waiting in the closet on the far side of the room where all the weapons we'd used when fighting the Shedu during the chase to find the dark wizard. There were laser pistols and rifles, canisters that Will forbade anyone to touch because one slightly mishandled could blow up the lab and everything around it, and plasma swords. Shivan reached for one of the swords, holding it carefully as he turned it over in his hands, looking for a sign that this was the one he'd used before.

Will touched a rough spot near the plasma coils. "It's the same one. It overheated a bit when you melted Tobias's medallion into the ground."

"Is it still functional?"

"Should be. My father would have removed it, otherwise."

Shivan clipped it to his belt. "I was never any good with it, but it feels right in my hand."

"And your sword?" Will asked.

"I've practiced," Shivan said with a laugh. "After you left, Kilfin spent many years teaching me to fight. He focused on the sword. My clumsiness with it was a personal affront."

Will knocked Kilfin on his asterisk. He might not be the best teacher.

"Where is he, anyway?" Drew asked as he reached for a pistol. "He might want in on this."

The last time Shivan spoke to the giant of a man, he was near Jeff's lair, contemplating crossing the bridge. It had been so long since anyone had come from the other side that no one knew if there had ever truly been foot traffic on the bridge, if the stories of visitors from other places were just that—stories— or if the world extended beyond Saint Francis and there were people on the other side. Kilfin had been trying to work up the nerve to cross the bridge and see for himself but hadn't been able to take more than a dozen steps onto it.

"He knows that if there's nothing there, if everything ends beyond where we can see, he might end with it."

"He'd probably just run smack into a wall," Drew said.

How far Kilfin would get depended on how vast the program was. There were no theoretical limits to the distances a visitor in the simulator could go; if Finn had added maps and images for the world, a person could walk anywhere he chose. He might run out of people to engage with, but there would be things to see and food to eat, and places to rest with the bathroom always on the left and the kitchen always on the right.

Will pulled a pistol from the storage closet and turned it, holding it out to Sean by the nose. "Have you ever fired one of these?"

"I've never even seen one of these."

Will slipped the ammo cartridge out and handed it over. "Jax, how long has it been?"

He huffed air between his lips. "Hm. Years. I think the last time I went to the range, Oz still thought Drew was gross and cried because he was coming for the summer."

"So, six, seven years ago?"

"She really cried?" Drew asked. "Not that it matters now, but I thought she'd always liked me."

You poured milk down her shirt. On purpose.

"Yeah, but we were maybe three and five then."

"She never cried," Jax said. "Well, the summers Carter was coming, there may have been a tantrum or two. She was never fond of your brother."

No one was fond of Carter, not until he realized he needed to grow the hell up and joined the army behind his parents' backs. Now he was the sort of man they trusted with their lives yet not with women. If Drew had his way, Carter would be locked in a massive room with all the women he'd used over the years, and they'd be given an hour to do anything they wanted to him.

"I love my brother," he'd said more than once, "but Jesus, he's an ass."

No one ever countered him when he said it, not even Carter.

"Is the clearing still there?" Will asked Shivan as he closed the closet. "Somewhere we can engage in a little combat training?"

The clearing where Shivan used to practice with the sword he could barely lift was just off the path of Market Street. It had disappeared for a time, when Tobias raised the old buildings of Saint Francis from the ground and replaced dirt paths with streets, but Kilfin resurrected it when Shivan asked to continue his training after we were gone.

"I'm not sure you want to fire those at bales of hay, though," he said. "The stack is good for stabbing with swords, not so good for lasers."

"Oh, I'm not planning on shooting anything." He grinned, and it was as evil a grin as I had ever seen. While he grabbed the computer tablet he had fished out of the center island and shoved it into his backpack, he added, "The King is going to shake off the cobwebs and prove to me he can fight."

= = =

Flat on his back, Jax spit dirt from his lips and groaned.

He'd entered the fight with confidence, and five seconds later he found himself painfully staring at the sky. No one laughed out loud, but Drew hid a smile behind his hand and Sean bit his lower lip to keep it in. Shivan had empathy for Jax; he'd sparred with Oz and found himself in the same position over and over.

Will stood over Jax, unsympathetic. "You're slow," he said, waiting for Jax to get up. "Oz could have done that to you when she was twelve years old."

Jax rolled half onto his side and started to get up, but before he found his balance Will kicked his legs out from under him.

"What the hell, Will?"

"Don't turn away from your opponent. I knocked you down. If I'd had a knife, it would be sticking out the side of your neck."

Jax got to his feet, and asked Drew, "Is he mean like this when you fight him?" He made the mistake of turning his head when he spoke, and Will punched him.

"Yep," Drew snickered.

It took getting knocked down twice more before Jax stopped looking away. Once he was paying attention, the blows Will struck were fast but not hard, and he explained how he made contact each time. "You left your ribs exposed. You dropped your shoulder a fraction of a second before striking. You're not blocking until you're sure of my aim." When he upended Jax again, he rested his heel just above Jax's groin. "It's a good thing you don't need those anymore. Next time, I'll kick and send them into your abdomen."

"And screaming out your nose," Drew offered.

Sean leaned toward Drew and asked in a loud whisper, "Am I expected to let him beat the hell out of me, too?"

"No," Drew answered.

"Good."

"That'll be my job."

Sean sighed and then turned his attention back to the fight building in the clearing. Jax was on the offense, trying to wear Will down. There were a number of times Will could have gotten inside Jax's defense and put him on the ground again, but he let his brother punch at him, and barely blocked his kicks. Ten minutes in, Jax was gasping for air, when Will scooped a rather large rock from the ground, and as he slung it toward Jax, he barked, "Shoot it."

Without thinking, Jax had his pistol in hand and blasted it to dust before it came within five feet of his face.

"Not bad," Will said. "And thank you for not putting me in the position of explaining the rearrangement of your face to Aubrey."

"I would have ducked," Jax said with a shrug. "And shut up. I would have."

"Never doubted it."

I did.

"All right. What am I doing wrong aside from telegraphing every move and leaving important bits exposed?"

"You're thinking too hard. You want to anticipate your opponent's moves, yes, but don't choreograph the encounter in your head. And when facing Tobias, shoot first."

If that's all you want, open the door, invite him through, and shoot before he gets his foot down.

"It's not that simple, Wick," Drew said.

I sat at his feet and looked up. *Oz is your wife. Do you want revenge, too?*

"No."

But you understand this.

"I think so."

All right. Go knock Sean on his keister.

He beckoned Sean into the clearing, but before he stepped forward, Will took his pistol.

"Just in case," he said.

"Friendly fight," Drew said when Sean stood to square off with him. "Light contact, the face is off limits. Just give Will a chance to see what you can do, so he can better judge how to use you."

Sean nodded and took a step back, using fists to guard his throat. "Anytime."

Drew started; he took a long, fast stride toward Sean, lifting his knee in preparation for a front kick. A second later, he was on the ground, curled up, trying to catch his breath. Sean hopped back, pleased with his knee strike to Drew's abdomen, and said, "Oh, yeah. I should have mentioned. Twelve years of martial arts and kickboxing."

The bare squeak of an F-bomb came out of Drew.

"And you said you'd be useless," Jax mused.

"I've never been in an actual fight," Sean said. "For all I know I'll fold and curl into a tight little ball of pathetic, sobbing loser. But I can spar. I don't suck at the sport side of it all. And I know the difference."

Will was less impressed than Jax. "For a student of the martial arts, you're in less than ideal condition. You were barely able to keep up when we walked from Union Square to Ghirardelli."

Sean stepped away from Drew, anger flashing across his face. "What the hell do you really expect? I've been scared to death. You dragged me into a future I wasn't prepared to see, and then brought me here, without telling me outright that we're not really a millennium away from where we were. You've given me so few details that my brain is racing, trying to fill in the gaps. I only wanted a few damned interviews with the King. And here I am. So, no, I couldn't keep up. I thought I was losing my damned mind."

"All right, that's fair." He handed the pistol back to Sean. "Ask questions when you're confused. Don't wait for the answers to come to you. Observation will only get you so far."

"Fine. I'll ask questions."

Drew moaned as he got up. "So what do you want to know?"

"Right now? Just one thing."

Will nodded.

"When the hell are you going to tell me you people can understand your cat? Because I'm tired of pretending you're not having conversations with him."

"I don't understand Wick," Jax said.

"Neither do I," Shivan added.

Hey, I understand all of you. Learn a new language already.

"Understand something fundamental," Will started, before

Drew could chime in, "our abilities, the ones you are aware of and the ones you may uncover, are state secrets. This goes beyond being off the record. These are things you cannot speak about to anyone else. You cannot hint that you know things about us."

"I know. I won't like the penalties."

"With that understanding...I have been able to converse with Wick since I was three or four years old. Drew's ability to understand him is roughly five years old."

"Mine is a gift from here." Drew gestured in a general, all-around-here motion. "I left here with the ability to hear the words beyond his meows."

"How old is he?" Sean asked. "If you were three—"

Tell him the truth. I want to see his head pop.

"Wick," Drew chuckled.

"He's at least four hundred years old," Will said.

"Holy—" Sean crouched near me. "So, protect Wick, I'm guessing. A cat that old has to be special. You're important, aren't you, Wick?"

We're all important. Like special little snowflakes.

"He's more than important," Jax said. "He's crucial to Will's life. So yes, we protect Wick."

"I swear," Sean said to me. "I've got your back if you need me. Jump on me, climb me, hide in my shirt, whatever you need."

With that, Shivan stepped forward and reached a hand to help Sean stand. "Come on. Let's find a nice, heavy stick. We'll use it to start you on some swordplay. And don't listen to them when they laugh. They're rude like that."

"Huh." Drew brushed the dirt off his jeans as they walked to the other side of the stack of hay bales to look for sword substitutes. "That's all it took for Shivan. If he'll take care of Wick, he can't be all bad."

= = =

Because Will was anxious about leaving Rhys in the village—despite Hyrum's presence—Jax declared a break was needed and he wanted lunch before opening the door to bring

Tobias back to Saint Francis. He understood Will's impulse to check on his son, though he was surprised when Will said he was tempted to take Rhys and Hyrum through the portal, leaving them with Finn in his birth When. They'd be safer, and, he thought, they would have more fun.

"Sure about that?" Drew asked as we skirted around the fire. Rhys was swinging on a rope tied to a heavy, low branch on a tree near Shivan's home, and Hyrum was perched in the tree, egging him on, trying to get him to swing higher. They were both bare-chested, clad in little more than strips of leather.

Will stopped, hands on hips. "Rhys. What are you wearing?"

He let go of the rope and landed on his feet, grinning. "Daddy! I'm Tarzan!" He tugged at the leather. "I don't know what it is, but Hyrum said it was okay because it covers my wiener."

"It's a loincloth," Will said. "And yes, it's fine. Are you having fun?"

"Lots of fun!"

Will looked up at Hyrum. "And you?"

"Uh-huh. Mrs. Lani read us some stories about a guy who lived in a jungle, and then made these for us. Is it really okay? I don't want Rhys to get in trouble."

"It's fine. You're not cold?"

"Nuh." He grabbed onto the branch and swung down, landing in a crouch. "What'd you guys do? Did you open the door?"

"Not yet," Will said. "I wanted to see if Jax could fight first. We'll go back after lunch."

"Mrs. Lani made lunch for us already," Rhys said. "We had grilled cheese and tomato soup. And Quinn used a straw to suck his soup up."

"Did he now? And I suppose you want to try that?"

"No. It made the soup come out his nose and he said it really hurt."

"I can imagine." He bent over to pick Rhys up and took him into the courtyard, setting him on his lap. "I need to talk to you. Hyrum, too."

Once Hyrum was in a chair and Jax was close, Will offered to take them back, to stay with Finn and explore the city where Will had grown up. "There's a lot of fun things to do and see there, and you wouldn't be stuck here, waiting for us to finish what we're doing. I might be gone all night, and—"

"Do we have to?" Rhys asked. "Darville said he would help us build a castle today. He has giant wood blocks and said it would be bigger than me."

"Maybe as big as me," Hyrum said. "And then we get to help Mrs. Lani bake cookies if we promise to not eat all the chocolate chips first."

"Grandpa will help you bake cookies," Will said.

"Daddy, please? I like Quinn."

"I'll watch Rhys, I promise," Hyrum said.

"They're safe here, Emperor," Shivan said. "We've seen to it."

Will wanted to know how. The village was in the woods; it was hidden from the city, but with one well-placed, fiery blast from a wizard-controlled dragon it could be gone in a flash. There was no protection from that.

Shivan pointed in several directions. "Friends of Jeff," he said simply. "They keep watch over the village. They'll give plenty of warning if someone approaches. You've seen what they can do to an enemy."

Shedu snacks.

"Give them another night here, at least," Jax said. "We can open the door in the morning."

Rhys and Hyrum looked at Will hopefully. He pulled Rhys tight and dropped a kiss on the top of his head, and then nodded. "Tonight is all I'll promise, all right?"

"We'll be good, Daddy," Rhys said.

"It's not your behavior I'm worried about. It's being out of reach."

He sent them inside to wash up, knowing the loincloths would stay on until bedtime, and he spent the rest of the day chewing on whether he would allow Rhys to stay. He had no control over Hyrum but trusted that if he asked him to go with Rhys, he would. Will was quiet through dinner, listening to Shivan's kids reiterate the day they'd spent with their new friends, and he stayed quiet until he and Jax were sitting on a log at the town fire while Drew and Sean played a game of hopscotch with Rhys and Hyrum in the dirt behind us.

"We don't have to give them a choice," Jax said, voice low to keep them from hearing. "With some appeal to your trust in his ability to care for Rhys, Hyrum will understand. And Rhys can be as mad about it as he wants to be. It won't be the last time he'll hate you."

"I expect it in adolescence. Not now, not when he counts on me to care for his feelings as much as I care for his wellbeing."

Promise you'll bring him back to play.

"I've considered the promise of a return, Wick, but the truth is with the speed of time here, by the time I did that, Shivan's children would be so much older. That renders any promise I make empty."

"You know he'll have fun with Finn."

"Once he gets over being upset, yes."

Finn might not even be there. He said he was going home, didn't he?

Will nudged his backpack with his foot. "The tablet I took from the lab is connected to the mainframe. I can get a message to him. If he's not there, one of his technicians will go through the portal and deliver it."

Is that new?

"Not new. We just didn't know about it last time."

"He'll get over it, Will," Jax said. "And you know as well as I do, if he's here, you'll be distracted. It doesn't matter how protected this village is, you'll worry. Distraction can get you killed."

With a sigh, Will fished the tablet out of the backpack and began typing. Once the message was sent, he turned to watch Rhys jump from square to square, and when he reached the last one, he pumped his tiny fists in the air and squealed, "I did it!"

It reminded him of a time we'd watched Hyrum from a distance, when he'd walked across the country in search of his sister. He had played a similar game by himself, and when he reached the last square, he pumped his fists, joyfully declaring victory. Tonight, he stood on the other side of the outline and clapped for his young cousin, just as happy for him as he'd been for himself.

Oh yeah. He'll go with Rhys.

It was Drew's turn next, and he hopped twice, then pretended to stumble out of bounds. Rhys giggled and proclaimed he should get a do-over, but Drew scooped him up and said that wouldn't be fair, then began blowing raspberries onto his bare belly. Rhys's shrieking giggles made heads turn and invited smiles from elves who were there to enjoy quiet conversation.

"I can't wait to see him with his own," Jax said.

"Indeed. He'll be as good a father as he is an uncle."

The tablet beeped, and Will turned back to it. He spent the next five minutes in conversation with his own father, and when he slid the tablet back into his pack, he said, "Finn will meet us outside the lab in the morning. He believes Rhys and Hyrum would be safe here but understands why I want them to leave. He'll take them back and entertain them until we're done here."

It'll only be a few minutes for them.

We could follow them in mere footsteps, and Rhys might believe we were all going home at the same time, but Will thought that wasn't fair, and considered giving Rhys at least a day with his grandfather. Time alone with Finn was rare for Rhys; he'd spent plenty of time with his grandparents, but it usually included his little brother and sister. A day with Finn and Hyrum would be fun-filled and exhausting.

Don't say anything until morning or he'll spend all night crying.

"I know, Wick." He got up and excused himself. There was only an hour until bedtime, and he wanted to play with his son until then.

"He's okay, Wick," Jax said. "In the back of his head is the idea that something could go wrong, and the moment he sends Rhys home is the last time he'll see him."

Then make sure that doesn't happen. Don't be stupid about this. If that happens? Oz will become Queen because Aisha will kill you.

18

Hyrum understood why Will wanted him to go home with Rhys; they'd gotten to play with their new friends, but it was time to have different fun with Finn. Rhys, on the other hand, didn't understand and cried most of the way to Union Square. Will had to carry him, and Rhys buried his face against Will's shoulder. When we reached the lab entry and he pulled Rhys away to talk to him, there was a large tear-soaked patch on his shoulder, and Rhys's eyes were red.

When Oz was three and Will upset her, she frequently balled her hands into tiny fists and stomped, yelling, "You're not my friend!" He was more amused than irritated with her and calmly informed her that it was fine, they weren't supposed to be friends. Rhys didn't yell or stomp his feet; he was wounded, and Will felt responsible for his pain.

Sean crept around them and went to Jax. "What if I offered to stay in the village with them?" he whispered. "Dragons are protecting the perimeter, and really all they want to do is play with their friends. I can oversee that."

"We may need you, Mr. McAllister," Jax said. "If this was yesterday? I'd take you up on that. But now we know you can fight, and we may need your skills."

"Rhys will be fine," Drew said, just as quietly. "Once Finn takes him back and puts a bowl of strawberries in front of him and then promises to take him outside to watch people flying with jetpacks, he'll forget being mad."

"That's a frighteningly bright little boy," Sean pointed out. "I don't think he'll forget."

That was half of why it pained Will to make him leave. Rhys would remember the feeling, and it might not be as easy for Finn to soothe him as it would be Alex or Charlie.

Will remembered being two and three years old. He had never forgotten the stings of slights thrown at him like angry darts. Rhys was, as Jax had pointed out more than once, so much like Will. His forgiveness could be counted on, but his forgetting could not. He was still holding onto Will, talking fast, trying to plead his case for staying.

Hyrum stepped away from them and walked over to where we waited. "He keeps promising to be good. Will keeps telling him he *is* good. I want to stay, too, but if he keeps arguing with his daddy, Will is going to get mad."

"Will understands," Jax said. "He won't get mad."

Tell him to ask Finn to take them to the castle. If Rhys gets to see a real castle, he might be happy.

"He can't," Drew said to me. "Rhys can't see that."

He's already seen it. We took them to watch boats, and it's right there on Treasure Island. Hyrum has seen it, too.

He promised to mention it to Will before Finn left, but he wasn't saying anything until then. Maybe Hyrum had noticed it, maybe not. He'd been fixated on the ferries; if he'd noticed the giant castle on Treasure Island, he would have said something.

"He's coming through," Jax said, turning at the very faint change in the sound of the portal. We could all hear it, except for Sean, but Jax could see it, and the color pulsed as Finn entered from the other side. "Don't feel bad if we basically shove you through, Hyrum. A long goodbye would be too much for Will and Rhys."

Only it wasn't Finn.

It was Aubrey.

She set down the pack she was carrying, then held a hand up and said, "Hear me out. Don't get excited or upset, but I need to talk to you two." She pointed at Will and then Jax. "Drew, take Rhys and Hyrum across the Square to play. This will only take a few minutes."

He took Rhys from Will and nodded in the direction he wanted Hyrum and Sean to follow.

"You came through alone," Jax sputtered. "How?"

Aubrey tapped at a spot behind her right ear. "I caved. I let Finn give me an implant. And I have a bitch of a headache right now, so don't give me grief over it."

"But you've always said—"

"I know. And we can discuss it later." She looked at Will. "I'm here to either take Rhys back or to keep him here and babysit. Aisha knows he's here and knows what you two are up to, and she's fine with him staying."

"You know what we're doing."

"Finn filled us in. And honestly, if the twins weren't sick, she would have come, too. But she sent a message for you: please `don't take this experience away from Rhys. As long as he doesn't see any of the fighting, let him stay and play."

Will remained skeptical. "How much of what he's doing is she aware of?"

Finn was able to give them a rough idea of what we'd already done and knew Rhys was spending his time with Shivan's children and his wife. He assured Aisha that the village was protected, no matter what stupidities we were about to engage in. Aisha wasn't as certain about that, but she had faith that we would keep the worst of it away, and that Aubrey could handle anything else.

"She knows as well as you do how dangerous this place can be. But she also knows how wondrous it can be and wants him to have a chance to see dragons in flight and to snuggle with Fluffy."

"If I allow him to stay, you cannot engage his sense of whimsy. He has a transponder. The computer will respond, and we might wind up with an army of Fluffy-sized cats and dogs. Or worse, he'll bring the story of Lazybones and the space monster to life."

Will looked past her to where Drew waited with Rhys. His eyes were still red and puffy, and he rested his head on Drew's shoulder, thumb stuck in his mouth.

"He hasn't done that in months," Will murmured.

"He hasn't wanted anything this badly," Jax said.

With a deep breath, Will nodded. "I don't like it, but I trust you to keep him safe. Did Finn leave instructions regarding how he wants to be informed of my decision?"

"If we're not back in two minutes, he's assuming we're staying."

I followed Jax and Aubrey to the steps that led down to the street that would never be used while Will went to get Rhys. They sat on the top step, and I waited until he'd collected a half dozen kisses, some inappropriately long. When I was sure they were done, and their spit was sufficiently swapped, I jumped onto Jax's shoulder, and head-butted Aubrey, rubbing my face against her.

"You came to snoop, didn't you?" Jax asked, reaching up to fluff my fur.

"Maybe he's hoping you're spoiling for a fight. I came knowing you might be angry about it."

"Angry? No. But I am surprised. You've always worried that these transponders were some sort of mark. *The* mark, the one separating the faithful from the lost in the end days."

"I know. But a few long discussions with my brother made me more open to the risk. Red pointed out that we know the world is here in two hundred years. If this were the mark, Will wouldn't exist. It would be over before his birth."

Deep down, she'd always known it wasn't what she feared. She allowed Oz to be implanted when she was a baby; she hadn't argued when Zed finally got one. She wasn't sure what her issue was, but religion wasn't it.

"You know why we're here?" Jax asked.

"You've mentioned every now and then that you wanted to find a way to go back and do the job someone else had, to end Levi's life. And I know Will offered this as an alternative. You're going to let him loose and go after him. A version of him anyway."

"And you're not dragging me home."

"Sweetheart." She reached over and set her hand on his thigh. "The man you look for here isn't my father. He's not even real. If doing this will help settle you—"

"It's a start. But it's still killing someone."

"If you wanted to go through a portal or use Will's teleporter to manipulate time in a way that allowed you to find Levi and actually kill him, I'd have a problem with that. This is a video game. A highly interactive, immersive video game. I've watched you and Will play those awful war games in your office...I didn't stop you then, and it would be hypocritical to stop you now."

"The video games don't shoot back."

She stood, and when he followed she awarded him with another kiss. "Don't get shot, then. But get it out of your system, because it's too soon for you to walk away from the throne, and I have a feeling that you're headed in that direction. Oz isn't ready to take over. She needs time to be a wife and mother and amazing business person first."

He didn't argue the point. They met Will in the center of the Square, where Aubrey had dropped her bag.

"How long have we been gone?" Will asked her.

"Ninety minutes or so. The last time I looked, they'd closed off Union Square, and at least a dozen officers were poking through the car that wrecked."

"Has there been an official announcement regarding our whereabouts?"

"Officially, you were already on your way down to the lab when the car hit the ground."

"People would have been watching," Drew said. "There were six of us. That's not easy to hide."

"Security footage of the King entering the lab will be provided," Will said.

Doctoring security recordings from around the Square was a simple enough matter; by the time the Guard's media technician was done with it, people would swear they'd witnessed the King casually stroll into the elevator seconds before the air car dropped from the sky.

"We'll take you to the village and show you where we're staying," Will said to Aubrey. Rhys was clinging to him, still sniffling, but he'd stopped crying. "Shivan can introduce you to his wife."

"I know the way!" Hyrum said, picking up her bag. "I can take her."

Aubrey reached for Rhys. "You boys get started on your mischief. Let Hyrum lead the way. He can explain to Shivan's wife who I am, and I'll get settled there."

"It's a good three miles," Jax warned.

"And I am perfectly capable of walking that far, Jackson."

He snuck a peek at her shoes, just in case. "It's flat terrain. Finn failed to account for the hills, apparently."

Those were a clue, Will said. Finn intentionally left them out to give unaware participants something to chew on—and it eliminated a measure of difficulty in construction of the simulator.

"All right." Will leaned over and kissed his son. "Don't make Aunt Aubrey carry you the whole way. And listen to her. If we're not back by dark, go to bed when she tells you to."

Rhys nodded and sniffed again.

"Don't worry if we wind up out all night," Jax said. "But I promise, we'll make our way back there sooner or later."

"Just don't do anything stupid," she said just before he kissed her. "And if you have to do something stupid, for god's sake, don't get shot."

19

Nearly five years earlier, Will stood at the center of Union Square and used his tablet to open a portal—a door—to the pocket universe he had created specifically to contain Tobias. The defeated dark wizard had expected and welcomed the certainty of his death at Oz's hands, but when the door opened to reveal his long-dead wife and children alive and waiting for him on the other side, he wanted his life. Still, he was willing to stay behind and die for the things he'd done and begged Hagar, his father-in-law and mentor—before he embraced dark magic—to go through and be with his family.

Will had no idea what to expect once he opened it this time. Miriam and her small children were there by his design; they were the ages they'd been when they died in a horrific explosion, an accident that Tobias blamed on the elves and used as an excuse to take control of Saint Francis and torment them. When Hagar and Tobias stepped through on that day, they reverted to the ages they'd been at the time of the accident. Will wasn't sure he would recognize them if he opened the door and they were in his sightline.

"I don't know how time flows there," he admitted. "It was not a parameter I considered. They may be the same as they were after stepping through. They may be five years older, twenty, or more. They may be dead."

For the sake of the children, he hoped there was a flow of time. Though they were bits of data on a solid-state hard drive, they were also self-aware and had expectations. Every little boy and girl, Will pointed out, has hopes and dreams about their adult years. To never achieve that would be heartbreaking.

"I hope they didn't age in reverse," Drew mused. "I mean, you did write code to de-age Hagar and Tobias. What if it became their universal law or something? The kids would be babies and Hagar would only be middle-aged. Or, ew. The kids would be... gone."

Will didn't look up from his tablet as he tapped on it. "You need to read something other than science fiction, Andrew."

"I could, but where's the fun in that?"

"What was that thing you had spread out on the table last week?" Jax asked. "You were using four tablets and had them lined up side to side. That was not fiction."

"It was just a chart I wanted to get a better look at. The book was one I borrowed from Finn on the quest to create sub-micro nanobots. Interesting, but I don't think the guy who wrote it is on the right track."

"And that track would be?" Will prompted, still not looking up.

"One other than mine."

Will snorted and gave the tablet one more tap. Twenty feet away, there was a flash of blue and white that hovered mid-air slowly expanded until it was ten feet tall, only an inch from the ground. The light briefly pulsated and then cleared, leaving the other side a bright picture of trees bare of leaves in winter, the ground bare of grass. It was bright and sunny, and in the distance, we could hear a woman laughing and the sound of quickly approaching footsteps.

Jax's hand went to the butt of the gun at his waist, and Will reached over to stop him from drawing. Anyone could be running up to the door; Hagar, Tobias, one of the kids, or a total stranger. He cautioned Jax: it could take time to find them, and even when we did, Tobias needed to be in this part of the simulator, and they were going to give him a fighting chance.

"You're not killing him the second he steps through."

Hagar skittered to a stop on the other side. When he realized who stood on the other side, he broke into a grin and grabbed the sides of his head in disbelief. He was far younger than he'd been the last time we'd seen him. His silver hair was now peppered with black, and the lines on his face had faded, leaving only creases at his eyes and on his forehead. He was in the same loose clothing; he wore brown pants and a red linen top tied at the waist by a brown belt, and he still looked like an overgrown garden gnome.

It amused me. There was a statue in Will's birth When depicting King Eli II dressed nearly identically.

"It *is* you," he breathed. "You have no idea how long we've hoped you would open this again." He let go of his head. "Emperor. Apologies. Hello. My manners are a bit rusty."

"It's good to see you again," Will said. "Step through. I'll leave it open."

Carefully, as if he didn't trust that the door wouldn't snap closed, Hagar crossed the threshold into the world of his creation. He looked up and around, soaking in the city he'd left behind, until his eyes settled on Shivan. There was a hint of recognition, but it was Yeosef he thought he saw, not the boy he'd last seen.

"How many years has it been for you?" Will asked.

Confused, Hagar said, "Ten. Almost ten."

"It's been almost five for us. But here, it's been twenty."

Hagar turned again to Shivan and realized who he was. The moment he knew, he grabbed Shivan in a tight hug and mumbled against his shoulder, "I can't believe it. You're a man now. I expected you to be, yet I also expected the boy I knew so well."

"I've missed you, old man." Shivan clapped him on the back and pulled away. "Everyone misses you, but I think I have more than most. I even miss your morning meal of the unborn."

"He means eggs," Drew whispered to Jax, who flinched at the idea.

"Your father and mother?"

"They're well. They've moved closer to the village to be near their grandchildren."

Hagar had not quite let go of Shivan, and his hands moved to his former student's cheeks. "You have children. I assume a wife? Please tell me you're married and happy."

"Very," Shivan said quietly, only for Hagar. "My children have grown up with stories of the cranky old wizard who did his best to help a boy become a warrior. I don't think they believe you're real."

"I hope I can meet them." His hands dropped away, and he looked to Will. "Is there a chance?"

"That would be entirely up to the village mayor. I have no say in the population of Saint Francis. I assume he will consent, but he might surprise me."

Hagar's eyes lit up. "Then take me to him. There's so much more I need to ask of him. Please tell me it's not that old brute, Killion. If he managed to get hold of the council, I might as well turn around and go back."

"It's not Killion," Shivan said. "What is it you need from the mayor?"

Hagar glanced at the portal. "My grandchildren have reached adolescence and will be grown before I know it," he said. "There's no one for them there. They only have each other to grow old with, and Miriam only has Tobias and myself for company...it's not ideal."

"You want to come home, and bring them with you," Shivan supposed.

"The children, yes. Tobias doesn't think he can convince Miriam to leave him, but if she will? He wants her to come home and build a new life."

"Explain," Will said before Shivan could answer. "I made sure there was a population. Why are you all so lonely?"

"They're filler, Emperor," Hagar said. "Bodies that move and wander, bodies that respond to orders and stimulus, but without any awareness of themselves. They would be good soldiers, but as friends, they're quite lacking. And filler does not make for a suitable mate. My grandchildren deserve more."

I've seen Will pale a few times, but only once—when given the news that six-year-old Oz had fallen into the bay and the search for her body was underway—had he paled to the degree he did when he realized what he'd consigned them to. He'd brought Hagar's daughter and her children back from the dead and left them to a life alone, which was not what he'd intended. He'd expected a happily ever after for them, not emptiness.

"I'm sorry," he said. "Truly."

"Thank you. But their welfare is what I'd like to discuss with the mayor. And the Emperor, I suppose, given that he's the one who brought them back."

"You want permission to return?" Shivan asked, hopeful. "You don't need to ask for that. Just come. Bring your grandchildren."

"I think I do," Hagar said. "I would prefer they live in the village, and not in my old hut. For that I need permission. They would be unexpected mouths to feed, and they need shelter. Miriam would need employment."

"And why would you need to ask me?" Will asked.

"Because you created our new world. You never gave permission to leave it."

Will shrugged. "It's up to the mayor, not me. But before he tells you his decision, you need to know why I opened the door. You may choose to go back and never speak with me again."

Hagar looked from face to face, taking in the discomfort on all but Jax, who looked defiant. "You're missing Oz and Aisha," he said. "And in their place, the King and—someone new." He glanced at Jax's hand, still on the butt of his gun. "You want Tobias."

"In a manner of speaking."

"He's not the man who left here, Emperor. He's settled. He honored his word to leave the dark behind."

"Not hard to do when there's no one around but your wife and kids," Jax said. "He moved on to have a nice, peaceful life, while my daughter had to live with the things he'd done to her."

Drew almost spoke up—Oz was not particularly bothered by what Tobias had done to her and was a peculiar sort of grateful because it spurred her into seeing a therapist for the things that Levi had done—but this was what Jax had come for. There was no therapy for the King, who wrestled with the history of Levi Munson's abuse of his daughter and son when they were under his roof, and the kidnap and torture of Oz after the bombing of Chicago.

His demons had never been exorcized.

Hagar reached through the door and crooked two fingers, beckoning someone to come closer. A few seconds later, Tobias loomed just beyond the opening, leaning against the edge as if it were a real door, his arms crossed over his chest. He waited, not speaking, but his mouth tugged up at the corners as he fought a smile. Most notably, he had his own face and looked nothing like Levi, which caused Jax to let out a heavy, disappointed breath.

"Let me guess," he said. "The price for allowing my family to leave here is my death."

"Not exactly," Will said.

"I'm amenable to the idea. I expected to die a decade ago, Emperor. Will you guarantee a home and support for my wife and children? You can draw and quarter me and then set me on fire if you can guarantee me that."

"Not so fast," Hagar said.

"Yes, that fast. What are my choices? Stay here, alone, for eternity, or go there and die, which would be a relief, frankly. I want my family to go home, where they belong."

"It's up to the elves' mayor," Hagar said. "Give me time to plead your case, and if it sways in our favor, find a home for them."

Shivan stepped forward, only a few feet from the opening. "Will they come?" he asked Tobias.

"Not if they know the truth. Bring them through, and then whatever your mayor decides, close the door." Tobias pushed away from the edge. "Either way, they'll grieve. They'll need the village. And Hagar."

"Will your wife step through before you?"

"If I have to pick her up and toss her through, she'll wind up there."

"That sounds like a lovely relationship," Sean muttered. "You gonna beat your chest first? Dropkick the kids from there to here?"

"You are?" Tobias asked.

"Mr. McAllister to you."

Drew snorted a slip of laughter.

Shivan ignored them. "Go get your family, Tobias. They'll be given everything they need, and they'll be taken care of. But you—if you step into this world, your life is no longer your own."

"Shivan, we need the mayor," Hagar started.

"The mayor consents," Shivan told him, not taking his eyes off Tobias. "I can't force you through this door, and I won't make it a condition of their protection."

"But you hope I will."

He didn't answer. Tobias stared for a time, and then took a few steps back, asking for time to get them. He told Hagar to stay put; it would be easier to get Miriam to come through if he was already there, and where she went, the children would follow. There would be no last night together in their tiny home in the middle of nowhere, no final meal. He wanted to move them before anyone could change their mind.

Five minutes later, three awkward, gangly teenagers appeared in the doorway. From a distance Tobias's voice boomed, ordering them to go through and go to their grandfather. The roughness of it made Sean shrink back a step, but Tobias's children laughed, and the youngest turned and said, "You and what army, old man?"

One at a time, they jumped through and went straight to Hagar. A minute later Tobias was back at the door with Miriam, and he made a grand gesture of sweeping her through. "After you, my love," he said, grinning.

She stepped ahead of him and turned, reaching a hand out to him. He took it, and without looking away from her, followed without a hint of hesitation.

"Hagar will take you to the village," he told his family. "He'll find whomever he needs to speak with to arrange housing. I need to stay here and speak with Shivan, who is, I gather, the mayor. He and I will discuss the conditions of our lives here while you get the children settled."

"You're not coming with us?"

"Not yet. You know the circumstances that brought me to you, Miriam. He needs assurances of my behavior, and I need to make amends."

"How?" She reached for his sleeve, tugging him closer. "If there are conditions, we'll go back."

Tobias nodded to Will, and with a quick tap on his tablet, the door closed. "That world no longer exists," Tobias said to Miriam. He set his forehead against hers and whispered, "They're not cruel, Mir. I was. If my life is uncomfortable for a time, or if it ends, it's a price I am more than willing to pay."

"And our lives?"

He kissed her and lifted his head. "Your lives will be wonderful. Our children will have friends, and in time, mates. They'll be able to explore Saint Francis the way you and I did when we were children. They'll work hard. And they'll be happy."

"This sounds like goodbye," she murmured.

He hesitated. "I never thought I would see you again, yet here we are. Even if the worst is the price I pay, I'll find a way to return to you."

His children erupted, angry and scared, begging him to go with them to the village. He let them rail for only a minute before barking, "Enough. Go with your grandfather. You can do well without me for a few days."

He kissed his wife once more and planted one on Hagar's forehead. "Take care of them," he said softly.

"Tell me you're sure," Hagar said softly.

"I have a debt to pay. You know that. We've discussed this."

When they were off the Square and on the path to the village, Tobias sighed. "Whatever you intend to do, wait until they're out of range. I don't want them to hear."

"It won't be that easy," Jax seethed.

"We'll do this properly," Shivan said before Jax could press on. "Tobias Avandeo, by your own admission you are guilty of treason against the former government of Saint Francis. You are guilty of acts of atrocity and cruelty, you have admitted to the enslavement of the elves of Saint Francis, destruction of the city, and you admitted to the capture of the Emperor William, the wizard Hagar, and myself, as well as the imprisonment of the Prince Andrew. You admitted to the torment and torture of the Princess Oz. The latter being an offense against a human of the world of our creator, his ancestor, it is deemed the most serious, and the blood debt is owed to her father. Do you accept his punishment?"

"As if there were an alternative?"

Shivan nodded. "You could die where you stand, Tobias."

"Do I get to hear what he wishes to do to me?"

"No."

"All right." He bowed to Jax, without a hint of sarcasm. "King Jackson, I admit and confess to acts of torment and torture against your daughter, the Princess Oz. I accept your punishment, whatever it might be."

Will held up a hand to stop Jax. "Parameters, Jax. We need them. The village is off limits. Anything within half a mile is off limits."

Jax nodded.

"Well?" Tobias said.

Jax set his hand back on the butt of his gun.

"Run."

20

Tobias didn't hesitate. When Jax told him to run, he bolted, cutting diagonally across the Square in the direction of Ghirardelli. He leaped down the stairs, and when he was back in sight, half a block away, Jax fired once, deliberately hitting the side of a building, a warning of his intent. Sooner or later, he grumbled to himself, the sound of a laser would not be a warning.

When Tobias was gone, Shivan mused that this wouldn't be a fair hunt, not really. Tobias was unarmed and no longer had his magic to rely on. The only thing he could do was run and hide, unless he picked up a knife along the way. There were no other laser weapons in Saint Francis, only the ones they carried, and the ones in the lab.

He's not little. He could use a broken tree limb to beat one of us to fleshy blobs of meaty goo.

"Well, that's a pleasant thought, Wick," Drew said. "And it's reason enough that maybe we should make sure none of us wander around alone."

Unless he can get into the lab, and then he'll have explody things to play with.

"He won't be able to break into the lab," Will said. "He couldn't last time, and that hasn't changed."

"Then we're chasing him until he wears down, that's all."

Jax thought that was the definition of a hunt. "Son, if we were hunting deer, they wouldn't be armed. All they can do is run and hope that they're faster than the person shooting at them."

The idea of killing a deer disturbed Shivan. "Why would anyone shoot a deer? What would be the point? Their pelt? Their antlers?"

"Their meat," Jax said.

Shivan was horrified. "We're not eating Tobias when this is over."

"Turn him into slop for the animals for all I care."

"I wouldn't do that to my pigs."

"You have pigs?" Drew asked, missing the point.

"Metaphorical pigs. I have chickens, though. And before you ask, yes, I make my children consume their unborn, and they enjoy it as much as I did when Hagar made me eat them."

"Maybe if you just called them 'eggs' and not the unborn, it wouldn't bother them so much."

"I could. But there's something amusing about standing at the foot of the stairs and yelling up at them, 'Get up! This morning we feast on the unborn!' My sons laugh, my daughter yells back at me."

"I am *so* doing that," Drew snorted.

"Do you have children yet?" Shivan asked him. "With Oz?"

"She's expecting our first." Drew broke out in a wide grin. "It's a boy. I can't wait."

Shivan glanced at Jax. "You married her first, didn't you?"

Jax grunted at them to get moving. He'd given Tobias enough of a head start, and he was running whereas they would walk.

"You must have," Shivan whispered to Drew as they moved. "The King would have your head otherwise."

"We've been married four years. But no, he wouldn't have lopped my head off, no matter how often he says he wants to." He raised his voice. "Jax *loves* me. Don't you?"

"I'm armed, Andrew. Don't push it."

"You call the King by name?" Shivan asked. "Doesn't that break a law or two?"

"I'm sure as hell not calling him 'Your Majesty' or 'Royal Highness.' I live with him. Half the time I just grunt in his direction."

"You live with him."

They could have taken the newly renovated apartment across from Will and Aisha, but before their wedding, Oz and Drew decided that they would be better off living in her bedroom, in the family apartment. They were both still in school, and Drew was dabbling in the things that would become Ozoo Enterprises and juggling all that and keeping an oversized apartment in shape seemed like one thing too many.

While they were on their honeymoon, Jax took down the wall that had separated Oz's room from Zed's and created a small in-home studio for them, and they stayed, even after they'd finished school.

"Aubrey has made it pretty clear that she'll be upset when we move, and there's plenty of space now that Oz's brother has moved out. Living with her parents is surprisingly comfortable, and they want us to stay even after the baby is born."

Sean rushed a few steps to catch up. "Gotta admit, I kinda wondered about that. You're staying after the kid comes?"

"Moving doesn't make sense. There's a vacant apartment in the building now, and we could take it, but staying means having family right there. Oz and I both work, and Aubrey wants to help. Hyrum wants to help. Will's kids are there three days a week, and your Queen is most happy when she has a bunch of tiny people pulling her in every direction. It really is amazing."

"Oh, man, I wasn't criticizing. Hell, I still live with my mom. It's nice to have someone else there to talk to, you know? And she cooks. I don't cook."

"Tell me you do dishes," Drew said, voice laced with *you-damn-well-better*.

"I rinse, she loads the dishwasher. But I clean the kitchen, and she sits at the counter and we talk. You know, catch up on what we're doing. Unless she's got a date, and I really don't want those details. Because, gross."

"Less talking, more walking," Jax called out. He and Will were getting further from us, but Drew didn't seem to be in any hurry.

"You know he probably changed directions," Drew called out. "He could be hovering in the shadows, watching us."

"Doesn't matter," Will said. "There are only forty-six square miles of this city. Fewer if you count the village, and fewer still if he does as I suspect and keeps to land north of Market. Perhaps add a mile or so for a pocket south of Market. He might venture to the fringes of Dogpatch."

Drew clapped a hand on me to keep me from falling from his shoulder and jogged a few steps to catch up, counting on Shivan and Sean to follow. "You know he's going to sneak into the village tonight to see his family."

"He damn well better not," Jax said.

Shivan was certain he wouldn't. He knew he'd be torn apart limb by limb and wouldn't expose his family to that. The worst he might do is perch where he could see inside their windows, but he'd also have to avoid being spotted by the dragons. If they saw him before Jax did, the hunt would be over.

Squishy snacky treat.

Will his family be welcome in the village?

"People will be happy to see them alive and well, and happier still that Hagar has returned," Shivan said. "Miriam was well-loved when she died, and she was mourned even after Tobias lost his mind. They won't press her about him."

"You don't know human nature very well, do you?" Sean asked.

"I have faith in my people," he said.

"How the hell did you become mayor, anyway?" Drew asked. "You're not an elf. You're an outlier."

"I was an outlier," Shivan said. His wife, on the other hand, was an elf and he'd lived in the village long enough to be one of them. "We're all human, Prince Andrew. It was just a class system designation. It no longer is."

"So they don't think of themselves as elves now?" Drew wondered.

"They'll always be elves. Now it's a matter of pride. It's a definition. The elves of Saint Francis take care of others. They're brave. They're loyal."

"But not forgiving," Will said.

Shivan sputtered, ready to dispute that, but Will went on. "You just said that if Tobias entered the village, he would be killed."

Jax snorted. "Well, what do you know? I'm an elf."

21

After wandering the bay coast and the woods for the better part of the day, Will convinced Jax to call it a night and head back to the village. There was nothing to be gained from searching in the dark; Tobias had found a place to hide, and they could speculate where it was and flush him out once there was daylight. Jax opened his mouth to argue; he stopped when Will reminded him Aubrey was waiting for him. She'd allowed Finn to implant a transponder—something she'd long sworn she would never do—and came through the portal, alone, for him.

"She didn't come to babysit, and you know that. Spend time with her before we're too distracted."

We arrived at the village entry at twilight. Aubrey and Lani were in the courtyard, with a dozen kids playing in the grass. Rhys and Hyrum were in their loincloths, along with Shivan's youngest. Jax paused at the end of the entry path to watch his wife; Aubrey's head was thrown back as she laughed, the way she typically only did with Aisha.

He wanted that for her. For too many years she'd only had acquaintances, until Aisha snuck back into their lives. He hadn't noticed what she missed until she had it again—someone to laugh with, someone to spend pointless hours with, someone to whom she could complain, usually about him. Away from being the Queen, she was bubbly and relaxed, and for the moment she'd found that in Lani.

Before he went to her, he handed his gun to Drew and asked him to stow the weapons someplace that Rhys and Hyrum couldn't get to; Will told him where he could lock them up, and together they headed for the courtyard. Drew set me down so I could follow, and I raced ahead to jump over the fence and onto Aubrey's lap.

"Wick!" She picked me up and kissed the top of my head as she stood up to greet Jax. That's all I wanted, a quick kiss. She held me close while she kissed him, too, and told him to hush when he complained that he'd gotten cat hair in his mouth.

Rhys leaped at Will and began talking fast. "Daddy! Today we went swimming and then had races and then chicken fingers for lunch! And then we built a racetrack and little cars and Quinn winned that, and then we played Tarzan, and then we had lasama for dinner!"

"Lasama?"

"Lasagna," Aubrey said. "And salad. Someone wasn't even picky about the tomatoes in his."

"Very good." He planted a long kiss on Rhys's forehead. "Where did you go swimming?"

"In the pool, Daddy," Rhys sighed.

"Well, clearly." He looked to Aubrey for clarity.

"Wading pool, Will. Six inches deep and just big enough for four kids at a time. Hyrum manned the hose."

"She means I squirted them!" Hyrum said with a giggle. "Is it bath time? I can give him his bath if you want to get something to eat."

It was bath time, but Will wanted to spend time with his son. Hyrum offered to make something to eat for everyone while Will kept an eye on Rhys in the tub, and they said their goodnights to Shivan and Lani. Jax and Aubrey headed for the fire instead of going inside, and I followed. My dinner wouldn't happen until after they'd eaten, anyway, and I wanted to watch the people who had gathered for the evening.

Hagar was there, sitting on a log with Aradyn, staring into the fire. Jax didn't know him well enough to interrupt, but I did, so when Jax and Aubrey had picked out a place to sit, I ran over to say hello. He didn't notice me at first, but I stood on my back legs and patted his knee until his eyes focused and he smiled.

"Hello, Wick. Did you have a nice day of wandering?"

I did. It was just a long walk, and I got to ride on shoulders.

"Wandering," Aradyn snorted. "They were hunting. And they left that wretch out there, alone, unguarded."

"That wretch is my son," Hagar reminded him.

"By marriage. You hated him for as many years as the rest of us, Hagar."

"I never hated him. He broke my heart. That's not the same thing."

"And all these years lost in another world with him? You forgave him?"

It wasn't forgiveness Hagar found; it was acceptance. Tobias had seen the horror of the things he'd done through his wife's eyes as he confessed to her, and Hagar had been witness to the long and rocky path she walked to reach a place where she thought she could allow him in. He was patient and never pushed, and his sorrow was genuine.

Aradyn didn't believe any of it.

"He came back," Hagar said. "He's trading his life for theirs. For mine. Willingly, with repentance."

"Don't expect me to feel sorry for him," Aradyn spat. He stood abruptly, but before he stomped off, he said, "He's here, and I can't stop that. I won't join the hunt. But I promise you, if I stumble across him before they do, I'll kill him."

To be fair, he had you killed first.

"They'll never believe in him," Hagar sighed. He pulled me closer as he stood and took me back to Jax and Aubrey. When he handed me to Jax, he said, "Ask the Emperor to meet me here in the morning. Before you truly begin searching for Tobias, there's something you need to see."

"He's very sweet." Aubrey watched him go; he shuffled toward the door at the end of the row, the one furthest from everyone else. "He seems broken, though I can't feel anything from him. I tried—"

"He's not real, angel," Jax said. "You won't be able to soothe him. Will can't read his mind, either."

She disagreed. She'd spent all day with Lani and her children, and they were very real.

"They're all part of a machine, Aubrey."

"And what are we, Jackson? We're gooey, soft, fleshy machines of our own making. Just because they were made in a computer, born from Finn's mind, doesn't make them less real. Don't treat them as if they're toys. They have feelings."

He knew better than to argue, though he wanted to.

"I understand why Rhys didn't want to go home," Aubrey said. "Lani is nearly effervescent. She pays attention to each of the kids and encourages them to explore and get as dirty as they need to. We spent a good part of the afternoon with a dozen of the neighborhood kids in the yard, and Rhys was so happy. I think he got a notion of what it could be like in a year or so when Alex and Charlie are a bit older. He'll have so much more fun with them."

"Give it just a few months. Marco will catch up to Rhys, at least in play terms. I don't think any of us will catch up to that tiny, incredible brain."

"He may have convinced Hyrum to pay attention to fractions," she said happily. "They were trying to divide the blocks equally among themselves and Lani's children, and Rhys did the math. Hyrum was stunned until Rhys explained it was just pieces of a whole."

"No arguing that it was minuses?"

"Oh, he tried to argue that, but Rhys pointed out you can add pieces to make a whole, too. They spent an hour putting blocks together and taking them apart just so Hyrum could visualize what Rhys meant. I haven't gotten that far with him in years."

"Wooden blocks trump construction-paper pizza slices, I suppose."

Hyrum had a basic grasp of fractions; he used them when he baked and cooked, but he refused to admit fractions were anything but minuses. It was one of the few things he'd thrown temper tantrums over; he had kicked the underside of the table repeatedly, yelling at Aubrey that it was minuses and he already knew minuses. He'd stormed away from their school time when she brought it up again. He'd even yelled at Will when he used the word "fractionally."

What he would never do is yell at Rhys.

"Enough of that," Aubrey said. She reached over and rubbed his thigh. "Come on, tell me what you did today. I don't think you found what you were looking for."

We spent the day learning the terrain; Jax was actively looking for Tobias, but Will's goal was to get a grasp on any changes that had happened in the time we'd been gone. The waterfront from Ghirardelli to the Marina had changed; there was a long strip of beach and grass between the bay and the city that hadn't been there before, but the inn we'd stayed at was still there. We made our way to Fort Point, hoping to find Kilfin, but he was gone.

"Apparently Kilfin is a giant brute of a man, tall and wide enough that Hagar once mistook him for a centaur," Jax told her, laughing. "Yet this massive person has been hanging around the fort, working up the nerve to walk across the Golden Gate Bridge."

You'd be scared, too, if it might mean you stopped existing.

"Bitching at me, cat? I know he's your friend. I'm not trying to make fun of him."

Yes, you are. But only a little bit, so I don't have to bite you.

From the bridge, we made our way to the Cliff House at Ocean Beach. I was happy to see it because it was where I had created Jeff; Will wanted to see it because it had once been Tobias's lair, and there was a chance he'd gone back to it. The glass in the door was still broken, so we were able to walk in.

"You have to see this place," Jax said. "It's nothing like it is at home. It's this massive, empty room, with a view of the ocean and Seal Rock that will make your mouth drop open. It's eerily quiet. When no one talks, you can hear every break of the waves."

"Take me there, then," she said. "This doesn't have to only be about the hunt for the man who hurt our daughter. We should spend some time together while we can."

From the Cliff House, we made our way back to the woods. Will pointed out things we'd seen along the way before, where the thick line of butterflies kept us from moving forward and instead pushed up to the beach, and where Drew freed the sprites. He and Drew argued over exactly where that point was, but Shivan urged them both forward until we reached a place on the path where we could see a faint glow coming from deeper in the woods.

Drew took a few steps closer, and the glow swarmed toward him. Sprites flitted around him, wings beating against his skin. They swirled and brushed his face, tiny kisses that made him laugh.

"They remember you," Shivan said. One landed on his nose and nipped at him; he blew air through his lips to move it along. "Stop. I would have freed you if I'd known how. Go home. You'll see Andrew again."

"Cute little things," Jax told Aubrey, "but Will was pretty damned serious when he said they'd eat a man down to his bones if he pissed them off."

"Then don't upset them." She leaned in for a kiss, and it was a really good one that Will interrupted by tapping Jax on the top of his head.

"Hyrum is pulling bread out of the oven," he said. "And Lani brought lasagna over. Dinner is served."

"And if I'm not hungry?" Jax asked.

"I feel pressed to remind you that this is a simulator. If the program fails, the hologram shuts down, and we're all in one massive room together. No walls. Consider what you want us to see before engaging."

"Killjoy." Jax got up and then held a hand out to Aubrey. "You know, they all have to sleep sooner or later."

"No walls," Will said. "Just blankets hanging between the beds. If your horny aspirations wake up my son?"

"I hate this hotel," Jax grumbled as we headed for the hut. "It's getting a horrible review online when we're done."

22

Hagar was in the village center at dawn, and we walked, with little conversation, to Union Square. Hagar led the way, followed by Will and then Jax, and they counted on the others to follow and not fall behind. Even without the hills, the pathways were laid out so close to the way the streets were at home that someone falling to distraction would be able to find his way there.

I rode on Will's shoulder, wishing he'd brought the Wickshirt along. Riding in the soft, fleece-lined pouch would have been more comfortable and certainly warmer. January in San Francisco wasn't always cold, but the mornings were nippy and I felt the moisture in the air cling to my fur. I could ask him to tuck me into his shirt, and he would happily oblige, but then I wouldn't be able to keep an eye on everyone.

Will looked like a man who had laid awake all night, not because he was troubled by anything, but because he'd spent eight hours with the feet of a three-year-old pressed against his back, his chest, and for an uncomfortable hour, one foot was resting on his forehead while the other was jammed against the side of his neck. Not sleeping wasn't new for him; nocturnal toddler gymnastics was something he was only recently learning to tolerate.

Drew looked somewhat rested, but Sean did not. I chalked that up to the frequent snorting that Drew did in his sleep and the proximity of his bed to Sean's. I could see their outlines from across the room. Every time Drew snorted, Sean twitched, and every time it happened Hyrum giggled.

Jax was the only one who looked well rested. He'd slept with Aubrey nestled against him, the big spoon to her little spoon. They'd heeded Will's reminder about the small chance the program could fail and resisted temptation, but it didn't stop the long, slow kisses before they fell asleep.

He was curious about what Hagar needed to show them but was still so wrapped up in the warmth of sleeping curled around his queen, an unexpected joy, that he didn't allow himself to consider the enormity of what it might be.

"He's not taking us to Tobias," Jax said as they got ready to leave, in the dark so that Aubrey and Rhys wouldn't be disturbed. Hyrum was awake; he always woke before dawn, a habit left from a childhood that forced it upon him. "We'll humor him, and then get on with our day."

They hurriedly downed the coffee Hyrum made, and Jax planted a kiss on the top of his head before we left and told him to have a wonderful day.

I had a feeling his day was going to be a lot more fun than ours.

Hagar took us to the spot on Union Square where his and Tobias's medallions had been melted into the cement. It was, he'd said, the thing that harnessed their magic. As it faded over time, so did their abilities, and his magic had been nearing its end. He'd felt it growing weaker, so he split the medallion and gave half to Drew and half to Oz, a gift that proved invaluable. Oz was able to use it against Tobias twice. Once, she thwarted his plan to use the things Levi had done as a way to goad her into giving herself over to salvation, destroying the baptismal font he wanted her to willingly step into, and later she used it to destroy Coit Tower, where he'd placed an array of computers in an attempt to access the mainframe.

He wanted to destroy Saint Francis and end the simulation. Instead, he wound up running, only to be chased down by Jeff and then hauled to the Square by Kilfin.

Shivan snatched Tobias's medallion from the chain around his neck, threw it down, and then used a plasma sword to melt and then bury it. Oz took the pieces from Hagar's, put them together, and with his permission, did the same.

Now he was standing over those indents. The edges had crumbled and grown soft over time, but the medallions were buried deep, and left alone would be hidden in another fifty years.

Hagar had other ideas.

"This is why I brought you here." He sounded sad, as if he was betraying someone by showing us a thing we already knew about. "You need to see this. Because if the possibility has occurred to me, it's occurred to Tobias."

He crouched and held his hand over the hole where his medallion rested, and soon after it began to sing to him. It was a squeal at first, but then thinned and became a gentle, melodious sound; when the song began, so did the light, a rainbow that beamed from below and bathed his face in soft colors. Half a minute later, I heard it scraping against dirt and then cement until it had worked its way out.

It sailed into his hand, and the song ended with a sigh.

"The magic was not lost," he said. "It was resting, and then waiting to be made."

"Remove his medallion," Shivan ordered. "Do it before he can."

Hagar stood, shaking his head. "I can't wake it, Shivan. Only Tobias can. It's wed to him, as this is to me."

"But Oz was able to use it," Drew reminded him.

"Because it was freely gifted. It's had twenty years to rest, Andrew. And I'm younger than I was. When the Emperor granted me those years, with it came a new surge of magic."

"Which means I granted that to Tobias, as well," Will said.

Shivan was horrified. "We let loose a dark wizard. Without a second thought, just let him go. I thought we were bringing back the man."

"So did I," Will said.

"He's not the same," Hagar said. "But once he realizes this? I don't know what will happen. He's been truly repentant since he stepped into that other world, and he earned my trust there."

"But?" Jax prompted.

"His medallion has a life of its own, and it will speak to

him," Hagar said. "Those sparks of dark are as wedded to that medallion as the light is to mine, and to me."

"Would he bother, though?" Drew asked. "He was out of his mind with grief when he went off the rails before. His wife and kids are here. He has nothing to fight against."

Hagar reminded him of the rain that Tobias brought down every night and the promise that it would peel a man down to his bones if he stepped outside in it. All the crops that were grown by day, only to be destroyed at night. He allowed the elves to fish on the bay yet forced them to shore with waves rough enough to capsize their small boats. "He's a showman, Andrew. He'll leave the village alone because his family is there, but if he comes for this, he'll use it against you. You won't be hunting an elf or a human. You'll be hunting a wizard who, no matter what he says, wants to live."

= = =

With that new information, Will wanted to check the lab and all the security cameras that were strategically placed around the heart of the city. He sent Drew and Shivan to the clearing to work with Sean a bit more, and when they were gone, he told Jax he would also do a visual check of the simulator's code.

"I don't know exactly what I'm looking for, but I'll know it when I see it."

He also said it would take a few hours; this was a good time to go get Aubrey and explore a bit. As long as they stuck to wide open spaces, they would be fine. Jeff could fly above, and if he spotted anything out of the ordinary, he would find a way to let them know.

"How? By lighting us on fire?"

"Possibly." He gestured to me. "Take Wick. Jeff and Fluffy respond to his wishes. I assume he can hear them, as well."

Only sort of. But if he wants to warn us, I'll know what he means.

"Your choice, Wick. I won't be offended if you want to stay here with Will."

You would be, a little.

"You'll enjoy it more with Jax," Will said. "This will be boring for you."

Oh. You need me to go, don't you? To report back if anything weird happens?

"Exactly. Aubrey needs someone to protect her against his horny intentions. Feel free to bite."

I climbed his leg, heading for his shoulder, but he plucked me off when I reached his waist. "I really wish you would wait to be picked up. That hurts, you little shit."

"The King is delicate, Wick," Will said. "Just sit there and scream at him when you want up."

He was getting better about walking with me on his shoulder. There were only three moments on the way back to the village when he thought I was going to fall and he placed a hand on my side to make sure I kept my balance. When we reached the guest hut, he poked his head behind all the hanging blankets and grabbed the Wickshirt from Drew's bed and slipped it on.

Aubrey, Hyrum, and Rhys were already outside, sitting in the courtyard with Lani. As soon as Rhys spotted him, he jumped up and shouted, "Uncle Jax! I petted a chicken! And then we got to feed him!"

Shivan did say they had chickens.

Don't tell him that's where chicken fingers come from.

"What do chickens eat?" Jax asked him, bending down to kiss the top of his head.

Rhys screwed his face up. "Chicken food."

"They have clothes on," Jax said to Aubrey.

"For now. Did you leave something behind?"

"My beautiful wife." He explained that Drew was working with Shivan and Sean—and surprise, Mr. McAllister could fight about as well as Drew—and Will was poking around the lab computer, so it opened up the opportunity to spend a little quiet time together. He soothed her concerns about safety by repeating what Will had said: just don't hide in the woods and have Jeff follow overhead, and reminded her that the village was off limits, so Hyrum and Rhys would be fine.

"I'll see to it," Lani said. "Go. Have fun."

Before Aubrey could say yes, a young, purplish-blue dragon perched on the roof, his long neck bent as he lowered his head to get a good look at everyone. He paid particular attention to Hyrum and Rhys, glanced at Jax, and then straightened.

"Holy hell, I'll never get used to that," Jax breathed.

"That's Scooter," Lani said, looking up at him. "Krisf and Jesf found him near the meadow when he was tiny and new, and they raised him. He's free to roam, but he chooses to guard the village most of the time."

"Scooter," Jax repeated. "Who named him?"

"He came with his name."

Jax nodded as if that made sense. Then, with a kiss to Hyrum and Rhys and a promise we'd be back in a few hours, he reached for Aubrey's hand, and we set off for the nearest clearing and a path that would take us to the coast. He wanted her to see the Cliff House in its quiet dignity, and to hear the music of the ocean lapping onto the beach.

Five minutes in, before we'd left the woods, Jax's head turned sharply at the sound of leaves crunching underfoot, and he stopped suddenly, pressing Aubrey against a tree while he stood with his back to her. His hand went to his gun, and he cautioned me against making any noise, so I kept my mouth shut even though I knew who he'd heard.

Since he wanted me to be quiet, I had to think what I wanted him to know, and a few seconds later the leaves rattled from the massive meow that boomed in the air. Fluffy came running, winding his way through the trees until he was close. When he spotted us, he leaped onto the path and then crouched down, inviting them to scratch behind his ears.

"Goddammit, Fluffy," Jax hissed. "I thought you were—"

Aubrey gently pushed him away from her. "You should have expected him. Where Jeff goes, Fluffy follows. No?"

"Damned if I know." He pointed at Fluffy while she awarded him with the head skritches he wanted. "You. Stay behind us. And thank you for coming."

"Sweetheart, only you could make gratitude sound like a threat."

A shadow swept over us, and he looked up. Jeff was circling overhead, waiting for us to reach the path out, and he bellowed once to make sure we were where he thought we were. Fluffy answered, loud enough to make my ears go flat.

"Wick, your children are unnecessarily loud," Jax grumbled. "Sure, let's just give away where we're at, in case anyone is following."

"Hush. Tobias is hiding somewhere. He's probably hoping you'll give up and go home."

"Are you?"

"No." She reached for his hand again. "Now come on. Hold my hand and whisper sweet things to me. Make Wick wish he'd stayed with Hyrum and Rhys."

"Sweet things. Way to put me on the spot, angel. Are we talking romantic sweet things, or are we in the mood for chocolate and peppermint or cake?"

"Yes."

I curled up in the pouch of the sweatshirt to take a nap. Otherwise, I would have died from Jax-induced diabetes, and that's not how I wanted to go.

= = =

"Don't fall. If you fall, I'll have to face the Blackshear wall of foot-up-my-ass. And half of them have huge feet." Jax set me on the wall that bordered the walkway around the back of the Cliff House. It was not quite as high as his chest, so falling to the sidewalk would be fine. I could do an artistic backflip, land on all fours, and call out *Ta-da!* It was the other direction he was concerned about. If I fell to that side, I would land in the Pacific Ocean, where there was a significant undertow. If I walked ten feet to the left, I'd fall to the beach, and that would incur several degrees of ouch.

Jeff perched on the boulder across the street where he'd first landed after I created him. Fluffy stretched out at its base and waited, swatting at Jeff's tail every time it flicked near, which was often enough that I was sure he was doing it on purpose.

They poked at each other the way siblings did, teasing and annoying, and I waited for Fluffy to start yelling at him the way Alex did when Charlie had touched her one time too many.

"This is beautiful," Aubrey said, words floating on breath. "I can't remember the last time I was at the beach. Or standing here, on the overlook."

When was the last time we had a family picnic? It was before Oz and Drew starting officially sucking face. Before the war.

He slipped his arms around her waist from behind and told her to listen. I wanted to warn him that half of what she heard would be the air going in and out of his nose and that might ruin the effect, but he wanted me to be quiet, too, so that she could hear the rush of the waves and the whispering sound of the breeze teasing its way around the rocks that jutted out of the water.

They stood silently for several minutes, until she said, "I miss this. Didn't we promise each other we'd slip away more often, just the two of us? Or even the four of us? We were going to take over Finn's apartment and play in the future."

"Hyrum came to live with us. Then Aisha had a baby. Then two more."

"And Zed couldn't keep his paws off Sophia," she said lightly.

"Life's been busy. But you've seemed incredibly happy. Otherwise, I might have—"

"I've been so very happy," she told him. "The last few years with Hyrum have been such a gift. And the days I watch Will and Aisha's babies? I love that, Jax."

She was a little less enamored with the rare times she had all of them plus Zed's kids, but that was mostly because of an endless stream of diapers and naps that never happened at the same time. The temper tantrums didn't bother her, and she could navigate toddler fights as if they were nothing.

"We should have had more," Jax said.

"We've discussed this. We have the family we were meant to have. I'm content, sweetheart. I wish I saw more of you, but I'm content."

"I wish you saw more of me, too."

"It's been harder since Will cut back, hasn't it?"

He refused to blame Will. Oz had picked up some of Will's slack, but she didn't have the experience to handle it all. Will's kids came first, which meant Jax had to step in more often. Jax agreed with that. It was the addition of Midlam and then Florida that added onto his burden. He hoped that as Florida's new Prime Minister found her footing, he would have less direct involvement in the running of that country, but he wasn't counting on it.

"Regrets?"

"A few," he admitted. "I wish we'd had time to create a strong provisional governmental framework before we took Florida. Or Midlam, for that matter. If it had been anyone but Shazia running Midlam, I don't think it would have worked."

"Red seems pleased with the way things are going."

"Red is just glad he's not in the political hot seat anymore," Jax chuckled. "Did he tell you, some woman stood up during the church's annual conference and threw food at him? She was angry about having been turned away from some church thing simply for not having testicles."

Aubrey knew and laughed along with Jax. Red was the head of the Church of Florida, and one of his major endeavors was to bring equality into every aspect of its workings. While he spoke to the church—five thousand in person and hundreds of thousands on a televised broadcast—about encouraging youth to explore science, without fear of any conflict with the church's teachings, a woman three pews into the congregation stood up, cocked her arm, and sent a giant wad of lime Jell-O at him. She then yelled about being kept out of the meetings where the matter of accepting the laws of science over long-standing traditions of faith were discussed. She had opinions but was turned away because she wasn't a member of the priesthood.

Red ducked, listened, and while the bishop seated behind him wiped green goop and tiny pieces of pineapple from his face, he agreed with her. The conference was televised throughout the country, and the head of the Church of Florida gave honest attention to a woman, and then openly agreed with her.

Everyone's opinion counted. Matters of faith were not gender-exclusive, and he would see that it didn't happen again.

There was grumbling amongst the men, particularly the older men who called for the new Quorum to be ousted and the church restored as the head of state, but there was no public traction to their demands.

Red thought it was less that the masses agreed with him, and more that they feared being in a rocking boat. One wrong move might capsize the whole thing.

"He's going to bring the church kicking and screaming into the twenty-sixth century," Aubrey said. "He'll wind up bruised and battered, but he'll do it."

"Beats the hell out of being stuck in the nineteenth."

"Let's promise each other something," she said, turning to face him. "This is a major milestone year for us. You turn fifty, I turn fifty-five, and it's our thirtieth anniversary. Let's grab Will and Aisha and go spend another week drinking shamefully large margaritas and making out in public places."

"I'm not making out with Will."

She poked him in the stomach. "Oh, but you don't discount the possibility of Aisha?"

He grinned but didn't answer that. "Maybe this time there won't be a gaggle of strange women stalking Will, trying to nab his DNA to create weird little emperor babies."

"Whether Aisha likes it or not, strange women will always stalk Will. In case you haven't noticed, he's hot."

Jax laughed but denied that was possible.

"Sweetie, Will is most women's dream man. He's kind and generous, he's gorgeous, he's got the body, and if he has a clue about how attractive he is, he doesn't care. He loves babies and little children, and isn't afraid to play their weird, wonderful games in public." She kissed him again, and then said against his lips, "And it's genetic. He's your great, great grandson, after all."

"He gets it from you. And goddamn, I wish he hadn't reminded me about all of this being in one big room. There are things I would really like to do with you right now."

The things they were tempted to do became a lot less

appealing when Fluffy hissed and Jeff roared. Jax and Aubrey startled and then twitched apart at the sound of a smooth, deep voice.

Tobias was fifteen feet away, standing in the walkway. "That's adorable," he said, a twist of amusement in his voice. "You've been together as long as creation, and here you are, professing sweet things to each other. It gives me hope."

Jax nudged Aubrey to get behind him. "Your hope will be short-lived."

"Hm. Maybe. But it's hope nonetheless."

Jax. His chest. He has his medallion.

Fluffy was on his feet, ready to pounce, and Jeff extended his wings, a clear warning. Tobias turned his head to see them and then grunted. "Cat, have your pets stand down. I'm not here to harm anyone."

Jax's hand went to his gun, but before he could get his fingers around it, it ripped from its holster and Tobias was holding onto it, one finger through the trigger guard. "Not so fast, King Jackson. I didn't sneak up on you to attack. This is a chance meeting."

"Chance, my ass."

"Were I out for blood, your prince would be dead, as would your Emperor and that ridiculous boy who once thought he could best me."

"As I hear it, he did."

"No, that was your daughter." Tobias's laugh was deep and throaty. "You know, I've woven her into many tales for my children. The mighty princess warrior, fearless and formidable. My own daughter wants to be just like her, the victor over the dark wizard of Saint Francis."

"You've turned everything you did into a fairy tale?" Jax growled.

"No. My children know the truth. They know the monster that I became. They appreciate the woman who bested him. They root for her, not me."

Aubrey stepped out from behind Jax, slapping at his arm when he tried to push her back. "You tortured our daughter."

"Did I?" He cocked his head as if he were considering the idea. "By whose accounting did you come to believe that? Hers or the Emperor's?"

"She—"

Fluffy got up quietly and began inching toward him.

"I don't excuse the things I did, Your Majesty," Tobias went on, cutting her off. "There's manipulation and mistreatment, and there's torture. I admit to all but one of those. But your daughter is not why I'm willing to die for my sins."

"I don't care if you're willing or not," Jax seethed.

Tobias ignored him and locked his eyes onto me. "Your pet is magnificent but call him off. His mass is no threat to this weapon, and if I feel as if he's about to bite, I *will* shoot."

Fluffy stopped just a few feet behind him, close enough that his breath ruffled Tobias's hair.

"I'll be hiding in plain sight, King Jackson. Come and get me."

"Stay out of the village," Jax warned.

"You will not see me there." He tossed the gun back to Jax. "Wizard's honor."

Before Jax could begin to think about flipping the safety and taking a shot, Tobias was gone. The air seemed to swallow him, and with the speed of a blink, he vanished.

23

Fluffy began walking at Jax's left. He nudged Jax away from his intended stroll through Golden Gate Park and steered him toward the orchards, head-butting Jax's shoulder several times until he took the hint. Jax worried that the orchards were too much like being in the woods, but I knew what Fluffy wanted: there were usually elves in the orchards, and it was less likely that Tobias would lie in wait there than he would in the park.

Tobias had used the park before, attacking with a tornado that ripped trees from the ground and sent elves flying out into the ocean, and Fluffy remembered.

The aroma of apples swelled in the air before we reached the orchard border, prompting Aubrey to muse that it was late in the season for apples; they should have been picked two months ago. Jax had no idea what the growing seasons in Sim-Town were, or even what an apple here would taste like.

"Sim-Town?"

"Holo-City? Fantasy Frisco? Finn really should have named the program."

"Saint Francis," she told him.

"Frank. Patron saint of the holo-people."

Once inside the orchard, Jax let go of her hand and jumped up, grabbing a low-hanging apple from one of the trees. He sniffed it, then turned it over in his hand, wondering again what apples grown in a pretend orchard would taste like. "I mean, the food we've had so far tastes like what it's supposed to. But all of that is provided for us if I understood Will."

Fluffy let out a sound that fell somewhere between a grunt and a growl and then batted the apple out of Jax's hand. When it hit the ground, he launched it in a straight line between the trees, and from the other side someone yelled out, "Oy! Stop it!"

"Fluffy wants to play?" Jax grabbed another apple and held it out to him. "Go ahead."

It rocketed high, curving over the treetops.

When Jax grabbed the third apple, Fluffy growled, and instead of knocking the apple out of his hand, he head-butted the center of Jax's chest and sent him sprawling. Before Jax could complain, Fluffy extended one of his long, sharp claws, and ran it across the curve of the apple, splitting it.

The skin parted like torn fabric. Inside was a mass of tiny metallic flakes, and as they spilled out, they disappeared into the dirt, leaving only the skin behind. Carefully, watching Fluffy to see if he would allow it, Jax lifted the skin and turned it over, running a finger over the now-silvery surface.

"I'll be damned," he murmured. "Drew is working on something like this. It's—"

I jumped into his lap and put my paw over his mouth to stop him.

"Dammit, Wick, your paw is dirty."

Stop talking.

He pushed my paw away. "Before Vicat pushed me through the portal, we were looking at one of Drew's projects."

I slapped my paw over his mouth again.

Not here. Not now.

"Sweetheart, I think he's trying to tell you that whatever it is you want to tell me, you need to stop talking about it."

Around my paw, he asked, "Is that it, Wick?"

I pulled away and then rubbed up against him.

"Fine. But I'm taking this to show to Will. He'll know what it is." He stood, picking me up with him. "Pass my thanks onto Fluffy. If I crossed some invisible line, I apologize."

Fluffy reared up on his back legs and slapped his paws against the tree trunk and began shaking it until several apples fell to the ground. He batted the closest one gently, rolling it to Jax's feet, then batted another toward him.

"I assume you don't want me to eat this." Fluffy sat down, flicking his tail at the apple. "You want me to take it with me?"

"To show to Will along with the skin?" Aubrey guessed.

They felt Fluffy's purr under their feet before they heard it.

"All right, big guy. I'll take a couple of apples to Will, and I'll tell him not to bite into them."

"I wonder what would have happened if he'd let you take a bite."

Fluffy stuck his tongue out and tilted his head to the side, and then slowly fell over. He rolled onto his back and stuck his legs straight up, twitched, then let himself roll over to his side.

"I don't think it would have killed me," Jax said. "Finn wouldn't have provided anything toxic in here. Would he?"

"You probably wouldn't have died, but you might have serious regrets," Aubrey said.

You might have turned into a cyborg.

Or a girl.

Those are kinda like the things that Mass used for Jay's surgery, and he grew all sorts of new parts.

He scooped me up and set me back into the pouch along with the apples. It was uncomfortable with the fruit pushing against my haunches, and he apologized for it. He would have carried one in his hand but thought he would eventually forget and take a bite out of it. I understood, but there was a tiny part of me that wished he would.

Having two queens would be awesome.

= = =

We took the long way to the lab instead of going back to the village. Aubrey assumed that no sign of Scooter meant that Rhys and Hyrum were fine, and she wanted to enjoy the city while free from trailing guards and curious people. Fluffy led the way out of the orchards and down the path that was Geary Street at home. There wasn't much to see because it was eerily quiet with no people around, but she seemed happy with what little there was.

They pointed out places they recognized, spots where they'd done nasty things to each other and places where they had wanted to but couldn't, including the tiny sandwich shop where he promised he would wait for her forever. It didn't matter how long it took for her to be comfortable with his touch, he would wait that long.

"The rest of the world can fade away," he'd told her, "as long as there's still you."

She thought that was both sweet and hysterical, rewarding him with a kiss while laughing under her breath.

Aubrey grabbed his hand, and we ran across the street just so they could sit on the withered red bench in front of the shop window. They didn't recall the bench, but the building was the same soft blue she remembered, and the door had been painted a deep, rich red. The hours once displayed in a large painted box on the window had long faded, leaving a shadowy outline, but there was enough left that Jax could make out what it said.

~

Monday to Friday, 6 a.m. to 10 p.m.
(if we feel like it.)
Saturday 6 a.m. to midnight
(unless we leave early for the bar.)
Sunday 11 a.m. to 9 p.m.
(unless there was drinking, then we open whenever.)

~

He laughed and then sat with her on the bench. "We need to see if it's open when we get home and if the sign is the same."

Has to be. Finn would have designed the sign based on what he knew.

"I hate that we had to stop coming here. I loved this place."

"It stopped being fair to the kids who worked here. People ignored me for the most part, until you came along. Then it was like they all had to see us together, though I'm not sure why."

Because she's gorgeous and you're not.

"You had a reputation, sweetheart. They wanted to see who was finally able to tame the crown prince. And a fair number of women wanted to see and then gloat that they got there first."

"A fair number," he sighed.

"An incredibly large fair number. You were a little slut, and you know it."

"I regret that, you know."

"And I don't." She snuggled a little closer, resting her hand on his leg. "You wouldn't have been half as patient with me otherwise."

He thought he would have, after she'd told him about the horrors of growing up with Levi Munson for a father. "And it's not like we waited an unreasonably long time. You told me, what, a month after we started dating? I don't think it was more than three months after that."

"It was longer than that, Jax. We didn't actually have sex until after you proposed. Before that, it was a series of long, sweaty attempts to make me comfortable with being touched and understanding that penises aren't weapons and that you truly would survive being insanely aroused without anything more happening."

"I enjoyed that, you know. Long evenings just holding you, being careful how I touched you. Looking at you even when you couldn't look at me. Feather soft fingers—"

"No walls, Jackson," she reminded him, amused. "Will could be ten feet from us for all you know."

"Fine. Just know that I got more out of those evenings than you might have realized."

"I used to wonder how you coped with it all. Hours spent lying naked in my bed, touching me, not being touched in return. I was too naïve to know that you were perfectly capable of taking care of yourself, and probably did right there in my bathroom before you went home." She laughed at herself and added, "Even with brothers, I was so sheltered. Whatever Red was up to, he kept it to himself."

"Probably afraid Levi would lop it off if he found out."

"You know one of the saddest things? To this day, I think my mother doesn't believe that women are even capable of enjoying sex. I doubt she knows what an orgasm feels like. And if she did, she would repent endlessly, because she'll never believe that there's a difference between a woman performing some sort of wifely duty and making love. It's all about men's wants and needs, and she'll deny she has any of her own."

"You took some convincing. And you had no idea—"

"I know. You had to tell me what had just happened to me. You're allowed to laugh about it now, Jackson."

"But I won't. And we need to stop talking about this." He got up and held out his hand to her. "Come on, let's find Will and show him the apples."

"Spoilsport. We could have had a perfectly lovely time and still kept our clothes on."

"And offended Wick while we were at it. Oh, and if you want your mood spoiled a little bit more, according to Drew, Hyrum has learned to masturbate and wants to sleep in the nude. So you might want to knock a little longer before opening his door."

She wasn't as shocked as he thought she'd be and reacted the same way he had. "Well, good for him. But if he has questions, I'm sending him to you."

After a bit, they agreed.

They'd send him to Will.

= = =

Three blocks down the street, Jax plucked me out of the sweatshirt and set me on his left shoulder. He didn't mind that I was bouncing against him, but he still had the apples, and my weight pulled the shirt down just enough that they pressed against things he preferred to not have abused by fake fruit.

I didn't mind. They were holding hands, swinging their arms like a couple of love-struck teenagers, and those fake apples were digging into my real haunches. On his shoulder, I had a decent view, and he was getting better about not knocking me off balance. One impulsive kiss, though, and I could go flying.

Remind me to have Will have a discussion with you about this. And no griping when I use pointy things as a reminder that I'm still sitting here.

He ignored me, as if he had no clue I was truly speaking.

I'm not kidding, dude. I have claws, and I know how to use them.

Crickets.

We need to get into a situation where the computer thinks I need you. Then maybe it would let you understand me. Like, forever.

"Wick, sweetie, are you all right?" Aubrey asked.

"He likes hearing his own voice," Jax said.

Fine. So don't do anything that would grant you access to all my wisdom. Your loss.

Four more blocks down, Jax paused in the middle of the street and gestured to a store on the ground floor of a six-story walkup. It all looked much like it did at home; retail space at ground level, apartments above. There might have been an elevator, but Will always described them as walkups, so I took his word for it.

Most people didn't share his love of self-inflicted torture via stairs, but he had a hard time wrapping his head around the idea that anyone would want a ride when only going two or three flights up.

"Sticky Slicks," Jax said as he pointed to the store. "The guy who owned it used to open it early four or five times a year, so my mom could bring me in for new shoes."

"That often?"

"She was a runner. She went through shoes like crazy and believed that once or twice a year for me wasn't enough. I could wear jeans an inch too short or t-shirts too big, but my shoes were going to be a perfect fit. She thought it was important, like setting the foundation for bone health or something."

Will's the same way. New running shoes like every other month.

"What, Wick?" Aubrey asked, tucking a finger under my chin. "You want to go in?"

Sure, why not. I've been there a hundred times, but sure.

Finn must have been in there a hundred times as well because it was laid out the way I remembered. The walls were lined with shelves displaying every shoe Slick had available, and there were seats in the center where someone could sit while they tried on a pair. For good measure, there was a track that looped the store so customers could run in their potential new shoes, and treadmills lined the back wall. Once a year Will ran on one of the treadmills while an employee stood behind him, training a camera on his stride. Then his feet were measured, the video was examined, and if there was any question, he stood in a box filled with goo to get an imprint of his feet.

"We're making sure my stride and fit have not changed," he told me. "A change could indicate an issue."

You run like a girl. Has that changed?

"That is not an insult," he insisted. "Try harder."

"Damn," Jax said as the door closed behind us. "Other than it not smelling like feet, it looks the same."

"How many hundreds of running shoes can there be?" Aubrey asked, not expecting an answer. She dropped his hand and stepped over to the sales counter, then behind it, drawn to the large framed poster hanging on the wall. "Jax, look at this."

He set me on the counter. "Wow. I've never seen this one."

It was a picture of a medal ceremony held at the center field of a track I didn't recognize. Three women were standing on risers, arms raised as they waved to the crowd. In the middle, on the platform that was a few inches higher than the others, was twenty-year-old Donna Domenico. Her face was flushed red, her black hair was tied back though strands stuck out, and her smile was exuberant.

Jax pointed to a figure standing nearby, his back to the camera. "Dad. This is the day she met him. He was there to congratulate Pacifican medal holders and then host a dinner for all the athletes we'd sent to the Olympics. He told me that when he went to shake her hand, he damn near lost his ability to think much less speak and once he'd gotten his wits about him, he made sure she was seated next to him at dinner."

Eli rarely talked about his early relationship with Jax's mother. When asked, he smiled and proclaimed those to be the start of the best days of his life, but he kept the details tucked away, something to be savored only by himself. Jax knew more than Eli had shared because he'd popped through portals to spy on his parents when they were in the earliest days of their relationship, hoping to understand how two staid, reserved people could fall in love hard enough to marry.

He knew it hadn't been an arranged marriage; his mother didn't come from royalty or political circles, and she'd grown up in a firmly middle-class home. He also knew she'd had options in her life that would have rocketed her to fame and possibly fortune. He wanted to see why she'd jogged off one path to another and given up that life for Eli.

"He never asked her to," Jax said, fingers lingering on the poster. "She once told me that when she realized she loved him and thought he was close to proposing, she knew she had to make a choice. The idea of choosing another Olympics over him was unbearable."

"I can imagine."

"He would have waited and given her that time. He was proud of her accomplishments and even when I was a kid, he encouraged her to keep running. I don't think she wanted to postpone life with him that long." He sighed. "I don't know. Maybe she knew it meant bringing their relationship into public scrutiny and she was private by nature."

Eli proposed to her at the start of her final year of university. She withdrew from the track team, and the public outcry astonished her. Pacifica's sports fans had pinned their hopes on the twenty-two-year-old to bring home gold medals in long-distance events—she had owned competitive distance running for nearly five years—and the masses were decidedly unhappy at the turn of events.

Eli reminded her that they had approached the relationship privately, seeing each other out of the public eye, and few knew about their involvement. The grumbling in the sports communities only abated when King Zachary issued a formal announcement of their engagement during an address broadcast worldwide, citing how happy he and the Queen were about the upcoming nuptials. He asked his citizens to welcome their new princess and share in their joy; for the most part, they did. A few pointed out that there was no law preventing her from competition, while others fired back that her presence in the games made every athlete on the field a target.

"No one ever asked her what she thought," Jax said. "She found it odd that people had an opinion one way or the other."

"Well, when you're that good—"

"She wasn't just that good. She was amazing. Look at some of the video taken when she competed. She blew everyone out of the water and made it look effortless. She could have dominated another Olympics, possibly two more, of that I have no doubt. It would have opened so many doors."

"Yet there was only one she truly wanted to go through."

He nodded. "One door and once she was through it, there was a giant 'Keep Out' sign in big bold letters on it."

"You're tempting me to go back and spy on them a bit, too. I know they loved each other."

"But they were reluctant to let us see," he sighed.

Aubrey stepped back and leaned against the counter. Her hand went to her lips as she laughed and said, "Oh, remember how angry she used to get with you when you came home late after being out with me? And the way she stared daggers at Will because she knew he was lying when he swore you'd been at his apartment playing video games."

"I had a hard time understanding why she was so against you and me together—"

"She knew who my father was, sweetheart."

"—*but*. That might have been part of it. But it wasn't until Oz and Drew became this *thing* that I got it. I was not happy when they stopped being friends and were determined to be more. I bit my tongue more than I needed to and didn't start warming up to the idea until Will reminded me about Aisha and what he'd left behind. He straight up warned me that I didn't want to be the reason Drew left Oz with her heart in her hand because he wouldn't take it. And if he didn't take it, it was likely to be because of me."

"But you were never angry about their relationship."

"I don't think she was, either. She was worried. She'd been

very good about ignoring the things I was up to, and here you were, someone who didn't deserve to have to put up with the boy I'd been. She wanted me to step up and be the man she was trying to raise, not that little hornball she'd had little control over."

Donna had been upset with the late nights and the sneaking around because she wanted this to be different. She wanted him to man up, treat Aubrey with respect, to understand that his previous relationships had been unacceptable, and she was worth more than that.

"When Drew sat down and explained how he felt about Oz and how his brother's examples had made him determined to never take for granted the things she was offering? When he straight up said he would wait as long as Oz need him to, because he wanted forever with her and not just sex, I finally understood what my mother had been going through. She wanted to push me to be the kind of man Drew already was when we sat down and talked, and she didn't think I was there."

She'd wanted to love Aubrey right from the start, but there was always a layer of uneasiness hovering. What if Jax screwed it up? What if he couldn't come to understand the horror of the man she'd grown up with, and pushed too hard too fast? Aubrey would turn and run, and Donna wouldn't blame her one bit.

Their age difference worried her, and she thought he was too young to marry at twenty, but she wanted Aubrey in their lives.

"I wish it hadn't taken hindsight for me to see all that," Jax said. "She wanted to love you as much as she was sure she would. The wall didn't come down until you showed her you could stand toe to toe with me, and I would happily take it all. When she realized I didn't just love you, but I adored you, she let it fall."

"Jax—"

"She loved me, I know that. But she understood my faults and was terrified I would hurt you. I just don't think she knew how to tell me all of that. She didn't know how to tell me I was being such a...dick."

"Will did that for her," Aubrey teased. "Deep down she knew you were a good man."

"I hope so." He crossed his arms, holding them tightly to his chest. "She wanted to grow old with Dad. She deserved that. And I *hate* that she didn't get it. She should still be here, glaring at all of us when—"

Aubrey inhaled deeply, her breath hitching.

"I'm sorry. I didn't mean to upset you."

She wiped a tear from her cheek. "It's fine. But I miss her, Jax. Perhaps she couldn't show me how much she cared in the beginning, but I felt it so much after we were married. And you're right, it doesn't feel fair. We were all meant to grow old together. Your parents, us, Will and Aisha. If we don't get that, I think I'll break."

"Ah, we'll get it."

"No guarantees, Jackson. Sometimes the worst is right in front of us, and we simply don't see it. We don't want to."

He turned and nudged her to face him. "I see what's in front of me, angel. Everything we ever wanted, and we'll have it forever."

New tears spilled over her lashes, and she reached for him. I waited quietly, until she finished crying, looking at the poster of the woman who would one day be Queen, how happy she was, youth glowing all around her, and I missed her just as much as they did.

24

Will draped the apple skin over his hand and ran careful fingers over it. He flipped it over three times, comparing sides, and then decided he needed a closer look at how it was held together. He took everything off the center island and hit the switch on the underside, activating the computer. The edges slid out, exposing hundreds of tiny projectors, and a keyboard appeared on the side.

Once it was booted up, he carefully set the skin on the center spot of the island and began tapping on the keyboard, until a three-dimensional display came to life, hovering above the countertop.

"Holy shit," Jax muttered. "This is the stuff Drew's working on, isn't it?"

"Similar." Will used his fingers to manipulate the display. "It's held together with unusual fibers."

"This is why you wanted me to shut up, isn't it?" Jax asked, hefting me a bit higher so I could see. "Who didn't you want overhearing?"

Drew, mostly. He hasn't gotten this far yet.

And Tobias. He might be able to use it against you.

"I would not mind Drew seeing this," Will said. "He has the concepts already and he's seen this system. He grasps the science. Somewhere in the back of his mind, this is already brewing."

"Before Fluffy sliced it open, it looked like an average red and gold apple. Once he split it, the inside was filled with nanobots, and they basically disappeared into the dirt."

Will wasn't surprised. Everything in the simulator was composed of nano-matter or projections that relied on nanobots for texture and firmness. The apple held onto the nanobots for weight and appearance, but once no longer needed, they returned themselves into the fabric of the simulation.

"It's partly how the images shift to give the appearance that we're moving through Saint Francis and not the simulator that exists beyond the northern wall of the lab," Will said. "They give texture and bio-sensory feedback to help your brain interpret all of this as reality."

"Interpret, or fool?"

"Six of one, half a dozen of another. But, Fluffy's concern was misplaced. Nothing would have happened if you'd taken a bite." He picked up one of the apples and bit into it, then showed it to them as he chewed. "It's a bit bland but still edible. And looks real enough."

"How the hell?" Jax sputtered.

"Perception matters here. You expected something when Fluffy cut the apple open, so the computer allowed you to see. There's no nutritional value in this fruit, but it won't hurt you, and it will appear real to you."

But you just swallowed a few hundred nanobots.

"Indeed, Wick. Nanobots and whatever else it's comprised of."

You're gonna turn into a girl. That might upset Aisha.

Oh. Maybe not. She's kinda flexible there, isn't she?

"William," Aubrey reached for the unmolested apple. "Won't those hurt you?"

"Not at all. The only effect will be a festive elimination later."

"He'll shit glitter," Jax said. "Come on, can you tell what the rest of it is?"

Will got his face as close to the skin as he could without disrupting the display, and without looking where he was reaching, he pulled a pair of tweezers from the underside of the island. Slowly, he pierced the underside and snagged one of the fibers and set it aside, then switched programs to analyze it.

"You know a hell of a lot about this place for only having been here once before," Jax said while Will studied the data coming up.

"I've had ample opportunity to discuss it with my father," he said. "I've seen all the code, and I now know where the lab-based access ports are in any given room. How food is distributed, how waste management is handled. He's still quite excited about how it all functions and was open to suggestions."

"Like being able to get messages out?"

Will nodded. "Knowing how seemed necessary." He bent closer to the display. "Fascinating. These fibers aren't composed of anything new. This is as old as life. It's spider webbing."

That caught Aubrey's attention. "Spiders? Here?"

"Not here. Part of the manufacturing process, I assume. The nanobots use it to hold certain shapes. Spun in ropes, it's incredibly strong."

And the nanobots can interlock with it the way they do the fabric of the suit Drew made.

"Indeed, Wick. In fact, a few centuries ago webbing was experimented with as a ballistic barrier, similar in Drew's use of nanobots. It was quite effective."

"What ended it?" Jax asked.

"There were drawbacks. The expense related to producing a single garment was too much to overcome." He flicked a switch and turned the display off. "I'll speak to my father about how he accomplished this. If it doesn't require new tech, I'll share it with Andrew."

"That kid is going to wind up filthy rich," Jax mused.

"That kid is already filthy rich," Will said. "He crossed that threshold with the release of the nanoglobes. His success with the technology licenses extended to Elysium has only added to it. And if Oz succeeds as well as I think she will with the Wastelands?"

"I should have invested early," Jax kidded. "I'll let them fund my retirement."

"You invested at the beginning. I saw to it. Don't you pay attention to the dividend statements I send you?"

"He doesn't," Aubrey said. "Whatever he tells you, he has no clue about them."

"Will will tell us if we go broke," Jax said.

"Possibly." He turned everything off, and the sides of the island slid back into place. "Wick, have you been a responsible chaperone today?"

Stuff happened. Jax made her cry. There was kissing. We saw Tobias.

Will twitched. "What? Where did you see Tobias?"

"By the Cliff House. He claimed it was a coincidence, but I think we know better."

He took Jax's gun. Like, it flew out of his holster. But he gave it back.

"Then he's using magic."

He had his medallion.

"Well, it's not unexpected. Did he threaten you?" he asked Jax.

"Not in so many words. But son of a bitch, Will, he vanished just like—" he snapped his fingers "—that."

That was precisely why, Will told them, hunting him would be difficult. His programming granted him access to parts of the program others did not have, allowing him to manipulate his environment. He'd been able to create a virtual dungeon, as well as the mile-long pool Oz had been forced to swim. He'd tapped into environmental controls and could move about freely. Had he been able to access the mainframe, he would have been able to delete the entire simulator.

"And taken himself with it," Jax said.

"That was his intention."

"Suicide?" Aubrey asked.

"His want was dual-purpose. To end his own suffering while making everyone pay for the accident that took his wife and children."

Aubrey looked pained, but Jax didn't care about Tobias's personal suffering.

"Wait. We're in the simulation. But you just said it's over there." He pointed to the wall where the weapons locker was. "Is this part of it or not?"

The lab was real; it was time-shifted, allowing its occupants in real time to remain in the lab while the simulator was in use. When in the lab, we were living in slivers of time neatly rearranged to fit around reality, while the simulation went on elsewhere.

"So, if the simulation ends and we're in here, the walls remain?"

"I believe so. I wasn't sure of it initially, but after discussing it with Finn...yes, the lab remains."

Jax shoved him toward the door. "Good. Get out. Take Wick and go get the others and go back to the village."

"Jax," Aubrey sighed. "Really."

Will scooped me up and headed out, laughing at Jax's boldness and Aubrey's discomfort. "Inflatable mattresses in the closet," he called out before the door closed.

25

We returned to the village by late afternoon. Scooter was still perched on the roof, but he had lowered his head to door level, a low growl rumbling from the back of his throat, and Rhys stood just outside the courtyard gate, head hung, heaving giant sobs. Will went from a casual conversation about inverted power supplies and new, beefier casing for the next computer to be launched to Elysium to thrusting me into Drew's hands and running in about the time it took for me to blink.

Drew trotted behind Will, pressing me against his chest. Rhys held pieces of a stick in each hand, tiny sparks flitting around his fingers, while Darville stood toe to toe with a much taller boy, loudly questioning his parentage while threatening to pound him into the dirt. Hyrum stood behind him, blocking his way home.

"What happened?" Will asked Rhys as he nearly slid on his knees getting to him. "Are you all right?"

"He broke it," Rhys sniffed.

"He grabbed Rhys's stick and broke it in half," Hyrum said. "We were just playing. It was mean."

The taller boy tried to shove Darville aside, but he wouldn't budge. "He was playing at *magic*," the boy spat.

"You didn't have to break it!" Hyrum was as angry as I'd ever seen him, including his spectacular meltdown regarding fractions. "He wasn't doing anything! We were just pretending."

Gently, Will turned Rhys toward him so that he didn't have to see Darville and Hyrum tussle on his behalf. He took Rhys's fists in hand and lifted them, looking for cuts and scrapes as he gently covered the sparks to make them stop. "He broke your stick?"

"It's my wizard wand," Rhys murmured. "Assmunch took it and broke it and told me I was bad."

"Asmonk," Darville corrected, amused. "It was only a game, Emperor. It was harmless."

"Ah. And what game were you playing, Rhys?"

He sounded smaller than he really was. "Harry Potter."

Drew turned on Asmonk. "He was playing a game from a *book* so you broke a damned stick? He was *pretending*. What the hell is wrong with you?"

"We don't pretend at magic," Asmonk shot back. "Ever."

"And I'll pull out the stick you have wedged up your ass, wipe it clean on your face, and give it to him as another wand," Darville growled. "He's a little boy. All little boys play." When Asmonk tried to refute, Darville shoved him back a step. "You used to pretend to be *Tobias*, you dimwit."

"And look what happened."

Darville looked down at Will. "He's an idiot. He fell out of a tree when he was pretending to cast a spell, and he broke his arm. Then blamed it on the dark wizard. There is no rule against playing at magic."

"There is!" Asmonk shoved back, his hand smacking against Darville's shoulder. "It's forbidden. My father—"

Shivan, who had been watching quietly, sighed hard and stepped between them. "There is no such rule, Asmonk. Go home and tend to your own business. If you bother anyone about this again, I'll report to your grandmother that you broke the toy of a three-year-old boy, made him cry, and refused to apologize."

He knew where the greatest threat was. Not his father, and not his mother. Shivan threatened to go to his grandmother, his family's matriarch, whose disappointment would sting the most. When the boy didn't budge, Shivan looked up at Scooter and said, "I suppose you could have him. Hungry?"

Scooter snorted, little balls of smoke puffing from his nostrils.

Will took the two pieces of stick from Rhys and held the broken ends together. "Close your eyes, and when I tell you to, blow, all right?"

"Will it hurt?"

"No. I promise. Just close your eyes." When Rhys did, Will pushed the pieces together, hard, and then stared at it. I knew what he was doing: in his head, he was imagining the wood unsplintering and becoming whole again, fixing the stick the same way he had helped Jefs grow his tongue. When it was ready, he whispered, "Blow."

Rhys sucked in a deep breath, and blew hard, tiny bits of spit landing on Will's arms and chin.

"Now open your eyes."

He peeked first, then opened his eyes wide. "Daddy, you fixed it!"

"Are you sure it was me?"

Rhys didn't have time to answer. Asmonk tried to get past Darville, his face angry and red, and he bellowed, "Wizard!"

Will finally stood up and turned to the boy. He was several inches taller, and the boy took a protective step back. "And if I am? Tell me, what will you do?"

"I'll tell. I'll tell everyone."

"Go home, Assmunch," Darville growled. "You'd better hope I don't spread that name throughout the school. You know everyone will use it."

He backed away, but as he turned to go home, Sean stopped him and whispered something to him. Asmonk flinched, glanced back at Will, and then ran.

"Daddy, can I still play Harry Potter? I was a good wizard, I promise."

"You can play anything you like." He bent over, setting his hands against his knees. "Darville stood up for you. What do we do when people are nice to us?"

Rhys handed the stick to Will and ran to Darville, throwing his arms around the older boy's legs. "Thank you for yelling at him. You did that like my big brother."

"You're welcome. What's your big brother's name?"

"Jay. Sometimes we call him JayJay. He's old like Drew, but he plays with me anyway."

"Nice. You can let go now, though." When Rhys didn't move, he said, "Really. You're breathing on inappropriate things."

"Rhys, you're annoying him now," Will said.

A tiny snort escaped him. "I know."

Darville snatched him up and held him high, swinging him around. "The last time Quinn annoyed me, I did this until he vomited."

"He lives upstairs from Prince Andrew," Will said. "This will be nothing new. He won't vomit, but he might pee on you."

"Not even kidding," Drew said.

He spun Rhys around several times, his laughter cracking through the air, and when he finally set Rhys to his feet, he challenged him to walk straight and not fall over. Rhys turned in Will's direction, took two steps, and sat down, hard. Where Charlie would have cried, Rhys laughed, then tried to get up and fell over again.

"You're like a drunk toddler," Drew said.

"I got drunk once," Hyrum offered. "Then Aubrey yelled at Jax and Will because they were only supposed to let me have two drinks and then we were going to shoot pool. But we didn't even shoot anything. All we did was poke balls around a table with really long sticks."

"I was there, hotshot," Drew said, amused. "We should do it again. That was fun."

Hyrum bounced on his toes, his hands held to his mouth as he giggled. "Aubrey will get mad. Can we really?"

"Legal drinking age is twenty-one. You turn forty-eight soon."

"Andrew," Will cautioned.

"He's a total dad, isn't he?" Sean asked Drew.

"You have no idea."

"Oh!" Hyrum lifted on his toes as high as he could, then bounced once more. "Rhys and I learned a trick! Wanna see?"

Darville warned Will they needed to go to the back yard if he wanted to see what they'd figured out. Asmonk might have eyes prying into their business, and it would only invite more trouble. We followed them around the house to a clearing where the grass had been worn down by tiny feet. There was a sandbox and an assortment of toys, explaining why Rhys was filthy every night.

Hyrum directed the adults to sit on the back porch steps. He and Rhys faced each other, pointy fingers extended, and when they each had a thread of light dancing at the tips, they touched. As the light grew, they walked in circles, making the strand of light twist into a rope, and when it was at least two feet long, Hyrum told Rhys to step back a few feet. The light extended between them, a bright white electric cord that they then swung up and down like a jump rope.

"That's only part of it," Darville said as he scrounged for another stick. When he found one, a long thin branch that had fallen into the sandbox, he held it upright for Will to see. "They can cut things."

He dropped the branch onto the rope, and it cut neatly in half, the ends burnt and sealed.

"Remind me not to mess with them," Sean muttered.

Rhys closed his fist, and the rope disappeared. "Show Daddy the ball!"

Hyrum flexed his fingers until they all sparked, and he worked up a small ball of light, then got to his knees and told Rhys to catch.

Will stood up, poised to stop them, but Rhys caught it easily and tossed it back, as if they were playing with a small rubber ball instead of enough power to burn down the woods. It took him a few seconds, but he found composure and relaxed.

"That," he finally said, "is very impressive. Hyrum is doing a good job of teaching you to control things, isn't he?"

"Uh huh. But he made sure Mrs. Lani was watching, and she had water in case we made a fire even though Hyrum said she might want sand instead."

Shivan stood up and whispered to Will, "I'll talk to her. She might not have understood what they were planning on doing. I assume you'd prefer to be present when they do this?"

Will gave a short nod and then went to Rhys. He checked

his hands and ran a soft finger over the bright red streaks that ran down his fingers and across his palm. "It doesn't hurt?"

"It tickles."

"I need you to remember something. You can hurt someone with this, all right? You need to be very careful."

"I know, Daddy."

"And don't let anyone play jump rope over it when you and Hyrum connect like that. It could cut someone's legs off."

"Daddy," Rhys sighed.

"We won't," Hyrum promised.

Doubt flickered in his eyes, but he sighed, "All right. It's very impressive, and I'm proud of you for not being afraid of it anymore." He nudged them toward the front of Shivan's house, where Drew promised to play hopscotch with them. Shivan asked his son where the other kids and his wife had gotten to— she'd taken them inside when they started fighting over a toy, leaving Darville to make sure Rhys and Hyrum were amused— so he went inside to make sure she wasn't sitting in the hall outside their bedroom with a bottle of wine.

"They're a handful sometimes," he said as he went in.

"They're breathing birth control," Darville muttered.

We sat on a log near the fire and watched Drew hop from square to square, and when they tired of that game, he drew a crosshatch in the dirt to teach Rhys how to play tic-tac-toe. He let Rhys win a string of games, but when it was time for Hyrum to play, he whispered loudly to Drew, "I wanna win fair, okay? If I have to lose, it's okay."

A couple of years ago, Hyrum wouldn't have noticed.

"He's far more astute than he gives himself credit for," Will said. "And while I enjoy seeing him grow, I also hope he doesn't lose himself to sudden maturity."

You want him to like playing Tarzan and stuff with the kids.

"I want play to continue to be fun, no matter what the game or with whom he's playing. It's important to him."

The kids are gonna grow up.

"I am aware. But there are many, many years before all the children have grown. Oz and Drew are not done by far, Zed's boys will be old enough to participate soon and he's not done, either. Jay has indicated he would like to have children. With luck, home will always have little ones running around."

He was reasonably certain about the children Oz would have. Zed was halfway there with his brood. But Jay was an unknown; Will had looked him up more than once, reading about the boy named Jimmy who had become a renowned artist in another timeline, one who had a wife but no offspring, who was close to his long-divorced mother until her death at one hundred thirty-four. But Jay had resources that Jimmy had not. Jimmy had waited until his mid-twenties to have surgery to correct his birth-assigned gender, and science had not yet caught up with biology. Jimmy was unable to procreate biologically and had, apparently, chosen not to approach parenthood by other means.

Jay had Will. Will had easy access to the future and a physician capable of not only correcting Jay's outward-appearing gender but his genetic code as well. He corrected everything, down to Jay's DNA, and there wasn't a lab test in existence that could tell him apart from someone assigned male gender at birth.

Jay would be able to father children.

Will and Aisha hoped he would get that. They wanted to fill the building with children almost as badly as Aubrey did. The day Jay announced that he and Navi were moving in together, and it was clear they intended a long-term commitment, Aisha turned to Will that night and said, "Those two will make beautiful babies."

If Jay doesn't, one of the other kids will. You'll get to be a grandpa, Will.

He didn't think he would be disappointed if that never happened. After all, he'd never thought he would have one biological child, much less three. He was supposed to be dead at forty-two. His life now was a gift.

"I will surely insert myself into the lives of Oz and Drew's children as much as I have Zed's."

Like with Oz and Zed? Except for those awkward teen years

when you were just the weird guy living downstairs, you've been a second dad for them.

"I was never the weird guy," Will snorted. Before I could counter, "All right, fine, they may have considered me weird, but I was always more than the guy downstairs."

They still feel bad that they grew apart from you for a while.

"They don't need to. Most of that was my fault. They were simply being teenagers."

Rhys sprang from the crouch he'd been in while watching Hyrum and Drew and he shouted, "Aunt Aubrey! Uncle Jax!"

Will turned to watch as they walked around the fire ring, and he laughed out loud. "Say nothing, Wick. We will not embarrass the Queen."

He should have warned Rhys instead. He scrambled over to her, and when she lifted him up for a hug and a kiss, he tugged at her collar. "Your shirt's on inside out."

Without missing a beat, she replied, "The other side is dirty. I didn't want it to show."

"Oh. Uncle Drew told me to do that with underwear."

"Nice." She set him down and followed him to the tic-tac-toe game, and Jax dropped onto the log bench with Will.

"Any further sighting of Tobias?" Will asked him.

"No sign of him on the walk back. But after we've had food and Rhys is in bed, I want to set out again."

"Are you sure you have the energy for that?"

"Reinvigorated. I want to find him and get this done. I know you don't like keeping Rhys displaced for very long."

He's doing okay.

It wasn't just that he wanted to avoid the illness that could come with playing outside of one's own time; Will didn't want Rhys aging away from home. It added up for a child; a few days here, a few days there, and over the years Rhys could be a year or more older than his birthdate indicated. Will didn't think it was fair to do that to him, even though the likelihood was that Rhys would age slower than his peers, as he did.

"Where would you like to start?" Will asked. There was no question about waiting; if Jax wanted to get going, we were going to humor him.

"Cliff House. He popped up there for a reason. If he was telling the truth and we met by chance, he may have been there because it's where he's hiding, and we surprised him by being there."

If he wasn't at the Cliff House, Will suggested we explore Golden Gate Park. When Tobias abandoned his lair the last time, he headed for the DeYoung Museum building and spent at least one night there. If he'd been there, he would leave clues. His ego would demand it.

Jax herded everyone to the guest hut for dinner—chicken and potatoes, which was no surprise to Drew and Will—and while Will helped Rhys get ready for bed, Jax and Drew stepped outside to discuss the things Drew could tell him about chasing Tobias.

I sat where I could see Will as he told Rhys and Hyrum a story and where I could hear Drew. He carefully avoided any mention of the tunnels under the museum, and he didn't tell Jax how one by one, people went missing.

They explored the Cliff House by moonlight. I bounced around, though not uncomfortably, in the pouch of Drew's sweatshirt, and peered into the darkness to see what they could not. Jeff and Fluffy waited outside, guarding against intruders. Inside, the former restaurant felt empty, and not only because there were no tables and chairs, or furniture of any sort. It hinted the hollowness of having been vacant for a long time; there was no imprint of human spirit in the air, and the only footprints were the ones we'd left before.

Outside, breath fogged in the cold night air. They split up and searched the exterior of the Cliff House in separate directions, meeting on the far side, not sure of what they were looking for. No one honestly expected to find Tobias there, either near the Cliff House nor on the beach. But we circled the building silently, alert and ready to spring.

Sean jutted his chin in the direction of the shack up the path, the one from behind Will and Drew had fired on the Shedu guards who protected the Cliff House, where Drew was shot in the hip.

"Any chance he's there? It looks creepy enough."

"It's barely standing," Drew said.

"And where would you go if you didn't want to be found? The place you'd used to hide, or the place no one would think you'd want to spend any time?"

I sent Jeff to snoop. He rose from his perch on the boulder across the street and took a long hop, wings extended, landing several feet from the shack's entry. His head cocked as he listened, and when he didn't hear anything, he butted a hole through the door and half of the front façade to get a peek inside.

When he pulled his head out, the shack folded in upon itself. Wood cracked and splintered, the joints creaked, and the walls fell inward after the roof collapsed. Jeff cocked his head again and then looked over his left wing, the closest to a shrug he could manage.

No one in there. Or if there was...not anymore.

"I still can't believe you guys have a dragon," Sean said.

"If you're nice to him, he'll give you a ride before we go home," Drew said.

"No freaking way. Nope."

Will pointed to the handles jutting out at the base of Jeff's neck. "Wick created him to carry people, if Jeff chooses to. It's entirely up to him."

"I just want to work up the nerve to pet him. I don't need a ride."

"Nothing to be scared about," Drew said. "He's careful."

No, he's not.

"It's not about being afraid," Sean said. "It's more about not wanting to use someone else for my amusement. I won't ride a horse, either."

Respect that, dude. Though Fluffy might grab him and plop him onto his back just to force a ride on him.

And don't forget, you refuse to waste meat for kinda the same things.

Jeff flew back to his perch and stretched his wings as wide as he could. He snorted lightly, tiny puffs of smoke popping from his nostrils, his neck bent as he gazed at us. He closed his eyes to slits, deliberately trying to make himself intimidating; Will and Drew weren't fooled one bit, but Sean took a step back, and Jax breathed out, "Damn."

"He's tame, right?" Sean asked, voice thin.

"He's friendly," Will said. "Don't mistake that for tame."

"He *has* eaten people," Drew noted.

"Before or after you jumped on his back for a ride? Maybe he was annoyed."

First, they petted him and told him he was pretty. He likes that.

Jeff stretched until his face was a foot from mine, and a tiny noise that sounded like a grunt and a growl had mated slipped from his mouth.

Stop it. You do, too, like it. You're pretty and you know it.

We sent him ahead to investigate the park. He circled over the meadow and the museum, and with every rotation his new red scales caught moonlight, glittering like tiny ruby stars. Fluffy tried to keep an eye on him as we descended the hill in front of Ocean Beach but kept bumping into Sean and Drew. After a few minutes and one near face-plant, Drew told him to run ahead, and we would catch up.

"Wait in the meadow. But if you see Tobias, turn and run. Let Jeff keep him at bay."

"That grunt is mean enough to hurt a cat?" Sean asked as Fluffy galloped down the hill. "That's pretty low."

"He systematically tortured an entire city for decades," Will pointed out. "He had them terrified. Hundreds perished. Injuring a giant cat doesn't seem outside the realm of possibility."

"What about kids? He would leave the kids alone, right?"

"He'll leave the village alone," Drew answered. "He won't do anything to put his own kids at risk."

Scooter would eat him. He probably knows that.

When we reached the meadow, Jeff was riding an invisible wave of his own making, dipping and flicking his tail at Fluffy, just above Fluffy's vertical leaping ability.

"They're playing with each other," Sean murmured.

"As siblings occasionally do," Will said. "I'm not sure I'd want to be near when they quarrel."

We stopped to watch. As badly as Jax wanted to find Tobias, he was fascinated and became lost in the moment, awed by the heights Jeff soared and the ballet-like movements they made as they swiped at each other. We waited for ten minutes, until Jeff made a low rumbling sound, and Fluffy stopped. Jeff landed near him and lowered his head to Fluffy's for a gentle head-butt, and then they turned to us.

"I *really* wish you could take them out of here," Jax said. "Can you imagine, sitting on the balcony, watching Jeff soar around Union Square? And Fluffy chasing the pigeons?"

"Can you imagine the panic if we could?" Drew said.

We started for the museum. "What do dragons eat?" Sean asked.

"I've only seen him eat people," Drew said. He tapped me on the head. "You would know more than the rest of us."

You haven't seen any Shedu around here, have you?

Drew grimaced, and Will said, "He is not eating the Shedu, Wick. He may not eat at all when we're away from here."

Maybe they have dragon food here. Like my canned food, only bigger.

"That would be a damned big can," Drew mused.

"Forget the can. Can you imagine scooping up after him?" Jax asked.

I bet he poops in the ocean. He's considerate like that.

"I can hear the conversation with Oz now," Drew said. "'What'd you guys talk about while walking around?' 'Oh, the nutrition and defecation habits of the native wildlife.'"

That's better than what you and Zed were talking about when we were walking across Colorado.

That made Drew laugh, and Will pointed at him and said, "And no further discussion is required."

"Aw, but that's when we realized that the Emperor is a warm-blooded human."

If you could understand me, I'd tell you, I said to Jax.

"Yeah, I don't think it would be news to Jax," Drew snorted.

Will directed everyone to just move along. He wanted to explore the museum and be back at the guest hut before Rhys woke up. It didn't matter that he would be fine if Hyrum and Aubrey were the only ones with him when he got up. He wanted to be there and to be the one his son turned to in the morning.

He was still itching to send Rhys back to stay with Finn. He'd given his young son several days to play with his new friends, and the longer we stayed chasing after Tobias, the more he wanted Rhys somewhere safer. Finn and Jo were also better capable of dealing with Rhys and Hyrum exploring their gifts, and after seeing what they were able to do when they worked in tandem, he was less agreeable about leaving them with Shivan's wife, as willing as she was.

"Aubrey can handle them," Jax said.

"I would like to send her back, as well. You don't need the distraction."

"She's not a distraction."

Even Sean laughed at that. Will reminded Jax that Aubrey once claimed that every time she went through a portal with him, it was like a switch flipped and he could barely stay off her. There was a reason she'd demanded he get snipped before she would visit Will's birth When for her fiftieth birthday; she was done having children, and she'd come back from one trip pregnant with Zed.

"There's no magical horny switch," Jax said. "When we go somewhere through the portal, there are no guards constantly trailing me. My every move isn't being watched and recorded. We both relax and just enjoy each other's company, and anything that happens is because we still have functioning hormones and are damned attracted to each other. Trust me, if Aubrey and I could wander around town alone, I'd be dragging her behind trees and buildings just for a long kiss or two."

"You're free to engage in some public displays of affection," Will said. "Just...not in the manner following your forty-fifth birthday dinner. Or what occurred in the alley upon going home. That would make the news."

That was the freedom Jax wanted. He pointed at Sean and said, "Mr. McAllister can take a woman to dinner, and they can stop to walk along a pier, sit on a bench, and make out like little fiends. As long as he doesn't cross a legal PDA line, no one will think twice. Aubrey and I have to be so...controlled."

"I'd need a girlfriend first," Sean said.

"You understand my point."

"Yeah, the point is you can go home every day to a wonderful woman who obviously adores you, and I can barely talk to them. It sucks that you can't publicly, I dunno, grope her but come on.

Appreciate what you've got instead of complaining about what you don't. I'd kill to have that."

"He's not wrong," Drew said.

"We don't feel sorry for you," Will said.

"Then you all can just bite me." We were close to the DeYoung. The observation tower was as we'd last seen it: burnt, crumbling, and tilting slightly. "Any chance he's here?"

"Only one way to find out," Sean said, taking a few steps forward.

Neither Will nor Drew were ready to go inside; the last time Will hadn't made it more than ten feet inside before the doors and windows sealed and the lobby filled with gas. When we woke, Will was gone. An hour later, Hagar vanished.

Neither said anything; there was a look exchanged, acknowledging the past, admitting their fears. Jax was following Sean, and with a sigh, we started after them.

= = =

The empty museum was pitch black. With no moonlight to see by and no flashlights on hand, we were less than twenty feet into the lobby when Jax admitted that there could be a hundred men waiting on the other side, and we wouldn't know until it was too late.

"So we save this for tomorrow and go look somewhere else," Drew said. "I mean, what are the odds he would come back here? He knows we know he used it before. It doesn't make sense—"

"I'm creeped out, too," Jax said. "I feel like I'm waiting for an ambush."

Walk the beaches. You have the moon to see by, and Fluffy can walk along the woods. He can see better than we can.

Will suggested we split up. He and Sean headed in the direction of city center, while Drew and Jax headed for the coast. Fluffy could get to Will quickly if Jax found Tobias, and Jeff could get Jax if he did. I went with Jax because Fluffy would respond to me faster than he would if they tried to explain things to him.

We cut through Land's End, and headed for Baker Beach, working our way toward Ghirardelli. Jax muttered several things from the Queen's bad word list when he realized he had to climb the stairs at Land's End, and again when he had to walk up the slope at Sea Cliff. He grumbled that Will had assured him all of Saint Francis was flat, and he would have taken a different route if he'd known.

Drew just laughed at him. He and Will often ran together up and down the hill at Ocean Beach, and when they'd done that several times Will always suggested—which was more of an order—they run the stairs. At first, Drew complained about it as much as Jax was now, but once he realized how much better shape he was in, he embraced Will's grueling workout routine and stopped whining.

"You two are masochists," Jax grunted halfway up the Sea Cliff path. "Wasn't walking across Colorado enough? You just keep compounding the pain."

"Says the guy who gets up in the middle of the night to run with Will."

"I get up to spend some time with Hyrum. And Will and I stick to running around Union Square. Basically, nice and flat."

"I spend too much time sitting while I work," Drew said. "I owe it to Oz to not fall into the trap of laziness. It would be too easy, and she might need me to be in the best possible shape someday."

"If it involves the creepy things you do to my daughter behind closed doors, I don't want to know."

"I stay in shape for the same reasons Will does."

Will saw his physical condition as a job requirement, and protecting his family was the biggest part of his job. He ran nearly every day, he trained with weights, he swam, and he kept his fighting skills honed by sparring with Oz, Zed, and Drew. Oz was the only one remotely close to his skill level, but he'd learned along the way that teaching was as important to understanding the art as was practice.

He pushed Jax to run, but he'd never been able to get him to learn more than a few basic self-defense skills. Jax didn't see the point; he had guards, and he would never be allowed to engage in any sort of fight. Will accepted that, but he could see the shortcomings of the guards and knew there were slim margins of time when Jax would not be under their watchful eye. Because of that, Will made sure he could defend his brother and King, and anyone else living in the royal house.

He'd made sure Oz could defend herself when she was young. His life had an expiration date that he was all too aware of. He wanted her to be sure on her feet and quick with her fists, and when he knew he would live, he pushed Drew and Zed to learn to fight, as well.

Jay dabbled. He paid attention and practiced enough to satisfy Will, but it was Drew who took the message to heart: that woman is your job, above all else. More than Ozoo, more than the projects that they sent to Elysium, Oz was it. Love her, cherish her, and protect her with your own life. If anyone is left standing in the end, it needs to be her.

"I appreciate that," Jax huffed at the top of the hill. "Really, I do. That doesn't mean I won't bitch like a teenaged girl grounded on prom night every time I have to go up a damned hill, though."

"There's a mental image," Drew said with a laugh.

"I never went to a prom," Jax said, seemingly out of nowhere. "I was looking forward to it, until my grades slipped, and my father pulled me out of one school and dropped me into another with classes segregated by gender."

"What, no prom in the new school?"

"It was academically intensive and there were no extracurriculars. It was also no fun."

But his grades shot up and he got into college. Don't let him fool you.

Will was also going to get Jay into that school and would have if he hadn't graduated early.

"Really?" Drew asked me. "Will wanted to send Jay to Suckage Central High?"

"Suckage Central," Jax chuckled. "Will wanted to send Jay there to get him away from some horrific bullying he endured at school."

"I thought Zed kept the jackasses at bay."

"He wasn't there for a while. Too busy hiking with you and Will."

Without Zed to stand as a barrier that kept the bullies in high school from turning Jay's life into a nightmare, he suffered. At sixteen, Jay was the size of a twelve-year-old. Because he was on medications to delay puberty, his voice was high, and he was reed-thin with little muscle mass. Other boys in his class sensed there was something different about him from the moment he stepped into their classroom in sixth grade, but as they grew and he did not, they paid closer attention. The more attention they paid, the worse he was treated.

While Zed was in the Denver safe house, and when he was hiking across Colorado to help find his sister, Jay was shoved into lockers and left there, he was beaten up, teased mercilessly, and harassed. Will had only been back in Aisha's life for a few weeks, but he knew where they were headed, and he wanted to protect Jay as much as he did Oz and Zed.

"What about you?" Jax asked. "Prom?"

"I wasn't interested in going stag to a formal dance."

"What, you couldn't get a date?"

"I didn't date in high school," Drew said. "I considered it once or twice, but it felt like cheating."

"You weren't committed to Oz then, Drew."

"Not officially. But I knew."

"Huh. Oz never dated, either. I didn't question it because I honestly didn't want to deal with it." Jax paused on the path "Wait. So you never—"

"Nope. When I kissed her on her eighteenth birthday? That was my first kiss, too. She was the only girl I'd ever held hands with, the only one I'd danced with, and she's been the only one for pretty much anything you can think of."

"Damn."

Jax was a whore.

"Wick," Drew snorted.

"He called me a whore again, didn't he?" He shrugged it off. "I'd like to say that if I knew then what I know now, everything would be different, but thirteen-year-old Jax would not have cared."

"Thirteen? Seriously?"

"Raise my grandson differently, Drew. I had far too much freedom to roam, and my dad turned a blind eye to a lot of what he knew was going on."

"Your grandkids have a hell of a lot of people keeping eyes on them," Drew pointed out.

"Still. I thought I was doing a better job than my parents, and then Zed—"

"That was one girl, Jax. One horny and determined girl who decided he was her next conquest. You can't fault him for that. Anyone else he was with, he was in a relationship."

"Then stress that. Relationships first. The chaos I could have potentially unleashed? And I still worry that out there are women who are damaged by the way I treated them."

"Worried there might be unknown Blackshear heirs?"

Jax worried that not only might there be children he never knew about, but if they surfaced and staked a claim, he wouldn't remember their mothers. He wasn't concerned about a claim to the throne—Oz was his formally declared heir, and nothing could change that—but knowing he wouldn't have been particularly kind about their births had he been aware at the time and knowing he would have been angry at everyone but himself gnawed at him.

"Will's decision to stay here when we were kids tamed me a hell of a lot," Jax said. "He shifted my focus away from the stupid crap I was getting into and just gave me a friend. I needed that."

"You didn't have friends?"

"I had friends, but Will was a *friend*. The same way he's been with you. I know you had friends in Chicago but think about how much more Will became for you. He's your brother as much as he is mine."

"Yeah, he is that," Drew agreed.

"If not for him staying when he did, I don't think I would have been the man Aubrey wanted. God only knows who I'd be now."

You'd still be a whore.

"Cat," he said when Drew translated, "I will turn you inside out."

No, you won't. You love me.

"He can still love you inside out," Drew said.

Will needs me right side out.

"Will has another anchor now," Jax reminded me. "You aren't the only thing holding him in this When."

He has lots of anchors now. Aisha and Jay and Rhys and Alex and Charlie. I can feel it.

"Seriously?" Jax asked.

I felt it when Aisha became an anchor. But I think maybe time finally let him go. He belongs in every When, I think.

"God, I hope so," Jax breathed.

We'd made our way past Marshall Beach and crossed over to a path that cut through the east side of the Presidio. Jax wanted to walk past Jeff's lair at Fort Point and then continue through Crissy Field. After that, he wanted to go back to the hut and try to get at least a couple hours of sleep before Rhys was up. Will would remind him to be quiet, but he was three; his idea of quiet and real quiet were different things.

The absence of light in the woods slowed them down. They kept talking, voices low, as Jax prodded Drew about his hopes for fatherhood and family. I listened quietly, without another Jax-is-a-whore comment; this wasn't a walk that would have happened when Drew moved from Chicago to be with Oz. He'd known Jax from the day he was born, he'd spent nearly every summer in San Francisco, but there was always a thread of fear wrapped around him, its end sticking out, trying to connect, where Jax was concerned.

I could almost see it; it was barely a thread anymore, more like a ribbon, and imprinted on its silky surface were patterns woven out of love and respect. Drew confessed things he had only shared with Oz: he was equal parts thrilled and terrified at the idea of being a father. He wanted this as badly as Will had when Aisha was pregnant with Rhys, and he'd thought he understood Will's fears then, but now they felt multiplied.

"More than anything I want to be the father this baby deserves," Drew said. "And I love my dad, like, an insane amount, but I hardly ever saw him, and I hate that I get as lost in my work as he did."

"Set office hours, son. Richard never did that."

Drew's father not only got lost enough in his work that he could spend days away from home, when he was home he inevitably spent his free time helping Shazia. Evenings at home were dedicated to reading paperwork to her and helping her memorize speeches so she wouldn't need to have notes in front of her.

"It's Oz, too. I don't want her to feel like she's been set aside because I want to spend time with the baby when I get home. I have no idea how to balance it all."

"Set your office hours," Jax said. "Stick to it. When you get home, the first person you go to is Oz. She gets the first hug, the first kiss, the first hello. When you wake up in the morning, she gets the first of everything, and you damn well tell her you love her. Every goddamned day, Drew. She comes first."

Drew was picturing it in his head: most of the time, when Jax arrived home, he sought out Aubrey. If someone else didn't get to him first, she was the one he gave attention to. There was always a kiss, always a smile. If he'd been away, it didn't matter who reached him first. They were told to wait, and he went to her.

"They're not just our wives and the mothers of our children," Jax said. "These women are our backbones. The soul of the family. And they're why our hearts beat. Toss out every bit of crap you've ever read about masculine stoicism and how men give love to get sex. Love her openly, and let the world see how much. If she never doubts your love, your children will be all the better for it."

Drew nodded as if he understood.

"Be worthy of her. That's all. And I'll straight up admit that's the advice Will gave me right after he introduced me to Aubrey. Be worthy of her. Do that, and the pieces will fall into place. You're going to be a good father, Drew. I have no doubt."

Jax wanted Drew to remind himself often: he and Oz chose each other and committed to each other for the rest of their lives. The kids would grow up and carve their own lives from the branches of the family tree they'd created. In the end, it would be the two of them, as long as they kept choosing each other.

They moved on to things less weighty. There was a long list of stupid things Jax had done in his teens, rash and ill-advised things that didn't involve his whorish ways. As we passed Jeff's lair and started for Crissy Field, he told Drew about stealing beer from his father's supply and taking it to the Presidio woods on several of Will's visits. They'd both hated it at first, Jax a little less than Will given that he'd been stealing it for a long time; they'd get pleasantly buzzed and talk until they were sober, and as Jax aged Will began bringing bottles of scotch along.

He hadn't had to steal them. Finn didn't mind providing one every now and then, and the last bottle he brought, on the visit when he spilled his soul and told Jax that the next time he came it would be to stay, he entrusted Jax with the last bottle Finn would give him until he was forty-two years old.

It was scotch meant for sipping, not the cheap scotch meant for getting drunk on. Jax created an alcove in his closet and placed a safe with a lock there and stored it until Will was ready for it.

"The Emperor's reserve," Jax said. "I still have the empty bottle. It was almost thrown out once, when we were too drunk to think of what that bottle meant to us. Fortunately, Aubrey understood the significance and grabbed it before I had a chance to trash it."

"And it helped that she was old enough to carry it," Drew guessed, laughing.

"There was an extra perk to falling in love with someone old enough to buy booze. But that was the day I realized pouring drink after drink down my throat wasn't as fun as I pretended. Damned middle of the day and I was loaded out of my mind, stretched out on a merry-go-round at the Dolores Park playground."

Fountain of vomit! Finally!

"Son, don't ever mix scotch, beer, soda, and—" He thrust his arm out, his hand going to Drew's chest, stopping him. We were on the dirt path that skirted the new Marina Green and sitting on the beach at the water's edge were a man and a woman, bathed in moonlight.

They knelt facing each other. Her hands were on his cheeks, and she looked at him as if she were searching for something. The words she whispered were lost to shadows; I couldn't hear her, and neither Drew nor Jax would be able to read her lips to guess at what she was saying. She was pleading with him, and when his shoulders slumped, she kissed his forehead, and let go when he dropped his head.

For a long, silent minute, she held his hands, waiting as his body heaved with sobs we couldn't hear. When he could breathe, her arms went around him to draw him close, and he rested his head in the soft space between her shoulder and neck. We watched, silently, waiting to see if Tobias had heard us and was waiting for Jax to make a move; there was barely a breath until I realized that Jax wasn't breathing at all.

His gaze was fixed ahead as if he were soaking in the image of the dark wizard and his wife, but there was an absence of light in his eyes. I counted, one, two, three, waiting for his chest to move just a tiny bit, but when I reached sixty, and he still hadn't, I risked breaking the silence.

Drew. Something's wrong. Jax isn't breathing.

He craned forward to look at Jax's face.

"It's just, like, a thousand-yard stare," he whispered.

No, Jax isn't...here.

He nudged Jax with his elbow and got no response.

"Jax," he hissed. "Come on."

Jax listed to the left a tiny bit when Drew's elbow made contact, but he didn't flinch. It was like watching a drone that had been powered down; there was no expression to tell us if he was in pain, if he was suddenly struck by what he was seeing and couldn't bear it. No breath, no blinking, no swallowing absently.

Tobias stood up and Drew reached for his gun, more to protect Jax than to end the hunt, but Jax took a breath and then set his hand on Drew's, and whispered, "Not now, son. Not in front of his wife. Whatever he deserves, she doesn't."

I thought we would wait there, silently, until Miriam left, but Jax turned and headed for the woods, leaving Tobias, alive, on the beach with his wife, and Drew scrambling to catch up and understand what had just happened.

26

Jax and Drew got three hour's sleep before they were woken by Rhys squealing, "Yay! Cereal!" Aubrey shushed him and reminded him that people were sleeping, but it was too late. Jax groaned and Drew called out, "What kind of cereal? The kind we like or the kind moms like?"

"The good stuff!" Rhys answered.

Drew rolled out of bed and started for the table but stopped when Aubrey pointed a spoon at him and growled, "Pants, Andrew."

He glanced down at his underwear, apologized, and went back for his jeans.

You've seen men in undies before. You've seen Drew in undies. What's the big deal?

She didn't need anyone to translate. "We don't come to the table without pants. It's rude."

"Finn must be controlling the food supply," Drew said when he came back, his shirt tucked into the front of his jeans but not the back. "The last guy had a hard-on for chicken and eggs. What kind of good stuff did we get, short stack?"

"There's chocolate puffs and honey puffs."

"Two boxes of each," Hyrum added. "Finn knows."

Will said to tell you there are hard-boiled eggs in the fridge, and you're supposed to eat two of them even if you have cereal. He wants you to have protein since we're going back out.

"Where is he?" Drew asked.

Outside. I would go with him, but no one will open the door for me.

"Normal cats scratch at the door when they want out." He got up anyway and opened it for me. "Holler if you want back in, in case I don't hear you scratching."

Or tell Will. He'll let me in.

He was sitting in Shivan's courtyard with Hagar, a mug cupped between his hands. The village was awake and bustling with kids scampering around the center as they yelled at each other to get going; it was time to leave for school, and if they were late, Scooter would fry them. As I darted between giant feet attached to gangly legs, Darville stumbled out the front door, blinking against the bright light. Therese was ten steps behind him, and she skipped from the porch steps to the gate.

Quinn followed her, grumbling when she closed the gate in front of him. "You're just a baby, Quinny. You don't get to come."

Darville bent over the gate. "Next year, sprout. And while we have to sit quietly in school, you get to stay here and play with Rhys and Hyrum. That sounds like more fun than math class."

I leaped over the gate, rubbed against Quinn's skinny leg, and then jumped onto the small table between Will and Hagar.

Hagar sighed. "I still cannot believe Shivan is old enough to have children. Especially one as old as Darville."

"It's been twenty years," Will reminded him.

"Here. My grandchildren aged only ten. They were unhappy to learn school was expected of them, along with the other village children. Miriam, however, was thrilled. She enjoyed teaching them when they were young but believes it's time for someone else to bear the brunt of their adolescent attitudes."

Will leaned back, setting his mug on the table. "Will the other children accept them? I haven't seen them outside since they arrived. I haven't seen your daughter, either."

I saw her last night. So did Jax.

Will's ear twitched; he heard me but wasn't going to give Hagar a hint.

"A few of the elves have come over to welcome her to the village, but most are wary, I'm afraid. Those who mourned her are feeling the pain all over again. But some of the children have come over to introduce themselves and stayed to talk. They don't remember Tobias or his reign of terror." He grunted. "Literal rain."

Tobias was with her. She was trying to make him feel better.

"I hope all goes well for them," Will said. He meant it, too; he wanted fairness for them and didn't believe that the sins of the father should be borne by his children. "I can't imagine this is in any way easy for them."

"And you would understand that, wouldn't you?" Hagar asked.

"I have some experience being the odd man out as a young teen."

Drew started to draw his gun, but Jax stopped him. He didn't want to kill Tobias in front of her. But before that, something went haywire with Jax. He froze. And I mean, he wasn't breathing, didn't hear Drew talking to him, or anything. He wasn't there, even though he was.

"Did you get fed?" Will asked me. "You're quite insistent upon being heard this morning."

Aubrey fed me. Rhys is excited because he gets cereal. You got that, though, right?

"I did. Rhys is as excited as any three-year-old whose father routinely insists on whole food at home would. Aubrey is feeding my son junk food," he explained to Hagar.

"And his mother doesn't also insist?"

"His mother is why my children know what chocolate tastes like."

Like you care.

"I would care if she showed no regard for my feelings on the matter, Wick," he said.

"As I recall, the lady Aisha is formidable enough that if she chose, she could make you believe her choices were your idea," Hagar said, bellowing out a laugh. "You need her here. Your mission would be a bit easier, I imagine."

"I'm surprised you'd be in favor of anything that made this easier."

"I understand the power of a very strong woman. You may be a powerful man in your own realm, Emperor, but she is, indeed, stronger. But no, I am not in favor of this hunt."

When the door to the guest hut opened, Hagar got up. He nodded to Drew but made his way out of the courtyard before Jax came out and was nearly home before Drew took the seat he'd vacated.

"I'd take that personally, but I know it isn't," Drew said. "Is he all right?"

"He seems to be. What happened last night?"

Drew told him what I had, adding that it felt like Miriam was telling her husband goodbye. He was broken and she tried to comfort him, and if they'd stuck around Drew wouldn't have been surprised to see her leave him alone on the beach, and he would have felt the heartbreak of Tobias watching her walk away. "Just a feeling. I might be wrong."

"Wick mentioned an issue with Jax."

Drew described how Jax had been, adding, "He was just vacant, Will. I could have pushed him over, and he wouldn't have noticed."

"Further proof he needs time off," Will said. "More than this. He needs—"

Drew's head jerked up at the sound of a slamming door, and he looked across the village center. "That's the kid," he said. "The assmunch."

Will looked over his shoulder. "Asmonk. The other children have left for school. Why hasn't he?"

"He frequently stays home," Shivan said as he stepped out of his house. "His parents don't seem to care, and he manages to be productive during the day. Today, I imagine he's afraid to go because of the name he earned here."

"Is he always such a dick?" Drew asked.

Will practically growled at him, but Shivan laughed. "Every neighborhood has an Asmonk, no? With luck, he'll outgrow it. If not, he'll be a very lonely elf. If he doesn't yet understand his behavior is his choice, he will sooner rather than later."

Rhys barreled his way outside, Jax on his heels. Shivan ushered the toddler inside with Quinn— "Lani is waiting for you. She has finger paints and a whole roll of paper." —and we got underway. Will wanted to go in the direction of the lab so that he could put his tablet on a charger and grab another one, and Jax didn't care. It was just as likely that Tobias had rooted himself downtown as it was that he was hiding in the woods.

We waited on Union Square while Will went inside to grab another tablet. Jax wandered the perimeter, peering down streets, while Sean stood near Fluffy, finally working up the nerve to scratch the giant kitty's chin. He glanced at Jeff, who had landed in front of the royal house but was still too wary of approaching him. I sat with Shivan and Drew on the ground. They rested with their backs against the side of the hut that served as the lab's entry, but they were actively observing everything around us.

"Look to the north," Shivan said. "Tell me what you see."

"Clear skies. Buildings a hell of a lot shorter than they are at home. Coit Tower." He paused and then exhaled sharply. "Coit Tower."

"The tower should not stand," Shivan said. "It was not repaired after Oz destroyed it."

"He definitely has his magic back, then."

You need to tell Will.

"I will, Wick. The question is whether we tell Jax."

Tell Will first.

"Why would you not tell your King?" Shivan asked.

"Will might want to shore up security in the lab first, to make sure Tobias has no access to the mainframe. That was his goal before, to get to the mainframe. He wanted to shut everything down."

"You'd be fine."

"But you wouldn't. I don't care if you're part of a computer program, Shivan. You're as real as I am. Your wife and kids are real. We're not about to let him end you."

"And I appreciate that. But take fewer risks than you did when we battled the Shedu, Drew. You have a wife, and she's expecting your child. When Lani was carrying Darville, nothing could have made me take the risks I did when I was a child."

"We'll leave before it comes to risking your lives," Drew said.

"Ah, there we go. I mention Oz, and you're in a hurry to leave. I see how it is."

"I'm not happy about the idea of missing any part of this pregnancy, even though I won't really."

"I drove Lani a bit insane with my hovering," Shivan admitted.

"I gotta ask you something, and it's super personal," Drew said. "Feel free to not answer and tell me to mind my own damn business."

Shivan nodded.

"How the hell do you reproduce here?"

Shivan considered the question, then said, "Well, Andrew, when a boy loves a girl—"

"Shut up," Drew chuckled. "I'm interested in the biology of it. And not in a creepy kind of way."

"You were present for the conception of your own child, weren't you?"

"Jerk. You know what I'm getting at."

"Yes, we have sex," Shivan said, laughing at Drew's interest. "Everything you do, we do. We were modeled after biological humans, after all."

But they probably do it way faster, since time here moves so quickly.

Super Shivan, faster than a speeding laser.

"He insulted me, didn't he?"

"It's what he does," Drew said.

Will's backpack was heavier than it had been when he went into the lab, enough that Drew noticed. When he pointed it out, Will said he'd taken time to make sandwiches, since he had no idea where they would go from here or what access they would have to food. Jax was still prowling around the Square, pausing at the heads of streets, and he was on his third lap around.

"Without being obvious," Drew said to Will, "look in the direction of Coit Tower."

"I noticed when we arrived."

"Pretty bold to recreate the place he stored all his equipment. There's not a snowball's chance in hell he thought we wouldn't notice."

"Is he there?" Shivan wondered out loud.

"I think," Will said carefully, "that its presence is a calculated message on Tobias's part. He reminds us that he has power still and is using it. I would be surprised if he spent all his time there, but I assume it's where he's spending his nights."

"Tell Jax?" Drew asked.

Will shook his head. "Not yet."

Drew's eyebrows knotted.

"Trust me on this."

Sean trotted over, flicking long cat hairs from his hands. "Stupidish question," he said. "And I don't know why I even thought about it. But if there are wizards here, are there witches?"

They all turned to Shivan.

"Remind me, I'll introduce you to Lani's mother."

Dude.

"Brutal," Drew snorted.

"Hagar's wife was a witch. Lani's mother is merely unpleasant."

"No others?" Drew asked.

Shivan thought it was possible, but no one would have admitted it after Tobias took control. Witches, warlocks, and wizards had no one to guide them; Hagar was the only known wizard apart from Tobias, and he had sworn to never take another apprentice. "I was technically his apprentice, but we never got to the magic part of everything."

"What's the difference between a wizard and a warlock?" Sean asked.

"Warlocks use spells and herbs and powders to cast magic. A wizard's magic is innate, as far as I know. Much like Rhys and Hyrum's ability to shoot things from their hands...it's just there."

"So there are no female wizards?" Sean asked.

Shivan didn't know, and the discussion ended because Jax had made his way across the Square and had a look of expectation on his face.

"Where to?" he asked Will.

Will wanted to explore SOMA and Dogpatch, going in the opposite direction of the tower. There were plenty of places to hide there; the Old Mint, which was not time locked here, the modern art museum, and unless it had been dismantled, there was an entire army encampment in Dogpatch. A tired wizard could make himself comfortable there, and he would be able to hear everything around him.

"Then he'll hear us coming," Sean pointed out.

"He knows we're coming," Jax said. "The question is, can he run fast enough?"

= = =

The Old Mint, as it turned out, was little more than a façade. Jax forced the door open and stepped inside, but there was no back wall, and the roof ended halfway across the top. Will guessed it was a choice Finn made to cut down on resource consumption, but if we'd needed it to be whole and the computer anticipated that before we entered, it would be.

"At least it doesn't have that godawful green tinge to it," Jax muttered, mostly to himself.

"The tinge you see is tied into the sound I hear," Will explained as we made our way down the steps. "It makes Oz nauseated."

"Yeah, I know the feeling."

"Every time Oz and I walk past it she says she wants to stab something." Drew mused. "We don't walk past it anymore. Just in case."

Jax headed down Mission Street to Third, and we followed that until we reached the crumbling remains of the ball park. The seating was long gone, as was the wall that faced the cove where eager fans often waited in rafts to catch balls that sailed over the wall. It was piles of brick turning to dust, and Jax wondered why Finn hadn't kept it.

"Resources," Will said again. "Should you ever develop a burning desire to play baseball, it would take only an hour or two of coding to make it whole."

"Baseball, hell. If you go to that trouble, we're staging a damned concert. Every band you ever wanted to hear, right here, live. Well, simulated live."

He'd never been to a concert. As a teenager, he'd wanted to travel to L.A. to see his favorite bands play in a massive expo, but the security demands and the imposition on other people persuaded King Eli to forbid his attendance. The First Friday concerts on the Square didn't count. He could watch those from his balcony if he chose, but more often than not he left the seats open for his kids. He'd wanted to be in the crowd, shoulder to shoulder with ten thousand other people, not sipping scotch in his own home while the band played.

"We're going to knock the entire thing down and bury ourselves, and no one will find us for a hundred years," Sean said as we made our way in.

"Nonsense," Will said. "The computer would note the absence of our life signs and inform whoever is monitoring the simulator."

"Well, that makes it all better."

Past the decay of what was once the framework for steps that led to spectator seats, over waist-high piles of rock and cement, was the field. It was now dirt and dust, looking out onto the cove. Jax went to the center and stared upward, turning to look in all directions.

"This is a lot less intimidating than it was during my coronation," he said after a while. "The noise was overwhelming. Between people shouting and the music that blared through all those speakers? I could barely hear my father, and he was right next to me."

Will grinned. "And he was telling you over and over, 'don't throw up. I told you not to get drunk last night.'"

"I wasn't drunk," Jax said. "Was I?"

"Fluthered," Sean offered. "The Irish say 'fluthered.' That sounds much nicer than 'shit-faced.'"

"I like that. I may have been a wee bit fluthered." Jax took a deep breath and stared at the spot where Aubrey had waited with Oz and Zed while Eli formally abdicated and then placed the crown on his head. "I was terrified that day. I was angry at having to give up my life for this. Sad because I knew what my kids were in for. Yet I was also beyond excited and so damned sure I would be the King the people deserved. Anything I was uncertain about, my father would be there to help with."

"And he was, for a time," Will said.

"Until the ghosts overwhelmed him, and he ran off to play with your grandfather." He turned to Will. "Don't let me do that to Oz. If I'm still alive when she takes the throne, I stick around."

"Presuming I'm still here."

"You'll be here. And fuck you, you know when I die. I hate that."

Will moved close because it felt like Jax was about to dive head first into his feelings, something that usually only happened when he was drunk. "I know when my great, great grandfather, the man in my history, died. The Jax I visit thirty-five years in the future may have a different end. As might you. You won't have the same threads of loss binding you. You very well might live far longer than either of those men."

"And Aubrey?"

"Do you really want to know?"

Jax blinked against the burning in his eyes. "Just tell me."

Softly, so that only Jax would hear, Will said, "She outlived you. It wasn't by much, but she was there for your end. And before you sink into sadness over it, you'll both have incredibly long lives if you pay attention to the details."

"You better be here for all of it."

"I intend to be. I know how long Aisha lived the last time around and I'd like to be here almost to the end."

"Almost."

They were still speaking softly, leaving the others standing awkwardly. "I don't want to outlive her, Jax. Every day I have is already a bonus, but life without her? I don't want that any more than you wish to outlive Aubrey."

"They'll have each other," Jax mused. "Might not even miss us."

"Aubrey will shatter without you. She needs you well, Jax. See to it."

Just kiss and get it over with already.

"I'm not kissing him."

Jax stepped away and pointed toward the opening we'd come through, and said, "Dogpatch, let's go."

We hadn't made it to the bridge that spanned the entrance to Mission Bay park when Scooter swooped down, his wings creating a breeze that fluffed hair and made everyone take a step back. He soared high, circling Jeff, roaring until he was sure he had our attention. Jeff dove down and landed, his head cocked a bit as he listened, and when Scooter landed next to him, they stretched their necks on the ground and waited.

"You want us to take a ride *now*?" Drew asked. "We're kind of busy."

A low rumble grew in Jeff's throat. He twitched his head, indicating that someone needed to climb on, and when no one moved, he looked at Fluffy. A second later, Fluffy circled behind us and began head-butting Will and Jax toward Jeff.

I think it's important.

Fluffy pushed Drew toward Scooter.

"Something's wrong," Drew said. He handed me to Will and whipped off his sweatshirt and told Will to put it on. "He'll be safer with you."

Instead, Will gave the shirt to Jax. "Sit up front and hold onto those handles tight. I'll keep an arm around you and a hand on Wick."

They scrambled for Jeff, but Sean remained rooted, his face pale.

"Ride Fluffy back," Drew told him as he mounted Scooter. "He's strong enough. Use his fur as a handhold and let him lead. He'll know where to go. It won't hurt him."

Shivan jumped onto Scooter; we didn't wait to see if Sean rode Fluffy or not. If he took a few hours because he was afraid to climb into Fluffy's back or still felt like it was wrong, no one cared.

Jax did as Will instructed and grabbed Jeff's handles as tightly as he could. I felt his knees dig in as Will's arm went around his waist, and then Will's hand cupped me in place. I only allowed my head to poke up from the pouch of the sweatshirt; if I hated it, I had no choice. Once Will was pressing me into Jax's stomach, there was no room to wiggle back under. The best I could do was close my eyes.

Unlike Jax, who hollered, "Holy shit!" joyfully at the top of his lungs, I was not a fan of thundering through the air without the confines of a car around me. The air stung my eyes and nose, and the noise hurt my ears. My view was largely the scales on Jeff's neck; he was an iridescent ruby red now, glowing under the light of the sun.

It suited him. He'd been more intimidating when he wore his black skin, but in the red his details were clear and his beauty astounding.

The red dot.

He was a flying red dot.

No wonder Fluffy wanted to pounce.

He streaked toward the village. Jax's excitement in riding on him waned as he realized where we were headed, and when Jeff landed just outside the entry, his heart was pounding, and he didn't wait for Will to tell him how to dismount. He slid down Jeff's side, clutching me to his stomach, and ran toward Hyrum, who was standing near the hut door, his hands clutching at his hair.

He began yelling when he spotted Jax. "I can't find them! I don't know where they went!"

Voices thundered in the woods, and Will shot past Jax, sprinting toward them. They were calling for Rhys and for Aubrey.

"What happened?" Jax asked. His hands went to Hyrum's, pulling them away from his head. "Come on, Hy. Take a breath."

Drew and Shivan ran past, too, and both dragons took to the air.

"I went inside to pee. Rhys was right here playing with his wand, but I came out, and he was gone. Aubrey went to look for him, but she's gone, too, and I told Lani and everyone got mad and started running and yelling."

I leaped from the sweatshirt and headed into the woods before Jax could stop me. There were a dozen elves that I could see pressing through the brush, calling out for Rhys, and others calling out for Aubrey. I caught up to Will and scrambled up his leg, but he didn't seem to notice I was there.

His voice boomed loudest, yelling for his son.

"Everyone else is looking over there," Drew said when he caught up to Will. "You take the left, I'll take the center." He turned and called back to Jax and Shivan, "Take our six!" and to Hyrum behind them, "Keep up with Jax, Hyrum!"

Jax swatted at a butterfly flitting around his head and nodded. He yelled for his wife while Will and Drew kept calling Rhys's name, and I stayed quiet, trying to listen between the pops of panic. Every few seconds Jax muttered to himself, cursing an annoyance, and I turned to see a dozen butterflies dancing around him and Shivan.

Will, look to Drew's right.

He turned. A fluttering blue and red wall streamed between the trees, and a thinner one formed behind Jax and Shivan. They'd saved us before, when we were headed down the same path as a female dragon teaching her offspring to hunt. Then, they pushed us toward the beach, avoiding the fireball that shot down the path we'd been on.

"What the hell?" Jax shouted.

"Turn," Will said. "They're guiding us."

His pace picked up, and I held on. The sound of the elves calling out for Rhys dimmed as the wall of butterflies thickened, and we ran deep into the woods.

Drew slowed down when one of the sprites flew straight at him, spiraling in front of his nose. It was followed by another, and then another, until there were a dozen surrounding his head. One hovered close to his face, and the others went for his hair, tugging on it as their wings beat loudly.

"What the hell?" Jax said when he was close.

"Don't anger them," Shivan told Jax. "They bite."

"But they trust Drew," Will reminded Shivan. "They're trying to talk to you, Andrew."

They were tugging him forward, until he said, "Show me. We'll follow."

We heard the dogs before we saw the light; Will snatched me from his shoulder and began running hard and Drew matched his pace, his arms pumping as he raced toward the angry barking.

The sprites made a sharp left turn, and as we turned, we saw the glowing light, the same light Drew had seen years ago, buried in the darkness that lived between the trees.

Will stopped abruptly. Rhys was eight feet up a tree, his arms and legs wrapped around the thin trunk, and on the ground under were five snarling dogs. They jumped and nipped, kept from their prey by a crackling net made from hundreds of tiny sprites.

"Don't touch it!" Hyrum shouted from behind us. "It's sparky! It'll hurt you!" He wasn't as out of breath as I expected from someone who chose to not run more than half a block at a time. "I can touch it. I'm a sparky sponge."

Drew pointed to the dogs. "Not until we can get past them."

Rhys was screaming, his breath racked in great sobs that sounded as if he were choking.

Jax had his hand on his gun, but before he could pull it, Hyrum splayed his fingers and sent heavy threads of hot light shooting forward. There was one thick electric rope for each dog, cracking against furry snouts. The dogs yelped and ran, but they stopped twenty feet away to lick their wounds and to growl, warning.

They'll attack again.

Hyrum wanted to tear the sprite's net apart but Drew reached for his hands and stopped him. "They're protecting Rhys. They won't hurt him. Let Will get him."

Will was already there, reaching up. When the sprites didn't part, Drew spoke up. "Please. He's the boy's father. We know you're trying to help and we're grateful."

Slowly, so that he didn't fall, the net parted and the sprites nudged Rhys down to where Will could grab him. When he was in his father's arms, face buried against Will's shoulder as he wailed, the sprites flew to where the dogs watched and spun overhead. One came to Drew and touched his head, waiting for the answer to the question that Drew heard inside.

"Not where the boy can see," Drew said. "Chase them toward the wood's edge, and when you're out of sight, yes. Go ahead. They're your reward."

"Wait." Jax grabbed at Drew's arm. "Do they know where Aubrey is?"

Drew shook his head.

Will turned back toward the village, holding Rhys as close as he could without hurting him. "Give him a minute, Jax. When he can take a breath without crying, he might be able to tell us where she went."

It took several minutes. When he was finally able to exhale without wailing, Will sat down, keeping Rhys on his lap, and asked what happened. "Can you tell me?"

Rhys hiccupped and then shook his head.

"Will you let me see?" Will's voice was barely a whisper, his lips near Rhys's ear and fingers already on the bare skin of his neck. When Rhys nodded, Will pulled him into a hug, and they sat quietly while Will listened to the memories playing in his son's brain.

There was an older boy, one whose face Will couldn't see. Rhys's view of him was legs in loose-fitting pants and bare feet. He heard a scratchy voice telling Rhys that he had puppies, and if he wanted, they could go play with them.

Rhys believed the boy because he could hear yapping in the distance, and when he was told that meant they were excited to meet him, he ran alongside until they encountered the pack of angry, hungry dogs.

There was a hard shove, knocking Rhys to the ground; he heard Aubrey calling him and he yelled for her, but the boy laughed and said she'd never get there in time, and he ran away. Rhys began to cry and knew Aubrey heard him because the sound of her voice became frantic.

The dogs were growling, creeping up on him, and he was afraid to move. He wanted to close his eyes, but there was a bright light, then another, and tiny voices urged him to get up and jump onto the closest tree trunk. They pushed him higher, begging him to hold on, until they'd formed the net that kept him from falling and kept the dogs at bay.

Aubrey was still calling for him. She followed the barking and then his crying, but when she was only a few feet away, the air around her pulsated, and she vanished.

"You did a very good job climbing the tree and staying safe," Will whispered to Rhys. "Can you tell me what happened to Aunt Aubrey?"

"I heard 'poof.' And then she was dis'peared."

Jax's hand went back to the butt of his gun, his knuckles turning white. "Tobias," he growled. "He was dead before. Now it will be painful."

27

The butterflies lifted out of the woods in bright ribbons that threaded through the trees, and we returned to the village. Hagar stood near the fire with Sean and a dozen of the villagers, with Asmonk on his knees in the dirt. No one looked any degree of happy, especially Asmonk, whose eyes were red and puffy, his nose dripping.

"He ran right past me," Sean explained. "And he had this." He held a stick out to Will. It was Rhys's magic wand; there was the tell-tale seam from Will's magical repair, and Hyrum had taped one end as a handhold for Rhys. "With everyone shouting Rhys's name, I figured he had something to do with it."

"That's him," Rhys sniffed. "Assmunch."

Jax stomped over and hauled Asmonk to his feet. "Where's my wife?" He grabbed the boy so hard his head whipped back. "Where?"

Asmonk pressed his lips together and glared through wet eyelashes, refusing to answer.

"Put him down." Shivan set his hand on Jax's arm. "Hurting him won't help us find her."

He shoved Asmonk onto his backside. "Son, you have ten seconds to start talking. Tell me what the hell you did—"

"No," Shivan said firmly. "That's not how we handle disruptions and disputes."

"I really don't care."

Shivan inserted himself in the space between Jax and Asmonk, who was still on his back in the dirt. "I appreciate your pain, Your Majesty, but you're not in charge here. You are the great grandfather of our creator, which grants you some leeway, and you are our guest. But you won't harm this boy."

"If he's responsible for my wife, you can damn well bet I will."

"And what good will hurting him now do? The only thing we know is that the Emperor's son saw her vanish, and it's likely that Asmonk drew him into the woods with the intent to harm him. He will be punished for that, but I will not allow you near him."

Shivan turned to Hagar. "Can you make him speak?"

Hagar gave a tight nod. "He'll speak."

Before he could do anything, though, the growing crowd parted as Asmonk's grandmother slowly made her way to him. She was small and light, thin bordering on fragile, but wasn't coming slowly because of age; she inched her way toward him full of rage, hands pressed into fists and jaw twitching as she ground her teeth together.

He got to his knees again, sitting back on his heels with his hands on his legs, head bowed. She stopped a foot in front of him and stared at the back of his head, then looked up to see Rhys nestled against his father; Rhys's eyes were as puffy and red as Asmonk's, and his breath hiccupped. Will met her gaze, his eyes hard and nostrils flared just enough to show his fury.

Without taking her eyes off him, she whipped her foot back and kicked Asmonk off his knees and onto his side. His head bounced against the ground, and when he sat up, there was dirt caked in his hair and ear. "Explain yourself," she snapped, her foot poised to take him down again if he refused to answer.

"He used magic." Asmonk's voice was thin and wavering. "He plays with sparks and light as if they were toys."

"You would feed a baby to the dogs for *playing?*"

He finally looked up, defiant. "He's a wizard."

Before he could brace against it, she kicked him over again. "And what of it?" she spat. "You think he's the only wizard here? That Hagar is the only one allowed those gifts?"

"Hagar was gone."

"And took all magic with him?" Her voice grew louder. "Magic is all around us. Why can't a little boy play with his sparks?"

He rolled onto his back, eyes wide and breath coming quickly.

"Answer me!"

"It's not...right."

She bent over and grabbed him by the front of his shirt and hauled him up as hard as Jax had. "And what are you, Asmonk Avandeo? From whose line did you spawn?" She spun him around by his shoulders and made him face Jax and Will. "Tell them. Tell them who your uncle is."

His *no* came out as a squeak.

"Tell them what you could do when you were as small as that boy."

"No."

"Speak your truth!" she shouted.

Thinly, barely above a whisper, he said, "No."

"Then you no longer have a home with me. Until you admit who you are and what you can do, you're banished. Until you make amends for hurting that boy, you're banished. You are no longer my grandson, Asmonk. I banish you from my family, and I take your surname from you."

She turned to Hagar. "Do what you need to do with him. If he admits who is he and makes amends, I'll take only your word."

"If he refuses?" Hagar asked.

"Send him to his uncle, if you can find him."

Asmonk's eyes went wide. "Please, no."

She walked away and didn't look back, even when he begged her to forgive him. He reached near-hysterics as her hand settled on the doorknob to their home, screaming, "Noni, please!" Without flinching, showing no sign that she'd heard him, she pushed the door open and went inside.

"Just tell us where the woman is," Shivan said to Asmonk. "You'll be given a chance to make amends with the Emperor and his son, but not if you refuse to tell us what happened."

He answered thinly, "I don't know."

"Those dogs yours?" Drew asked. "They didn't attack you."

Asmonk nodded. "I'll call them back."

"No point." He leaned closer, his voice low so that Rhys would not hear. "They're long gone now."

Asmonk's head snapped up and his eyes filled. "What did you do?"

"Personally, nothing. A band of sprites saw the danger you'd put Rhys in and protected him. Now, they gave the dogs a running start, but I've seen what they can do when they're pissed off and hungry." Drew pulled himself upright. "For some reason, the sprites like me. And I imagine they'll come if I call."

"I don't know where she is," Asmonk insisted. "I ran, I didn't stay to see what happened."

"Then you were willing to kill my son, yet didn't have the nerve to watch?" Will passed Rhys to Hyrum and asked him to take him into the guest hut and close the door. When he heard the click of the latch catch, Will had his hand around Asmonk's throat, and no matter how hard Shivan tugged on Will's arm, he couldn't get him to let go. "I won't kill you. But I *will* make you wish that I would."

Shivan begged Hagar to stop this.

"I said he would speak. I didn't say how it would happen. Asmonk, the Emperor is of unusual strength and is incredibly patient. He can, and will, hold you there hovering between life and death until you tell him what he wants to know. Now, I already know the answer to this, but it's incumbent upon you to answer. Tell him who your uncle is."

His answer caught in his throat, causing Will to let up enough for him to speak.

"Tobias. My father's brother."

"Damn, dude," Drew said. "Your dad must be old as dirt."

"Yes."

"Answer truthfully, Asmonk," Hagar warned. "I already know. Do you show signs of magic as well?"

"Not permitted," he squeaked.

"That's not what I asked. Do you show signs?"

"Yes."

"Then why," Will growled, "would you attack a little boy for the same thing?" He released the pressure on Asmonk's throat but didn't let go. "He's three years old. He's a baby."

"He shows the same magic that my father said Tobias did when he was little," Asmonk replied. "He's touched by the dark. I refuse to use my abilities. It's wrong."

"Yet you didn't try to lure Hyrum into the woods," Shivan said. "You've seen them both playing with sparks and light, yet it was the little boy you went after. Why?"

"I don't know."

Hagar's hand went to his medallion, and when he lifted his hand to point a finger at Asmonk, Shivan stepped away and pulled Will with him. Sparks danced from Hagar's fingertip, and a moment later Asmonk was shrouded in soft light.

"You won't be able to lie," Hagar said. "Do you know what happened to the Queen?"

"No, I swear."

"Did you intend for the boy, Rhys, to die?"

Softly, "Yes."

"Are you willing to make amends to him and his father? Amends as they wish?"

"No."

"Not even a simple apology?"

"No. The village needs protection from the things he can do."

"You understand what banishment means?"

"I have to leave."

"Alone, with nothing but the clothing you wear. You'll take no food, no water. You won't be given time to tell your parents goodbye. One more time, will you make amends?"

"No."

Hagar bent his finger to his palm, and the light around Asmonk winked out. "Your grandmother was clear on your punishment. Your name is no longer your own, and you are no longer part of the Avandeo line. You are banished from her home, and because she presides over the family, you are also banished from your parents' home. They won't speak with you again, Asmonk. You will truly be alone."

His mouth dropped open.

It wasn't over.

"I will give you a saving grace." Shivan stepped over to him again. "You have one week. You may not return to the village unless you become willing to make amends. If you haven't by the end of one week, you may never return. Amend, and return with the welcome of all who reside here. Refuse, and you're on your own, forever. It's entirely up to you."

He turned his back on the teenager, and then one by one the other villagers did as well. Only Will, Drew, and Jax continued to face him, until Shivan cleared his throat. Jax turned first, then Drew, but Will stared at him as long and hard as he dared, until tears ran down Asmonk's face and dripped from his chin. When Will finally turned his back on Asmonk, the boy's breath hitched several times, unbelieving, and then he ran.

28

The village no longer felt safe. After an argument between Will and Jax about racing after Tobias to find Aubrey—we still had no idea where he was hiding, and Will thought it would be a futile attempt without more information—and with Hagar's assurance that he would get quick word to us if Aubrey appeared in the village, we set out for the lab and the security of heavily locked doors and multiple cameras focused on the terrain around the Square.

It was less about protecting ourselves against Tobias than it was using the security system to keep an eye on Saint Francis, and keeping Rhys and Hyrum safe.

The first thing Will did was message Finn, asking him to come to get Rhys and Hyrum. While waiting for the reply, he directed Drew, Shivan, and Sean to empty out the broken weapons locker and move everything downstairs, where Rhys and Hyrum wouldn't accidentally get to any guns or grenades. While they moved things, he pulled inflatable mattresses from storage and set them up in the offices and behind the island, made sure the fridge was well stocked, and then sat at the table with Jax.

Jax had dropped into a chair at the table in the tiny kitchen, head resting on his folded arms. He groaned about having no idea where to begin looking for her. He was sure if he found Tobias, he would find Aubrey, but other than traipsing through the woods and the city, how was it even possible? He could be anywhere. He could have her anywhere.

"He could *do* anything to her," he said, choking on the thought.

"He is not Levi," Will reminded him.

"But the son of a bitch used him to get to Oz," Jax hissed. "He knows which of Aubrey's buttons to push to hurt her."

Will made sure Rhys and Hyrum were in the office, too far to overhear, and glanced in Drew's direction when he came back. "He used Levi's face. He made sure Oz understood he was aware of the things Levi had done to her."

"Tobias never touched her," Drew said, as if realizing it for the first time. "He never touched any of us. He moved us around like toys, but he never touched us."

"He didn't need to," Shivan said. "The perception was enough."

Jax lifted his head. "He feels pain?"

"We do."

"Good. Once Finn has come for Rhys and Hyrum, we're setting out. I have no idea which direction to go, but we're going somewhere. I can't just sit here and wait."

Will agreed and began scanning the video feed from the cameras. He made no effort to gather supplies, and Jax didn't seem to notice. Drew did; he made coffee and set a mug in front of Jax, and began pulling staples from the pantry, trying to come up with food we could carry, taking his cues from Will.

After the first hour, Jax began to fidget. After the second, he asked if there was any reply from Finn. At the third hour, he pushed away from the table and went into the bathroom, kicking the door closed behind him.

"What the hell are we doing?" Drew asked Will.

"Waiting to hear from my father. I assume he's been unavailable to receive the request. I'm also continuing to scan for movement outside, any sign that Tobias or Aubrey is near."

"The tower?" Drew asked.

With a side glance to the bathroom door to make sure Jax was not on his way out, Will said, "I have eyes on it. I have eyes in it. He's placed more computer equipment inside, but I haven't noted any movement there."

"What's he doing?"

"I'm not certain, but he's aware I'm looking. Even if he recreated everything exactly as he'd had it before, there were no working interior cameras in the tower. He's placed them there intentionally."

"He wants us to see?"

"I assume so. The bigger questions are why, and what is he doing?"

"He wanted access to the mainframe before, to shut everything down. Why do it the same way when it didn't work?"

Jax is coming. I hear his hand on the doorknob.

"We need to get out and start looking," Drew said. "For his sake."

You could shut everything down, right? Without killing the program? Like, move it to another part of the hard drive? Then she'd just be across the room.

"Indeed," Will said, but I wasn't sure if he was speaking to me or to Drew, or both.

"What about Rhys and Hyrum?" Drew asked as Jax approached. "We can't leave them down here, alone, and we can't take them. But we definitely need to get out there."

Sean, who had been sitting quietly at the table, volunteered to stay in the lab. "I can keep an eye on the video feed and search from here. Just leave me a way to contact you."

"I knew you'd be useful, Mr. McAllister," Jax said.

Will paired his and Sean's phones to the system computer, leaving Sean's docked to a port in the office. He wouldn't be able to call, but if he hit the system alert button, it would activate Will's phone, and they would be able to communicate. "The microphone is here" —he tapped a tiny mesh dot near the alert button— "and speak normally. Try not to shout, even if everything is falling apart here. And use it for important matters only. If Rhys asks for something that you're unsure he should have, leave it up to Hyrum. He knows what Rhys is allowed and when."

"So, if he wants cookies for dinner and Hyrum says it's all right?" Sean joked.

Will gave him a tiny grin. "He won't. But he might ask for strawberries. They're tucked behind the milk jug in the fridge."

"Sandwiches okay?"

"That's fine." Will paused. "No peanut butter. There might be a jar in the pantry if you want it, but don't offer it to Hyrum. It's better if he doesn't even smell it."

"If Rhys wants it?"

"He won't. He knows the aroma will upset Hyrum." He started to turn. "If, by chance, Hyrum does tell Rhys they should have cookies or ice cream, or any other junk food they can find, don't stop them. They've had a horrible day, and it won't hurt them."

Yeah, that was more for you than him.

While Jax and Drew checked their ammo supplies, Will took Rhys and Hyrum into the second office to explain why they needed to leave. He showed Hyrum how to work the video monitor to find suitable entertainment and asked him to make sure Rhys was in bed by nine. "I might be back by then," he said as he pulled Rhys onto his lap. "But if I'm not, listen to Hyrum. He's in charge."

"Are you gonna bring Aunt Aubrey here?" Rhys asked.

"As soon as we find her," he promised.

Hyrum waited at the door while Will gave Rhys a hug and a kiss, and before Will could leave, he said, "Tell Aubrey I said sorry."

"For?"

"It's my fault. I was supposed to keep an eye on him."

Will took Hyrum by the arm and gently pulled him away from the office. "This is not your fault."

"But I went inside and left him playing alone, and I know better. I'm *really* sorry. I should have made him go in with me."

"I promise you," Will said, drawing him into a hug, "none of this is your fault. Aubrey was outside, too. What happened to Rhys was Asmonk's fault, and what happened to Aubrey is Tobias's."

"You couldn't have stopped either of them," Shivan said when Will let Hyrum go. "Asmonk was waiting for everyone to be distracted. If he hadn't gotten to him when he did, it would have happened later."

Even Scooter didn't see in time.

"Wick is right," Drew added. "He even waited until Scooter was looking the other way."

Hyrum wasn't convinced.

"Hy," Jax said, gently, "none of us blame you. Do you think if we did, we'd leave you in charge while we look for Aubrey? Will still trusts you with Rhys. He wouldn't leave if he didn't."

"Sean's here to watch us, isn't he?"

"No," Sean said. "I'm here to keep an eye on the video feed."

Hyrum finally nodded. He promised to make sure Rhys had dinner and a snack, and they would both be in bed at nine. He didn't have a book to read from, but he'd memorized most of Rhys's favorites, so they would be able to curl up and tell each other stories in the dark.

Still, Will gave Rhys a long, sad look before we left.

"He's fine," Drew said. "He knows he's safe in the lab with Hyrum."

"For now," Will said. "But the long-term effects? I should have insisted Aubrey take him home when I first asked. We knew who we were dealing with, and we knew the simulator places people in unfortunate circumstances."

If you want to pick it apart, we're only here because Jax wants to kill a man.

Why haven't we discussed the wrongness of that? I only thought he wanted to kick him in the nads, not hunt him.

"I know, Wick," Will said, reaching over to tap me on the head. He'd heard me. "We'll find her, one way or the other."

You'll shut everything down if you have to?

"Indeed. There are only so many places to hide."

You have a reason for letting Jax do this? Letting him hunt?

"Yes. Drew packed plenty of food for you."

Let me guess. Chicken.

That made Drew snort. "It's always chicken, Wick, unless you're Rhys or Hyrum, and then you get whatever your little heart desires."

"I noticed that," Jax said. "They get variety. We get...rations."

"Should have been with us last time," Drew said. "That made this seem like a beautifully laid out buffet. Seriously, nothing but eggs and chicken. And some bread."

There were vegetables once. In the Cliff House.

"Canned crap," Drew said. "And Aubrey's cooking has spoiled me. If it's not fresh, I'm not terribly interested."

"She hates anything fake or processed." Jax chuckled, and added, "My mother loved that about her. Aubrey took over the kitchen and insisted on cooking for everyone. Even when we lived downstairs. She'd get home from school, grab the kids from Will, and head upstairs to start dinner."

Will laughed with him. "She made Eli wash dishes. That's what your mother loved."

I forgot about that. He didn't believe her at first when she said he was going to pull his own weight or not eat.

"No one had ever spoken to him like that," Jax said.

Aubrey was terrified at first. In her world, the family patriarch ruled with an iron fist, and all the cooking and cleaning was women's work. Her father would have beaten her mother senseless if she'd suggested he pick up a dishrag and help. But Aubrey saw Donna's exhaustion and her irritation when Eli left the table, leaving behind not only his plate but a scattered mess of used napkins and crumbs on the table and on the floor.

"My grandfather was the same way," Jax said. "Without Levi's violent streak. I think in his head, being King was enough. When he was at home, he just wanted to be. Dad saw that, and even though he didn't really agree with it, he picked up the habit."

"And yet, you did not," Will pointed out.

He didn't because, even as Eli left detritus behind, he insisted that Jax clear the table and help with the dishes. Aubrey saw that and saw the irony in Eli's insistence that the work didn't belong solely to Donna while not considering that he needed to pitch in, too.

"She waited until a day when she knew Mom was completely wiped out. She'd had half a dozen appointments on Dad's behalf, spent part of the day touring the kid's ward at the med center, and she was just emotionally and physically spent. When dinner was nearly over, Aubrey told her to go rest...Dad would clear the table and help me with the dishes. Damn, his jaw dropped. I think he was trying to figure out a way to politely tell her to fuck off when she got up and informed him that everyone at the table had worked all day, Donna more than anyone, and if he was going to eat the food they'd prepared, he could get off his ass and help clean up."

"Oh my god, I wish I'd seen that," Drew said.

"It was priceless. She and Mom went out onto the balcony with a bottle of wine, and I had to teach my father how to wash dishes. But damned if after that he didn't make sure that at least on the days he knew Mom had a full schedule, he helped after dinner. It spurred him into learning to do his own laundry and cleaning up after himself, too. I think if he'd known how little time he had left with her, he would have made even more of an effort."

"She was content with what he did," Will said. "And she knew he adored her."

"I wish I'd seen that more than I did." Jax took a heavy breath. In public, and in front of their son, King Eli and Queen Donna stayed at arms' length. They held to old traditions of royalty avoiding public displays of affection; he could recall few times when he'd seen them touch outside of home—the day he climbed the bridge was one—and it was still rare in his presence.

I saw it.

They laughed together a lot. He could make her laugh so hard she'd throw up.

Jax stopped walking, which made everyone else pause with him. "What about affection, Wick? And I don't mean sex. Were they affectionate when no one else was looking?"

They were tender with each other. He was always sweet to her when you weren't around.

Jax's eyes rimmed red. "I wish I'd seen it more."

They had pet names. She called him 'Nicky-bit' and he called her 'my cherry.'

Drew scrunched his face. "Those are odd."

"Nicholas is his middle name," Jax explained. "He went by Nicky while his grandfather was still alive. When he was a boy, cherries were rare, so much more than Rhys's coveted strawberries. And they were his favorite thing. I think he told me he'd had them only a dozen times, ever, and I felt bad for him because they were so close to being extinct. He said it was all right, he'd found the last cherry he ever needed, sweeter than anything he'd ever known, and nothing would ever top that."

Jax let out a slip of a laugh. "I honestly thought he was talking about fruit. Do you know how fucking hard I pressed for new growth in the Pacific corridor? I spent billions of tax dollars to bring back the cherry for him."

"Does he know he's why you did that?" Drew asked.

"I never specifically told him, but why else would I pour so many resources into a single fruit?"

"It led to agricultural renewal in other areas," Will reminded him. "Strawberries, for instance. There are hundreds, if not thousands, of food items that were very nearly gone and now thrive because of that."

"But I had no idea that would happen. I just wanted my dad to have his favorite thing, even if it was only one more time. He was probably laughing his ass off at me. Goddamn, he meant my mother."

You know that other thing?

Yeah, they weren't just affectionate.

"I don't need to hear that, Wick," he said, ignoring Drew's laughter.

You're not the first person to think up handcuffs and chocolate pudding.

It wasn't remotely true, but everyone was laughing, and for a moment they weren't overwhelmed with horrible visions of what Aubrey was going through. Will nudged him in the direction of Coit Tower, and for a minute or two, at least, they were amused.

= = =

"Oz blew this shit up," Drew said, sounding both puzzled and amazed that it looked the same as it had when we'd explored it five years earlier. We entered to a room lined with computers stuffed into refrigerators and a wall lined with monitors. The tower-high metal support beam was again filled with neat clusters of wires in varying colors, and at the top of the stairs was the same electrical globe that generated the power that brought pounding rain every night.

The only difference Will noted was that the cables to the globe had been severed, melted to uselessness on the cut ends. The tower was too newly rebuilt for any of the elves to have come in and cut them; even if they had entered the tower, he mused, it wasn't likely that any of them would have known what the cables led to, nor that those specifically should be disabled.

"You think Tobias cut his own cables?" Drew asked.

"If he had no use for them and wanted no one else to gain control, yes. He wouldn't risk someone using his equipment against him."

Jax was opening the refrigerator doors, checking inside, but he turned his head to see Shivan. "You know what all of this is for. Would any of the elves?"

"They would understand the concept of the computers, but not how they work. I believe that knowledge has been withheld from us."

"Hagar and Tobias have access to a significant part of the database that the elves do not," Will said.

"Why them and not us?" Shivan asked.

"The code that contains their magic needed to be separate from the elves' daily lives."

"Your father gave that sort of power to a man like Tobias," Shivan said, not at all happy about it.

"It was merely part of a story he created for use in a simulator, Shivan. He never expected that as the program waited for participants that its characters would achieve this level of awareness. It was a game intended to serve as a holding pen for those who might seek to end their lives by portal-jumping too far into the future, or to stop those who had jumped forward unintentionally."

Before Shivan could express righteous indignation at being referred to as a character in a game, Drew jumped in. "The fact that you got this far says a lot about the consideration to detail Finn put into this. He wanted you to be whole characters, not two-dimensional tropes. He could have made all of you filler, but he didn't."

"Which was my mistake in the world I created for Tobias and his family," Will said. "I populated it with filler. It's not surprising he was eager to come back here, even knowing what waited for him."

Jax slammed the refrigerator door closed. "Now do you understand the law against AI?" he asked Drew. "Imagine letting Tobias loose in Pacifica."

Drew understood the law and worked carefully to avoid breaking it. But for now, he nodded and let Jax make his point.

"Hell, for that matter," Jax went on, "running around Elysium."

"Less of an issue," Will said. "On Elysium, he could be shoved out an airlock."

Drew grimaced, but Jax laughed.

We better find her before he completely loses it.

As we left, Will used his laser pistol to fuse the door shut. It wouldn't keep Tobias out, but it sent a strong signal to him: we know where you like to hide, and we're coming. From there Shivan suggested we skirt along the city and get to Dogpatch, where we'd been headed when Scooter came for us.

"If no outliers are living in the tents, he might be there. It's comfortable enough, and the elves never go there."

"If it's comfortable, why not?" Drew asked.

"Too far. They prefer to stay close to the village now. There's a perception of safety in the woods, and they're within a few minutes' walk to the orchards and fields."

"Downtown?" Jax asked. "Do they make use of it?"

"Not really. The elder elves fear how suddenly the buildings appeared and Hagar no longer lives near, so there's no real reason to venture to this side of Saint Francis. The younger elves explore, looking for trouble."

"As a young person would," Will said.

"Yeah, they're looking for quiet spots to hook up," Drew snorted. "I'm guessing no one has told them about tent city?"

"No," Shivan chuckled. "I knew, though."

"And every girl you took there told someone else," Jax said. "So your generation at least had the energy to walk that far."

"There was only Lani," Shivan said. "I would be surprised if she told anyone. The tents have been our private place to get away, even now. We send the kids to her mother, go build a fire, and spend a day or two in a tent soaking up how joyfully quiet it is."

"How private will it feel later if that's where Tobias is hiding?" Drew asked.

"As long as he's not there, I won't mind."

"He won't be there long," Jax said.

Drew and Shivan fell behind Will and Jax, letting intentional space grow between them. "Do you often hunt with the King?" Shivan asked him.

"Never. He's not a hunter. He won't even go fishing."

He barfs if you kill something in front of him.

"Will told Zed and me about having to hunt with Jax once, when he was eighteen or so. King Eli had dumped them in the middle of nowhere with the idea they had to get by on their own. Will caught a rabbit and Jax threw up when Will had to gut it. He just doesn't have the stomach for it."

"Odd," Shivan said. "Do you do anything with him? I avoid my mother-in-law, but I enjoy spending time with Lani's father."

"He's crazy busy. Hell, so I am. But a couple times a month he and I and Will go out for drinks. Sometimes Zed and Jay join us.

"Zed and Jay. I recognize the chosen name of Prince Zealand, but I don't know Jay."

"Jay is Aisha's oldest son. His given name is James, chosen name is Jay."

"And Rhys is the Emperor's oldest?"

"Oldest biological kid. He considers Jay his son, too. Jay's got four parents laying claim to him, and oddly, they all get along pretty well."

Except when George tried to kill Will, sure.

"All right, they get along *now*. It was sticky at first."

"Perhaps bring them to visit sometime when we're not hunting Tobias," Shivan said. "Only don't wait twenty years. I don't want to be as old as the Emperor and King."

"I never intended to wait as long as we did. And I keep thinking I want to bring my son here after he's born, but with the difference in how time moves, you'll be years older anyway."

Ask Will to change the time parameter. Slow things down here.

"If it's possible," Drew said. "It seems to run normally while we're here."

How many days have we been here?

"Four or five. I'm not really sure."

In our clock time, it's been less than a day. Look at your phone.

He dug it from his front pocket and flicked the screen on. "Holy hell. According to this, it's the day we left, twenty-two hours later."

I feel it. You feel the pull of the environment.

"Will," Drew called out, "check the time and date on your phone." He scrambled to catch up and held his phone out for Will to see. "What the hell? Wick said we've only been here for a day, and according to this, he's right."

Will checked his own phone, raising an eyebrow. "That would explain why Finn hasn't answered my message. He just sent Aubrey here, as far as he's concerned. He might not check back with the lab for hours still."

"Was it like this before? Were we here for less than a week?"

"One might assume. It also explains how the population here gained awareness so quickly after Finn wrote the code for it."

"Can you slow it down?" Drew asked. "Match their clock to ours?"

"I can certainly ask my father to consider it. Shivan? Is that something you would want?"

He nodded. "I'm not thrilled with the idea that I'm aging rapidly, now that I know. It would be nice if I weren't old if it takes another five years before you visit again."

"You would be fifty-five," Jax said.

"I know. Old."

"You never told me he was mean," Jax said, gesturing for everyone to get walking again. "I turn fifty this year."

"So, five years past being old."

"My wife will be fifty-five."

"Beautiful women never grow old, Your Majesty."

"Smart boy," Jax snorted. "Speed up. That beautiful woman is waiting."

The tent city felt like an abandoned town. Door flaps clicked under a gentle breeze, and burnt logs in the fire pit were cold. Fog threaded between the long tents and hovered inches from the ground, prompting Jax to mutter about Finn's sense of physics and weather, and why the hell was it so cold?

They split up, each taking a quarter of the circle the camp was built around, pushing the tent flaps aside using the nose of their guns. Will was the most careful, pausing to listen at each one, while Jax stomped from tent to tent, shoving the flaps aside with a hard pop.

Doesn't he ever watch war or spy movies? He'd be dead in the first twenty minutes with all the noise he's making.

"I think he grew up on video games," Drew said. "The ones where you start from the place you left off every time your player gets killed."

Will warned him he would be killed here, right?

"He doesn't believe they're here, that's all."

Where do you think they are?

"I thought they'd be in the tower."

The last time he moved people he held them in the royal house. Where the pool is supposed to be.

"Mention that to Will. If I do, Jax will overhear and we'll find ourselves running there."

We met the others near the cold fire pit. Jax wanted to move on, but Will pointed to the tent once used as a dining hall and said he needed to take a break. There were chairs there, and a table. He didn't care if no one else was hungry, but he wanted food and was sure I did, too.

I would not refuse something.

"I could eat," Drew said.

Jax admitted that it wouldn't kill him to take a few minutes to eat and recoup. He was disappointed that Tobias hadn't been at the tower nor was he here, but as desperately as he wanted to find Aubrey, it wouldn't do her any good if he ran out of energy.

I jumped onto the table while Will dug into his backpack for sandwiches and did as Drew said, reminding him about the little jail cells Tobias had once created in the royal home.

"I know, Wick," he said. "You have a choice. Canned chicken cat food, or reasonably fresh baked chicken."

I don't want to take food from a person.

"There's plenty. If you prefer the fresh, you're not taking food from any of us."

"And I packed my own," Shivan said.

Drew leaned over to get a look at the paste-like stew Shivan had in a shiny metal container. "That's kinda gross. Is it food-food, or simulated food?"

"You would not want to eat this," he answered. "To me, it tastes like beef stew with potatoes. But I realize that we have no cattle, and to you it might taste like a medieval history lecture."

"But you can eat real food?" Jax asked. "Will said you could, but—"

"I can."

"Where does it go?" Drew wondered out loud. "I have this mental image of your legs filling with chewed up chicken and eggs. Sooner or later, there won't be any room."

"I unscrew my legs every week and dump it out," Shivan said dryly. "My internal anatomy functions similar to yours. The difference is that when I consume food, no nutrients are extracted from it. It's simply broken down and eventually eliminated."

"Yeah, but how?"

"He shits, Andrew," Jax said.

"I shit," Shivan concurred.

Aubrey would be jabbing her pointy finger at you two right now. No shit talk at the dinner table.

"I learned that right off the bat," Jax said. "The day we met, she warned me, she had little tolerance for rough language. I tried to take it to heart, but Will?"

"She chastised me on a regular basis," Will said.

"I know Will introduced you," Drew said. "And I've seen the picture he took when he realized that you and Aubrey had pretty much forgotten he was there. But damn, how the hell do you get from 'Hi, I'm Jax' to realizing you just met the woman who will be your actual queen?"

"Your jaw drops," Will said, "and you stammer, 'Hello. I think I love you. Marry me and have my babies.'"

"I did not," Jax said. "But by the end of the day? I knew I would fall hard and fast, and I needed to change everything about myself if I wanted to keep her."

29

Will met Aubrey, accidentally on purpose, at the coffee shop where she worked the early morning shift. He was the only customer at the counter at four in the morning when she clocked in, and he sat there quietly, a cup of coffee resting on the bar between his hands as he watched her pass back and forth. She felt him watching as she went about prepping for the breakfast crowd, and after twenty minutes of his unwanted supervision, she set a bag filled with sugar packets in front of him and told him if he was that interested, he could restock the holders along the counter.

She was caught by surprise when he took the bag and said he'd be glad to. She was even more surprised when he told her that despite appearances, he had not been watching because he intended to hit on her. Equal parts relieved and offended, she asked what his intent was, then, and he came straight out with it: he knew, without a doubt, that she was a perfect match for the crown prince and wanted her permission to introduce them.

"She was speechless," Will said. "But only for a moment."

There was no doubt about his sincerity and no question about whether he knew Prince Jackson or not. They were seen together frequently, and the Emperor—his name was not known; it would be nearly twenty-five years before anyone would call him by his given name—was just beginning to merit mention in the news. It was no secret that King Eli had taken him under his wing, so to speak, found him a place to live, and given him employment. That he was emerging as the prince's best friend was new gossip fodder.

Will sat in the coffee shop until nine, when she clocked out to head for her first class of the day, one in which there was no chance of running into the barely eighteen-year-old prince. He had just begun his second semester at the university, and she was engaged in post-graduate studies; he majored in history, she majored in education, and their academic paths were still a summer term apart from crossing.

"I still remember the first words she said to me," Jax said, sitting at the table in the tent, clutching a thermos the same way Will had held his coffee mug all those years ago. "We went into the coffee shop where she was waiting, Will made the introduction, and after I stupidly gave her this weird half-bow and kissed her hand, she sighed and said, 'So what now, I curtsey for you?'"

"Technically, yes," the young Emperor said to her, "but truthfully, no."

"I can't imagine you ever being any step below me that would require you to curtsy," Jax breathed.

She cocked her head, just a tiny bit. She wasn't buying any royal smooth talk. Not yet.

He asked her all the right questions about her studies and work, the things she was interested in, and when she claimed she would rather not discuss her family—ever—he didn't press. They quickly found common ground in their love of education. Jax knew when he was a young teenager that he wanted to teach history, and he was passionate about it. Aubrey already had a degree in early childhood education and was less than two years away from earning her master's degree in secondary education. She harbored notions of continuing to a doctoral degree and studying child psychology along the way but admitted that was a long shot.

"I have abused the goodwill of Pacifica's educational scholarships long enough," she told him. "Perhaps after I've paid taxes long enough to not feel guilty about it."

When they'd only known each other for half an hour, they were discussing the future and the similarities in the things they wanted. The Emperor realized that he hadn't been spoken to after telling her she didn't need to offer any sort of genuflection to the prince, and he slipped out of his chair and across the room, where he snapped a photo of them, their heads close together and the rest of the world someplace else.

"I was never sure where Will went to," Jax said. "But we sat in the coffee shop until it started getting dark, and I asked her if she'd allow me to take her to dinner. When she said she would, I damn near shouted 'yes' and knocked my chair over when I stood."

Aubrey was afraid he'd meant somewhere worthy of his royal title and that she'd be out of place and underdressed, even though he was in jeans. Instead, he took her to the diner near Union Square, the place Will sometimes took me because the servers catered to my whims and allowed me to sit at the table, as long as I was in a towel-covered high chair. It was bright and very public, with giant windows for the world to see inside, and there was no chance that he would attempt anything improper.

"I was afraid my reputation had preceded me," he admitted. "I didn't want anything scaring her off."

After dinner, when they'd sat long enough that their server stopped checking on them or offering refills and dessert, they stepped outside, and he told her he would like to walk her home but understood if that was too much for the first day they'd met. He could call a cab for her, if she preferred, but she reached for his hand and tugged him along.

He did not get an invitation inside and was not surprised by the lack of one.

"I didn't even try to kiss her. Which, for me, was unbelievable. But I stood outside her door and asked if she would have lunch with me the next day. After she agreed, I knew I needed to leave, but something was tugging at me."

He was still holding her hand. He took a half step back, glanced down at their hands, and when he looked up, into her eyes, he said, "I already know I'm going to fall hopelessly in love with you."

She let go of his hand and set hers on his cheek. "Then don't mess it up, Prince Jackson."

He had never been more determined to get something right. He kissed her at the end of the second day they'd known each other, but only after telling her he wanted to, if she didn't mind. He kept his hands to himself, asked her out to dinner nearly every night for a week, and at the end of the week, she invited him inside for a drink at the end of the evening.

There was no room left for doubt: it was only a drink, and no alcohol would be served. "We sat across from each other at her kitchen table, and she told me then that she would not be an easy person to date. She had issues, and intimacy was going to be a significant problem. If any other woman had said that to me, I would have gotten up and left. But this woman? I would have waited forever for her."

"When did she tell you the reasons?" Drew asked, immediately followed by, "Hell. Tell me to fuck off. That's none of my business."

Jax didn't tell him to fuck off.

"It was early on, maybe two months, probably less. That might have been the hardest damned conversation she'd ever had. She begged for my secrecy, told me who her father was, and then over the next couple of hours explained why she'd run away."

Jax was the first man she'd been comfortable enough with to tell the entire truth. He was not the first she had dated since landing in San Francisco, not the first kiss, and not the first crush. But he was the first to stay seated when she said anything physical was going to take time and work, might not happen, ever, and he was the only one to stay long enough to hear why. "I straight up told her that if I pushed the boundaries too hard, she had license to haul off and hit me. And I would inform my guards that if she did, I deserved it, and they were not to react."

"How long before you caved and told her you loved her?"

"That night, actually. I told her I had no problem waiting as long as she needed because I loved her."

"Mr. Romance," Shivan snickered.

"Yeah, it didn't go over as well as I'd hoped. She didn't want to hear it then, not in response to what she'd just told me. So I promised I'd say it again, later. I called her the minute I stepped out of the building, just to tell her I loved her. And then again halfway home. And when I got to Union Square."

The last time he called her that night, just before getting into bed, she answered her phone with, "I love you, too, Jackson. Now stop. It's late, and I have to be at work in the middle of the night."

"What'd you do then?"

"Masturbated furiously," Will chimed in.

"Asshole."

"I'm not wrong, am I?"

Drew saved him from answering. "How the hell did you not go after Levi Munson then?"

"I wanted to. I wanted to tell my parents who her father was, though they knew and just hadn't said anything to me. I promised her that if they knew what he'd done, every bit of justice Levi had coming would rain down on him like apocalyptic fire. She asked me not to, and when I was reluctant, she begged me. She had siblings and her mother to think about, and like it or not, they were better protected from the church with him around. And back then, it was probably true. If Levi had been unseated from the head of the church before Red was old enough to take over, everyone's lives would have been far worse."

Drew's scowl prompted Will to say, "She considered more than just her own family, Andrew. She considered what the leadership would have done to every person in Florida."

"The Second Minister at the time was Lloyd Young," Jax said. "Older than dirt and if he'd had his way, women would have been less than property. They would have been hidden away and used only for breeding. He advocated for the so-called release of women too old or unable to bear children."

"Release?"

"Euthanasia," Will said. "Young believed that females were a waste of resources, and only required what was needed to get them through puberty, then bred until they could no longer reproduce. After that, they were disposable."

"I think most of Florida celebrated quietly when he died. Hell, even Levi likely did. There was no state funeral for Young, which spoke volumes."

"Young." The name pricked at Drew's brain. "Any relation to Simon?"

"His grandfather."

Simon Young was the boy who ran from Florida with Aubrey. He was seventeen and had been promised as her groom when he turned eighteen. She was only fourteen. They'd spent just enough time together for her to understand that if she married him, there would be no family, no children, and only the amount of affection a brother might have for his sister. He would protect her, no doubt, and he might even love her, but the marriage would have been chaste and confining.

When his father beat him for admitting that their match was a poor one, they ran.

"Hey, did she ever convince you to meet him? I know Jay's father was willing to help her touch base with him."

"We've had coffee a couple of times. Met at Fuzzy's once for drinks. I don't think we'll ever be fast friends, but he's nice enough that I tolerate it for Aubrey's sake."

He and Aisha like each other. They like to talk about James.

"They like to dish about James," Will said. "His habits affected both of them at various times and—"

He stopped when his phone rang. There was only one person it could be, and he paled a bit as he answered.

"You're on speaker," he said when it was on.

"Emperor. I'm looking at Union Square. Tobias is out there with Mrs. Blackshear. They're just...sitting there. Talking."

Everyone got up and headed for the exit. Drew scooped me up and shoved me into his sweatshirt, and they left what remained of their dinner on the table.

"Don't open the door," Will cautioned Sean. "Not for any reason, understand?"

"Even if Mrs. Blackshear wants in?"

"Not for any reason." Will started running, counting on us to keep up. "Tobias cannot have access to anything within the lab. I don't care if she's banging on the door, you do not open it."

Jax wanted to argue the point, I think, but he was too busy trying to run faster than he'd ever run in his life.

30

It was dark when we arrived at Union Square. Aubrey sat on a wooden stool ten feet from the little hut that hid the lab's entry, and Tobias was on a duplicate stool more than ten feet from her. He was just close enough that she could clearly hear him, but far enough that she had a running start if he did something stupid. Jax and Will had raced up the stairs ahead of us and bolted toward Aubrey, but halfway there Jax suddenly slowed.

She was laughing with him.

There was enough moonlight to see her broad and bright smile, and the sound of her laughter sliced through Jax. He drew his gun and held it in front of his face, staring down the scope as he ordered Tobias to get up and step away from her. Will remained a half step behind and to his side, where he had a clear view of Aubrey, but he didn't pull his gun.

"Jax, stop," Aubrey said, getting up.

Tobias did as he was told. He stood and took several steps to the side, holding his hands up in surrender. "I didn't harm her." He spoke as if it were a matter of fact, and without fear. "On the lives of my children, I never touched her."

"You took her."

"I did."

"Jax, stop," Aubrey repeated. "He saved my life."

Jax twitched and glanced away from Tobias. "What?"

"I was running into something I wouldn't have gotten myself out of, sweetheart."

Tobias was in the woods, hoping to run into his children or his wife. Instead, he heard the screams of a terrified little boy and then saw a bright streaking light. His first worry was that the sprites were attacking a child and he ran toward them. As he neared, he realized they had formed a mass to protect him, but Aubrey was running straight into a pack of frenzied, hungry dogs, and there was no time to reach her.

"I cast a protective shield around her, and we moved. I hadn't considered where, and we reappeared at the ocean's edge, at the far end of the beach."

"And yet you didn't then move her back to the village," Will said.

"I couldn't. I was spent. I needed time to recover, but even after waiting an hour, I didn't have enough energy to move anyone."

Aubrey went to Jax, setting her arm on his, pushing the gun down. "We walked, Jackson. He helped me find the village, and one of the elves told me you'd moved here. I was willing to come here on my own, but he refused to let me walk all that way with daylight fading."

"Which elf?" Jax asked.

"I don't know all their names," she said. "Does it matter? He was small, and his voice is raspy. And he hoped you would return to the village soon."

"Jesf," Tobias said. "Which one of you returned his voice? I assume it was the Emperor, but the prince seemed equally obvious."

"The Emperor repaired the damage you inflicted upon him," Shivan said. "All those years. He was mute before I was even born, and only now can speak."

"I had his tongue cut out," Tobias said when it looked as if Aubrey was confused. "The educated are the enemy of the dictator. Teachers breed knowledge, and I knew if he could speak, he would continue sparking hope among the elves. Knowledge is power, and I refused to give any of mine away. It's not a choice I would make now."

"What would your choice be now," Shivan challenged. "Leave his tongue but kill the man? Oppress the elves even further? Would you lengthen their days in the fields and rob them of night and rest? How much worse would it be?"

"I would leave them alone, Shivan Adomondai. Hindsight is a horrific thing, you know. All the tricks I used to keep them in check, to torment and torture? I could have used those to bring back my wife and children, and everyone else lost that day. I could have saved them, and yet all my grief showed me was revenge."

"You understand the code," Will mused. "You couldn't have accessed the mainframe to alter it, though."

Had he chosen another path, had he invited the elves to share his grief instead of punishing them for it, every effort expended to hurt them could have been spent on garnering goodwill and their help in getting to the main computer. "A wasted allocation of resources. You did in an hour what I didn't conceive until I had my family in front of me again."

He took several more steps back, extending his arms. "Get it over with it."

Jax shoved the gun back into its holster. "Nah. I'm not feeling it right now. You earned one reprieve, Tobias. On my wife's grace, take the chance to run while you can."

His hand went to his medallion. There was a spark, and he swore under his breath, but with a second try, he vanished.

"You sure you're all right?" Jax asked Aubrey.

"I'm fine. My feet are sore from walking so far, and one of you is cooking dinner for me because I'm famished, but I'm fine."

"Good." He pulled her into a tight hug, burying his face against her neck. "You're not allowed to leave me first. I couldn't bear it."

When they pulled apart, Will leaned over and kissed her cheek, lingering a fraction longer than usual. No one else noticed, but I did and I understood why.

He was making sure she was real, and not an invention of Tobias's cruelty.

When she was through the door, Jax on her heels, I asked.

Did you hear thoughts or clicking?

Wait. You let her go inside. She's real.

"Indeed, Wick." He stopped Drew before he could go in. "Don't repeat that to Jax. Don't give him a reason to second guess."

= = =

The moment he heard her voice, Hyrum exploded off the inflatable mattress that he and Rhys were sitting on and bolted from the office. She had just enough time to brace herself before he threw himself at her, grabbing her into a massive hug. Jax was right behind her, ready to catch her if Hyrum had jumped; he often ran at Jax and Will, leaping into their arms. Hyrum squealed her name on repeat as he ran across the room, and when he was finally touching her, bouncing, his voice cracked. "I'm sorry. I shoulda made Rhys go inside with me."

"Sweetie." She extricated herself from his surprisingly strong, gangly-armed hug. "You didn't do this. Rhys is a very fast little boy when he wants to be. I saw him leave with Asmonk. I just couldn't catch up."

Rhys lingered in the doorway. He was ready for bed, dressed in an old t-shirt Hyrum found in the storage closet, one that swallowed his tiny frame whole and made him look no older than Charlie. He glanced at Will, but it was Aubrey who captured his attention; his thumb went to his mouth and his breath hitched, but he remained silent.

She squatted and motioned for him to come to her. "Baby boy, I am so sorry I couldn't get to you before Asmonk pushed you down. Are you all right?"

He nodded but still didn't move.

Will twitched in Rhys's direction, but Aubrey glanced at him, a clear message: *Don't. I need him to come to me.*

"Do you forgive me, sweetie?" she asked Rhys. "You must have been so scared."

The thumb came out of his mouth. "The puppies wanted to eat me."

She sat all the way down, and he finally ran to her, flinging his arms around her neck. "That must have been awful for you," she said against his cheek as she kissed him. "How did you get away?"

"The lightning bugs picked me up and helped me climb a tree. Then Hyrum did the thing and made the puppies run away."

She tilted her head to look up at her little brother. "Thank you, Hy."

"Did the bad man steal you?" Rhys asked. He let go of her neck and settled on her lap while she stroked his arms gently.

"No, sweetie. He thought the puppies were going to turn on me, so he helped me jump away. He would have made you jump, too, but he saw the lightning bugs and knew they were going to help you."

She's taking away the fear, isn't she? I asked Drew.

He nodded.

"The lightning bugs singed to me," Rhys said. "They made up a song just for me."

"Do you remember?"

He nodded and then sang, "Climb the tree and don't be sad. Daddy's coming, he's not mad. Don't be scared, hear our song. Don't be scared, just hold on."

"That's beautiful," Aubrey whispered to him. "I know you were scared anyway, sweetheart. Are you okay now?"

"Uh huh. Hyrum gave me some strawberries and chocolate milk and said that makes everything better."

"Hyrum always tells the truth, you know."

"He was scared, too," Rhys whispered. "I'm sorry. I won't be bad anymore."

That made Will interrupt. "You've never been bad, Rhys. Never. You're a very good boy, always."

"Listen to your daddy," Aubrey whispered. "He doesn't lie, either."

After another hug and kiss from Aubrey, Will took Rhys back into the office to get him settled while Drew began scrambling eggs for Aubrey. Hyrum leaned against the counter, not sure what he should do, until she went to him and reached for his hand.

"Are you sure you're all right? You must have been terrified, too."

"I'm okay."

She pulled him into another hug anyway, until he grunted, "I know what you're doing, Aubrey."

"Then hush and let me do it."

"It's gonna take you all night to make everyone feel better," he said against her shoulder.

"I think there's only one more person who needs to." Her eyes flicked toward Jax, who was waiting patiently. "I promise, I'll take my time with him."

Hyrum laughed and pulled back. "I know what that means."

"Hush." She swatted at his backside, playfully. "That's not what I meant."

"We're in the lab," Drew said as he scraped the eggs onto a plate. "The walls will not come down. Just in case. Please be quiet."

"I'll sleep in the other room with Drew and Sean," Hyrum said.

"My wingmen," Jax chuckled as he sat down to keep Aubrey company while she ate.

She jabbed a fork in his direction. "I'm exhausted, Jackson."

"I'll do all the heavy lifting. No problem."

"I. Will. Stab. You."

He sat with her while she ate and didn't complain when she offered to let me lick her plate when she was done. He washed the dishes while she showered and then told Drew and Hyrum to go to bed. It didn't matter if they were tired or not; he was making tea for her and wanted the kitchen clear if she wanted to sit up and talk, and it was a discussion to which they were not invited.

She's tired, dude. Let her go to bed.

"Cat, I know you're insulting me."

No, not really.

"You could sneak in and jam a cold nose up Will's backside if you're bored."

I might do that to Drew, later. I don't want to risk Will yelping and scaring Rhys.

He sat at the table to wait for Aubrey and didn't even yell at me when I jumped up to sit with him. "I'm sorry we're dragging you all over the place, Wick. I imagine you'd rather just go play with Fluffy and Jeff."

I just wanted to see them to be sure they're okay. And they're okay.

"You take good care of us, you know that?" He reached over and rubbed the top of my head, right between my ears. "I hope you're still here long after I'm gone, taking care of Will. My gut says he's going to outlive us all."

Except maybe Finn. Finn's going to live a freakishly long time.

"I know the other me that he visits is in his eighties. Sometimes I grab onto that and think, fine, I have a lot of time to get it right. But then he reminds me that things have changed, and our lives have taken a turn from that timeline. But you'll hang around for him, won't you?"

Sure, but I hope not much after that. If I do, I might forget him again. I'm tired of forgetting.

"You won't forget, Wick." Will crept out of the office, carefully closing the door all but an inch. "Your memory was impaired by the programming of your transponder. That's why everything flooded back when Dad flipped the switch."

I still have gaps.

"I know. But they'll come to you." He poured himself some coffee—decaf, he asked Jax to be sure—and sat down. "What's the plan, Jax? Do we set out again first thing and see if we can find Tobias's trail?"

"Maybe. Or maybe we'll just look while we walk to the beach. Rhys and Hyrum might enjoy playing in the sand. Actively hunting Tobias can wait until Finn answers your message and comes to get Rhys."

Sure, run across Tobias and wind up shooting him in front of a little boy.

"Wick," Will sighed. "No. The beach is not a giant litter box."

It could be.

I'm certainly going to turn a few spots into one.

You know if Jax knew how you change what I say, he'd be ticked.

"Next time," Will said, "I ask Dad to provide beer."

"What's the little shit complaining about?" Jax asked. He might have even cared, too, but Aubrey came out of the bathroom in the old gray sweatpants and sweatshirt Will kept in the lab, holding her hands against her lower back, and he forgot I was there.

"I swear, my back hasn't hurt this much since I was pregnant."

"See?" Will said. "We need beer."

"Honestly, William, right now I'd take something stronger. How do you and Drew manage to run to the beach and back and still have a full day?"

"Booze," he snorted.

Maybe she really is pregnant.

"She's not pregnant," Will said.

"I'd better not be." She jabbed her pointy finger toward Jax. "If Mass messed up—"

"I went to all the follow-up appointments, angel. Nothing to worry about. Besides, you're not half as cranky as you were with Oz."

"Give me ten minutes. Or alcohol."

Will promised a few days in his birth When with a stream of head-sized margaritas and a case of Finn's home brewed beer.

Maybe it's a phantom pregnancy.

"Wick, stop," Will said.

You don't know. I moved to the other side of the table and sat in front of her. *How's your uterus? Quivering? Expanding?*

She made him tell her what I said, word for word. Instead of expressing the same irritation he had, Aubrey picked me up and dropped kisses on my head. "You remembered. I felt so silly, but you crawled on me and started purring harder than I thought possible."

"Remembered what?" Jax asked.

"When I realized I was pregnant with Oz." She gave me one more hug before setting me back on the table. "It hit me so hard, and you weren't home. Wick was the only one there, and he's the first one I told that I suspected—he followed me around the house talking to me until I caved and took the test, and then he cuddled with me."

She said it felt like her lady bits were quivering.

Inside ones, I mean.

"Wick, do you remember what you were telling me as you chased me around the house?"

Pee on the stick. Pee on the stick. Pee on the stick.

I wanted to know.

"There was more than that," she said. "If only I'd known you were honestly speaking to me."

I wanted to know if you were going to have a litter. I was disappointed when you only had one.

"You were not," Will said, chuckling. "Why do you like babies so much? They're loud, usually sticky, and when they learn to crawl, they start chasing you."

Why do you like babies? They don't chase you, but they pee and throw up on you.

"Babies need us," Will said. "They're hope for the future, as well."

But you like other peoples' babies, even the ones that don't need you.

"Indeed. I simply enjoy them."

Well, there you go. Babies are fun. Then they turn into kids, and kids like to play with me.

"This isn't a mocking question," Aubrey ventured, "but I am curious. Do you and Wick spend a lot of time in deep discussion?"

"He's a good sounding board," Will said. "All those years I went day after day without sleep, he often kept me company and tolerated my incoherent babbling."

"You're such a good boy, Wick," Aubrey said.

I am, aren't I?

"Wait a minute." Will reached over and poked me. "You get upset when I tell you you're a good boy."

Because you say it like I'm a dog. She says it because she loves me.

Jax got up and ruffled the fur on my head. "Good boy, Wick. Good boy."

I hate you.

He held his hand out to Aubrey. "Come on. I'll rub your back and keep my horny intentions to myself."

"Just so you're aware," Will said as they headed for the office, "sound does not carry as much as I've led Drew to believe. My father designed the offices intending people would sleep here. Including himself with my mother."

Okay, Aubrey might hate you right now.

"I will survive."

He picked me up and carried me into the office he was sharing with Rhys, and I waited on the floor while he carefully settled onto the air mattress. Rhys rolled toward him and curled up against his side, and when I was sure I wouldn't wake Rhys, I climbed on and settled on Will's chest.

He didn't have to ask; I knew he wanted me close, where I could reach a paw out and touch Rhys's head to listen to his dreams. If they were filled with fear, no matter what Jax wanted, we were going home.

31

He dreamed about riding his tricycle while chasing Fluffy around Union Square and later dreamed about playing with his brothers and sister. Jay provided large sheets of paper and finger paint, and before they were done, they had painted the floor and the walls, and eventually, each other.

His dreams were happy. There were sprites in one dream, but they flitted around his head like a crown and made him giggle.

"You didn't sense any fear?" Will asked, quietly, while Rhys ate breakfast across the lab.

No. Even when he dreamed about painting the entire apartment, he wasn't worried about getting in trouble. In his dream, Aisha came in and said, 'You're so pretty!' and you wanted to paint, too.

"Thank you. You were awake all night, weren't you?"

I can sleep in Drew's sweatshirt. Or on the beach, if we really go.

"We'll see what Jax's mood is before mentioning it to Rhys and Hyrum."

Are you really going to let him hunt and kill Tobias?

"I am."

You better have a good reason.

"I do. I promise, Wick, this isn't because I enjoy the concept."

It's not really about revenge, either, is it?

"No. And I'd like to leave it at that for now, all right? I'm not keeping it to myself because I worry that you'll say anything. The reasons are complex and personal to Jax."

I left it alone. Aubrey called me over for food; everyone was at the table, the level of conversation a nice, almost-too-loud rumble that felt like home. No one rushed through breakfast, and when they were done Sean and Drew did the dishes while Will checked the security cameras.

Sean volunteered to stay and man them again.

"Mr. McAllister," Jax said as he put his shoes on, "today we leave no one behind. We're all going out, and we're going to the beach. I feel like building sand castles with Hyrum and my nephew."

Will called out from the office, "Hold that thought. You need to see this."

I ran in and jumped on the desk, which had been shoved against the wall to make room for the mattress. Union Square was covered in a thick blanket of white, and more was falling.

"Is that snow?" Jax asked, peering closer. "What the hell?"

"It can rain here, so why not snow?" Will mused.

Rhys pushed his way past Drew and Sean so that he could see. His eyes went wide, and he gasped, "Daddy, can we go outside? I never played in snow before."

"Does he have enough clothing?" Aubrey asked. "Do any of us?"

There were sweatshirts and Will dug through the storage closet to find things to layer for Rhys. There was abuse of a roll of duct tape to make them fit, but it was enough to allow him some time outside. The stairwell leading up was frosty, and when we made it outside, Drew plucked me off his shoulder and shoved me into the pouch of his sweatshirt, declaring it too-fricking-freezing for someone as tiny as me.

Rhys turned his face up toward the sky, squinting at the giant, fluffy flakes drifting around him and grinned. There were at least three inches on the ground, enough for snow angels and snowballs, and for the next half hour he and Hyrum pelted Will and Jax with as many as they could.

Just as Aubrey decided it was time to go back inside, before Rhys had frostbite, Shivan came onto the Square carrying a large bag, breath fogging around his face.

"Warm clothing," he said. "I have things that will fit Rhys and Hyrum, and perhaps Her Majesty, as well. Lani would like it if you all came for lunch, and the children are excited about playing with Rhys and Hyrum in the snow."

"Has it ever snowed here?" Drew asked him.

"Not in my lifetime. It took me a few minutes this morning to remember what it was even called." He followed as Aubrey started nudging people toward the door. "School was called off for today. It seemed mean to make the children spend the day inside when we don't know how long it will last."

"Do you got lots of snow?" Hyrum asked.

"Heaps. Enough to play in and maybe even build a few snowmen."

"Snowmen!" Rhys started jumping up and down. "Daddy, can we go play with Quinn? I'll be good, I promise."

Will snatched him up. "You're always good. And yes. If we can't go to the beach, I don't see why we can't go play in the snow with your friends."

Jax started to list his reasons until Shivan spoke. "Hagar put a spell of protection around the village. They'll be safe. And I imagine they'll spend half the day inside warming up."

"Still."

"I'll make sure there's always an adult watching carefully," Aubrey said. "Full attention."

He couldn't argue; he was the only one with reservations. Shivan opened the bag and pulled out heavier pants and a jacket for Rhys, things Quinn had outgrown, and he brought clothes Darville had outgrown for Hyrum. There were gloves and knit caps; the only thing lacking were warm shoes, but Will grabbed water-proof bags from the kitchen to put over their feet.

"If an adult tells you it's time to go inside to warm up, no arguing," he told Rhys, and by extension, Hyrum. "We're not trying to be mean. We're just making sure you don't get chilled."

He carried Rhys on his back most of the way, until we reached the edge of the protective spell Hagar placed around the village. Shivan called out for entry, and a few moments later Jesf was there with a remote controller, lifting a section long enough to let us in. "We're taking turns," he said, his voice less raspy than it had been just a day before. "No one wants to stand out in the cold very long."

The children didn't share his discomfort. All around the fire, which had been fed more wood and now burned high, there were small elves engaged in battle, throwing snowball after snowball, and the din of laughter filled the village center. Quinn waited near the courtyard gate, and when he spotted Rhys, he ran toward us, snowball in hand, arm cocked back. He let it fly with a wild giggle but stopped suddenly when it landed on Jax's forehead.

Eyes wide, he wasn't sure if he should laugh or run.

Jax quickly bent to scoop up a handful and said, "You little monster. Just for that, I'm aiming for your face."

Quinn barked out a laugh and ducked, yelling for Rhys to come play.

"He'll never forget this," Aubrey said to Will. "When he's Oz's age, he'll still remember the time he played in the snow, in the place with the dragons."

"And I hope Aisha will forgive me that she's not here for this."

Aubrey leaned against him and whispered loudly, "It's all fake, Will. She'll be there for the real snow."

"But not for this joy." He didn't have time to wallow in it; Hagar was more than halfway across the circle, waving at Will.

"You brought them back! Very good. Are you staying? The village is safe now."

"I thought it was safe before," Will said. "Tobias agreed, this was off limits."

Hagar nodded thoughtfully. "And I take him at his word. But Asmonk gave no such word, and he's out there, wandering around."

"Asmonk?" Aubrey asked. "The boy who—"

"No worries," Hagar said. "He admitted his crimes and has been banished. He can't enter the village now."

Aubrey didn't express the relief he expected. "You *banished* him? He's just a boy!"

"A boy who tried to kill your three-year-old nephew," Jax

reminded her. "And you. Those dogs would have ended you, Aubrey."

"But he's still just a boy and it's *cold*. It's snowing. What did he leave here with? Anything? The clothes he was wearing? He'll *die* out there, Jackson."

Jax inhaled deeply and asked the question he already knew the answer to. "What do you want me to do?"

"Find him! Get him to shelter. If he can't come back here, find somewhere else for him that's safe and warm. And make sure he has food. I'll keep an eye on the boys."

Jax turned to Shivan. "Is there any way you can scrounge up something warmer for her to put on?" When Shivan nodded, he told Drew and Sean to stay in the village and to help keep an eye on all the kids. "This kind of cold isn't common here, I'm sure. Don't be shy about making kids go inside. Any of the kids."

"Don't tell Rhys who we're looking for," Will said. "Don't frighten him."

Hagar offered to go with us; he knew of several places Asmonk could stay, and a familiar face might go a long way into getting him to listen. "If he sees the two of you, he'll hide. He might speak with me."

You made him confess. He might try to kill you.

"Possibly. Nevertheless, I'm going."

They headed into the woods, with no direction in mind, all with the same thought: Where would a teenager in Saint Francis hide? Jax knew of the places in the Presidio woods he used to go to when he wanted life to fade away for an hour or two, and the places he and Will used to sit while they enjoyed beer purloined from Eli's refrigerator. Hagar knew where teenagers went before Tobias took control of St. Francis, but there was no wandering the city after that, and he had no idea what the kids did now.

"The places to which teenagers drift largely remain the same from generation to generation," Will mused. "We simply pretend to not notice that our children are discovering the same freedoms we once believed were unique to us."

"Start there, then," Jax said. "Where did a teenaged Hagar take his girlfriends?"

"Was I ever a teenager?" Hagar wondered out loud. "I feel as if I were born old."

Where did old Hagar take his wife to make out before she was his wife?

"That no longer exists," he said, amused. "When I courted her—"

"Courted," Jax snorted.

"—there were private spaces near Ghirardelli, before the land fell into the bay. I believe you once referred to it as the aquatic park?"

There were places to find shelter there now. We'd once spent a night at an abandoned inn near Ghirardelli, and even though the sparse amenities inside disappeared after that, it was someplace out of the cold and the snow. It was a place to start the search, though I thought it might be as fruitless as wandering around looking for Tobias.

Saint Francis was seven miles from the Bay Bridge to Ocean Beach, and another seven from the Wharf to the southern edge of the city. In straight lines, it was a simple matter to explore, but everything in between could take years.

I can ask Jeff to fly around and look.

"That would be helpful, thank you," Will said.

"Do dragons mind the cold?" Jax asked, absently.

He can think extra thick skin for himself. It's a perk of being made by me.

"Tell me if you start feeling chilled, Wick." Will patted the pouch on his sweatshirt. "This won't be warm enough sooner rather than later. I may need to tuck you under my shirt."

I gave him my promise. While they pressed on, I concentrated on Jeff hearing me, and a few minutes later his shadow shot past us, mottled by the cover of trees. Hagar and Jax looked up, but Will kept his eyes on the ground, and once Jeff was out of sight, he stopped.

"Footprints," he said, pointing to light indentations in the ground. "They've been covered by a light dusting of snow, but these are fairly fresh."

"How big were that kid's feet?" Jax asked. "Anyone notice?"

That would be a weird thing to pay attention to.

"Well, it would sure as hell be helpful right now, furball," Jax said. "Are we looking at his footprints, Tobias's, or someone else's?"

We followed them anyway because it was the closest thing to a trail that we had. They wove between trees, and a hundred feet before we reached the border of the woods, they stopped.

"What the hell?" Jax muttered.

Maybe Scooter snatched him up for a midnight snack.

"Scooter didn't eat anyone," Will said. "Besides, had he landed here to grab the boy, there would be other signs."

"Well, these prints belong to someone," Jax grumbled. "Maybe the cat is onto something."

"Think." The voice cracked from above. "There are directions other than forward."

Jax's hand went to his gun, but he didn't draw it. Tobias jumped from the branch he'd been perched on, landing in a crouch.

"So, what do you think of the snow? I admit, I'm proud of it."

"You did this?" Hagar asked. "Whatever for?"

"I'd hoped the children would enjoy it. Mine have never seen snow, you know that. I presumed none of the villagers had, and those old enough might not remember."

"You wanted your kids to play in the snow," Jax sighed, somewhat annoyed.

"Don't tell me you wouldn't do this for yours if you knew it was something they wanted." He looked at Hagar. "Be honest. Were they happy to see it? Were the other children? I'd hoped to find a way to spy on the village to witness the fun, but you've cut it off. I couldn't even get a seeker past it."

Hagar admitted, the village children were excited and having fun. Tobias's kids were just as happy to see the ground covered in snow but spent part of the morning trying to be more mature than their desires wanted them to be. Half an hour after breakfast, however, they bolted out the door, and within minutes Hagar heard joyous shrieking as his grandchildren were pelted in a snowball fight.

"They're being treated as friends," Hagar told him. "And that's what you wished for, isn't it?"

"If simple things can bring them joy—" He swallowed hard. "This is it, then? You found me. I won't fight you."

"No time for that," Jax said. "It's fucking cold, and a kid is wandering around out here. I'd leave the little son of a bitch, but my wife wants us to find him and get him to shelter."

"I haven't seen anyone else this morning," Tobias said. "Whatever possessed him to come into the woods on such a cold morning?"

"He was banished," Hagar said. "The boy who wanted to feed the Emperor's son to the dogs."

"Ah. Isn't that the point of banishment? He's no longer your problem."

"Yeah, well, my wife doesn't see it that way," Jax grumbled.

"How is she today? I was concerned about the effects of being suddenly moved."

"Fine, if it's any of your business. You're safe for now, Tobias. We need to get moving and find this kid before he freezes."

"I still—"

"It's Asmonk," Hagar said.

"Who?"

"Your nephew."

Tobias blinked rapidly, trying to reach into the depths of his brain for any memory of a nephew. "My brother named his son *Asmonk*?" He then waved it off. "No, I'm not surprised. I suppose he has a daughter named Asnun."

Hagar gave a slight shrug.

"No," Tobias said, disbelieving. "He wouldn't."

"Her name is Vestal. Philip is rabidly religious," Hagar said. "I haven't spent much time with him, but Shivan's wife is a wonderful fountain brimming with village gossip. There's an entire sect dedicated to the worship of the creator of Saint Francis. Philip wishes for his children to dedicate themselves to it."

"Oh, holy hell," Tobias spat. "They do know their creator is a human sitting at a computer? Not some god?"

"My father will be equally disturbed," Will said. "Religion was never supposed to be part of this."

"If they want to worship anyone," Tobias said, "it should be those who delivered them from me. Your father created them, but the princess saved them."

"She would say it was a group effort," Jax said. "Come on, we need to keep moving."

Tobias trotted alongside Hagar. "Tell me where you're headed. I'll search in another direction."

Will outlined the places he thought we should look first: along the water, to the inn, the parks, and the orchards and wheat fields. Asmonk would look first for a place to sleep and get out of the cold, and then for food. Will also didn't think he would wander too far from the village, not yet. There was a chance Shivan would change his mind, declare he'd learned his lesson.

"That won't happen unless he makes amends," Hagar said.

"No, but a young teenager would certainly hope."

Tobias said he would check the Cliff House and down the beach, then Golden Gate Park. There were hundreds of places where someone could hide, and there were buildings for shelter if he found a way in, all spots a village elf might know. "I'll cast a spell of seeking," he said. "If I stand in the meadow, it should point to a general area to look."

"Spells," Jax said. "I thought spells were for witches. Isn't that what Shivan said?"

"What?" Hagar and Tobias said together.

"Witches and warlocks use spells to cast magic. Wizards are born with it. He was unsure if there were female wizards." Jax sighed. "I don't know, I heard about the conversation after the fact."

While Tobias laughed, Hagar said, "We're all one and the same. The magic comes from within, but a spell here and there helps."

"Your son," Tobias said to Will. "Here, he would be considered a wizard, perhaps of limited power."

"And you know this, how?"

"I asked Her Majesty. I wanted to know why your son had

been lured into the forest and why the sprites protected him." He considered it. "Your family is bestowed with human magic, and it will grow if nurtured."

"If he were part of a simulation, perhaps," Will said.

"I've read your family history and somewhat of their future, Emperor. You can move through time. Find your father in his later years and ask him. You might be surprised."

"God, if my grandkids can levitate..." Jax sighed again. "Hell, just give us a hint."

Will held up a hand to stop him. "The future he speaks of might not exist, Jax. I may have changed everything."

"No shit. I hear that at least three times a month."

"Look to the castle," Tobias said. "Look to your son. He holds the threads that bind you all together."

With that, Tobias winked from view.

"Son of a bitch," Jax spat. "Whose son?" he asked Will. "Yours? Mine?"

"Ask him later," Will said. "Someone else's son is our job right now, and as cold as it is, I don't think we have much time to find him."

= = =

When we were almost to the inn, close to the place the remains of Fort Mason should have been but were lost to the bay, Hagar paused in a clearing—it could have been a small park or a remnant of the old Marina Green, but the details were covered in snow, and I wasn't sure where we were—and decided it was a decent place to do as Tobias planned, and cast a spell of seeking.

He stripped off his gloves and held his hands out, palms up. His middle fingers twitched up, and he lowered his eyelids; his eyes weren't closed, but he stared at his hands through eyelashes and began muttering.

"Show me the way," he said softly. "Seeker go quickly, find the boy."

The space between his slightly upraised middle fingers filled with bright blue light. He raised his hands and said,

"*Requaero,*" while flicking his fingers forward. The light shot off, a bright thick line that spun until it found its center, and then sped away like a pulse from a laser gun.

"So," Jax ventured, "We just stand here until you get an answer from a flying glow stick?"

"We can keep walking. It will find me. Although, if we wait, we might save ourselves the effort of looking where he isn't."

Jax opted to wait. He bounced on his toes for warmth and grumbled that Will should look as cold as he felt. "You're kind of a freak, you know."

"I have been informed," Will said. "Wick, are you all right?"

For now. I might duck my head down soon. Don't freak out if I do. I'm just warming my ears.

"Is it just me or is it too cold for this?" Jax asked. "I've never felt this kind of cold in the mountains."

"Tobias isn't familiar with winter weather," Hagar said, searching the sky for his seeker. "He may have dropped the temperature more than it needs to be."

"Can't you fix that?"

"His work, his issue," Hagar said. "If I could undo his magic, the elves never would have suffered under him."

"Why elves?" Jax asked. "They're men."

Hagar glanced at him, then went back to looking for the blue light. "Please tell me you're not like Andrew, expecting tiny pointy-eared men who live in trees."

"No, when I hear 'elves' I think of a warrior class. Tall, lean, and fierce."

"Ah. The Emperor is an elf, then."

"I am not," Will said.

"Yeah, you basically are," Jax said. "By my standards. The Emperor Elf."

"No."

"Elves are the working class, that's all," Hagar said. "Although now there is no class system. After Saint Francis fell, there were elves and outliers, but now there are only elves and a scant number of others who come to the village to trade. Shivan says the outliers essentially vanished, though a few joined the village."

Why doesn't anyone live downtown? There's lots of space.

"Those buildings aren't habitable," Will said. "Essentially, they're shells and facades. But Wick has a fair point. Why have the elves remained in the village? There's plenty of land to expand upon."

"I haven't been here. I don't know." Hagar extended his arm to catch the returning light. It plunged into his palm, and he closed a fist around it, then sighed. "He's not on this side of the city. It searched to the bridge. There are a few people, but none of them are Asmonk."

"Then we work inward," Will said. Tobias was searching from the coast into the park; if we went a few miles southwest, Hagar could use another spell to look, and perhaps Asmonk's location could be found through simple attrition.

"I'm fucking freezing," Jax said. "And I'm getting a bitch of a headache. We need to find somewhere to warm up for a little bit. I don't think I have two miles in me."

"We might as well press on to the inn, then," Hagar said. "Can you make it to Ghirardelli?"

Will stopped them. "I don't think he needs to. Where we stand is close to Scott Street, at home. Can you make it as far as Webster? Near the Marina Green Triangle?"

It was only a few blocks. Jax nodded, and Will took the lead. We walked along the new marina, with its long beach and pathways. None of this had been here before, the houses that had cropped up along the rough-trodden main path were new and looked every bit like they did in the When where I met Luxor and older, Other-When Jo learned her son was alive.

With each small section of the block we walked, the more familiar it felt. Will finally stopped at a house with a large courtyard, and he smiled warmly as he tapped out a code on the security panel near the gate. It beeped, then the gate clicked and swung open. I'd been here before; the yard had been home to more cats than anyone could reasonably keep track of, and they hissed at me because I was the intruder.

"My mother's house," he said as he opened the front door. "My father would not have left it out, not once he knew about it."

"Your father was unaware of a home owned by his wife?" Hagar asked.

"In another When, their marriage did not survive," Will explained "But my father is now aware of that possibility, and of the home she owned on the marina. He's visited it a few times now."

Jax wasn't as interested in Finn's trips through time as he was in the warmth to be found here. He barely noted the grand staircase and the luxury that nearly dripped from each wall. Will pointed him to the library, where there was a fireplace. It was in that room where Jo, a future Jo, was presented with the son she'd lost so many years earlier.

The ladder is still there.

Will set me down so he could light the fire. "As are all the books. I half expect Luxor to come walking into the room." He glanced at me over his shoulder. "Please don't create another Lux."

I miss him. When can I go see him?

"Soon. Once we're home, if you want, you can visit."

We could stop on our way back.

"I don't want Jax to meet himself. One of them at a time is enough."

Jax had settled onto the sofa. The fire had barely started, but the warmth had already filled the room. "What makes you think I haven't gone and met me? Oz and Drew went to see themselves."

"Yes, and their meetings have been carefully arranged to avoid conflicts. They embrace the concept of letting life meet them as it comes."

"Bullshit," Jax grunted. "They just haven't figured out that you're not the boss of them."

"And yet, they're quite clear on that point about you."

Jax set his head on the back of the sofa, pressing fingers to his forehead. "Exactly how I want it. Jesus, this headache. Please tell me there are functional meds here in your mother's pretend house."

The house had access to the same things we did in any

building. Will went into the downstairs bathroom and rifled through the medicine cabinet, and when he came back, he had a bottle in one hand and a small patch in the other. Jax leaned forward so Will could stick the patch on the back of his neck, and then took three of the pills he was offered.

"The patch will offer near-immediate relief," Will explained when Hagar asked. "The pills will keep the headache at bay for a few hours."

Is he okay?

"His neck and throat have been exposed to the cold," Will said. "It's probably from the constriction of blood vessels and tightening of muscles. Our delicate leader isn't used to extreme cold and physical exertion."

That doesn't sound right.

"You can fuck right off, Emperor," he said, rubbing his forehead again. "But thank you. It's already easing up."

"Five minutes more, it should be gone."

We waited the five minutes, and then a few more, until Jax sighed with relief. He pushed off the sofa with a soft grunt, and said, "Come on. If the cold did this to me, it's probably killing that kid. Part of me doesn't care, but the bigger part knows Aubrey is right. Let's find his sorry little ass and get him to where it's warm. No one deserves to die in this."

Can we take him back to the village?

"No," Hagar said, though he seemed upset about that. "There are other places, Wick. Where we take him depends on where he's found."

What if he froze in the middle of the night?

What happens to elves when they die?

"They're taken to the orchards or the fields and left for their remains to be absorbed into the ground. It doesn't take long."

Like that apple Fluffy cut open.

Jax explained about the apple, and how the insides spilled out and went into the dirt. Hagar nodded and said it was much like that. "We don't stay to see it happen because that's too stark a reminder of what we are, but we return to the things of which we are made, essentially."

Then why is the beach still stained with Shedu?

"There's been no reason for the stain to fade," Will said. "The things they were comprised of were absorbed, but the color remained. If the elves wish to change it, they can."

Then why didn't Aradyn and all the others return like that? They were bloody messes.

"Because we expected a human-like end to their lives."

A lot of this would have been helpful to know the last time around.

"Indeed. It would have been helpful to know from the start that we hadn't truly jumped forward a thousand years. I believe that anyone new reaching the simulator will be informed."

Finn needs to make a simulation that looks like outer space. People will think they're floating.

"That would invite terror, I believe."

Yeah, but think how relieved they'll feel when they realize they're not about to die.

"Unless they drop dead from a heart attack," Jax said.

Risks. You take one every time you walk into a portal.

= = =

We followed a line across the city that cut it neatly in half. We knew where Asmonk wasn't—he was not in the northern part of the city—and Hagar didn't think he would venture into SOMA. We put the Presidio woods, the orchards and fields, and Golden Gate Park between Ocean Beach and us, working inward, overlapping places Tobias would search.

Every mile, Hagar stopped to release his seeker. He found small groups of people, elves and outliers, most playing in the snow, but not Asmonk.

"What are elves doing this far from the village?" Jax asked.

"Residence in the village isn't a requirement," Hagar said. "According to Shivan's father, some of the elves who lived apart from it before Tobias's reign moved back into the homes they'd been forced to abandon."

"So what do they do in an emergency?"

Hagar didn't know. "In my youth, the population was far denser, and help was a voice yelled from a window away. There was always someone nearby. I have no idea what those who choose life away from the village do. Perhaps…die."

They probably wish really hard. I bet someone always comes.

"Or," Will ventured, "there's something in place Hagar is unfamiliar with. I can't imagine their government would fail to account for all its people."

"I haven't seen any hint of a government," Jax said. "Shivan is the elves' mayor. He hasn't mentioned anything else."

Maybe Shivan is it. He was the only one who decided what would happen to Asmonk.

"Indeed," Will murmured.

Do you think he would have banished him if he'd known the snow was coming?

"I don't know, Wick. I would hope Shivan has retained his compassion."

If we hadn't been there, if it had been an attack on someone else, Hagar was certain Asmonk wouldn't have been kicked out of the village, not permanently. But he attacked the creator's grandson, and his few days back in Saint Francis had convinced him that religion was more than a concept and was now actively forming. Penalties against those who offended anything of the creator would be harsh.

"Shivan knows we're merely men," Will said. "Surely he doesn't believe any hype surrounding a creator."

"Shivan will respect the beliefs of his people. At least, the boy who once lived with me would have."

"What about crime?" Jax went on. "Is there some form of law enforcement? Who takes care of the town drunk when he's on an angry bender? If one elf attacks another?"

His musing was rhetorical; with religion would come the defense of those beliefs, if not outright fighting over forcing it on others. With religion, there were always laws. Would those rules become the law of the land? Would the village cut itself off from Saint Francis to protect its new church?

"The path to theocracy is bloody and dangerous," he said. "We've seen it over and over. It's never peaceful."

We stopped again so Hagar could let his seeker fly. "Why does it matter to you, King Jackson? These aren't your people."

"I'd be kind of a dick if it didn't matter."

Hagar glanced at Will. "Is he kind of a dick?"

Amused, Will said, "Sometimes."

The seeker returned, quicker this time. "Still nothing." He closed his hand around it, and with a sigh, began walking again. "Word of advice, Your Majesty."

"Just Jax. And sure."

"Don't be a dick."

= = =

An hour later, a red light similar to Hagar's blue one zipped overhead, hovered as if it were observing us, and then took off. We were closing in on each other. Jax grumbled that if Tobias had not found the boy by now, he might have ventured further out than expected, and if that was the case, we needed to find someplace to warm up again.

"That may have been his signal that he's near and knows where we are," Hagar said, preparing another seeker of his own.

When it sped by again, he was certain of it. He let his fly, but instead of zooming away, it chased the red light, and they hung together in the sky, spinning around each other.

"He's found the boy," Hagar said. He flicked his fingers upward, calling both seekers to him, and when he closed his fist around them, he nodded. "The lake in the park. And your wife was right, Jax. The boy is not well."

"How fast can we get there?"

Hagar began moving his hands, casting a reddish glow that enveloped all of us, and before Jax could ask what he was doing, we were near Stow Lake, where Tobias knelt near the still form of a young teen.

"He was curled up in the bushes," Tobias said, not looking up. "He's barely alive."

"Where can we take him?" Jax asked. "Someplace warm. With food."

Hagar wanted to know about the condition of his old hut. It had moved, but if it had been resurrected as it was before, with the fireplace and beds, we could take Asmonk there. Food could be procured. He volunteered to stay with him and make sure he was all right.

Tobias looked up. "No. You need to stay with Miriam and the children. You swore, Hagar."

"In these circumstances—"

"He's your nephew. You stay with him," Jax said to Tobias. "We'll get firewood and food, but your job now is to keep this kid alive. Otherwise, the Queen will be royally pissed off."

"I can summon food and wood," Tobias said, picking the boy up. "So, you'll know where I am. Tomorrow the snow will be gone and the temperature pleasant. Assure your Queen that the boy is all right and I will care for him. On my wife's life, I swear."

"I'm not sneaking up on you in the middle of the night to kill you," Jax said.

"Tomorrow," Tobias repeated. "Otherwise we'll keep running around Saint Francis, and I know the city well enough that you won't find me on your own. I'm sure you have a life to return to."

In a blink, he was gone.

"Jesus, we need to get somewhere warm," Jax said. "I can't feel my feet."

Will wanted to stick me inside his shirt while we headed for the DeYoung building; it was close and would be warmer than being outside, but before he could move me Hagar waved his hands around, and the next thing I knew we were in the village, right next to the fire.

Drew and Sean were sitting on a log close to the courtyard where Rhys and Quinn were tossing handfuls of unpacked snow in the air, giggling as it rained down on them. There were fewer kids outside now, and the noise level had dropped considerably. "They just came back out," Drew said before Will could express ire over Rhys still being out in the cold. "Aubrey and Hyrum are inside making hot chocolate, and Shivan is over there—" he pointed across the fire "—yelling at Aradyn about something."

"Aradyn does not seem like himself," Hagar said woefully. "It feels like my old friend is gone."

"Did you find the kid?" Drew asked.

"He's with Tobias in Hagar's hut for now," Will said. "Jax, you need to get inside. You won't get much warmer standing by this fire. We'll start another inside."

Jax nodded and headed toward the door. Will watched Rhys for another moment, soaking up his little boy's glee, and asked Drew to bring him inside in a few minutes.

There was already a fire roaring in the small fireplace that butted up against the wall between the kitchen and sleeping area. It seemed like a bad idea to me—fire where the furniture was made of hay—but someone had carefully swept near it, and no sparks were popping out. Just above the opening, warm air blew from a vent, and the hut felt toasty and warm.

Aubrey was at the small stove, stirring the hot chocolate. She turned when the door opened, and before she could get it out, Jax said, "He's with Tobias. It was close. I think that kid was half frozen, and another hour would have killed him."

There was no I-told-you-so. She set the spoon aside and went to him, slipping her arms around him for a hug. "Jax, you're freezing, too."

"I've been warmer."

"Will?" She let go of Jax. "Are you all right?"

"I run warmer than most," he said. He prodded Jax toward the fire and grabbed a blanket off the closest bed to wrap around his shoulders. "The outside temperatures will begin rising soon. By morning the snow will be gone, and the cold should abate."

"Fucking wizard," Jax muttered.

"Jax," Aubrey sighed.

"He did this. The cold, the snow. There's no way he didn't understand that the people here aren't prepared for winter weather. He gave some bullshit excuse that he just wanted the kids to enjoy a day of snow, but you don't just spring that on people. If you can control it, you warn them."

"Or," Will said, "he failed to consider the ramifications and thought only of his children. They'd never seen snow, and he wanted to give this to them while he could."

"Don't defend that bastard."

"Jax, I am acutely aware of who and what he is. My job is to present other sides to you. This is one of them."

"That's not your job."

"It is, and we both know it."

"Yeah, well, then you're fired."

"Wonderful. Aisha will be delighted," Will said as he dropped onto the hay bale across from Jax. "She's always wanted a trophy stay-at-home husband. Very considerate of you to give her that."

"Trophy," Jax snorted. "Participation trophy, maybe. Tiny little thing, everyone laughs at them. Kind of like your—"

"Jax!" Aubrey nodded to Hyrum, who was at the table waiting for hot chocolate. "Stop."

Will didn't take the bait. "You realize you're insulting Aisha with that statement. The insinuation is that she's only good enough to get the participation trophy."

"Eh, she had an off day. And then came you."

"*Veni, veni, veni,*" Will said, grinning.

"You're both impossible," Aubrey sighed. She went back to the stove and began pouring the hot chocolate. Hyrum was about to get up and call Rhys in when the door opened and Drew came in, carrying him, with Sean right behind.

"Daddy!" Rhys squealed, wiggling to get down. "We made a snowman!"

"I'm sorry I wasn't there to see that. Are you sure it was a snowman? Perhaps it was a snow woman."

"Daddy," Rhys groaned. "It was a man."

Will pulled Rhys close, as much to see how cold he was as to hug him. "Snow people can be women, too, you know."

"It didn't have boobs."

"Some ladies don't have boobs," Hyrum snorted. "My sister, Elle, is flat as a b—"

"Hyrum," Aubrey said, pointing a warning finger at him. "Be nice."

Jax laughed. "He's telling the truth, angel. Your sister is not...endowed."

"Aubrey, do you remember Brother Dave?" Hyrum asked.

"I do. He lived next door," she said.

"He had boobs." Hyrum held his hands a few inches in front of his chest. "Like this."

"Enough." She was not half as irritated as she wanted them to think. "Everyone grab a mug and go sit by the fire. I want you to warm up."

She told Jax to stay right where he was and brought it to him, dropping a kiss on top of his head before she sat next to him. For a few minutes, no one else in the room existed for them; she snuggled close, trying to help him warm up, smiling when he leaned close to whisper in her ear.

I jumped up onto the hay bale next to Will and Rhys where I could see them better.

Remember when the power in the royal house went out and the only thing we had all night was the fireplace? Or maybe you don't, you lived in that apartment and Jax hadn't even met Aubrey yet.

"I remember it," Will said. "Jax was so delicate that he came to spend the night on my sofa rather than suffer a cold December night at home with his parents."

It was right after his birthday. Queen Donna didn't want to let him go, but Eli thought that a newly minted eighteen-year-old should be trusted to spend a night with his friend.

"That must have been before he realized I was stealing his beer," Jax said. "What'd they do that night, Wick? Do you remember? I've always had a hard time picturing what they did together when they were alone."

"Same thing you two do," Drew said with a chuckle.

"They weren't nearly as affectionate," Jax said.

They were private. But I remember that night because she wandered all over the house looking for me, calling my name, and then made me stay in the living room with them so I could curl up by the fire.

"She loved you," Jax said. "She's why there are cat flaps to every room in the building."

She loved everyone more than you supposed. Eli most of all. He came first, even before you.

"I hadn't noticed that."

"She didn't want you to notice, sweetheart," Aubrey said.

She told me once that Eli was the most important person in her life because they had chosen to love each other and spend forever together. You were the most important person to the two of them together because you were a reflection of their love. But the night the power went out, the person they talked most about was Will.

32

While Donna flitted from room to room, calling for me, Eli searched for the fireplace lighter. I was curled up in Jax's bedroom—Oz's room—between the pillows on his bed, creating my own little pocket of warm, and listened to him grumble about never being able to find anything in the damned house, and why the hell couldn't anyone put anything back where they'd found it.

Donna brushed past, reminded him that he was the last one to use the unusually long wand lighter, and headed into Jax's room, her voice light as she sang my name, stretching it into two light syllables. "*Wiii-ick.*"

I poked my nose up and meowed so she would know where I was and that I was fine. She reached across the mattress, mumbling about the unmade bed and the general state of chaos in Jax's bedroom and scooped me up. By the time she'd cuddled me and told me how awful it must be, sleeping in that boy-stinky bedroom, Eli had the fire going.

"Twenty minutes," he told her. "The room should be warm by then."

"You'll stay with me until then," she said as she kissed the top of my head. "What about the guards, Eli? The poor boy on door duty must be miserable."

He promised that he'd seen to the guards; there were battery powered heaters in the staff kitchen and guard's lounge, and the desk guard had one under the desk pointed at his feet and another he could move around to keep the rest of himself from freezing. "They know how to keep warm. Stop worrying."

"I'll worry as much as I care to," she retorted. "This kind of cold is unusual, and they're not dressed for it."

That made him laugh. "They have winter uniforms. They're fine. The only ones likely complaining are the maintenance workers on the roof looking for the reason the solar lines aren't recharging the building's energy reserves. We should have power."

It's those pigeons. They're pecking at the lines.

She handed me to Eli, telling him—not asking—to keep me warm while she made them some tea. He lifted me to his face level, frowning. "You were warm where you were hiding, weren't you? She worries too much."

This is fine. I like sleeping by the fire.

He set me on the hearth, where soft, warm fingers were beginning to reach out. In a few more minutes it would be roaring, and I'd have the comfiest seat in the house.

They snuggled together on the sofa under a quilt. Eli's giant feet stuck out the end, and she kept trying to cover them up until he finally told her he was airing them out on purpose. "You're hot, you know."

"Thank you." That earned him a quick kiss. "Did you call Jax to make sure they have power tonight?"

"They're fine," he sighed. "If it's cold in the Emperor's apartment, they can cuddle together on the sofa and drink hot tea and worry about the cat together."

"As if that boy would let Jax anywhere near him."

"He prefers to keep to himself," Eli said. "It's not personal. Don't take it as if it were."

"He won't even shake hands, Eli. It's quite...rude."

"That's not his intention."

She went through a list of possible reasons Will was a weird little touch-phobic teenager: religion, fear of germs, sensory issues, outright cluelessness. She'd seen him share a drink with Jax, ruling out a germ phobia. He was otherwise polite and often gave half-bows when greeting her and Eli. He'd never mentioned religion, and in her experience, people tended to speak about their beliefs even when they weren't proselytizing.

She settled on sensory issues.

"Everything that boy wears is skin tight. It borders on obscene. Maybe he needs a special sort of touch, and the tightness of his clothing provides him with that."

Eli chuckled. "He's showing off, that's all. The Emperor is extremely fit and wants every girl he passes to know it."

That made no sense to her. What was the point in flaunting anything if he couldn't bear the touching that would surely follow?

"What makes you think he's not engaged in quite a bit of touching, privately?"

I promise you, he does a lot of private touching.

She allowed for the possibility. "Oh. It might not be girls he's trying to impress. Do you think he and Jax—"

"They're friends, that's all. And if Jax's track record is any indication, that's all they will ever be, even if the Emperor wants something else. And I'm certain he doesn't."

"I wouldn't mind," she said. "I just wish he wasn't so...odd."

"He's not odd. He's Scottish."

If you knew he understood me, you'd think he was super odd.

"And the name," she went on. "'The Emperor.' It's bad enough he's taken a title as his name, but why on earth do we refer to him as *the* Emperor? Imagine how it would sound if I started referring to our son as *the* Jackson?"

"I address him as 'Emperor' only. When discussing him—I have no idea. It sounds less clunky, I suppose."

"Then explain why he's 'Emperor' at all?"

Eli knew why, but he couldn't share that with her. There was a time when I knew, but I'd forgotten, and it would be decades before Finn would flip the switch that made me remember.

"Where are his parents?" she asked. "Surely they wouldn't—"

"They know where he is," Eli said. "I've spoken with them. This is the best place for him to be right now, Donna. He's capable of caring for himself, but I've given my word that I'll keep an eye on him. And he's been good for Jax, you know he has."

She couldn't argue that. Jax had tamed considerably in the short time since Will had chosen to remain in San Francisco. He spent more time with the Emperor and more time at home than he had before, and she worried less about the girls he had clearly been stringing along, one after the other.

There was the matter of how he had seemingly not aged in the years since he'd plucked Jax from the Bay Bridge, but she decided to let that go for the moment. He was odd enough without complicating things by examining them too closely. He was a good friend to Jax, Eli clearly cared about him, so no matter how worrisome the Emperor's traits seemed, she welcomed him into their lives and promised Eli she would relax more around him.

There was a knock on the jamb of the open door; one of the guards stood just outside and waited until Eli got up before he took a step in. The issue with the solar system had been found and would be repaired by morning. "Lines leading into the batteries and backup system were compromised," the guard reported. "There are several bird nests on the roof, and the technician assumes they are the root cause of the problem."

Pigeons. I told you.

Donna got up, taking the quilt with her. "How are the guards faring? Is the lounge warm enough?"

"Yes, ma'am," he said, a slight smile tugging at the corners of his mouth. "There are heaters running in the lounge and in the kitchen. The guards are comfortable."

"Told you," Eli said.

"I didn't doubt you, old man. I wanted to be sure they're *still* warm."

"Son," Eli said to the guard, "you're dismissed. Unless you want to witness the proof to your Queen about how not old I am."

The guard left quickly.

I went to sleep because I didn't need to see it, either.

But I remembered it, because no matter what they wanted the outside world to see, I saw the tenderness and gentleness, and heard the music of their laughter.

= = =

I can still hear what her laughter sounds like. Sometimes it was like a cackle, but alone with Eli a lot of the time it was music.

"I wish I'd seen some of the things you did, Wick," Jax said.

They loved each other the way you and Aubrey do. She just couldn't do it in front of anyone.

"We probably drove her a little bit nuts," he mused.

No, she was happy that you were never afraid to show the world how much you love Aubrey. People like knowing that their king and queen are together because they want to be and not because they have to be.

"For the same reasons you wanted everyone to know Oz and I chose each other," Drew said. "That it wasn't an arrangement."

She also wanted Levi Munson to witness the love story that had enveloped his daughter. Donna never let on to Aubrey that she knew who she was, and she guarded that secret as well as she could. She swore Eli to silence. While she had no idea the abuse that Aubrey had endured under Levi's roof, especially at his hand, she knew he was a hard and horrible man, and the only way Aubrey was in Pacifica was because she had run away; there was no other reason she could have been there.

She made sure Aubrey had the fairy tale wedding, over the top and broadcast around the world, knowing he wouldn't be able to resist watching. What she wanted for her new daughter-in-law was all the love she hadn't had as a child, though she was never quite sure how to show it.

"Wick," Jax said, patting his lap to invite me over, "I am so damned glad you have most of your memories back. And I might ask you to tell me more stories later if Will doesn't mind helping you. For some reason, my mother has been on my mind a lot lately."

Will did not mind and Drew understood without being told why Jax didn't want him to act as translator.

I had a hundred things to tell him about his parents, but for the rest of the evening, they sat by the fire and listened to stories about Rhys and Hyrum's adventures with Shivan's kids. Will paid attention to all the things Rhys didn't say, and when there was a hint of what Asmonk had done to him, when he'd heard the sound of a dog baying in the distance, Will gently closed his hands over Rhys's to snuff out any potential sparks.

We were using hay for furniture.

Sparks were probably not in our best interests.

Aubrey noticed. "Will, have you heard from Finn yet?"

"No, but at this point, it doesn't matter. We know where Tobias is, and he's expecting us to end this tomorrow. We can go home afterward, and then I can explain to Aisha why I didn't send him home right from the start."

33

Breakfast was quiet, nearly somber. Rhys pouted because Will had already told him to expect that the snow had melted, and Hyrum was quiet because he suspected this was our last day here. He'd watched Will and Drew packing things away, and as Aubrey cleaned the kitchen, taking great care to place even the smallest crumbs she could find into the mulch bin. He didn't seem upset but stayed quiet to keep Rhys from having another reason to pout, or worse, cry.

"He's less upset by the idea of going home than he is with the snow being gone," Will said as Rhys and Hyrum ran out the door to find their friends. "I can promise him a trip to the mountains to play in the snow again."

"But?" Aubrey said. "I heard hesitation in there."

"But. Aisha was not here for his first encounter with snow, manufactured or not. It was real to Rhys and that moment is lost forever."

She'll get over it. Think of all the firsts you saw with Oz and Zed. You didn't even tell them about a lot of them.

"Listen to Wick," she said. "Whatever he's telling you, he's probably right."

"He's telling me I'm an ass."

Jax leaned back in his chair. "Well, look at that. I don't get to see your colors change very often. I think that's the first time you've outright lied to me."

"What color?" Aubrey asked. "I know what Ozzy sees. What do you see?"

"Orange. Not a lot of it. He's a tight ass even when he's lying."

"I lack control where the feelings of my children and wife are concerned," Will said. "And guilt is enough to lower one's defenses. I should not have allowed him to remain here."

"Sweetie, Aisha knows where he is. She knows how this place is. She won't be angry with you."

Drew nudged Sean and nodded toward the door, and they left quietly.

"She should be," Will said. "This isn't a place for children, and we both know that. She understands that the circumstances here can turn—"

"Knock it off," Jax said. "Even if she's pissed off, you'll have an argument, you'll apologize, and that'll be it."

"No, it truly won't, Jax."

"She'll see that he's fine—"

"But he might not be fine. He might be scarred for life. He's three years old, and I placed him in a position that could have cost him his life and may have instilled in him a lifelong fear of dogs. He's asked about a puppy, Jax. He wanted one. Now he might be terrified of them."

That was something Will could fix. Jax reminded him he had the ability to pluck a memory from his son's mind, and he could easily replace it with something warm and fuzzy that would result in getting him a puppy for his birthday. "Make him think he had a fucking great time with the little bastards."

"Jax," Aubrey sighed.

He scowled. "It's just a word, Aubrey. The kids aren't here."

"But I am, and I hate it when you swear like that. I really wish you wouldn't."

The chair creaked as he pressed back. "And? What about what I want? I respect your not wanting me to swear around the kids, but we're adults here. They're just words. They don't mean anything unkind unless I use them that way. And every now and then, I *fucking* want to."

We should leave.

Want to go outside and play?

"That you use them around me is an unkindness," she said, voice soft.

"And you know me better than that. Just let me be unguarded when there aren't any small kids around. I've earned that by now."

Dude, she has a pan in her hand, and I think she wants to hit you with it.

She might have been about to, but the door popped open and Drew was there. He didn't bother coming in. "Aradyn is throwing a fit. Hagar just let Tobias into the village, and they're coming this way."

Jax jumped up, grabbing his gun and sweatshirt. Will was right behind him, and I followed along with Aubrey, waiting by her feet when they all stopped in front of Shivan's house. Asmonk was limp in his arms, head, and hands hanging. Tobias walked quickly with Hagar and Shivan on either side, and he went straight for Will.

"He's dying," Tobias said as he placed Asmonk on the damp ground. "He's barely breathing. I spent my magic keeping him warm all night and can do nothing for him now."

Will knelt beside the still boy and placed fingers against his neck and then on his chest. He waited, counting silently, then said, "I can barely feel his heart beating. He's only drawing shallow breaths."

"You can heal him," Tobias said. "I know you can. You helped the elves regrow their tongues. You created a dragon. If you can do that, you can fix him."

"I don't know that I can," Will said. "I'd need to know exactly what's wrong with him."

"He's dying, that's what's wrong. Please."

Jax bent over to look at Asmonk. "What's it to you, wizard? One more dead elf. So?"

"His nephew," Will said.

"And he had no idea he had a nephew. I doubt it's from a deep family connection. Really, Tobias, why do you care?"

Tobias dropped to his knees, ignoring Jax. "Please. I'm spent, I have no magic left to give him. With Hagar's help, maybe you can do this."

The three men set hands on Asmonk's chest. Hagar and Tobias's eyes closed, concentrating on the things going wrong inside Asmonk. Will moved his hands a few times, checking the boy's pulse and setting his hand across his neck to see if he could do anything there. They were quiet and still for several minutes, until Rhys jumped off Shivan's front steps, where he'd been standing with Darville and Quinn, and ran over.

"Daddy, what's wrong with him?"

Drew tried to pull him back, shushing him, but Rhys jerked away and leaned over Will's shoulder.

"I don't think we can help him," Will finally said. "His heart has stopped."

"Please," Tobias breathed. "He's so young."

"Daddy, I know what to do. I saw it on TV. He needs zapping in his heart."

Will turned his head. "Sweetheart, I appreciate that, but we don't have a defibrillator here."

Rhys held his hands up. "I can do it. I just touch him and go, 'surprise!' and then he jumps."

Hagar looked at Will. "We have nothing to lose."

"Other than the long-term effects on my son if it doesn't work."

Tobias didn't wait for an answer. He ripped Asmonk's shirt down the front and pushed the fabric out of the way.

"You're asking my toddler to save a man's life," Will said. "If he fails—"

"If he *succeeds*," Hagar countered.

Rhys already had light glowing around his hands. Will sat back on his heels, and held his son's forearms, watching as the light danced around his fingers and the palms of his hands. "Not too much, all right?"

"Only enough to scare him. Like saying 'Boo!' but with sparky things."

"He hurt you, Rhys. You don't have to do this."

"But if he dies, he can't say he's sorry."

"He might not say that, regardless."

"What about his mommy? She'll cry."

Will nodded and scooted out of the way, warning Hagar and Tobias to back up. Rhys did exactly what he said he'd do: he slapped his hands on Asmonk's bare chest, right above his heart, and yelled, "Surprise!"

The teenager's body jerked upward.

"One more time," Will said.

"Okay." Rhys slapped a bit harder this time, sent more electricity through Asmonk, and yelled "Surprise, Assmunch! You're it!"

Asmonk jerked, then sucked in a hard, ragged breath. Will bent to listen to his heart, then probed his neck with two fingers.

"Good job, Rhys," he said as he sat up. "His heart is beating."

Rhys clapped his hands together and then jumped up. "Yay! Can he wake up now, Daddy?"

"He might need rest." Will bent over the boy again, listening, and pried his eyes open. "Asmonk. Are you in there? Can you hear me?"

He answered with a groan but didn't open his eyes.

"Say something, boy," Tobias pleaded.

His voice failed him, but he managed to mouth, "Hurts."

Rhys bent toward Will and whispered loudly, "Daddy, don't say he peed. He'll be 'barrased."

"Andrew," Will said. "Take him home and explain to his parents what happened. Do you know where he lives?"

"I know!" Hyrum said. "I'll show him!"

Will got up as Drew lifted Asmonk, and then he picked Rhys up. "You are an amazing little boy, Rhys Blackshear. And don't be too upset if Asmonk doesn't apologize to you. He might not be well enough for a long time."

"Nor might he be here," Shivan said. "He can't stay."

"You can't possibly hold him to that banishment," Aubrey said. "He's just a boy."

"I can't take it back. He no longer has a home in the village."

"He's just a—"

Shivan held a hand up to stop her. "I know."

Darville stepped off the porch, leaving his little brother there alone. "He's only a year older than I am. What if that were me? Would you banish me?"

"You would never do what he did," Shivan said.

"I've done plenty of stupid things. Ask Mom about all the things she's never told you."

"But you never tried to kill someone," Shivan said, irritated.

"Why are you defending him?" Jax asked Darville. "Just curious."

Darville glanced over his shoulder. Drew and Hyrum were at Asmonk's door, knocking hard. "I've had time to think about it. He's not much different than you, Dad."

"Than *me?*" Shivan was outraged. "I have never tried to hurt—"

"You tried to kill *him*," Darville said, pointing at Tobias. "You wanted to rid the world of dark magic. To save everyone from the harm that it delivers. To do that, you thought you had to kill the wizard. That's all Asmonk wanted. We've grown up with stories about the mighty and brave Shivan Adomondai, House of Blackshear, Lord of Prophecy, facing the dark wizard, Tobias. How you spent your younger years training for battle, and your one goal, your *only* goal, was to kill the man."

"Enough," Shivan barked.

Darville didn't back down. "What did you and the elders expect? That we would hear those stories and not take them to heart? Asmonk has heard for *years* about the dangers of magic left unchecked, and when he saw it happening it frightened him beyond reason. Of course, he tried to do something. He thought he was protecting us. All of us."

"You did want to kill me," Tobias said as got up from the ground. "And rightly so."

"It's not the same."

"It is to *him*," Darville shot back, pointing to Asmonk's home.

"What would you have me do," Shivan asked, sucking in a deep breath. "Reversing an order of banishment has never happened before. I don't have the power to do that."

"You're the mayor."

"Take a chance," Jax said. "What's the worst thing they can do? Fire you?"

"Banish me," Shivan said. "While I would survive exile, it wouldn't be fair to my family."

"Then make them listen. Remind them that this boy is just that, a boy. He's supposed to be stupid right now."

"You do it," Tobias said. "You unbanish him."

"I'm not the King here," Jax said. "Shivan has reminded me of that."

"But you are. You're the great grandfather of our creator. And our creator lives under your reign and your rule. By extension, that gives you dominion over Saint Francis. Your word is as much law here as it is in your own world."

"Will?" Jax asked.

"The argument could be made. It would amuse Finn."

"And if I do? How pissed off will you be? The offense was against your son."

Will reminded him that he had, in a roundabout way, lifted George Denton's banishment from Pacifica, and the man had tried to kill him in front of Jay. He'd tried to take Jay. If that didn't bother him, allowing Asmonk to stay in the village would not.

"Stop banishing children," Jax said to Shivan. "Figure out a system of fair punishment but stop shoving them out to survive when you damn well know they can't."

"Is that a royal declaration?"

"Sure. Whatever works."

"Terrific." Tobias took a few steps backward, his heels bumping against one of the log benches surrounding the fire. "Now let's get this over with. If we don't, we'll simply spend the rest of our days running around Saint Francis. You'll never catch me out there, and frankly, I'm already tired of running."

He held his arms out from his side. "I have nothing left in me to fight back with. My magic is spent. Just do it."

Will handed Rhys to Sean and asked him to take Rhys to the guest hut. "Get a snack," he told Rhys. "Take your time."

Once the door was closed, Jax pulled the gun from its holster. "Don't beg," he said. "It won't work."

Drew came running back, alone. He'd sent Hyrum into the hut, asking him to help Rhys with whatever he was going inside for.

"Your daughter told you what I did to her, didn't she?" Tobias asked, baiting Jax. "The *torment*. I listened to her mind, King Jackson. Her secrets. I played on her fears. One by one, I plucked from her side the people she trusted. I placed her in jeopardy over and over, and I *adored* the possibilities. And when she didn't break, I forced her to strip off her clothing and then swim across the city, where she had no choice but to get out and walk, dripping, in front of a thousand of my men."

Jax's hand twitched. "Shut up."

"I tried to shame her. I held her on display, cold, wet, and naked, and wanted her to feel shame. Yet, she never blinked. She stood fast, and only bent to my will to cover when I threated the life of the Lord of Prophecy. Even then, when she followed me to where I held your precious Emperor, she refused to give in to what I thought were sterling mind games. I used the things her grandfather had done believing she would give in, and she refused. She would not bend. She would not break. I hurt her, and she didn't flinch."

"Yeah, bud, you didn't hurt her," Drew said. "If anything, you made her realize she needed help. But there was nothing you did that touched her."

"Well, the torment was genuine. That was some of my best work. The pool, the street filled with Shedu warriors, snatching your Emperor away, with Hagar and Shivan. And the baptismal font? I thought that was a stroke of genius. I knew he had held her under the water until she thought she would drown."

"By then we knew it was a game. She's determined, though. She wanted to win."

Tobias concentrated on Jax, urging him to pull the trigger. "Do you know how I tormented her? Did she tell you? Shall I don the face that I hoped would bring her to her knees?" He grabbed his medallion with his right hand, and looking down, blew on it until it glowed. His dark hair faded to white, his shoulders curled forward, and when he looked up, it was Levi Munson staring back at Jax.

"Oh my god," Aubrey uttered. "No. Don't do this."

"You don't know what he really did to your daughter," Tobias said. "How he touched her. How *intimately*."

"Shut the *fuck* up," Jax hissed.

"He ran his hands over her, licking his lips as he cupped her breasts," Tobias went on. "And then he *jammed* that thick, dull wire into her flesh, slicing it upward. He laughed at her pain and told her that all little whores deserved what she was getting. He promised it was only the beginning of his game, and she would beg him to take her before it was over."

"We know all this," Drew said.

"You do, perhaps. Surely, she has shared her nightmares while lying next to you with the lights out. But her father? No, he has no idea. No clue that while his daughter lay racked in pain and bleeding from the beatings Levi Munson ordered, he pressed up against her, grinding until he found satisfaction. He has no idea that Levi promised that if she survived the holidays, she would serve him entirely. Repeatedly. Daily. And that he described in agonizing detail the things he'd done to her mother."

"She's worked through it," Drew said to Aubrey. "Don't listen anymore."

Aubrey couldn't help it. Her eyes were red and filled with tears, silently pleading with him to stop.

"Look at me, King Jackson," Tobias said. "The face of the man who violated the women you treasure and adore. What does *he* deserve?"

Jax's finger twitched on the trigger, but his attention diverted when Hyrum ran from the guest hut, shouting to Aubrey that Rhys wanted toast, but he couldn't find the bread, and—

He stopped in his tracks, eyes wide. His hands went to his chest, and in a choked breath he cried, "Daddy?"

Hyrum caught Tobias by surprise, and he stumbled back, nearly falling over the log. Drew took a few steps toward Hyrum, but his attention was focused on the man in front of him; he didn't hear when Aubrey called to him and told him that it was someone else, someone who looked like their father.

The fear in Hyrum's voice evaporated. He stopped between Jax and Tobias, tilting his head as he considered what he was seeing, and then said, "Daddy, you're dead. How can you be here if you're dead?"

Tobias looked over Hyrum's shoulder, silently asking for help. Will reached into his backpack for his tablet and spent the next fifteen seconds furiously typing. When he was done, he looked at Tobias and then nodded at his tablet. A moment later, the information settled in Tobias's brain.

His eyes filled when the horror of what he now knew hit him.

"Hyrum," he said, his voice mostly breath. "No, I'm not your—"

"You're supposed to be with Jesus. Oh!" His hands went to his mouth the way they did when he was surprised or had said something he wasn't supposed to. "You went to the other place, didn't you? I was afraid of that. Did you tell Jesus you were sorry? You just need to say sorry."

"Tread lightly," Aubrey warned.

Tobias sat on the log, hard. "Sorry doesn't make up for some things. Certainly not for the things you went through."

"It's enough for Jesus. He loves you even when you're bad."

"Perhaps he's not the one who deserves the apology. The offenses were against you and your sister, Hyrum. People should pay for the things they do to hurt other people." He looked up at Jax. "Even me. Especially me."

"But if you mean it, sorry is okay." Hyrum went to his knees. "Jesus loves you even if we think you're a dick."

In that moment, Tobias broke. He stopped looking for a way to apologize to Hyrum without it sounding as if it were coming from him and jumped right into pretending to be Levi Munson. Jax tensed when he realized what was happening, and Aubrey sniffed back the tears that threatened to become a full-on wail.

"I never gave you credit for the incredible things you can do, did I?"

Hyrum lifted his hands and looked at them. "You didn't like what I can do. No one did."

"I was jealous," Tobias said. "You were beautiful and incredible, and I was simply average. But I can tell you now, what you do is impressive. It's truly a gift, and it can only have come from above."

With a shrug, Hyrum dropped his hands. "I guess."

"I'm sorry I didn't treat you better because of it."

"I'm sorry I set your hair on fire."

Tobias smiled, though his eyes went wet. "I'm sure I deserved it. You deserved none of the horrible things done to you. Please tell me you know that. You were and are an extraordinary person."

"It wasn't just me," Hyrum said. "You did those things to Aubrey and my other sisters, too, except maybe the baby. And David is a dick because of you."

"Your brother," Tobias said as he searched the information Will had given him. "You used your talents to blast him in the face. Well, he deserved it, too. I'm sorry he was so mean to you. I'm sorry for everything."

Hyrum stood up and crossed his arms. "Are you sorry because you're sorry or are you sorry because you want Jesus to think you're sorry?"

"Right now," Tobias said, standing, "I am more concerned with your feelings than I am with the Lord's. Don't forgive me, Hyrum. I don't deserve that. But I am sorry."

I thought that was it, Hyrum would step away, and I hoped someone would shield him before Jax pulled the trigger, but instead he took a step closer. His voice caught as he asked, "Why didn't you love me, Daddy?"

Tobias blanched, and he had no idea how to answer.

"I tried to be good. I did everything I was supposed to, and I don't know why you didn't love me."

Aubrey gasped, quietly, and when she blinked the tears spilled over.

"What makes you think I didn't love you?" Tobias asked.

"You said you didn't. You said you never would. You said I was broken and stupid, and nothing good would ever come from me. You said I would never grow up, and no woman would ever want me because I was a giant man-baby. And you said that even Jesus wouldn't want me because I was full of the kind of wrongness that only comes from Satan."

"Please," Aubrey said, "stop."

"The only broken and stupid person there was me," Tobias said. "You are absolutely wonderful. I was a mean, evil person, and the things I said were because evil people say things to hurt others. I was wrong. So very, very wrong."

Hyrum nodded.

"And I lied, Hyrum. You were loved. You were always loved. Please remember that. The man whom you lived with could never say it, but I can. You were *loved*. And I'm happy that you live with your sister now because she will never hurt you the way I did. Do you understand? You're a good man. And you're a well-loved man."

"Okay."

Tobias looked over Hyrum to Jax, his eyes pleading, *not in front of him*.

"Take Hyrum inside, Andrew," Jax said.

"No." Hyrum jerked away from Drew. "I know what's going on, Jax. You're going to shoot him."

"I don't want you to see this," Jax said.

"But he's already dead. Even if we can see him, he already died."

"I don't want you to see this happen, either," Tobias said. "I need to find my way, and Jax is going to help me."

"To Kingdom come," Jax uttered.

Silence fell over the village, a collective of held breath as everyone waited. Darville closed his eyes, not wanting to see, and Hagar forced himself to look Tobias in the eyes, wanting to be the last thing Tobias saw.

Jax shouldered the gun, taking aim, holding his breath to make sure he didn't falter when he squeezed the trigger.

Tobias waited, unmoving.

"See what's in front of you," Tobias said when Jax didn't fire. "Look. See what's right there."

Jax swallowed hard.

"Listen to the voice inside your head. What's it telling you?" His voice became a whisper. "Why are we here, King Jackson?"

Jax's breathing increased, and he had to reposition the weapon twice. He blinked rapidly, trying to focus, and when he was able to see through his own fog, he lowered the gun and set the safety. "What the hell is wrong with me?" He handed the gun to Will. "No, really, what the hell is wrong with me?"

"You didn't shoot, that's what," Tobias said. "Come on already."

Aubrey slipped her arm around his waist and drew close, but it was Will Jax looked to. "Emperor. What the hell is wrong? Don't lie to me. There's something wrong."

Will swallowed against a lump in his throat before he could answer. "Cognitive impairment. Slight changes in personality. Unguarded emotion. Irrational impulses and rationalization of those impulses. Temper. A tendency toward maudlin introspection."

Aubrey buried her face against his neck.

"So?"

She clutched at his shirt, grabbing fists full of fabric.

"She's been on your mind lately," Will said. "You admitted

as much last night. Think carefully, Jax."

"My mother," Jax breathed out. "Why didn't you tell me?"

Will shoved the tablet into his backpack and picked it up. "I could have. I could have told you that you were more emotional than is typical and that you had moments that deeply concerned me, and knowing you? You would have shut me down. You needed to get this" —he gestured toward Tobias— "out of your system, regardless. So now you know, you are your daughter's father, and have the grace to grant life to those who, perhaps, don't deserve it."

"Son of a bitch," Tobias spat. "Do it already."

"No," Jax said softly. "I won't."

The silence that had taken hold of the village broke and Aradyn stomped forward. "If you don't, I will. He never should have been allowed to come back. Kill him."

A familiar voice rose above the others. "Oh, fun. A public execution. Who are we killing?"

Everyone turned to the voice that came from behind the fire. Finn hopped over a stray piece of wood and strolled toward Will as if nothing were going on.

"Me," Tobias said.

"Oh. Hello." Finn stopped and regarded him for a moment. "Will brought you back. And now you want to die?"

"I deserve to die."

"Of course, you do. I designed you to die. That doesn't mean it's a requirement."

"Dad," Will said. "What are you doing here?"

"I got your message. You wanted me to take Rhys back?"

"About a million weeks ago," Drew snorted.

"Ah. Yes, well, we played around with the time parameters a bit. I take it things are a bit out of synch?"

"That would be an understatement," Will said. "And we're ready to go home."

"No!" Tobias bellowed. "Not until we end this."

"If they don't," Aradyn started.

"If you kill him, you'll be exiled," Shivan warned. "Murder is murder, regardless of the victim."

"Would it make you feel better to die?" Finn asked Tobias. "I can bring you right back if you feel like you need to be killed. I don't imagine it would hurt much."

Aradyn was horrified. "No! Don't do that. It's...horrible."

"What do you mean?" Hagar asked him. "In what way?"

"The Emperor brought me back, and I wish he hadn't," Aradyn said. "I'm not the same. I feel like I'm missing parts of myself. If you resurrect Tobias, there's no telling what he'll miss, and it might be his conscience."

"Then don't bring me back," Tobias said.

"That would suit me well," Aradyn hissed.

"Enough," Shivan barked. "You're standing in front of your creator, arguing about the lives he's granted you. Show some gratitude."

"The what?" Finn said.

Will snorted out a laugh. "You're their god, Dad."

"Ew." Finn scrunched his nose. "Good lord. Worship the dragon or giant cat or something else worthwhile."

"Do you want him dead or not?" Shivan asked.

"Eh. I don't care either way. Let him live." He squinted at Tobias. "You've got a family, right? Go play house. Have fun. Stop being evil." He drew a cross in the air in front of Tobias. "So sayeth Finn."

Shivan turned and said to the crowd, "You heard him. The creator has granted him peace."

Aradyn opened his mouth but thought better of it.

"That doesn't mean you're wanted in the village," Shivan said to Tobias. "Find a place near Hagar's old hut to build a home for your family. You're not banished, and we will trade with you and make sure your family is fed but living here would be a mistake."

"I truly don't deserve this."

"No, but your wife and children do." He looked across the fire, to the house at the end of the row. "Go tell them. They can stay until your home is done."

"You can stay in my hut until then," Hagar said.

The elves, disappointed but unwilling to protest the

decision of their creator, began walking away until there were only Shivan, Hagar, and Darville standing there. Sean brought Rhys from the guest hut, and he scrambled across the dirt, jumping at Finn with a loud "Grandpa!" that cracked in the air.

"We'll have to tweak the code a bit," Will said to Shivan. "You need laws and a way to enforce them. But we'll make sure you continue on."

"Make sure they're coded to know I'm not their king," Jax grumbled.

Shivan ignored him. "Will you make sure our time aligns with yours? I'd like to see you all again, but before I'm an old, old man."

Will assured him that could be done, and he hoisted Rhys up along with his backpack, laughing when Jax complained about the long walk back to the Union Square portal. "Like I said, delicate."

"Why go so far?" Finn asked.

"That's the closest access point I know of," Will explained.

Finn sighed, hard, then said, "Access portal." Where the guest hut had been, there was now a large glowing blue doorway. "I suppose I should write some instructions. You can get out no matter where you are in here. It's all basically the same space."

"I knew that."

Drew poked Will in the back as we headed for the door. "Sure, you did. We believe you. Totally."

"Shut up."

PART FOUR

35

We stopped in Will's birth When to leave Vicat a message that she could return home at her leisure—just go to the lab, someone would escort her through—but there was still the matter of the car crashing into Union Square. Aubrey knew that at least ninety minutes had passed when she entered the portal four floors above the apartment; our second stop was there, leaving her to wait, reluctantly. She wanted to wait in the lab with us, but Will felt it was more important for her to be seen. "Step out onto the balcony and watch some of what's happening on Union Square. Allow people to see that you're unconcerned."

"A car crashed, William. I should be concerned."

"By now you would have been informed of any injuries. What people will look for are signs that you've been told the King is injured. Let them witness curiosity, but without apprehension."

We headed for the lab using Will's transporter; there were three of Finn's techs sitting at the table, but when we appeared, they quietly got up and went back to work downstairs.

The lab kitchen was a safe place for Will to jump to when he was testing the device. The techs had gotten used to his sudden appearances a long time ago and rarely excused themselves from his presence. Rod often asked where he'd been and when, though this time he was sitting at a monitor in the future, having made sure we had food and water in the simulator.

The King, on the other hand, was reason enough to make a polite escape.

Jax sat at the table and stared into the cup of coffee Will set in front of him. He didn't move while Finn set up Rhys and Hyrum in his office with cookies and cartoons, nor while Will and Drew texted Aisha and Oz. He didn't react when Finn dropped a cup into the sink. When Will finally sat down with him, Jax sighed, "I really wish Aubrey were here."

"Half an hour more, we can leave. They're almost done with the cleanup."

"And then I have to face reporters, and God knows what else. I just want…" He sighed. "I don't know."

"Guards are waiting at the elevator, and when the door opens, you'll be surrounded and escorted across the street. Reporters can shout all the questions they want, but you won't be given time to even think about answering."

Jax finally looked up. "Better get someone on Mr. McAllister. He might take a verbal beating for having unfettered access to me all this time while they get nothing."

"He'll be taken care of."

"I'm not supposed to die, Will," Jax said, softly. "You went to my eightieth birthday."

"That Jax, yes. He survived. But it was hard fought, and he resisted the symptoms."

"How much do you know? From history books?"

There had been many afternoons and evenings spent with Jax's future self, discussing his illness and how resolutely he had refused to admit it was happening. He dug his heels in and stood in the way of treatment until his Aubrey threatened to leave before she had to watch him die.

"As I understand," Will said, "he felt as if he were being bullied into admitting there was something wrong in order to explain behavior that he felt was entirely fatigue and apathy induced. I didn't want this to reach the point of Aubrey feeling as if she had to hurt you to get you to listen."

"You wanted me to see it for myself."

Will nodded. "I've known this was coming for some time, Jax, all the while hoping it wouldn't. I've had time to think about how you could be helped to reach the conclusion that your behavior was a touch off before anyone else began berating you for it. When you invited a college reporter into your life and then granted him more than one simple interview, I suspected. But when you began speaking of retirement in that wistful way—"

"That's not cancer. I don't want the job anymore, Will. I'm tired. Anyone else can just walk away from a job they're done with, and I'm stuck. But it's not cancer. Deep down, I want out. I want to quit."

"Will you?"

"I don't know. If I can't find a good enough reason to stick it out? Yet, do I want to do this to my daughter? Dump it all on her?"

"Ordinarily you would not."

Jax leaned his head back, staring at the ceiling, and was quiet for a long stretch that Will wasn't compelled to interrupt. He waited, arms folded, until Jax spoke again.

"Holy hell." He closed his eyes. "The way I spoke to Aubrey this morning."

"She understands."

Jax lifted his head, and his eyes snapped open. "She knew. That's why she let Finn implant a transponder and why she came instead of him."

"Don't be angry."

"Angry? Son of a bitch, Will. You *know* why she refused that transponder for so many years. It goes right to her core, her roots. She's always been afraid it was the Mark. That woman is risking the wrath of God for me. She surrendered eternity for me." His eyes rimmed red. "Jesus, Will. I need to get home."

"I'll call the guard. One way or the other, you're leaving here in five minutes."

"What do I tell the kids?" Jax said softly as if he hadn't heard Will. "They saw what their grandmother went through. They know how broken my Dad—"

Will called Drew over from the other side of the room, and

Sean slipped into the office to watch cartoons with Rhys and Hyrum. As Drew sat, Will asked, "Do you understand what's going on?"

"I have an idea. You'll be all right, right?" he asked Jax. "I mean, there's a cure—"

"It's not that simple," Will said. "Other cancers are simply treated. This one is a particularly stubborn hybrid glioma, and the treatment is long and difficult."

"And half the people with it die anyway," Jax said.

"But you didn't," Drew sputtered. "I've met you. The other you. I've gotten drunk with him and let him beat me at nine ball."

"Like hell you let him," Jax said.

"Talk to Oz," Will said to Drew. "Stress to her that this is likely early in the disease process and that we'll get him to see Mass as quickly as possible. Before the end of the day."

"Should we tell Zed?"

Jax thought he should be the one to do it, but Will nodded and told Drew to handle it delicately.

It took ten minutes longer to leave the lab than Will had promised but waiting outside the elevator were a dozen guards, and they surrounded him before anyone else could get near. He had a guard at each side, holding his arms to propel him forward, and they jogged across the Square and down the steps, leaving Will to face the people waiting to ask questions.

Rhys clung to his back, his tiny arms around Will's neck. There was a small cluster of media waiting, expectantly, and the questions began the moment the door slid closed behind us. Drew snorted and told Will he could have all the fun because he wasn't answering a damned thing. "Not my job."

Will started to answer the first question he heard—how did we manage to get into the elevator so quickly—but Rhys clamped his hands over Will's mouth and said, "No! You're my horsey! Horseys don't talk!"

"You heard the man," Drew said. "His horse is nonverbal. Questions will have to wait."

They got five steps forward when more questions were fired at Will. This time Hyrum stepped in front of Will and shouted, "Stop it! He's Rhys's horse right now. Go away. He can talk to you later when he's the Emperor again."

Drew made sure I was secure in his sweatshirt and then told Hyrum they should all be horses. They galloped across the Square, and I rested my paws on the top of the pouch, listening to Rhys and Hyrum laugh as the confused buzz behind us faded.

= = =

Aisha waited for us at the top of the stairs. She knew something was wrong because Jax and Aubrey were standing in the middle of their living room locked in an embrace that felt nothing like happy. She listened while Rhys squealed about his adventures—there was snow, Mommy! And I saw Jeff and Fluffy and I was Tarzan and Hyrum taught me to make a sparky rope and Quinn eats his boogers and Daddy gave me lots of rides on his back and there were lightning bugs that looked like *people*—until she silenced him with a kiss and suggested he take a breath, and then tell Oz *all* about it while she talked to Daddy for a few minutes.

Drew took Rhys from her and asked where Alex and Charlie were; Oz had taken them into her room for pre-nap story time, so Drew prodded Hyrum in that direction and told Will they would watch the kids for a while.

"What happened?" Aisha asked Will. "Did someone get hurt?"

"Physically, no. I have more than a few things to tell you about the simulator and Rhys will surely wish to share everything he can with you, but this is about Jax." He peeked into the living room; Aubrey was leading Jax to the table, so he gestured toward the balcony.

"No one was hurt, but you're scaring the hell out of me, Bilbo," she said as she sat down. "What happened?"

"Something I've been expecting, though it seems to be happening far ahead of schedule," he said. "You recall the discussions we had with older Jax regarding his stubbornness in seeking treatment?"

Her eyes went wide. "That's happening *now*? Will, I really thought it wouldn't happen *ever*. Everything is different. He has a much better doctor. Mass won't dick around—"

"I'd hoped it wouldn't. And I could be wrong, Aisha. I may be reading more into his behaviors than is truly there. Jax may simply be turning into a grumpy, emotional middle-aged man."

"You know he's not."

"I know," he sighed. "How are the kids? Are they feeling any better?"

"An amazing recovery occurred when Oz mused that sick little boys and girls probably shouldn't have pudding because it might make their tummies hurt. They have colds, that's all." She got up and reached for his hand. "Come on, it's chilly out here."

He wanted to tell her everything, but she thought it could wait.

"You'll be furious with me, Enzo," he said. "Perhaps we should get it over with."

"I have plenty of time to be angry with you. Jax probably needs your support right now."

Aubrey was doing exactly what I thought she would do—whether he wanted it or not, Jax was getting hot tea and cookies.

"My mind wants to tell me these are stale, and you'll break a tooth on them," she said as she set the plate on the table. "They've been sitting out since I left."

"Two hours ago," Jax reminded her. "Maybe three. Are you sure I'm allowed to have one? I haven't had lunch yet, and I know the rules."

She declared rules suspended for the afternoon. He could have cookies, he could have a beer, and if he really wanted to, he and Will could duck out and go get drunk at Fuzzy's.

Will declined getting drunk. "Take a few minutes to breathe," he told Jax. "Have some cookies, but then you're seeing Mass."

"Mass might not have an opening today."

"Brian Massimo is your personal physician. He will make time for the King."

"He might not be here," Jax argued. "He might be in surgery two hundred years from now, crafting functional junk for some terrified teenager."

Will mused that he was perfectly capable of jumping that far and getting him; either way, Jax was seeing the doctor before the end of the day. There was no point in sitting there stewing over the possibilities, and there was every advantage in getting answers as soon as possible.

"How long have you known?" Jax asked Aubrey.

"Will told me he suspected a few weeks ago but was more certain the night you brought Sean home for that first interview," she said. He'd also told her about his discussions with the other Jax, how hard he fought the idea that anything was wrong, and how close to broken he became before admitting he needed help. "He felt that had he been given the opportunity to see his symptoms for himself, he would have agreed to treatment sooner, and it would have been far less stressful."

"You're not suggesting I'm stubborn, are you?"

"No, sweetheart. It's not a suggestion."

"You are much like your mother in that vein," Will said. "Even when she knew something was wrong, she refused to admit it. And Eli tried hard to not see it."

"Dad," Jax breathed. "Don't tell him, not yet."

They agreed; Eli didn't need to know anything until Jax had something to tell him. Still, a part of Jax wanted him there, because he was the best font of information about Donna. While he hadn't wanted to see her pain, he remembered it. He would be the one best able to tell him what to expect if Jax's disease had progressed as far as his mother's had when Eli realized something was wrong.

"Don't say that," Aubrey said, very softly.

"Presume it has not," Will suggested. "If it had...he would have pulled the trigger and killed Tobias."

Aisha opened her mouth to ask—how the hell was Tobias even there?—but Will promised to explain it all later, and then stand there and let her beat the hell out of him if she wanted.

"I would have killed the man," Jax agreed. "No, I think what I want most from Dad is how he finally accepted there was something wrong with Mom."

She tried to kill me.

Will flinched. "What, Wick?"

That was how he knew there was something wrong. She tried to kill me.

36

There was a crumb on the counter.

Everyone, save Will, had been home for dinner the night before. That was nothing unusual; Aubrey gradually took over cooking for Eli and Donna, and they had dinner together as a family, every night. Oz and Zed were small and sloppy, so there was almost always a bit of food on the floor and on their chairs at the end of the meal. Whoever cleared the table was responsible for cleaning up the bits and pieces that hadn't made it to their mouths, and whoever washed dishes was responsible for wiping down the counters.

Donna was picky about the state of the apartment. Anyone could pop in at any time, she argued. Visitors would not leave with the impression that the royal family was untidy, even if she had to get on her hands and knees to scrub the floor. She'd spoiled her husband and son, who rarely saw the effort that went into keeping their home spotless, not until Aubrey forced the issue.

On this morning, Donna was agitated. She'd made breakfast for Eli, but he only had time to grab coffee before he needed to leave for a series of meetings at city hall, and she wasn't amused when he said one of them was important enough he might get to sit on the throne—she always laughed when he said that, even if only for his ego. She sat at the table and stared at food going cold, and then stomped about as she threw everything away, complaining about the waste. Plates clattered as she shoved them back into the cupboard, and a glass cracked when she slammed it down next to the sink.

I watched from a chair at the end of the table, not knowing what to do to make her feel better. No one knew that Will understood the things I said to him, so I wasn't sure that running downstairs and telling him something was wrong would do any good. What was he supposed to say? Hello, how are you, the cat reports that his Queen is distressed?

He was probably hip deep in his babysitting duties, anyway, and there was no reason to expose the kids to their grandmother's bad mood.

I decided to stay put and watch, hoping that I would be able to figure out what she needed most. She often enjoyed it when I touched my nose to hers, and a few sour moods had been made a bit better with a gentle head butt. I waited while she put food back into the refrigerator—butter and bacon and jam—and I managed to not flinch when she slammed the door so hard that Oz's drawing of a purple unicorn with blood dripping from its horn flew off and floated to the floor.

She scraped bacon grease from a cast iron skillet and then wiped it dry, and when she turned around to put it away, she noticed the crumb on the breakfast bar. "Who the hell left that?" she hissed. "I spend all this time cooking and cleaning, and they can't be bothered to clear off a damned crumb?"

Now, something I should have considered was that Donna did not like me on the counters and table any more than Jax did. But the crumb was something I could fix for her; it didn't matter what sort of crumb it was, I could eat it, and it would be gone, and she would be happy.

So I jumped from the chair to the breakfast bar and swiped at the crumb with my tongue, pleased when it was gone on the first lick. I heard the elevator door slide open, and turned to see who was coming home, and only saw the shadow of the skillet as Eli entered the living room.

She swung it as hard as she could, aiming for my head, screaming that she'd had enough, and I knew I wasn't supposed to jump up there. I sensed it coming and leaped at the same time

Eli yelled her name, and a half second after, the skillet crashed down onto the countertop.

She swung it again. "Goddamned filthy cat! Never again!"

Eli was across the room and had her wrist in his hand before she could swing it a third time. He pulled the skillet away and tossed it to the floor, staring at her in horror, lips parted to speak, but he was unable to ask why she'd tried to hit me.

I cowered at the end of the breakfast bar; I should have jumped down and run, but I waited there and watched as she replayed the moment in her head, and as what she'd just done registered. She sucked in a deep breath and tears rolled over her eyelashes, and Eli let go.

"Wick, what have I done?" she cried.

Normally, I would have walked across the counter and gone to her, but I couldn't make myself move.

She sunk to the floor, wailing, sitting with her knees drawn to her chest. She cried with fists pressed to her lips, and Eli stood there with his mouth open, still not sure what was happening. I finally moved and jumped down, moving carefully toward her. I stood on my back legs and reached up, and tapped her arm with my paw, wanting her to know I wasn't mad.

The wailing became an agonized groan. "I killed Wick, I killed Wick, I killed Wick."

Eli snatched me up and set me on the table, ordering me to stay there. I thought he was going to sit on the floor and try to comfort her, but instead, he pulled out his phone and called for an ambulance. He watched her writhe on the floor and listened to her scream, helpless, until three guards rushed in with the medics, afraid to move, afraid to touch her, afraid to breathe wrong, and she was still crying when they wheeled her into the elevator.

= = =

Spoilers. She didn't kill me.

"Wick," Aubrey croaked. "Oh my god. How terrified were you?"

Probably not as much as Eli. But that's when he admitted there was something wrong.

"He told us she'd had a bit of a breakdown," Jax said. "I had no idea."

"It was your crumb, wasn't it?" Will asked Jax, dryly. He fished his phone from his pocket and flicked the screen on, tapping at a single number. Everyone remained quiet while he waited for an answer, and when it came, Will said, "The King will be in your office in fifteen minutes."

He didn't wait for a response.

Will went to Oz's room to ask her and Drew to watch the kids a bit longer, and when he came back, he said that once everyone was down for their naps, Drew would explain everything to Oz and Hyrum, and then they would tell Zed.

Take me with you.

"There's no need, Wick."

I got left behind when Eli took Donna out, and she was never the same. Please. Take me so I can see what Mass does to him and hear what he says. Don't make me stay here and worry. Don't make me stay here and think he's never coming back.

"All right, that's fair." He tapped his shoulder and I jumped up. "Stay with me unless Jax specifically asks for you."

He might need to be purred on when he talks to Mass.

"I might," Jax said when Will explained why I was going. "Will's purring is substandard. And weird."

"Not half as weird as the fact that my purring abilities even occurred to you," Will said. "However, if you like—"

"Bite me."

"It truly was your crumb, wasn't it?"

= = =

Mass was dressed in blue professional pajamas, and he waited for Jax in the hall outside his office. This was the first time he'd been summoned to see the king, and he seemed surprised to see Jax coming down the hallway without a compliment of guards. They were hovering, waiting in the hall around the corner, and others were circling to cover the hall behind where Mass stood.

"Here or there?" he asked Will before he said anything to Jax.

"There," Will said, gesturing to the portal that was just behind Mass.

Jax told them to wait a minute. "Don't you want at least a clue?"

"I know your history, Your Majesty," Mass said. "We'll do all the requisite scans to confirm and compare against the files preserved from your counterpart, but you have a tumor running through your brain. It's a rare hybrid, referred to in simple terms as a threading glioma, so named because it sends tendrils— threads— throughout the brain and until recently has been extremely difficult to eradicate."

"What's new?"

Mass turned and headed for the portal. "I am."

"He's not wrong," Will said as we headed through after Mass. "The other Jax had Jacobsen treating him. He employed an archaic approach in treating the tumor and refused to attempt more contemporary methods until he was threatened with the revocation of his license."

"Who threatened him?" Aubrey asked.

"You did," Will chuckled. "I believe you also threatened to bring a writ of treason against him, as he was clearly attempting to shorten the life of Pacifica's King."

"He always was a bast—" Jax stopped, just a few feet outside the portal. "Hell. Did we just transport to a ship or something?"

"Same hospital, same location, different building," Mass said. "Why?"

"He has a fascination with twentieth and twenty-first-century science fiction television programs," Will explained. "Show him how to open a door. Go on. It will be like watching a two-year-old discover the automatic doors at the grocery store."

We stopped at Mass's office. He unlocked the door and stepped back, gesturing for Jax to go inside. When the door opened with a swoosh, he grinned and stepped through, letting it close behind him. We waited while he went in and out several times until Aubrey told him that was enough; he was here to get his brain peeked at, not play with the doors.

"I can do both," he grumbled.

He was less impressed by the exam room across the blue brushed-metal-walls hall. It was spacious and brightly lit but contained only a platform surrounded by several monitors—on the wall behind the platform was a monitor that was at least seven feet long—and a desk tucked neatly to the side. On the ceiling, there was an oblong fixture four feet wide but only a few inches wide.

"That's a bio-scanner," Will answered when I asked about it.

Mass told Jax to get onto the platform and lie down, arms at his sides with his palms face down on the table while he accessed the scan he wanted.

"Clothes on or off?"

"You can get naked if you want, but it's not necessary." He looked up from his computer. "Either way, everyone in this room will see the outlines of your body. Inside and out."

Aisha started to back out of the room.

"You've seen naked men before," Jax said. "No need. I don't care."

"Aubrey might," Aisha said.

"I need you here," Aubrey said, softly.

Aisha moved away from Will and went to her, reaching for her hand. "All right. I'll lie and promise to not check out your husband's assets."

Jax stretched out on the table and closed his eyes, swallowing hard. He sucked in a deep breath and held it when Mass told him to, and the room was quiet other than the hum of the scanner moving on the rail overhead. We watched as images formed on the monitor on the back wall, starting with his head, and two minutes later we were looking at the innards of the King, outlined faintly by his skin.

The other monitors displayed individual areas; his head, his heart, his kidneys, his liver. Mass pushed away from the desk and told Jax he could get up, and when Jax was on his feet, he slid the platform out of the way and moved close to the back monitor.

"Aside from the tumor," he said after a few minutes, "you have a minorly damaged valve in your heart, equally minor scar tissue on your liver, four kidney stones, a sinus infection, and you dress to the right. I can fix all but that last one."

"He has heart disease?" Aubrey asked, horrified.

Mass pointed to the monitor displaying Jax's heart. "Not disease. This looks like a micro-tear covered with a bit of scar tissue. Have you ever taken a hard blow to the chest? It might explain this and your liver."

"I don't think so."

When you were little. You used your bed as a trampoline and fell on the footboard.

"I don't remember that, Wick."

You broke a bunch of ribs. I think you were Rhys's age. Maybe a little older.

"Wouldn't the liver have healed itself?" Jax asked Mass.

"If the laceration were significant enough?" He shrugged. "Clearly, the bleeding from it was treated. I'd have to see those records to know what your doctor did at the time."

"It doesn't matter," Aubrey said. She fixated on the monitor displaying his head. "We're here for that."

The tumor was lit in bright white. There were two marble-sized masses, one near his right ear, the other toward the back of his head, with thin tendrils winding through both sides of his brain.

"That's not awful," Mass said. "I've seen worse."

"It's horrible," Aubrey seethed. "This is what killed his mother. Don't you dare—"

Mass held a hand up to stop her. "I only meant that this is entirely treatable. A week in the tank, and he'll be fine. Everything your mother-in-law suffered? That won't happen. When we pull him out of the tank, every tiny thing wrong in his body will have been repaired. He'll literally be as good as new."

"Swear to it." She wasn't giving an inch. "On your life."

"My life, my wife's life, my mother's life."

"Don't do that," Jax said. He was an inch from the image of his brain, staring intently. "Surely there are odds against me.

Does anyone here ever come out of that tank…dead?"

"No. The mechanics won't allow for that possibility."

"But?" Jax prodded. "What's the failure rate?"

"Miniscule. One-eighth of one percent is stretching it, and those are patients with tumors worse than this and much older than you. And I, personally, have never lost someone, not to this."

Jax turned away from the monitor. "Your specialty isn't cancer. Your specialty is gender correction. What have you lost a patient to?"

"Suicide," Mass said bluntly. "And not here, in this timeline. In yours, I've lost two patients to post-surgical suicide. I was not as aggressive in insisting they follow up with psychological treatment as I should have been. Not everyone's family is as accepting as Jay's."

"That's not on you," Aisha said.

"I still count those as losses," Mass said. "But to this?" He pointed toward the monitor. "I've never lost a patient in or out of the tank."

Show him the tank. Once they see it and you explain they'll all feel better.

We moved down the hall to the operating room. Mass pointed to the blue line on the floor—don't go past that—and gave Jax and Aubrey some quiet time to take in all the details. This was the same room where Jay had undergone surgery; it was the same tank. He then explained the procedure: Jax would float in the gel, and he would have a few hundred thousand nanobots scurrying throughout his body, removing all traces of the tumor, all the scar tissue, and the kidney stones. His sinus infection would be cleared.

"When you come out, you might even feel a few years younger. If you'd like, you can look it, too."

"That would be difficult to explain," Jax said.

"And I'm already older than he is," Aubrey said. "Let's not make it more."

Mass raised an eyebrow. "You can spend a few days floating, too. A little rejuvenation here and there. It wouldn't be obvious, but you'd feel it."

"Tread lightly," Jax warned. "You just told the Queen she looks old."

"Scan her," Will said suddenly. When Aubrey objected, he added, "You've never had an exam so comprehensive. We're here, and Jax will be in that tank for several days. Take advantage of it."

Her eyes narrowed. "What do you know?"

"You have arthritis. Why not see where it's at, and take care of it now?"

Mass headed for the door. "Well, then. It's family examination time. You're all getting scanned. Even Wick."

= = =

Aubrey's arthritis was not pronounced, but it was visible and affected her spine, hips, and shoulders. Mass told her it could wait if she really wanted, but there was no point in putting it off until she had obvious pain from it. "You have tiny grandkids," he said. "Take care of it now so that getting down on the floor with them will be easier later."

Will, he pronounced, had abnormally tiny nipples and apparently dressing to the right was genetic, neither of which he was willing to treat.

"Holy shit, Will," Jax said, looking at the scan. "*That's* not genetic."

"It skips generations. A gift from my great grandfather, I believe."

Dude, he wishes.

"No wonder Oz is so happy," Aubrey snorted.

"He has two great grandfathers, you know," Jax grumbled.

"I have no notion concerning the state of Drew's genitals," Will chuckled. "But, indeed, Oz seems...content."

The amusement abated when Aisha slid off the table. Mass tilted his head as he looked at her scan, and without turning around, he said, "You're going in the tank. No argument."

"Like hell."

Mass pointed at the monitor to his left. "That ovary needs to be taken care of before it spreads."

"That's a simple treatment at home—"

"And no guarantee it won't recur. Do this now, and you're done with it. Your only real decision other than agreeing to treatment now is how much I program the system to do for you. We can just do the ovary, or we can take it a few steps further and ablate the uterus. No more menstruation, no more cramps, and no risk of pregnancy."

"Will already had—"

"Vasectomies can fail, and you're still fertile." Mass gestured to the monitor. "Based on the size of your unaffected ovary, I'm guessing you have ten to twelve more years until menopause."

"Do this," Will said quietly. "If not for yourself or me, do it for the kids. Don't make them see you go through treatment. Don't risk them overhearing that something is wrong."

With a heavy sigh, she said, "Fine. But only because I enjoy the idea of you shuttling between three rooms, keeping an eye on all of us."

Mass patted the table. "Come on, Wick. Let's peek inside you, too."

"Is this programmed for feline anatomy?" Will asked as he set me on the platform.

I rolled onto my back, paws in the air.

"Pick any living, oxygen-breathing, earth-born creature," Mass said. "It can diagnose anyone."

The table hummed under my back as the scan began, and a minute later he told me I could sit up. There was a tiny bit of scar tissue in my head where Will had removed a transponder, but other than that the system proclaimed me to be a healthy domestic feline roughly five months of age.

"Five months," Will breathed out.

Was that how old I was when Eli's friend sent me to null space?

"You were perhaps a few weeks younger. This explains quite a bit about my father, as well. He's aged, but not nearly as much as one might expect."

"Might explain you, too," Jax said. "You're a year younger than me but you still look like you're in your thirties. Maybe all that time in null space altered Finn's...issue."

"How old do you think I am?" Mass asked him.

"Fifty?"

Mass grinned. "Nice. I'll take that. Late sixties. We age a little slower here. And if it helps, compared to a forty-nine-year-old from the early twenty-first century, you look about thirty-eight. Our life spans are extending, and our aging is slowing down with it."

Aisha turned to Will. "I am *so* opting to have a few years shaved off. Now that it's possible, I don't want to be eighty with a fifty-year-old husband."

"We'll do it incrementally," Mass said. "A couple years here and there over the next decade or so, until you two are caught up to each other."

"Or until you die of old age," Will said, amused.

"I know how old I am when I die," Mass said. "There's probably not a single person who returned from being displaced that hasn't looked up their information. If I hold to the lifespan of the Mass who stayed in that When, I'll live another hundred ten-plus years."

"So, you'll basically still be alive when you're born," Jax mused.

"If time holds. Hell, think of how many Finns are running around."

"In this When?" Will asked. "Three, I think. My father, my predecessor's father, and Liam Finnegan."

"Those are the ones you know about. There must be hundreds—"

Will stopped him. He already felt obligations to the ones he knew, and he didn't want to extend that any more than he had to. He was close to his own father and the slightly older Finn, and he occasionally humored Liam Finnegan, but adding onto that would feel like work.

"Finnegan," Mass said. "Does he still want your DNA?"

Liam Finnegan had once sent women to get Will's DNA by any means; they failed and collected George Denton's DNA instead, which led to Isaac. Will allowed for the possibility that he would give the much, much older Finn a sample that would allow him to raise Will's clone, but only after he and Aisha had procreated.

"His focus shifted when my mother offered hers instead," Will said. "He's content with the notion of raising my sibling, and my father had no issue with her participation. He knows that if it were him, having lost me, he would want the same consideration."

"Is there a tiny Emperor sibling running around now?"

"Not yet. The first attempt was unsuccessful, but the subsequent one seems viable."

In the first operating room, Mass declared he would go in order of time needed in the tank—longest first—and handed Jax a pair of paper shorts to change into. Jax looked at them with a frown, wondering what the point was. They were coming off before he was put in the tank, weren't they?

"These are far easier for us to remove than, say, your underwear. And since most people want their family with them before going under—"

"I don't care."

"I do," Aisha said. She gave Jax kiss on his cheek and went to the hall to wait.

"Well, it's not like she didn't get an eyeful from the scan," he mused. He handed the shorts back to Mass and started pulling his clothes off. "How long will Aubrey take?" he asked Mass.

"A day, maybe two."

She folded his clothes as they came off.

"After he wakes you up, go home," Jax said to her. "Don't wait here. Head back, and I'll be a few minutes behind."

"I'm not—"

"Promise me," he said. "Tell me you won't wait here for days, watching me float in that tank. Go home. If you won't, I'm not getting in."

"I'll stay with him," Will said. "Aisha will only take as long as you, I presume." He looked to Mass for confirmation. "You can go back together. Head for the coffee shop downstairs, and we'll be right there."

"Order me a giant mug of hot chocolate," Jax said. "And coffee cake. The one that's loaded with cinnamon. Or a head-sized cinnamon roll with so much icing you won't be able to stop yourself from lecturing me about it."

"Agree, please," Will said. "Clearly, he's freezing in here."

"I hate you," Jax said.

"Of course, you do." He waited while Jax sat on the table next to the tank, and as Mass explained what would happen—he'd have a respirator, he'd be injected with a serum loaded with nanobots, then placed in the tank—and in roughly a week he'd be pulled out and woken up.

Oh. Tell him how they get the nanobots out.

Will did not translate that.

Instead, we went out into the hall so that Aubrey could give Jax a semi-private goodbye kiss. Twenty minutes later Jax was in the tank, and we were headed for the operating room next door, where Aubrey would have her arthritis removed, and once she was floating, we moved another door down.

Aisha didn't need an explanation of the procedure. She'd watched Jay as he was prepped for his surgery, all but the ouchy parts, and she'd sat by his tank for four days while his body was re-sculpted.

"You know, if you didn't want partial rejuvenation, you could sit upright in a waist-high tank," Will told her as she changed. "You'd be awake, and it would take less than four hours."

That didn't sway her. "Allow me some vanity, Bilbo."

"You'll still be out first," Mass said. "Eight hours, maybe nine."

"Why so fast?"

"We're not rebuilding the structure of the ovary. We're removing it. The ablation will occur at the same time, so no added time there."

"And how much pain will I be in when I'm done? Jay hurt for a week."

"Cramps at worst," Mass said. "We'll give you something before you're awake and it won't bother you at all."

Will stayed for all of it; the injections, the placement of the respirator, and he watched as she was moved to the tank. When her body settled near the center, he asked Mass how long it would really take.

"Eh. Six, maybe. I'm hedging the time in case it takes longer. If she were older, it might take the full eight, but we're only taking a couple years off her."

"And Aubrey?"

"As long as nothing fractures while the nanobots remove the rough bits from bone and no disks rupture when they're in the spine, she'll come out soon after Aisha. The timing is comparable, but I can only supervise one extraction at a time."

"Fair enough."

"Technically, Aubrey could take up to two days," he reminded Will. "I doubt it, but spine work is delicate. If a disk blows, the rebuild takes time. Aisha's surgery is pretty straightforward and typically goes quickly."

"Good to know." He pulled a chair from the corner and sat as close to the tank as permitted, reminding me that I was not allowed on the floor at all. I waited in his lap, watching tiny bubbles form around Aisha, and the techs that had come in to monitor her.

Will only got up once, when I needed to pee because nothing else was keeping him from her.

37

"My boobs are bigger."

Aisha stood in the center of the operating room, stark naked, hair dripping wet from the absurdly thorough cleaning she'd been given before being woken up, and she cupped herself. Mass barked out a clipped laugh, and his technicians looked away, though I saw the one who had been monitoring her vitals grin before she turned. Will tilted his head as if considering the matter, humoring her.

"Not bigger," he said. "Perhaps firmer?"

"Everything will sag a little less." Mass snatched up his computer tablet. "Time to rouse the Queen, and then you two can be on your merry way."

"She'll want to see Jax first," Will said before Mass was to the door.

Aisha was still fixated on her boobs. "Did they float in the gel? Like weird little alien orbs, wiggling back and forth?"

They did. Like aliens with pointy hats.

I thought it was warmer in the tank.

"Not that I noticed." He prodded her toward the room where her clothes waited. "Are you in any pain?"

She left the door to the changing room open. "No. Mass said he would give me something for the pain before I woke. But..."

"But?"

Her eyebrows knotted together. "Oddly, my ass hurts."

Oh. Tell her.

"The nanobots have to come out somehow," he reminded her.

They shoved a vacuum cleaner up there.

"Wick, they did not shove a vacuum cleaner—"

"Yeah, they kinda did," she said, laughing. "Did Mass say how it went?"

Will nodded. "The offending ovary is gone, and you are now effectively rendered sterile."

"And the more important thing—no more periods. No more cramps from hell. No more PMS."

"You still have the usual complement of hormones, Enzo. You'll continue to cycle through them until you reach menopause."

She called him a name right off the Queen's list.

We waited for Aubrey in the hall; no one with her could tell her how firm her boobs looked, other than Mass, and he wouldn't think to comment. I asked Will to hold me up to the window so I could see, and then he could pass along the message, but he refused, claiming it was inappropriate to discuss her body regardless of my intent.

But she might want to know.

"Jax will tell her later."

You better remind him to notice.

"And how will that conversation go, Wick? 'Jax, I know you just had a massive amount of cancer removed from your brain and the only thing your wife cares about is that you're all right, but you need to tell her that her breasts are perky and spectacular?'"

Yes.

"That would work on me," Aisha said as the operating room door slid open.

"I am not telling Jax to inspect and comment on Aubrey's breasts, no matter how wonderful they are."

"Oh, do," Aubrey said as she stepped into the hallway. "If he doesn't notice that I'm far less wrinkled than before, my feelings will be hurt."

"You weren't wrinkled," Will sighed. He got up, as he always did when a woman entered the room.

"Not where *you* can see."

"Fair enough."

Aisha opted to wait in the hall while Aubrey and Will went in to see Jax. She didn't want to offend his sense of modesty, while Will didn't care if it upset Jax that he saw him naked again. I stayed on Will's shoulder so that I would have a better view of the tank. Jax was floating in its center, his arms dangling an inch, knees bent, head leaning back. It looked uncomfortable, but Will assured me it was not.

"If you could get over the panic of being in water, I could show you," he said. "It's quite a bit like floating in the deep end of the pool. There's little sensation, yet you feel entirely supported."

Aubrey stepped up to the blue line. She crossed her arms as if trying to hold herself, and her breath hitched.

"He's fine," Will told her softly. "In fact, he's not just sedated. He's asleep and dreaming."

She glanced at the monitors. "You can tell that by peeking at all this data?"

Mass snorted. "He can tell that because REM sleep tends to cause erections."

"Aubrey, if you say you didn't notice, I will give him hell for years to come."

"I wasn't going to point it out, William." She tried to sound annoyed, but it made her laugh. As quickly as her amusement came, however, it vanished. "How can I just leave him here alone?"

"He won't be alone. I'll stay with him, and when he's done, we'll meet you in the coffee shop near the hospital. We'll be fifteen minutes behind, twenty at most."

She pointed out that they could time it to step through the portal less than a minute after her. There was no reason to leave the surgical floor; they could go to the coffee shop together.

"Because that's what he asked of us, Aubrey. We could be a minute or two behind, but it will take longer for us to make our way out. The guards will want to clear—"

"I know," she sighed.

He wants an excuse to have the giant cinnamon roll. With extra icing.

The corners of her mouth tugged up a tiny bit because I was right.

"Things are going well," Mass said from his spot near the tank. "Scar tissue and kidney stones are gone, and his heart valve has been repaired. Everything is now focused on the tumor, and there haven't been any hiccups."

Will slipped his arm around her and tugged a bit, urging her to leave. When she finally did, the moment she was in the hall, she grabbed Aisha into a giant hug and stood there, trying not to cry.

"Wick, you're going home with them," he whispered to me as he picked me off his shoulder.

In case she needs purr therapy?

"Exactly."

I can do that. It's not like I can help with the surgery, anyway. But you'll be bored.

"I can amuse myself."

You didn't bring your backpack. Your tablet is at home.

"I can borrow one from Mass. There are a dozen books I've wanted to read. I'll start there."

He handed me to Aisha, kissed her, and gently shoved them in the direction of the portal. Aisha took Aubrey's hand in case she wasn't thinking about where we needed to go and hoped the portal computer would accept her destination over Aubrey's. Half a breath later, we were a few feet from Mass's other office, and a few feet beyond that were the first set of guards waiting for Jax.

She told them that Jax would be a few minutes. Her own guards stepped from their positions; her personal guard asked where we were headed, then lead the way. I spotted several more of the royal guard dressed in regular clothing, lingering in chairs along the way, some pretending to read or listen to music, but they made note of her and that she was not with the King.

One of them got up when he spotted us, and casually strolled in the direction of the exit. He hesitated for a fraction of a second, not long enough for anyone but Aubrey's guards to notice; his hand twitched, one finger lifting a quarter of an inch in the direction of two reporters who waited in the lobby near the front desk.

Jax's entry to the hospital had been noted, but their own security hadn't allowed them past the desk. The first reporter to spot Aubrey jumped up and rushed in her direction, calling out questions, but was stopped by her head guard with a firm hand to his chest.

The other reporter waited quietly, patiently, and when she was close, he took a step away from his chair and bowed his head before saying, "Ma'am. May I ask how the King is?"

She met him halfway across the floor. "He's fine," she said, voice even. "He had a headache that turned out to be a sinus infection, nothing horrible. He'll be down when he and the Emperor are done taking juvenile swipes at Dr. Massimo."

"Boys," Aisha snickered.

Aubrey turned to a guard behind her. "Call up and tell Jackson's guard that Mr. Butler is waiting to speak with him. He should give him a few minutes, if for no reason other than to assure everyone that he's fine and his visit is simply because of his sinuses."

Make him blow his nose and show snot as proof.

"Know him?" Aisha asked once we were on the sidewalk outside.

"Terrence Butler. He's reported on the royal family for over thirty years and has always been careful and respectful."

"So, one of the good guys."

"Oh, he can be brutal. He doesn't let polite consideration get in the way of a story. I have no doubt that before he leaves here today, he'll use a public information declaration to get a look at the records of Jax's visit with Mass."

"And the message was to make sure his sinuses are on that record."

"It's not a lie," Aubrey answered. "He does have a sinus infection. Given that his other issues were treated elsewhere, there's no reason for that treatment to be on record here."

"But Mass will keep that information somewhere."

"There, I hope," Aubrey said. "If he brings any of it home, it's discoverable. Imagine trying to explain that."

Nanobots ate my brain. Story at eleven.

The coffee shop was unusually quiet; there were people at three tables, and a few of the guard had been directed to get there ahead of us, but the noise level that usually cut through me when the door opened was only a dull buzz and not at all unpleasant. The aroma of coffee, tea, and hot chocolate, and the sweet scent of cinnamon and baked rolls and scones hit me before the low rumble of conversation. What I did not smell was bacon. Will always got me a slice of bacon.

"Heads up," Aubrey said as the door closed behind us. "Your ex is here."

James was at the counter. Aisha looked around the coffee shop for George, spotting him on the far side, pacing in a short line between tables. He was holding Isaac, who had his head on George's shoulder and an arm looped around his neck. The three-year-old's eyes were closed, and he was pale, and his father looked pained.

Instead of going to the counter to order and to greet James, Aisha headed for George and Aubrey followed.

Without saying hello, Aisha's hand went to Isaac's forehead. "He's warm," she said, as if George didn't know. "What's wrong?"

Isaac's eyes fluttered open. "Yeesha." He lifted his head and reached out for her, and she took him, patting his back when he settled his head on her shoulder.

"You don't have to," George said.

"Hush." She didn't have to comfort her ex's husband's tiny clone, but Jay considered him to be his little brother every bit as much as Rhys and Charlie were, and she'd spent enough time with him to feel an attachment. Isaac spent many afternoons in her home, playing with Rhys while Jay babysat. It didn't matter from whose DNA he sprang; he was a little boy who loved her, and she loved him back.

"There's nothing wrong that his doctor can find," George said. "He's listless, won't eat, he runs random fevers..."

"How long has he been here?" she asked, meaning this When, not the coffee shop.

"Three weeks."

"That would be pretty quick for time to start picking at him," Aubrey mused.

Isaac had spent months in a row in this When; he'd never shown any sign of the sickness that befell the anchorless migrants from the future, and George thought he might be a child of both Whens, without the need for one.

"Jay noticed a pattern," George said, gesturing for them to sit. "In the last six months, the time between trips here and there have shortened, and Isaac always has a stomach ache or loses his appetite before we go home. And each time it seems worse."

"How long do you stay there?"

"Just long enough for me to re-center."

James brought his and George's coffee over. "He needs an anchor here."

"I thought it would be you or me," George said. "Even Jay."

Get him a cat. Or even a puppy. Maybe he just doesn't want to go back there and gets a tummy ache. But get him a cat anyway.

"You probably have all the answers," George said when he heard me speak. "Where's the Emperor when I need him to translate?"

"He'll be here soon," Aisha said.

I jumped onto the little table and tapped Isaac's back, then meowed. No words were riding on it; my straight meow was different, and Aubrey had learned to tell the difference.

"What are you trying to tell us?" she asked.

I tapped my paw against Isaac's back and meowed again, then turned and sat in front of her. When she still didn't get it, I went back and rubbed my face against his hip and returned.

I did it twice more, rubbing my nose with my paw each time I sat.

He needs a pet. He'll anchor to a pet.

"You think he needs a cat?"

I rubbed my face against her arm.

"It worked for Will," Aisha said.

"George hates cats," James said.

"I'd tolerate one for his sake," George said. He got up and held his arms out for his son. "Maybe when we come back. Jay's taking us home for a bit. But I'll certainly think about it."

"We're getting a cat," James said, trying not to squeal.

"We're getting a cat," George sighed.

"Two?" James asked hopefully.

"Don't push it." He nuzzled his face against Isaac's head, breathing in the scent of little boy. "Fine, if he wants a bonded pair, yes. But no more than that, James. And the litter box is your job."

Aisha watched as they wound their way to the door. "Proof that people can change," she uttered. A guard opened the door, and Jax stepped in; George gave a short nod of his head and said, "Your Majesty," as he waited for Will to step inside.

"Did you ever imagine this?" Aubrey asked. Will shook both James's and George's hands, and they took a moment to speak. Will reached out to rub Isaac's back, and he nodded to whatever George told him. "Civility, yes, but they're almost friendly."

"George told Navi he despises the man Jay grew up with as a stepfather. He's actually grateful to Will for being the man Jay needed."

Jax was tired. He smiled when he spotted Aubrey, but his eyes didn't light up the way they usually did, and he was slow to make his way across the coffee shop. Will set a steadying hand on his back; to anyone else it was a warm, brotherly gesture, but to Aubrey, it was a warning.

"Headache, that's all," Jax said before she could get upset. "Mass said the drugs will kick in soon. I didn't want to hang around until they did."

She wanted to hug the stuffing out of him but worried it would look odd. She settled for a quick kiss and then asked what had taken so long.

"Once we were back, Will made me stop to shave. And as you requested, I gave Butler a few minutes."

"And your record for seeing Mass today?"

"He made the appropriate entry," Will said. He pointed to the patch on Jax's neck. "Make sure he leaves this on through the rest of the day. It will cure that annoying sinus issue."

It's for pain, right?

"Yes, Wick. But if anyone asks, it's for the infection."

Will grabbed a chair for Jax, but before he could sit, the

door opened, and Eli barreled his way in. He pushed past his own guard and bellowed, "Where the hell is my son?" at Jax's head guard.

I thought he was in New York.

"He was," Will said.

Eli sped across the shop when the guard pointed in our direction. His eyes were red and lashes wet, and when he grabbed Jax into a hard hug, he began sobbing, begging for the kids to have been wrong. "Not you. Not like this."

Will had his phone in hand before Eli could get another word out. "I'll alert them that they need not worry."

It took a full minute before Jax could extricate himself from his father's arms. He leaned back just a touch so that he could see Eli's face, the corners of his mouth tugging up just a bit. "Dad. It's all right. I'm all right. I promise. I'm fine."

"You saw what this did to your mother." Eli's voice cracked, and tears ran down his cheeks.

Jax asked Will to step over. "Dad," he said, softly so the few people in the coffee shop wouldn't overhear, "I can't explain it here. Will can tell you silently if you'll let him."

Eli didn't wait. He grabbed Will in a hug as tight as the one he'd given Jax. Will's hand went to the bare skin on the back of his neck, and a few seconds later Eli sagged with relief. He now had, in perfect images, everything Will knew and everything Will had seen, from the moment we stepped through the portal until Jax was pulled from the tank.

"I promise you, he's fine and the cancer is gone," Will whispered when Eli finally let go.

"That quickly?" Eli sat in the chair Jax scooted toward him. "Finn called me less than an hour ago."

"How the hell did you get here so fast?" Jax asked.

Eli tugged on his shirt sleeve and showed him the transporter bracelet Finn had taken to him. "I'm supposed to return this to you, Emperor," he said. "He sent me to Dr. Massimo's office, and I've been chasing you from there." As Will unclipped the bracelet, Eli went on, "Why didn't you call me? Why didn't you let me know before running off to Will's When?"

"Why would I worry you? I should have asked the kids to not call you at all. I intended to tell you after."

Loud enough for everyone to hear, Eli barked, "I am your *father*, Jackson. I deserve that much consideration. I need—"

"You need coffee," Aisha said. "Double mocha, extra sweet?"

"Yes, thank you. Now see that, Jackson? She's considerate. Thoughtful."

Jax refused to bite. "You needed to not worry, Dad. There was nothing you could do, and there was no firm diagnosis until we were through the portal."

"But I could have *been* there," he argued.

Aubrey reached across the table for his hand. "Seeing the scans would have broken your heart, Eli. They broke mine, even when I knew he would be all right regardless."

"I couldn't do that to you," Jax said.

"I *want* my heart broken," Eli hissed. "Every important thing, good or bad, let me decide how invested I should be."

"People can hear, Dad."

He jerked his hand away from Aubrey. "I don't care. Let them hear. I can't bear the idea of something happening to you. I don't care if they know."

Woman at the table just past the door is recording this.

"Her audio will be less than ideal," Will said. "At best, she'll have video proof that the King and his father had an argument, based on body language."

Eli didn't flinch, but he also didn't want their argument to flame public speculation. "Fix this, William."

Will went to the counter where Aisha was putting a lid on Eli's coffee and spoke to the cashier. By the time she had returned and set the cup in front of Eli, Will was moving from table to table, handing out gift cards along with an apology for disrupting their afternoon. All was well, it was a simple misunderstanding between father and son.

When he reached the woman who was recording everything, he sat with her. I waited for him to take the phone and delete the video, but instead, she lifted it and recorded his explanation for what she'd been watching: King Jackson's father had misunderstood a message and was worried about his health. Surely, this would be the sinus infection that went down in history...and a reminder to the King that he is someone's treasured son, and he should call his father more often.

"Yes, he should," Eli scoffed when Will related the message he'd agreed could be uploaded and shared online.

"You live downstairs," Jax pointed out.

"I live in New York. I have an apartment downstairs."

"Do I need to call my daddy every day?"

"Yes. You do. Call me every evening. Shoot me a text every morning."

"Every morning," Jax repeated.

"Why not? Aubrey does."

Jax turned to her. "You text him every morning?"

"Just to say good morning."

"And she tells me she loves me," Eli said. "When was the last time you did that, Jackson? Hm?"

"Fine," Jax said. "I'll start sending messages when I get up at four to spend time with Hyrum. 'Dammit, good morning, you cranky old bastard. I love you.'"

"Thank you."

"I do love you, Dad."

Eli lifted his coffee cup. "If you loved me, you would have fetched my coffee instead of letting Aisha do it."

"I would have, if not for this headache." Jax pressed fingers to his forehead. "Ow."

"Snowflake," Eli snorted. "It's a sinus headache. I didn't realize you were so fragile."

"Of course, I am. I grew up with an oppressive father, always in his shadow, never knowing if I was loved or simply tolerated." Jax sniffed pretentiously. "It was horrible. My self-esteem never grew, and—"

"Aye, you're so full of it. Come on, get your food and drink and then take me home so I can see my grandkids and then get the little ones so riled up they can't sleep tonight."

= = =

Sean McAllister sat at a table near the bakery with Hyrum; he typed furiously on a computer tablet while Hyrum dug donuts from a bag, setting them carefully on napkins before licking the frosting from his fingers. He spotted Aisha first and smiled, but then saw Eli behind her. He thrust his arms in the air, hands in fists, and he shouted "Eli!"

Eli stopped where he was and pumped his fists in the air, too, and yelled, "Hyrum!"

"Mr. McAllister didn't even flinch," Jax mused.

"He's spent enough time with Hyrum to be used to the outbursts," Will said.

He stood when we were closer, and while Hyrum leaped from his seat to hug Eli, Sean held up the tablet. "I was just typing out a note for you, sir," he said to Jax.

"Oz said I could come outside if I wanted," Hyrum interrupted. "I promised to not go far. It's okay, isn't it?"

"You don't need permission, sweetheart," Aubrey said. "As long as you let someone know where you'll be, you can go anywhere you want."

"I didn't say I was getting donuts," he told her, half whispering. "The babies were going down for naps, and I didn't want them to feel bad."

"You can't possibly need more material for your article." Jax took the seat next to Hyrum and nodded toward Sean's chair so that he would feel free to sit. "What's up?"

"This isn't about the article. It's what I overheard when I was in the lab with the cops. About the car that wrecked."

That got everyone's attention.

Sean had waited at the kitchen table, surfing online with a tablet Finn lent him. The officers sat with him, discussing the wreckage and the men who had walked away from it without a scratch between them, while they typed up reports on laptops.

"I'm kind of nosy. I could see the one guy's screen and got names, and then looked them up. They're both from Florida, Graham Hinkley and Zeke Nelson. Those names kinda poked at me because they seem so, I dunno, Florida-ish, so I dug around online. The first mention I found was a listing of delegates for the

Prime Minister's reception—they were part of the grunt crew, the guys who handle the piddly errands and stuff. But digging a little deeper? They're both members of the Coalition to Restore Faith."

"Newly formed group protesting the acquisition of Florida," Will explained when Aisha and Aubrey looked confused. "They intend to return the church to Florida's government and break away from Pacifica."

"By all means possible," Eli added.

Sean wasn't done. "The thing is, these guys are like bottom feeders. They have no status in the coalition. They're errand boys, same as they are in the Florida delegation. But one of them, Hinkley, has been all over social media bragging about his new status within the group, and how he was going to bring big things to the table. Like, this week. And a couple days ago he posted to the Florida Faithful Forever message board that he would see everyone in the celestial kingdom."

He handed the tablet to Will. "The responses make it seem like he was just saying goodbye for the time he would be here, and it's just the messed-up way people talk to each other there, but honestly? My gut reaction was that these guys were on a suicide mission, and they fully intended to kill the King."

"How would they have even known he was here, on the Square?" Aisha asked.

Sean shrugged. "That's beyond my pay grade. But I saved all the info I pulled up, and it's attached to the note I was writing. I thought you should know."

"I'll have to wipe your tablet once I've pulled off what I need," Will said.

"It's your dad's. I hope he doesn't mind that I took it out of the lab, but—"

"He will not."

"Sir, you don't seem surprised," Sean said to Jax.

"There are thousands of people who want me dead," he said, beckoning his head guard over. "The only real surprise is the public venue and the startling sloppiness of the attempt."

Aubrey reached over and patted Sean's hand. "Thank you. This is invaluable."

"You're welcome." He got up, thinking he would leave everyone to the rest of their afternoon, but hesitated. "Mr. Blackshear, are you okay? I mean, with everything and that—"

"I'm fine. It's been taken care of. Or will be, in a couple of centuries."

"And off the record, I understand."

Jax nodded. "Officially, it was just a sinus infection. And if I keep saying that, I might start to believe it."

"Sir, I'm not sure I'll write the article, anyway. I'm starting to feel like it would be intrusive, and we don't have a right to your personal life."

"Write your article, Sean." Jax got up and extended his hand. "Tell the truth as you see it, minus the things you know you can't reveal."

Sean shook his hand, but his jaw dropped.

"What?" Jax asked.

"That's the first time you've called me by name."

"Huh. Maybe. Mr. McAllister has an alliterative ring to it that I enjoy. Future use of it is not personal. It's just fun to say."

"I swear, the tumors were removed," Aubrey sighed.

When he was gone, Jax told Will to comb through the information Sean had given him and to forward it to the head of the guard. She would expect it soon and would take it from there. Aubrey thought he was a bit too calm about it—that wasn't just a threat, but an active attempt on his life—and wondered why he wasn't demanding their heads.

"We don't behead," he said lightly. "We only threaten to."

"Jackson."

He bent over to kiss her. "Angel, right now I'm just glad to be alive, and I want to go home and see my kids and grandkids, tell them I love them, and put all this behind me."

"Good luck with that," Will said. "They'll all hover for the next month."

"Like you won't."

"Eh." Will half-shrugged. "You're in no danger of dying now. But I do think we need to hit Fuzzy's and celebrate."

He'd keep an eye on Jax as much as everyone else, and he knew it.

Aisha started to get up when Eli and Hyrum did, but Will reached for her hand and stopped her. "We still need to talk. Away from the kids."

"Bilbo, whatever it is, it can't be that bad." She looked up at Aubrey. "Can it?"

Aubrey kissed Will on his cheek. "Remember, it was my fault."

"It truly was not."

Jax offered to take me inside, but I wasn't moving. If she took a swing at him, I wanted to be there. I especially wanted to be there if she kneed him in the groin.

Witnesses are important.

38

Aubrey had gone into the simulator for two reasons: she hoped Jax was close to an epiphany about his health, and Aisha had mused that Rhys and Hyrum were probably having the time of their lives and wouldn't want to leave with Finn. If Aubrey hadn't wanted to be there for Jax, she would have stayed home and watched Alex and Charlie so that Aisha could go and play with her old friends in Saint Francis.

Without telling Aisha why she needed to be there, Aubrey made it clear that she wanted to be the one to go.

"I knew he was with you, Bilbo," she said, a bit amused at his discomfort and horror over the decisions he'd made. "I also know the simulator is a risky place, but since we were there, Finn added tighter safety protocols. There's no chance in hell those dogs would have gotten to Rhys. The sprites might have some weird allegiance to Drew, but I'll bet you real money that Finn programmed them to protect anyone not part of the simulation."

"That doesn't change the potentially life-long trauma inflicted—"

"Will. Stop. You're overthinking. If he's terrified of dogs, we'll deal with it. Quit focusing on that one thing and focus on everything you gave him by taking him with you. He had time with his daddy away from his little brother and sister. He got to ride on a motorcycle, and then he played games while he floated in the air. He met the dragon and giant cat from his favorite stories. He played in the snow. He and Hyrum began working on their gifts together. And he saved a life."

"Still."

"He saved a life," she stressed. "He saved the boy who tried to hurt him. All those good things are what he'll remember if those are the things we remind him of. And now we know what kind of person he is. He's not just a good boy, Will. He's a good person. And that Asmonk kid proved it."

He wanted to believe her. He also wanted her to get angry, to yell, because if she did, he would have a reason to defend himself and let go of the guilt.

She wasn't going to give that to him.

"He'll want to go back," Will said. "He doesn't understand the concept of simulated people and counts Quinn as a friend now."

"Of course, he does. He found a playmate. He doesn't really have that here. We'll take him back every now and then."

You were gonna go back before and look how long it took.

"I know, Wick," Will said. "But this time we'll have a little boy reminding us that some things shouldn't be put off."

Like teaching him to better deal with the things he can do? Closing your fist over his hand won't work anymore.

"It might, for a while."

He can do more with it than you know, I think. He controlled how much power he shot into Asmonk's chest. He doesn't know what else he can do, but it's coming.

"How old were you when you were truly aware of the things you could do?" Aisha asked him.

"When I could articulate it? Roughly Rhys's age. My parents realized before I did."

Don't make the same mistakes they did. Or that Valerie did with Hyrum. Don't keep him isolated.

"Never. And he has the advantage of siblings, something I did not." Will looked up to the balcony where Jax and Eli were now sitting. "I'll learn from my parents' mistakes, Wick. We'll teach him to share the burdens of what he's been given, along with the wonders of it. Something I wish I had been able to do when I decided to stay here."

"Finn never should have insisted you keep things so secret.

Jax would have accepted you, and so would Eli. They would have understood why you stayed."

"Eli knew," Will snorted. "He'd met me as a little boy, and I had no idea."

"And Aubrey would have helped you learn control all those years ago."

But then there would be no Jay because you two would have started doing bouncing things when you were teenagers, and everything would be different.

"Stop using logic when we're talking like this," Aisha said, tapping my head with her pointy finger. "We know. That doesn't mean there aren't regrets or that we don't wish for the years we missed out on."

Fine.

I turned and looked at the balcony, too.

How long does Eli live? I'm just curious.

"No telling," Will said. "His circumstances have changed as much as the rest of us."

Did the other one live long enough to see Oz end the monarchy?

"He did," Will said, getting up. "And from what I read? Holy hell, he was pissed."

I turned to Aisha. *Will said "pissed."*

"According to Drew, we're turning both Hyrum and him into real live boys, Wick."

"I swear, I'll stop translating for you," Will grumbled.

That's fine. I still have Drew. And probably Hyrum in a few years.

"Good." He scooped me up and set me on his shoulder. "Go live with Drew and Oz. Talk at them until three in the morning. The quiet will be nice."

You have toddlers.

You don't get to enjoy quiet for about twenty years.

= = =

Will set me on the floor once we were up the stairs. I was

less interested in the quiet conversation coming from Oz and Drew's room than they were, so while they went to check on their offspring, I headed for the balcony where Eli and Jax were enjoying an expensive bottle of scotch and the outdoor heater Oz had given Drew for Christmas.

Tiny warm fingers reached out from its base and massaged my furs. Even when I jumped to Eli's lap, I could feel it wrapping me in a warm hug, and I wondered why it had taken so many years for someone to think of getting one. I was almost willing to trade my hover cart for one.

Almost.

And totally theoretically.

"My brain—no, my soul—went numb," Eli said to Jax as his hands went to my back. "It was as if I couldn't comprehend what they were telling me. I'd just witnessed the love of my life trying to kill this incredible beast—" he fluffed my fur a bit "— and while I knew something was very wrong, I wasn't prepared for the truth. I sat in that room and stared at the images of her brain, lit up like a Christmas tree, and the news simply would not settle."

They walked through the next weeks as if lost in the thick fog that often curled around the city. Eli performed his duties by rote, and Donna hid at home, sometimes staying in bed for days on end. She got up when she had to, for appointments and treatments, and she bent to Aubrey's will when her daughter-in-law insisted that she sit out on the balcony for fresh air. She accepted Aubrey's authority over her diet, forcing herself to take at least small bites of the meals made specifically for her. She stopped taking care of the apartment, pretending not to notice that Will often slipped in and cleaned when no one else was looking.

Words left her mind in complex sentences but exited her mouth in frustrated clips that she often had to repeat to make herself understood. Most days, she welcomed me onto her lap so that I could purr for her, and other days she believed she'd killed me and was terrified of my ghost.

Her behavior remained erratic, and there were days when

she couldn't remember what was wrong with her. Eli stopped reminding her, because it brought the grief of the diagnosis to the surface all over again, something neither of them could handle.

"That last major appointment, though," Eli said with a sigh. "I'd taken her to someone new because Jacobsen admitted he had exhausted his ideas. Jerome DelOro. At the time, he was the most sought-after expert in the field. We sat in his office while he pored over the scans and treatment notes, silent, barely breathing, and when he finally looked up, he seemed as sad as we were. He said that at this point he could throw everything at her again and combine it with centuries-old treatments based on radiation and chemicals, but the truth was that she still had less than a ten percent chance of survival, and she would suffer horribly."

While Eli tried to digest that statement, one he couldn't make sense of—of course, she would survive, she was his queen—Donna stood, and with more clarity than she'd displayed in months, she announced that she was done. Eli was still trying to swallow, and she had already digested. No more. She'd reached the end of it all and just wanted to enjoy what little time she had.

"Even then, I don't think she honestly believed she would die. And for all her bravado, she was terrified."

"Except that last week," Jax mused.

Donna's last week was soft and relaxed. Though they didn't know it until years later, Will had gone to her and set his hand on her forehead, giving her all the things he knew, the answers to the questions that frightened her most, and the truth of the happy life her son would live along with the joy of who her grandchildren would become. He told her who he was and how he'd come to be there and made sure that she felt as loved as she truly was.

"I wish I'd known William had done that," Eli whispered.

"Will prefers to give of himself quietly, and it was private. He didn't understand that your grief would have lessened a little bit if you'd known."

"My grief never lessened. But my guilt would have."

Jax wished that Zed hadn't called Eli. There was no need to frighten him with information that was surely going to change before the call had ended.

"To be fair," Eli said, "I heard 'brain' and 'cancer' and panicked. I hung up on him and called Finn, and wouldn't listen to him, either. I just started begging him to get hold of one of William's transporters and then come get me."

"Well, I'm glad you're here, but I wish you'd come for some other reason. Like, Sunday afternoons. Every week Aubrey wishes you were home for the big family dinner."

"This has been a hell of a wakeup call, Jackson. More so than when I agreed to stay put for a few months."

Jax wanted to know how. He'd done as he promised, he came to live and stayed until he was needed to take the slot as representative to the Consortium. They understood why he was gone more than he was home.

"Eh. I don't need to spend so much time in New York these days. I want to move my offices here. I miss my grandkids and great grandkids. I miss the fog. I miss the cat."

"What you miss is Aubrey's cooking," Jax teased.

"Who wouldn't? But what struck me when we walked across the Square this afternoon was how much I miss Hyrum. The unbridled joy in that boy..."

"You realize he's almost as old as Will and I."

"And you realize I still think of you both as my boys. I've come to love Hyrum just as much."

"Hard not to. I'll cut the bitch who tries to get him to leave here."

Eli laughed, hard. "Did you just call your mother-in-law a bitch?"

"If the shoe fits... I mean, I get it. She felt tied down because of him, and she couldn't defend him from Levi. But she sure as hell should have done a better job at protecting him from knowing that she's happier with him living here. She never sees him."

Hyrum didn't really want to see her, either.

The door creaked open and Will came out, warning them

that the apartment was now overrun with kids and grandkids. Everyone was there, including Jay and Navi, and they were doing their best to whip the little kids into a frenzy.

"There is discussion about having a slumber party, complete with matching pink pajamas. I left before I could be convinced to agree."

"You'd be outvoted anyway," Jax said. "I hope you like pink pajamas."

"I'm stunning in pink."

He has pink underwear.

"Indeed, Wick, I now have pink underwear. So do Jax and Eli. Hyrum gifted them to us for Christmas, and I wear them often."

"Most damned comfy things I own," Eli said. He turned at the sound of the door opening and smiled when Oz slipped out.

"Oh my god, the noise," she groaned. "Four toddlers, four grown men who are acting like toddlers, and a baby looking at all of them like he's just waiting for his turn to scream. And mom is sitting there like it's all perfectly normal."

Jax reached for a chair and pulled it next to his. "She doesn't mind the noise. That's one big reason why you were allowed so many huge parties when you were a teenager. She enjoys seeing kids having fun and believes they should be allowed some noise."

"Has she had her hearing checked? Because it's insane."

Aisha was in the thick of it but had a bottle of wine close by. Jax agreed, another drink was a good idea, and pulled the bottle of scotch out from under his chair.

Oz's hands settled on her belly. "That's mean. No one else should be allowed to drink until I can, too."

No one else was agreeing to wait until she'd had the baby and then weaned him. "Besides, Sophia isn't drinking," Jax said. "You can whine about it together."

"If she were home," Oz grumbled. "She's at some meeting with a realtor. She and Zed bid on space at the Ferry Building and they're one of the top contenders."

"Management is going through the motions," Will said. "Her competition is another coffee shop. There are already two in the building and several others in the area. Her café is far and away better suited to the space."

"Also," Jax said, "he cheats and knows things." He leaned back and considered Will for a moment. "We've been there, haven't we? Sof-why-Z."

"Sof y Z," Will said, pronouncing the Spanish 'and.' "And yes, we have. It will look different, but it's the same café."

"Sophia and Zed," Oz murmured. "He calls her Soph all the time."

"I just thought it was a clever way to spells "Sophie's," Jax said. "And I know, we keep it to ourselves, you heartless bastard."

"If you told her, you'd spoil her joy when she's awarded the lease. Give her that."

"You're still a bastard," Jax said. "But don't be one when I tell you this. I want to go back into the simulator. I feel like I need to settle up with Tobias."

"Dad, why?" Oz asked. "You let him live. That's settled up enough."

"I feel like I tormented him and his family without good reason, Ozzy. I *hunted* the man, and his wife knew what I was doing. How horrific was that for her?"

"They're all data points on a hard drive," she reminded him.

"Those data points are self-aware," Will said. "They learn. They have lives that continue even when no one is using the simulator. All of it takes place on the hard drive, but the program doesn't pause for them, and their lives feel every bit as much real to them as ours do to us."

"I need to go back and right my wrongs," Jax said.

Oz didn't yield. "Even if they are aware, it's still a computer-generated game. It gives you what you need, Dad. Not what you want."

"I didn't need to kill anyone."

"Neither did I. And that was the point. The point was making me understand what I really needed."

"And that was?"

"Help. I needed help to deal with everything Levi Munson did to me. To admit what it really was. And when Will realized what was happening, he let it play out so that I could get to the end game and do whatever the hell was necessary so I could see that."

"So, what was the game trying to make me see?"

"Same thing, Dad. Something was wrong, you couldn't see it, and needed to. Tobias doesn't need an apology. He was a tool, doing his job."

"He just wants to go play some more," Will said. "Eli, do you want to see the simulator?"

"I do not." He got up. "I just want to see the babies play, and then ask Hyrum to read a story or two. I miss that."

"He's in the thick of everything," Oz warned.

"Good." He took a step and then turned to Will. "Find me office space close by. Daddy's coming home to stay."

"Is it just me," Jax said when the door closed behind his father, "or is it a little bit creepy when he says stuff like that?"

"It's a bit creepy," Will agreed.

Little hands slapped at the door, and when he couldn't push it open, Charlie pressed his face against the glass. It fogged around his nose, and spit dripped down the glass where his tongue pressed up against it. Will sighed hard and got up to open it for him.

"Daddy!" he squealed. "We habin' boobie night! Come see!"

"I'll be there in a bit."

"Unca Jax! Boobie!"

"I've seen a few already, kiddo."

"Come see!"

"Whose boobs are we inspecting?" Jax asked as he got up to help Oz wiggle out of her chair.

"Movie," Will said.

"Damn. I was hoping for—"

"Dad," Oz groaned.

"Oh, like you don't flap yours around Drew's face every chance you get."

"Oh. My. God."

He held the door for her. "Darlin', I did not die this week. I dodged the metaphorical bullet. If I want to celebrate with boobs, then I should celebrate with boobs. Presuming the owner of the boobs agrees."

"You're drunk."

"Maybe. But I'm a happy drunk. And drunk me wants boobs, and to go back and deal with the wizard. In that order."

= = =

Oz and Drew curled up together in Aubrey's comfy chair while the movie played, sound low because everyone under five had fallen asleep on the floor, and the sofa was taken by Zed and Sophia. After promises by Jay and Navi to watch Rhys and the twins, Will and Aisha fled to the quiet of their apartment upstairs. Eli was snoozing in Jax's chair, and Hyrum had given up and gone to his room.

"He's super active tonight," Drew said, his hand splayed across Oz's belly. "This is awesome. I don't think I'll ever get tired of this."

"Says the guy who doesn't get woken up at three in the morning with a heel stomped into his bladder. One of us is tired."

"Cut back your hours. The Wasteland park will wait."

It wouldn't, and he knew it. Oz had a deadline to meet and investors to appease, overactive baby or not. "That's not the reputation I want to build. Until he's born, I'm getting the work done."

"And after that? You're taking time off, right?"

"As much time as you are."

"Good. Because I told Will I was taking a couple of months. He can hold down the fort."

The Wastelands project was part of Ozoo Enterprises. Will was going to be a busy man.

"Hey, look down the hall," Oz whispered.

Jax and Aubrey were standing just beyond their open bedroom door. Her hands were on his face, fingers gently caressing his ears. His eyes were closed, and his breath hitched just before she leaned in to kiss him.

"Is he crying?" Drew asked.

"He's had a hard day. A car almost landed on him, he wound up in another When, did a bunch of crazy stuff and then tried to kill a wizard. And then there's the whole brain cancer thing. It takes a toll on a guy."

"I can't believe he wants to go back. There's nothing to make right with Tobias. He gets to live, and he gets his family. There's nothing about any of that Tobias won't be happy with. And the rest of them can suck it if it bothers them."

"You're going with him, right?"

"If he'll let me. Will's going, but I don't know if he wants anyone else there."

Her hand settled on top of his. "I'd go if not for this guy. There's not a snowball's chance in hell I'd risk it now."

"We'll go after he's born. Just so Shivan and Hagar can meet him."

"Can you take pictures in the simulator? I want a picture of grown-up Shivan. And of Jeff and Fluffy."

Drew turned to look at Jay. "Oh man, I should take him so he can meet Jeff and Fluffy. And then get him to paint them on the nursery wall."

"Sure, give our baby nightmares because the giant cat and dragon might eat him. Besides, he's sleeping in the room with us for at least six months. Just get pictures for now."

"If I can."

Hyrum's door creaked open, and he headed across the hall to the guest bathroom, stark naked.

"Hey," Drew said, "no one wants to see your wiener."

"Your mom does." He stopped, eyes wide, and clamped his hands over his mouth. "I'm sorry."

I'm not sure Drew heard the apology. He was laughing too hard, hard enough that Oz got off his lap.

"It's official," she said when Hyrum darted into the bathroom. "You've turned him into a real live boy."

"Between him and Will," Drew snickered, "my job is done."

PART FIVE

39

Shivan was just outside the portal, and several steps beyond him Hagar stood with his hands clasped at his back, looking every bit as hopeful as Hyrum and the kids had at Christmas. Will and I came out first; Drew followed, and when Jax stepped out he headed for Shivan. "Do you just wait here all the time, in case someone pops in for a visit?"

"Your Majesty." Shivan gave a little bow, more from amusement than loyalty. "No, I don't. I get a sense when someone is about to enter, and where. Part of my existence is to greet visitors as they enter, and to begin their program."

"Creepy that you know it's a program now," Drew said.

"Not really," Shivan said. "When your alarm goes off in the morning, you know it's time for work. This is no different."

"Do you get many others showing up here?" Jax asked.

"A few, lately. People who clearly work with Finn come in to check on things, but they rarely engage with us. I see him every now and then, too, but he waves hello and then goes on about his business."

"And the masses are unaware that he visits," Hagar added. "They've built a religion around him. It's better if they don't know their creator is nearby."

"There was a man who came recently," Shivan said. "He only wanted to meet Jeff and Fluffy. We spent time with them on Ocean Beach, watching them play. Then he went home."

"Who was he?" Jax asked.

"I only know his name was Eli."

"Young or older?" Drew blurted. "Like, old enough to be his father?" He gestured to Jax.

"Don't answer that," Will said. "That's not information Drew needs."

"I don't need it, but I want it."

"It wouldn't be helpful. Age won't tell you which Eli it was."

Future Eli didn't know about the simulator, anyway. It had to be King Eli.

"Time travel," Drew said. "It's a thing."

"Still."

"Was he alone?" Drew asked.

Shivan grinned, just a touch. "Is this a visit for the sake of visiting, or something more?"

"Come on," Drew groaned.

"Both," Jax said. "I have unfinished business with Tobias."

"He's been remarkably well behaved," Hagar said. "And he's grateful for the opportunity to redeem himself. He won't be as willing to let you hunt him, not now."

"No hunting. I just want to talk."

Tobias was in the village. After Finn had ordered his life spared, he gathered his family and headed across town square, intending to move into Hagar's hut near Market Street, but was blocked by a group of elves at the exit. They wanted him where they could keep an eye on him, and where he could be forced to become a productive member of Saint Francis. "We'll have to provide food for his family regardless of where he lives," Krisf pointed out. "There's not enough trade outside the village and few places he can grow edible crops. Make him hand over his medallion to keep him from doing magic. But keep him where we can see him."

The lack of a medallion wouldn't strip him of his magic, but it would weaken the strength of his spells. Shivan agreed with the small group over the protests of Aradyn and Lerym, with the warning that the first step out of line would have him removed from the village, whether his family followed or not.

"He's thrown himself into being the village mule," Shivan said. "If there's heavy lifting or manual labor to be done, he sees to it. Asking for volunteers is unnecessary. He just does it."

"How long has it been?" Drew asked. "We were here six weeks ago."

"Same," Shivan said.

"My father synchronized the time parameters," Will said. "Time should flow equally in both locations."

That meant there wouldn't be twenty years between now and the next time someone visited. Quinn would be disappointed that Rhys hadn't tagged along, but Will was resigned to the idea that his son might have a social life within the simulator, at least until he started preschool.

"There aren't many children Quinn's age in the village," Shivan said. "There are so few little ones at all that it's becoming a bit worrisome. I don't think there will be more than sporadic expansion beyond the village if people don't start having children. Outliers rarely come here because of the isolation. The elves are going to die out."

"Are your kids considered elves?" Drew asked. "Just curious."

"Their mother is an elf. Even so, they would be welcomed as elves. It's not a species, Drew. It's not much different than calling yourself a Pacifican."

"Technically, you're a Pacifican. I mean, apropos to nothing, I suppose. But you exist within Pacifica. San Francisco, even."

"And yet, I can never see the land of which I am a citizen."

Drew snorted. "Look at you, getting all grammarish on us. Sometimes you sound a hell of a lot like Will now."

"I will endeavor to refrain," Shivan chuckled. "But seriously, by your logic, I can never lay eyes on my own homeland, if Pacifica is my home."

We were at the entry to the village, where Fluffy waited. He began purring when he spotted us, and Drew went to him to offer chin skritches. "What if you could visit San Francisco?" Drew asked Shivan as Fluffy pressed his massive head to his hand. "Would you want to?"

"Of course."

"How?" Jax asked. "Doesn't he need the projectors and nanobots and Finn's magical fairy dust to exist?"

Fluffy jutted his head so hard that Drew fell backward, landing on his backside. "Those space shows you like," he said as he got up. "One of them has a character who is nothing but a hologram, and he can move anywhere in the ship. He's got this thing he wears…"

"Mobile emitter," Jax said when Drew couldn't cough up the name. "It's fiction, Andrew."

"Yeah, well, so was all of this at one time." He gestured toward the village. "So were flying cars, air bikes, the weird things Will can do, and time travel. It wouldn't be difficult to create something he could exist in outside of the simulator, especially if I piggy-backed it onto a drone."

"Slippery slope," Jax said.

"You would be an illegal entity outside of the simulator," Will explained. "There are limits to artificial intelligence, and you fall firmly in that definition."

"Afraid I'll take over your world?"

"Not you, specifically," Jax said. "But once you're introduced to the world, others here will want the same opportunity, and some will want to stay. The next thing I know I have an entire class of AI demanding rights equal to humans. And then the problems begin."

You're going to work on it, anyway, aren't you? And you already have ideas about how it can be done.

Fluffy stuck his tongue out, aiming for Drew's face. If he had an answer for me, it was lost in his scramble to back away from the affection Fluffy wanted to inflict. "No freaking way, cat. Your tongue has, like, a million tiny knives on it. I'd like to keep my skin."

The tongue stayed out, and Fluffy got up, inching toward Drew, eyes twinkling.

"I mean it, furball." He took several steps back. "That would hurt."

Fluffy crouched, his butt and tail raised and wiggling.

"Oh, hell no." He jabbed his pointy finger toward Fluffy. "Stay. I mean it. Stay. Wick, do something about your kid."

He loves you.

"Stop teasing him, Fluffy," Shivan said. "Be good and sit down, and I'll send Krisf to give you lunch soon."

Fluffy did not sit.

"Fresh fish. Today's catch was enormous. You'd have your fill for once."

Fluffy sucked his tongue back into his mouth and sat down.

"Good boy," Drew uttered.

Will touched my feet to make sure I was balanced on his shoulder, and we turned to head toward Shivan's house. Before we had gotten four steps in, Drew launched past us and fell chest-first into the dirt, and Fluffy was on all fours, his head cocked to the side.

Shouldn't have called him a good boy.

You know better.

"Well, I do now."

= = =

Shivan sent Darville in search of Tobias. His son thought he was outside the village cutting trees for firewood; an elf wandering past suggested that Tobias was hauling brick from an old building near Golden Gate Park to shore up a section of newly built seawall. Darville groaned at the idea of running around the woods and all the way to the park to look for the wizard but gave his word that he would find him and not stop for any distractions along the way.

"His current distraction is called Becca," Shivan said. "He's known her his entire life, yet somehow she recently became... interesting."

"Funny how that happens." Jax sat at the round table in Shivan's front yard and pointed at the guest hut. It had been remodeled, with a new façade and thick, heavy wood door, and a second story had been added on. "When the hell did you do that?"

Shivan glanced over his shoulder. "Right after you left. The council of elders requested it, in case you returned."

"Me? Why?"

"A king should not dwell in the quarters of a commoner," he said. "Their words, not mine. I argued against it. A warm bed and hay to sit on seemed sufficient for your needs. You don't seem like the fussy royal type to me."

"I'm not. And I'm not their king, no matter what Tobias says. You even agreed that I was not."

"The elders beg to differ."

"Follow the trail," Will said. "I'm sure their logic hasn't changed over the last six weeks. You're their creator's king, therefore you're also their king."

"Eh." Jax's lip curled. "I don't want to be the king here."

"Good luck with that," Drew snorted.

"What's the point? When I come here, presuming I return, I'll want it to be for fun." He jutted his chin toward Shivan. "He's the mayor. What else do they need?"

"Someone who knows more than I do," Shivan answered. "Someone who knows more than Finn, at least regarding the running of a government."

"He never expected the degree of autonomy you would achieve," Will said. "At this point, he presumes you'll make your own rules and regulations based on the government that existed before Tobias took hold of Saint Francis."

"Stories," Shivan said. "We honestly don't know at what point the backstory he created ended and we began. Our history is rife with kings and queens and a Saint Francis that bustled with people and trade, but as far as we know, it's fiction. When did we begin? The moment you first stepped into Saint Francis? Are our collective memories simply part of that story?"

Will thought they began, in the true sense of awareness, the moment Finn activated the simulation. There surely were kings and queens, and the outliers were likely transient visitors, but as quickly as time moved, in the few months between the day Finn turned the program on and the day Will stepped into the simulator with Oz and Drew and Aisha, those people became history.

"Your evolution is real," he said. "As is your need for governance."

Jax continued to argue the point; they were fully capable of managing their own lives, and he had his own country to deal with. Pacifica's size had exploded since he took the throne; Midlam was now an equal part of the mix, and Florida presented more headaches than those two combined. "Whispers are coming from New England about becoming part of the new United Kingdom. The Consortium has issued a request to study the potential effects of eliminating borders across North America. We're a few drunken decisions away from becoming the United States all over again, and you want me to add Playland to that?"

Shivan and Will answered in unison, "Yes."

"There's not enough scotch in the world..."

"Just meet with the elders," Shivan urged. "Once. Hear them out."

Jax looked at Will. "Tell me there's alcohol here."

"That means yes," Will said to Shivan.

"Jesus Christ," Jax muttered. "All I wanted to do was settle things with Tobias."

"Consider what Oz told you," Will said. "Here, you're gifted with what you need, not what you want."

"Christmas is nothing but underwear and socks here, isn't it? Get Finn. I want him to suffer right along with me."

Will fished his phone from his pocket and a few taps on the screen later he said, "Summoned."

"You can do that?" Hagar asked. "Contact the real world from here, and he'll come?"

"When he feels like it." Will held the phone up. "This is new, being able to send messages out. He added it as part of renewed safety protocols following our first visit here."

"Ah," Shivan uttered. "That explains why I felt compelled to tell our other visitors that this was a simulation and to proceed at their own risk."

"Visitors, plural," Drew said. "Who was the other one? Come on."

"He doesn't need to know," Will cautioned. "He's fishing for information on his future family."

"What if it were a child of yours?" Shivan asked him. "Wouldn't you want to know?"

"My children have been born. I won't be surprised if one or all of them come here someday. My problem will be getting them to come home."

"Yeah, sure, but you'd be pissed if some rogue dragon ate one of them," Drew said.

"Were any of our children consumed by friends of Jeff?" Will asked.

"Jeff's friends wouldn't eat our kids," Drew said.

"Baby dragons lack control," Shivan answered with a laugh. "But no. They simply came to meet Jeff and Fluffy."

"No curiosity about everyone else here?" Jax asked.

"A few questions about specific individuals."

"Rhys," Drew said, popping the top of the table with his hand. "He wanted to know how old Quinn was. Right? I know I'm right. He brought Eli here and got the date wrong. If Quinn was still a child, he skipped right to introducing Eli to Wick's children."

Are they my children?

"You created them," Will said.

That means everyone else here is Finn's child.

"Finn's creation lacked the intention that yours did. His interest was clinical, and I don't think he has an emotional attachment to the people here, other than common humanity. You, however, have definite feelings about Jeff and Fluffy. You care about them."

But in a different way than I do the babies. Or even you.

"I know. All the same, you care. You want what's best for them."

"They're like grown kids, Wick," Drew said. "You brought them into this world and let them go."

I gave them up to Krisf.

"Because you couldn't stay here," Will said. "They've been well cared for."

Have they been happy? I want to know.

"They're still here," Drew said. "They have free will. If they weren't happy, they would have moved on. Right?"

Maybe. I never told them they had a choice.

Jax leaned to the side a few inches, trying to see past Drew. Six elves sat on logs near the fire, watching us, and they didn't look away when they saw that he had noticed. "Who are they, and why are they staring?"

"Council of elders," Shivan said. "They're waiting to speak with you."

"Elders," Jax grunted. "Not one of them looks much older than I am."

"They are, by far," Shivan said. "Jesf, you've met. Logan, Nicolai, Ambrosia, Persephone, and Chip."

"Chip."

"Chip," Shivan repeated.

"And what is it they want?"

Shivan glanced over his shoulder, toward the path that cut between the colorful row houses. Beyond, there was a clearing, and on the other side, an enormous barn-like structure. "For you to take the throne."

= = =

"Was this here before?" Drew whispered to Will as Chip and Jesf pulled the barn doors open. "I don't remember it, but I don't think I came this far into the village."

"It might not have been here as recently as yesterday," Will said.

It was almost the size of the bonus room upstairs in the royal house, with polished wood floors and bright lights lining the ceiling. There were several people inside, stowing tools into bags and carrying away stacks of cut wood and leather panels; when they saw Jax, they scurried away from the object of their labor, where a taller man was on his knees, screwing something to the floor.

"Oh holy—" Jax sighed. "You meant a literal throne."

It was directly across the floor from the door. Trimmed with leather and made of heavy, dark stained wood with reddish highlights, it rested on a pedestal with four steps up. The wood was polished and caught the light in a way that made it seem as if it were sparkling, and as he got up, the man working on it brushed away dirt that we couldn't see.

When he turned, Jax uttered another "Oh holy," and started toward him. "They weren't kidding when they said you looked like me," he said, extending his hand as he neared Shivan's father. "Jackson Blackshear. Jax."

Yeosef Adomondai accepted Jax's hand but also gave a short bow. "Your Majesty."

"Really, just Jax."

"And I'm just Joe." He took a step back, sweeping his hand toward the throne. "I hope this meets with your approval. I'm a cobbler by trade, but quite proud of this."

"Cobbler," Drew snorted. "The dude made armor out of leather and wire, and it *worked*."

The throne was magnificent. Jax stood with his hands clasped behind his back and examined it from the floor, soaking in all the details. It wasn't fussy, which he hated, and it wasn't covered in gold and jewels, which he found abhorrent. The red seat and back were thick and velvety and were the most royal-like things about it. "If I could have chosen a throne for myself," he said, "this would be it."

He turned to Will. "Why can't I have something like this at home? I might actually use it."

"You don't have a personalized throne because you refuse to spend the taxpayer's money on one," Will said.

"Well, my birthday is coming, and it's a big one. I want this."

"Noted."

"Take it for a test sit," Drew suggested.

If he sat in it, that was as much as agreeing that he was the King of Saint Francis. They had their own government, Mayor Shivan and the Council of Elders. His reign was not necessary to their day to day function, and he didn't have the time to dedicate to overseeing their progress.

"Our government is basically Shivan," Yeosef said. "He consults the council, but the burden of everything falls on his shoulders. There are no written laws, no plan to advance the citizenship of Saint Francis, nothing upon which he can truly rule. They genuinely had more direction under Tobias's thumb, as horrific as it was."

"And the laws that predated him?" Will asked.

"We have no record," Jesf said. "Krisf and I can retell the history of our people, but the nuts and bolts that hold everything together are long gone."

"Tobias," Yeosef said. "Whatever remained of life before him, he destroyed. Basic rules of life are simple, but the elves are faltering and want direction."

"Hence, the religion that has sprouted around my father," Will mused.

"And having learned that their creator has a ruler?" Shivan said. "They want him. They want their King."

"The King doesn't want to be a king," Jax said. "The King wants to return to his life as a teacher, or even reinvent himself as a beach bum."

"And I'd like to go back to being Hagar's pretend apprentice," Shivan said.

"So? Why not go do that?"

"Because I grew up. This is what life needs of me, and until it no longer does, this is what I will do."

"This will always be in the way of what you want," Jax said.

"No, it won't."

"Unless there's someone else waiting in the wings, you're stuck, Shivan. Trust me, I know the feeling."

"One day," Shivan said, quite serious, "I will grow old and will no longer function well enough to lead anyone, much less all of Saint Francis. I won't be Hagar's apprentice, I will never learn his magic, but I will have my life back."

"When you're old. Who wants to wait that long?"

"We were born into this service, Your Majesty. Like it or not, this is what we will do."

Jax turned and headed for the backside of the throne. "Yeah? Well, I don't want to."

Under his breath, Drew mocked him. "And you can't make me."

When Jax was behind the throne, inspecting it with Yeosef, Shivan asked softly, "Is he well?"

"His tumors were removed," Will answered.

"That's not what I asked. Is he well?"

Will wanted to say he was. Jax had the surgery, his health was good, and he had a long life to look forward to, but instead, he gave a light shrug and said, "We'll see."

"I thought the surgery was supposed to fix this," Drew whispered. "What gives?"

"The surgery couldn't correct things that had nothing to do with the tumors. He's felt the itch to pull away from the throne for a while, but now he's vocal about it."

Is this a time thing? Trying to assert itself?

"I don't know, Wick," Will said. "In the previous timeline, at this point, he was roughly a year from abdicating. I had expected he wouldn't feel that same pull, given the change in circumstances."

"So maybe it wasn't just your death that did it. That might have compounded his feelings, but if he's been chewing on it for a while, it might be something he just has to do."

"At Oz's expense," Will reminded him.

"We won't be happy, but she can handle it. She has you, and even if he quits, he'll still be around. He'd still help."

"She's not ready, Andrew."

At least Drew isn't King of Midlam. He was by now, wasn't he?

"He was, and it was difficult." Will glanced at the throne. "Oz has other things brewing that she didn't have before. She's wholly in charge of the property development arm of Ozoo, and two years from now she'll be even deeper into her business dealings. The Wasteland project is only going to expand."

"She'll have to delegate. We'll have to step up."

"You're having a baby," Will said. "Your focus should be on him, not a looming ascension to the throne. The other Jax would reverse the decision if he could. It was one of his regrets, leaving before he needed to."

"Does the other Oz blame him?"

Will shook his head. "She understood. That doesn't mean it's what should happen now."

"I don't really blame him. I never wanted the job, either. I just got lucky."

"You didn't want it because you were keenly aware of Oz's strengths over yours, and you have other things the world needs more. Jax is just tired. His responsibilities at work and home increased dramatically over the last four years."

"Should Oz and I move out?"

"Absolutely not. He would be crushed. Even joyous events, Hyrum coming to live with him, and his grandchildren being born, are stressful. Those are the things he would choose over the monarchy if he could."

"But everyone being there is still added responsibility."

You help with Hyrum a lot. Oz even says you turned him into a real boy.

"Crudely," Drew said with a laugh.

Jax came around the throne. "Mocking me again? I heard that comment, Andrew. And no, you can't make me."

"Laughing at something Hyrum said. You know how he's always muttering 'No one wants to see your wiener.'"

"And the kids are picking up on it. Aubrey is not thrilled."

"Yeah, well, not too long ago Oz and I were sitting in Aubrey's chair, and he walked from his room to the guest bathroom buck naked, and I said it to him. No one wants to see your wiener. Without missing a beat, he shot back, 'Your mom does.' That might be the funniest damn thing he's ever said to me."

"Hyrum," Jax said, surprised. "If only he'd do something like that in front of his mother."

"I would pay to see that," Drew said. "Like, real money."

"Hyrum," Will explained to Shivan and Yeosef, "is the Queen's younger brother. His mother would likely have a stroke were he to speak to her like that."

"Deserves it," Drew grumbled.

Jax probably had a dozen opinions about his mother-in-law but became distracted by a swelling of voices outside the barn. Tobias approached, followed by a mass of curious elves. They stayed several feet behind him, just far enough that he could pretend he was alone despite the noise that flowed in a wake between him and the village center. Jax didn't wait for Tobias to come to him; he started for the door and met him outside.

"Sire." Tobias gave him a sweeping bow. "I'm told you wished to see me."

"Jesus, don't do that."

"I researched the etiquette. Would you prefer 'Your Majesty?' I'm given to understand 'Your Royal Highness' is more appropriate for the Prince." He nodded toward Drew. "I have no idea how one addresses an Emperor who is not regent."

"I would prefer Jax."

"King Jackson," Shivan said to Tobias.

"Holy hell," Jax muttered under his breath.

Shivan ignored him. "Emperor is a name more than a title in this case. Address him as Emperor."

Will didn't tell him to call him by name, and Drew was too amused by it all to even think about what he wanted the elves of Saint Francis to call him.

"And you?" Tobias said, looking at me.

Wick is fine.

"Mister Wick," Will said.

"Or Master Wick," Shivan said.

He's just trying to goad Tobias, isn't he?

"Wick finds either acceptable," Will said.

With that out of the way, Tobias clasped his hands in front of himself and asked Jax what he could do for him. "Your wish, and all that."

The throng of elves who had kept a comfortable distance pushed forward so they could hear.

"I would prefer to do this with your family present," Jax said.

"Miriam is waiting for me by the fire, but the children are in school. Will her presence, as well as her father's, suffice?"

Jax nodded and gestured for Tobias to lead the way back. The elves parted to allow them through and started to follow until Shivan cleared his throat loudly, reminding them that the

Emperor and Prince Andrew were to follow the King, before anyone else.

"They weren't like this," Drew whispered to Will. "None of them were fascinated by royalty when it was you and me and Oz. What gives?"

You were the Trident. All they wanted from you was freedom.

"Growth, one might assume," Will said. "The desire for effective leadership is natural. The want of compassionate leadership is innate. As they learn more about life outside of Saint Francis, they may yearn for that."

Hagar and Miriam waited on a long bench on the side of the fire closest to Shivan's home. Lani stood near, their conversation disrupted by a hundred voices riding on air. As Tobias neared, Hagar and Miriam stood, both looking confused.

When he reached her, Tobias took her hand in his and said, "The King wishes to speak with us."

She grumbled but turned toward him.

"I'm not here as anyone's king," Jax said. "I'm here as a man who made a colossal error in judgment, whose choices were so overwhelmingly stupid, and who is as mortified as he is embarrassed. What I did, and what I put you through, are more levels of wrong than I can comprehend."

Tobias spoke softly. "Not nearly as wrong as the things I inflicted on these people, King Jackson. I understood and am grateful for your compassion in allowing me to live."

"You were ill," Shivan said before Jax could respond.

"Illness is no reason," Jax said. "It's an excuse, and a poor one at that."

"I understood," Tobias repeated.

"And I appreciate that. Nevertheless, I'm here to apologize. I am deeply sorry for the trauma I caused by forcing you to wait for a violent end to your life, at my hands." He looked at Miriam. "I am sorrier, still, that I put you and your children through the agony of waiting and wondering when you would lose him. For seeing me here in the village, knowing why I was here and what I was doing. I don't expect forgiveness, but I do deeply, sincerely apologize."

Tobias opened his mouth to accept, but Miriam dropped his hand and crossed her arms defiantly.

"I reject your apology. Suffer with what you've done. You'll get no absolution here."

40

The noise behind us exploded. It began with a collective gasp, and then the anger of a hundred elves shouting their upset, demanding that Miriam accept the apology of the King. There were expletive-laced reminders of the reasons Jax wanted Tobias dead, cries of names of elves lost during his tyranny, and a renewed demand that he pay for his crimes.

Miriam disregarded them all; she glared at Jax, waiting for him to erupt along with the elves calling for the blood of the dark wizard.

Instead, he nodded and said he understood and accepted her rejection.

"I don't care," she seethed. "You wanted to hunt my husband like an animal. I stepped into this world suspecting he would die for his crimes, but what *you* did was cruelty beyond my comprehension. My children suffered through every day they were expected to behave as if they'd been given this wonderful gift of returning to their home, while knowing that at any moment their father could die by your hand. I sought him in the woods so many times, every day, only to find myself telling him goodbye for the last time. Over and over. How many final kisses did I sob through? How many times did I think I was telling him I loved him for the last time? You *tortured* us. I will never forgive that."

"I tortured his daughter," Tobias said, softly. "It was my just reward."

"But not hers," Jax said.

"Can you even imagine?" Miriam bellowed at Jax. "Think of your queen. What would she—"

"Enough," Hagar snapped. "You were dead, Miriam. Your children were dead. Consider the King's actions as payment for a blood debt. His brother brought you back to life, and he brought your children back to life. His daughter could have killed Tobias all those years ago but let him live, and he was returned to you because she asked that of the Emperor. His anger and wish to see Tobias suffer is a small price to pay for the gift of your lives."

"It's not," Jax said. He turned to Shivan. "How can you ask me to be your king when I've done this?"

Tobias took a step forward. "You are our king *because* you did this. You rule with compassion and offer remedy for things you fear are missteps. I accept your apology, Your Majesty. I accept it on behalf of my children, as well. One day, they'll understand."

"And yet, I worry most about your wife and what I've done to her," Jax said. "I can't fix this. I don't know how. I did to her what you did to my daughter. I will never expect forgiveness, but I would like peace for her."

"I will—"

He stopped at the sound of a little boy squealing, "Daddy!" Everyone turned, and the low rumble of gossip turned into a buzz as the crowd parted to let Rhys and Finn though. Aisha and Aubrey were a few steps behind; Aisha scrambled to grab Rhys's hand, but he shot forward and jumped at Will when he was close enough.

"Daddy, I came to play with Quinn! Is he home?"

"I'm sorry," Aisha said. "He heard us talking and nearly exploded with the idea that you were here without him. I couldn't think of a good reason to say no."

"Quinn is taking a nap," Lani said to Rhys. "He'll be up in a bit, and then you can play, all right?"

"Okay." He wiggled out of Will's arms. "I'll wait."

Aubrey was equally apologetic. She knew what Jax was here for and wanted to be by his side. "I also wanted to thank you," she said, turning to face Tobias. "You protected me when you didn't have to, and I am grateful."

"It was my honor."

"There," Miriam barked at Jax. "He saved her life, and you *still* wanted him dead. That wasn't enough? You're a horrible, vile man, and I wish nothing more for you than the pain you inflicted on me. Tobias might accept your sorrow and your rule, but I never will. I would rather see you die."

"And that's fine," Jax said.

"Fine?" Aubrey's demeanor switched with a blink, and she took a few steps toward Miriam. "What is your problem? You want him dead?"

"Aubrey." Jax tried to reach for her arm by she shrugged him off.

"No. We can hash this out, just the two of us, and honey, I am still so angry at what your husband did to my daughter that I will *not* fight fair. He tormented her with all the little things she was afraid of most and forced her to parade down the street in front of a thousand men without a stitch on. Nothing. She was cold and wet and *naked*. He tried to humiliate her, and—"

Miriam turned sharply toward her husband. "You did *what?*"

"That's what bothers you?" he asked. "I tortured your people for years, and many of them died. Yet the notion of a naked teenaged girl angers you?"

"You have a daughter," Miriam hissed. "How could you?"

"Fine, I owe the Princess Oz an apology as sincere as the King's. Perhaps she will be as gracious in accepting it as she was in allowing me to live, and more kind about it than you are about his."

"No fighting," Rhys said with an irritated sigh. "We're supposed to play today."

Tobias chuckled under his breath and crouched down to be at Rhys's level. "You're right. No more fighting. Not today. Today we play nice."

"What happened to your face?" Rhys asked him. "It's different."

"Weren't you inside when that happened?" Tobias asked.

Rhys whispered loudly, "I peeked out the window, and I saw you change."

"Is that a bad thing?"

"No. A face is just a face. But you should always let people see your real one."

"Are you angry I showed a fake face before?"

Rhys shook his head. "Maybe it wasn't fake. Faces change when you grow up. Maybe this is your grown-up face."

"Out of the mouths of babes," Tobias murmured as he stood up.

Lani ruffled Rhys's hair. "Go inside and wake Quinn. He'll be happy to see you."

He scrambled to get to the gate before she could change her mind. Will called after him, "Be nice about it, Rhys. Don't jump on his bed and yell at him."

"He's going to jump on the bed," Aisha sighed.

"Quinn will survive," Shivan said. "What about it, Miriam? Will you yield?"

"I don't want him as my king," she said, sounding less certain than she had.

"I don't want to be your king, either," Jax said. "I don't want to be anyone's king. The job kind of sucks, frankly."

"But you *are* our king!" someone from the back of the crowd shouted. "You rule the creator. You rule over us."

"You're going to get a God complex, aren't you?" Will asked Finn, who had been standing there, quietly, observing.

"It's fascinating, really. I never conceived that they would latch onto the idea of religion. Or that if they did, they would leap from the notion that there is a creator who controls all to there being someone who can control their creator."

"It doesn't have to be me," Jax grumbled.

"They built him a throne," Will told his father. "It's rather nice, too."

Finn wanted to see it. Jax let out an exasperated huff and followed reluctantly when Will led the way back to the barn, grumbling under his breath the entire way.

"Don't let him fool you," Will said as he crossed the threshold. "He likes it."

"Impressive." Finn swept an arm in the direction of the throne. "Well, go on. Sit on it."

Jax didn't move.

"Come on. They went to all that trouble, the least you can do it is to try it on for size."

"No, the least I can do is stand here and not move."

Shivan had enough. He ignored the gasps behind him when he grabbed Jax's arm and spun him around. "Stop. You're unhappy, we get that. You think I enjoy being mayor? I didn't choose this. There was no election. It was decided, without my input."

"My entire life—"

"It doesn't matter. Neither of us has had the life we would have chosen, King Jackson. Do you think I would have left my parent's home when I was still a boy if I'd had a choice? That I would have gone to live with a cranky old wizard and spent my waking hours learning to wield a sword I had no business being near? I was never given a choice, either. From birth, my life was consecrated to the service of others. First in being the Lord of Prophecy, destined to defeat the dark wizard. Then in being the mayor here. I had perhaps five years to be a child between those things. No choice. No more than you had."

"I'm sorry for that," Jax said. "But you can walk away, you know."

"And to what end? What becomes of the elves if I take those selfish steps? Someone has to make the decisions. And the truth is that I cannot and should not do it alone. I can arbitrate, I can make small laws, but I should not *reign*."

"And I should."

"You already do. They already see you as King. They already accept that if you take the seat of the throne, your laws are ours. The laws you've already crafted."

"I can give them access to that information," Finn said. "It's not like you'd have to actually do anything."

Jax twitched. "King in absentia?"

"Eh. Maybe visit every now and then. Toss a law or two their way. Confer with Shivan. Come when he calls if there's an emergency."

"I cannot call," Shivan reminded him.

Finn pulled his phone from his pocket. A minute and a few dozen taps on his screen later, Shivan's eyes flew open wide as information flooded his mind.

"I can call," he murmured.

Finn proposed placing a computer in Jax's home office, one Will could monitor and bug Jax with details as needed. Most of his decisions could be fed to Shivan through the system if any were needed.

He yielded. With a heavy sigh, he climbed the few steps to the throne and sat in it, looking out over the elves who stared, now mostly quiet. He glanced at Aubrey and then at Shivan before settling back on Finn. "By the storyline here, Shivan and I are related, right?"

Finn nodded. "He was the last of the House of Blackshear. Don't ask me to count how many generations."

Jax looked at Shivan. "Formally change your name from Adomondai back to Blackshear," he said. "Your father as well. Reclaim the family name."

"I will."

Yeosef stepped from the shadows. He was holding a crown, gleaming gold and encrusted with more gems than I could name. Jax sighed and then said, "That's a bit, uh, overdone, don't you think?"

"Every stone that we knew to be worthy of your crown," Yeosef said, a hint of humor in his voice. "The children designed it, and I crafted their wishes. They're proud of their effort, King Jackson."

Jax huffed a short laugh through his nose. "As am I. It's... beautiful."

With a deep breath, he settled into the throne and managed to not flinch when Shivan placed the crown on his head. "I want confirmation from the villagers. Do you accept my rule over Saint Francis and agree to abide by the laws of Pacifica and the decisions rendered on behalf of Saint Francis?"

There was a low rumble that began to swell until Jax held a hand up to silence them.

"Raise your hand. All who agree, raise a hand. All who oppose, you'll get your chance."

Of the two hundred elves in range, as his request filtered out the door to those in the rear, all but two raised their hands. Miriam stubbornly refused, and Aradyn was busy pushing his way to the front.

"Aradyn," Jax said when he had finally made it to the base of the pedestal. He gestured for everyone to lower their hands. "What can I do for you?"

"Before I swear to your reign, I want your word."

Jax waited.

"No resurrections. Never again should a dead elf be returned to his life."

"You benefitted from the Emperor's—"

"And I was never the same!" Aradyn seethed. "I feel apart from everything. My anger is always there, eating at my soul. I should have been left near the wizard's lair until I crumbled back into the earth, as I was meant to. We all should have been."

"How many did you bring back?" Jax asked Will.

"All who died in battle. More than a hundred."

"How many of you are here right now, who died then?"

Nearly half the hands went up.

"How many of you feel as Aradyn does?"

Every hand save one went down. Jesf stepped forward and stood next to Aradyn. "Respectfully, I disagree with Aradyn. My life has been the same. Better. I am not angry. I am grateful."

"It's moot," Hagar said. "None of us can bring back the dead. Only the truly living have that ability."

They were learning to control the world around them, Aradyn argued. The dragon played with his skin. The cat learned to control his prey. Children were learning to access the system, and they delved into human history. Eventually, they would figure out how to get to the information that would teach them how Will raised the dead and Oz healed the injured.

"You'll never be able to access that," Finn said. "Truthfully, you can only get to the bits I allow you to. And I won't give you that. Ever."

"Then no one else will go through what I have?" Aradyn asked.

"Not on my watch," Finn answered.

"Swear to it on your son's life."

Finn shrugged. "Sure, why not? Will, no more vampires."

"Then I agree," Aradyn said. He raised his hand. "I agree to your reign and swear fealty."

"And those opposed?" Jax asked.

No one, not even Miriam, raised their hand.

"All right then. I have only two things for you today, and you may take them as *ex cathedra* pronouncements. The first is that I hereby elevate Shivan Blackshear to Prince Regent, to rule in my absence. You will accept his decisions as my law and presume that he has consulted with me in anything he declares from this throne. The council of elders will serve as his cabinet, and he will meet with them regularly."

He looked at Shivan. "Do you accept?"

"I do," Shivan said, loud and clear enough for all to hear.

Jax leaned forward a touch, speaking only to Shivan. "When you speak from the throne, your word is law. Only take the seat when ruling. Otherwise, you might sit here and casually tell someone they can marry someone else's daughter, and it's a done deal. Be very careful about the words you use when seated here."

Shivan nodded.

"Good. Then as I am your King, elves of Saint Francis, he is my eyes and voice here."

"What was the other thing?" Krisf called out.

"You're dying out. Spread out. Live beyond the village. Rebuild the city. But mostly, have babies. Lots of babies."

"You're ordering us to spawn," Yeosef said, chuckling.

"Well, maybe not you." Jax stood and stepped from the pedestal, setting the crown on the seat. "Do what I wish I could. A lot of nothing and spend as much of that nothing as you can playing with your grandkids."

41

"Did you get what you needed?" Aubrey asked Jax, watching Rhys swing on the rope still hanging from the tree branch. We were in Shivan's front yard with a bottle of Finn's homebrew; Drew was playing with Rhys and Quinn, shaking the tree, making them shriek as loudly as he could. Will and Aisha sat on the side of the table closest to the gate, where they could leap over it to get to them if needed.

He wasn't sure. He'd apologized, but it hadn't felt like enough. It felt like there was more he needed to do, but he didn't see a way to do it. "Amends are not easy to make," he mused.

"Perhaps that wasn't the problem."

"Kinda was."

"Sweetheart." She set her hand on his. "Your fight was never with Tobias."

"Kinda was."

"He'll see it soon," Will said.

I wanted to mock him, but he was too serious to take it the right way, and he was looking at Will. "You fixed the hunt. I was never going to find Tobias to kill him, was I?"

Will gave a slight shrug. "I may have played with the code a bit. You were able to find him, but only in moments I was sure you would not fire."

"You knew I wouldn't kill a man who was with his wife," Jax mused, thinking of Tobias kneeling on the beach, raw and mourning his end with Miriam. "You knew if his children were near, he was safe. I could have chased him around Saint Francis for a year and never found him."

"You had two weeks," Will said. "And I was just as surprised as everyone else when he offered himself to your judgment, wanting to end the hunt."

"Would you have let me kill him?"

He might have, but Rhys yelled out, "Assmunch!" and he let go of the rope, running to catch up to the barefooted boy heading toward the gate. They stopped just in front of it; Asmonk was pale and visibly trembling, but Rhys was excited and clutched his hands to his chest the way Hyrum often did.

"Are you okay?" he asked Asmonk. "Do you feel better?"

"Yeah, I'm okay. Why are you even talking to me?"

"I didn't hurt you?" Rhys held his hands out, flexing his fingers. "I did the sparky thing on your chest. Is it okay?"

"Yeah, it's fine." He bent over so he could look Rhys in the eyes. "I came over to say I was sorry for what I did to you. It was mean."

Rhys looked confused. "I'm sorry your dogs ran away."

"That's not what I meant. I shouldn't have taken you into the woods."

"But I got to see the lightning bug people! They made sure the dogs didn't bite me. Did they come back? Did you get your puppies back?"

"They came back later," Shivan said quickly. "They're fine."

"I just..." Asmonk looked at Will helplessly. "I'm sorry I scared him, I really am. I'm sorry for everything."

"Clearly," Will said reluctantly, "Rhys believes everything is all right."

"I hope it is."

Will gave him a short nod. "Your apology is accepted, Asmonk."

"We're playing Tarzan," Rhys said. "Want to swing on the rope? It's lots of fun."

He didn't want to, but he went over to the tree anyway.

"You changed Rhys's memory, didn't you?" Aubrey asked Will.

Will's gaze was fixed on his son. "I did not. I'm not sure how he remembers it this way. He was terrified and screaming."

"Asmonk is terrified right now," Shivan said. "I've never seen someone tremble so visibly."

Rhys showed him how to grip the rope with his feet to keep from falling and held him steady while he got the rope around one foot. His hand lingered longer than necessary, and when he let go, Asmonk had calmed. The trembling faded, and he smiled.

"Did he do that?" Jax asked, his voice barely above a whisper.

"Touch doesn't work here," Will said. "I tried with Aradyn once. All I heard were clicks."

"Intent," Aisha said. "He's human and has a transponder. He can wish something and make it happen here."

But how did he know?

"What do you mean, Wick?" Will asked.

How did he even have the idea that he could make Asmonk feel better by touching him?

"Can he?" Aisha asked. "Could this be another gift?"

"It could be coincidence," Will said. "But if it is, thank you great, great, great Grandma."

"Good lord," Aubrey sighed. "Stop making me feel so old."

Jax was still watching Rhys. Tiny sparks were dancing around his fingertips, but he was laughing and didn't notice.

"Sweetheart?" Aubrey said.

"I am so goddamned glad I get to know that kid," he said softly. "I can't wait to see everything he'll become."

Aisha jabbed her pointy finger in his direction. "Hey. No rushing this. I want my babies to be babies as long as they can."

Just then, Rhys let out a long, drawn belch, that ended in a fit of giggles.

"Too late," Will said. "He's one hundred percent little boy now. We'll never be able to keep up."

= = =

The afternoon slid into evening, and as the light began to fade from the sky, more wood was thrown onto the fire. Jeff circled overhead and dipped low, blowing fire to stoke the flames, and they soon leaped high enough that we could feel the heat from Shivan's yard and couldn't see people who sat near it on the other side.

Rhys and Quinn were playing on the other side of the gate, jumping from square to square that they'd etched into the dirt, dust flying up from their shoes as they landed. Jax wondered what the point was; they weren't playing hopscotch, there was no obvious game. Aubrey watched for a moment and then said, "They're enjoying being little boys, sweetheart. Little boys love to jump and get dirty."

"Yeah, well, Rhys is taking about a pound of dirt with him when we go home."

"The dirt doesn't follow," Aisha said. "He could be caked in mud, and once we get through the portal, he'll be as clean as he left."

"Huh." Jax glanced around the yard and then asked Shivan if he had a hose. "Wet the little suckers down."

Part of me hoped they would, but a voice bellowed from near the entry to the village, "Kilfin! Kilfin's back!"

That got them up and out of the yard. Kilfin came through the village center with his horse pulling a cart, and the cart was stacked with pink bakery boxes. Shivan let his inner fifteen-year-old out and squealed the giant man's name and then ran at him, throwing his arms around Kilfin's neck.

"Where have you been?" Shivan demanded when he let go. "We've been worried."

"Shivan's been worried," Hagar said. "The rest of us appreciated the quiet."

Kilfin dropped the horse's reigns, his mouth agape. "You came back," he said once he'd gathered his wits. "You were leaving forever."

"The story is long, and we'll tell you about it later." Hagar gestured to Jax and Aubrey. "The King and Queen, Kilfin. You've missed quite a bit."

"I would guess that I have." He brightened. "I bring gifts, and the first should go to our royal guests."

"*Our* King and Queen," Shivan said. "Not guests."

Kilfin gave a short bow of his head. "Even so." He grabbed

a pink box from the top of the stack and held it out. In bright gold script, the top read *Princess Sweets*, and I could smell what was inside before he opened it. "There are thousands of people in Sausalito. I spent weeks exploring, and I think I met most of them. But before I left, I found a shop near the water, and the owner insisted I bring these to share."

He pried the box open for Shivan and the others to see. "Cupcakes!" he boasted. "I hadn't seen a cupcake in more than forty years, and there they are across the bridge of gold, more than anyone could hope for."

Drew took a step closer. "No freaking way. He found cupcakes."

"You had cupcakes last week, Andrew," Aubrey said.

"I know, but... Oz. You know, when she tried to run away. She was looking for cupcakes. This means something. It has to."

"It means," Jax said, taking two from the box and turning to give them to Rhys and Quinn, "that once they've had these, it's time to go home."

"Aw." Rhys groaned as he pulled the wrapper away from his cupcake. "We're not done playing."

"I'll bring you back in a couple of weeks," Will said.

Rhys bit into the cake, chocolate frosting smearing his nose. "Promise?"

"I promise. If I can't, Mommy or Andrew will."

"Or I will," Aubrey said. "Andrew might be preoccupied, and I wouldn't mind coming back."

Kilfin looked past Drew. "Where's the princess?"

"Home." He held his hands out in front of himself as if he were cupping his stomach. "She's a little bit pregnant."

Kilfin stepped close, so close Drew had to crane his neck to look at him. "You're properly wed?"

"Why are you people so concerned with marriage?" Drew grumbled. "Yes, we're married. Great, big ceremony and a huge honking reception after."

"Good." Kilfin stepped back, and then clapped his hand on Drew's shoulder, hard. "Congratulations, then."

"Really, why?" Drew asked, looking to Finn.

"Why not? I gave them a moral code, thinking it would be interesting to see how many generations it would take for it to be broken."

"How many?" Will asked.

"First," Finn snorted. "But overall, they've stuck to pair bonding and nuclear families."

"Heteronormative families?" Will asked. "Please tell me you didn't fall back on old stereotypes."

"No, there's no moral code regarding pair types. Although I may have failed to account for same-gender couples wishing to procreate. I might want to—"

His train of thought derailed when Rhys yelled, "No fighting!" He thrust his hand forward, and pulses of energy shot forward, stirring the air as it sped through the narrow space between Jax and Will. There was no light, no electricity. In the same sliver of time Tobias yelled out, "Miriam, no!" and she flew backward.

She was twenty feet away, on her back, and a long carving blade was on the ground at her feet.

"That's not nice! Knife things aren't toys!" Rhys barked, stomping away from Quinn. Sparks flittered around his fingers, crackling. Will scooped him up before he could get any closer to her, and he closed his hand over Rhys's, trying to snuff them out. "She wanted to hurt someone, Daddy. I didn't really hurt her. I threw air and not sparky things."

"I know," he said softly. "We'll talk about it when we get home."

Hagar was already at Miriam's side. "She's fine. He could have lit you on fire, daughter."

"You're lucky he didn't blow your hand off," Tobias spat. When he was close enough, he kicked the knife out of her reach. "What were you thinking? Why?"

She had no answer.

Aradyn, on the other hand, had plenty to say. He stomped forward, "I warned you. I told you that it changes people. The old Miriam was never like this. Never angry. She was kind and sweet and killing anyone would have never crossed her mind."

"She wasn't resurrected," Will said. "She was recreated."

"Same thing," Aradyn spat. "Leave the dead alone. Leave them to find peace."

Jax didn't want to get into it. "You can argue amongst yourselves and figure it out. Shivan will let me know what you decide."

Tobias picked the knife up, and held it out to Shivan, handle first. "We'll leave the village. We should have left before."

"We leave, and he'll still be King," Miriam hissed.

"And that is our just reward," Tobias said without looking at her. "Hagar, will you stay here, with the children?"

"No!" Miriam cried.

"Aye, I'll stay," the wizard sighed. "You brought them here to be among people. Until they're ready to be on their own, I'll stay." Before Miriam could protest again, he tugged on her sore wrist. "You'll see them. You're not banished. But you need to be away from here. Both of you. Go to my hut."

She snatched her hand away from him.

Tobias finally turned to his wife. "Our place here must be earned. We were foolish to think you could step back into your old life, with or without me."

"Go," Hagar whispered to his daughter. "Before they decide that you deserve worse."

"If this happened at home," Shivan ventured once she and Tobias were beyond the fire, "she'd be executed, wouldn't she?"

"If it could be proven that my wife or I was her target," Jax said. "Yes, she could be executed. Rhys stopped her before anyone else saw her, so we can only presume. But if you're concerned about a death penalty becoming part of your law...no. Attacks on the royal family are the only things punishable by death in Pacifica, and truthfully, we haven't enacted that in my lifetime."

"It's happened? People have tried to kill you?"

"Someone always wants me dead. Watch your back, Shivan. As Prince Regent, chances are someone will want you dead, too."

= = =

"That was a cheery note to leave on," Aubrey said when we were standing on Union Square at home. "Do you really feel like your life has a constant threat against it?"

Jax pointed at the scars in the concrete where the air car had crashed. "Comes with the job."

Will still had Rhys in his arms. The chocolate frosting that was smeared across his face remained in Saint Francis, and the dirt on his shoes was gone. He put his hands on Will's face and squished his cheeks together, another thing he picked up from Hyrum. "Daddy, are you mad at me?"

"No. Why would I be?"

"I hurted that lady. But she was going to hurt Uncle Jax."

"I know. It's all right. You're not in trouble."

"I made sure I hit her knife. I didn't know it would hurt her hand and knock her over, too."

Jax reached over and took Rhys from Will. "Kiddo, you're my hero right now. Don't worry about her hand. She'll be fine."

Rhys leaned close to Jax's face and giggled. "I should get a parade."

"Will you settle for pizza? I'll make your dad let you have root beer with it."

"Can we?" Rhys leaned back so hard he dangled from Jax's arms and looked at everyone upside down. "I'm hungry."

"You just had a cupcake," Will reminded him.

"A cupcake that probably stayed behind," Drew said. He fished out his phone and said he would call everyone at home and tell them to meet us at the pizza place a block away.

Rhys rode on Jax's back on the walk across the Square. Will and Aisha walked behind them, trailing far enough to talk without being overheard.

"What are we going to do about him?" Aisha asked. "He's learning to control how he uses his hands, but not when. And that...that was new, Bilbo."

Will had no easy answer. He wanted to know what else Rhys could do, if anything, but he understood they couldn't hide him away until he was old enough to recognize how people would react if they saw him do anything.

"I refuse to isolate our children," Will said. "I know that pain."

"Well, what's the alternative?"

"We take our chances. Teach him how to judge the situations he's in, and help Hyrum teach him more control. And then we hope against hope that neither Charlie nor Alex have gifts, at least not as visible."

People won't notice, not really.

"How can they not, Wick?"

Dude, I've been alive for as long as they can remember, and no one asks. I was Jax's cat when he was a baby, and no one's bothered to question why I'm still around.

"They assume you're not the same cat," Will said.

No. They just don't think about it. If Rhys gets all sparky in public, they'll come up with another explanation for what they saw. At least the people without gifts will.

"Without gifts."

You can't be the only ones. There are more hiding in the shadows. They'll notice. And once they do, and they realize the royal family has people just like them and treats them as normal, they'll seek you out.

"And then?"

And then Zed builds a castle and teaches them to speak for the dead so they can hide in plain sight.

Will stopped walking.

"Rhys didn't exist—"

Hyrum did.

"You think that's what happened?" Aisha asked, prodding him to get moving again. "The school wasn't just Zed fulfilling a childhood wish?"

"It would explain why he granted admission to children," Will mused. "Wick, how do you know?"

I get bored sometimes. I read a lot. No matter which When we're in.

"I don't recall ever seeing you access a computer."

Who says you're with me? I go places without you, you know. I visit Lux a lot, especially at night when everyone's asleep.

"At least no one there can talk to you," Will sighed.

Hyrum can.

"Hyrum hears you every now and then."

That was a long time ago. He's learned how to listen. And he's awake a lot, so we talk. He helps me use his computer. There are people like you out there, Will. They'll need protection.

"How did Zed come to own Treasure Island?" Will asked me. "Do you know?"

It was a gift, as far as I can tell.

"Given when? And by whom?"

That'd be telling.

"So tell me."

We were almost to the door of the pizza place. Jax and Aubrey were already inside, and Drew had made a beeline for the pool tables.

Go ask Drew. Old Drew, not this Drew. And remember, time is like spaghetti. Find the places it sticks to itself. And then do what he tells you to do.

PART SIX

42

THE KING AND I
SEAN MCALLISTER

I'm not a reporter. I'm barely a writer. I'm a student, exploring as many different things as I can before I'm jettisoned out into the world to become a functioning member of society. As a student, I couldn't pass up a guaranteed A in my second-semester journalism class. Early on we were presented with something that on the surface seemed to have a low level of difficulty: get a one-on-one with the King, just meet him, talk to him, provide proof, and you're guaranteed an A for the semester. It was only good for the first student to present proof, and the instructor did everything but laugh out loud at those who seemed interested.

It wasn't meeting the King that we jumped at; it was the guaranteed grade. I knew the instructor's expectations were low. Who could possibly get past his guards or secretaries at city hall? The odds that he would have time to spare were slim. It was a nonstarter, but the incentive dangled like candy on a string, and a few of us wanted it.

I listened as the others discussed how to approach His Majesty's handlers. It was a guaranteed race to city hall, and I'm not the quickest person on the planet. My odds of getting there first were about as good as getting the interview.

Instead of city hall, I went to the royal residence, thinking that at the very least, I could speak with the guard on duty. Maybe he or she could get me an appointment, and if I had proof of the time and date, I might be the victor. I wanted the grade; if I got it, that meant one less class I had to obsess over. My needs were selfish, and I knew that. But still, I went straight from that class to the front desk just inside the door of the building where our King and Queen and their family live.

The desk guard took down my name and phone number but was not optimistic that I would get anything more than a call from another guard, informing me that His Majesty was unavailable. But while I swallowed hopeful disappointment, the guard slid out of his chair and stood at attention, facing the stairs.

Descending the stairs, right in front of me, were the King and his brother, the Emperor. Before I could turn and run out the door, which is what my gut told me to do, the guard nodded at the King and then told him who I was and what I was there for. My expectations crashed; not only would I not get proof of meeting the King, but he was also going to laugh and send me on my way.

Instead, he smiled and held out his hand as if I were more than a twenty-year-old kid impeding on his day. He made me feel as if he welcomed the intrusion, claiming that talking to me would get him out of a meeting or two. He sent the Emperor in his stead and invited me upstairs, where we could speak at his kitchen table, and where I could meet the Queen.

Now, I sort of knew the Queen. To me, she's Mrs. Blackshear, my fifth-grade teacher, the one who made me love reading and who taught me that despite the pain of my early years, I was worth as much as anyone else. She encouraged me to explore outside my comfort zone and was a good part of why I'd taken the chance and shown up on her doorstep.

It had been ten years, but she remembered me. And I got the feeling that if you were ever her student, no matter how far back, she'll remember you, too.

I had expectations as I went up the stairs with King Jackson.

He is our King, after all. Surely, I was about to enter a residence of palatial proportion, decorated richly, with expensive things on display. I presumed that, would not have been surprised by it, and honestly, thought that our royal family deserved that.

I entered to see a toddler streaking, naked, down the hallway. Another toddler was on the floor engaged in a typical two-year-old's temper tantrum because she didn't own a blue unicorn t-shirt. A third was stretched out on the sofa watching a cartoon, trying to drown out his sister's wailing by notching up the volume. There were toys strewn about, a stack of diapers on an end table near a chair in the corner, kids' books scattered across the coffee table, and there was nothing—literally nothing—that told me this was where royalty resided.

It was all perfectly normal.

Within a few minutes, everyone had clothes on, the tantrum was over, the volume turned down, and the Queen's brother sat on the floor to play with the Emperor's three youngest children while we sat at the table and talked. I got my proof—the Queen took a picture of the King and me—but I left there with more than I bargained for: another meeting. They wanted me to take the time to formulate a plan, decide what I most wanted to write about, come up with the right questions so that when it was over, I would have enough information to write a good article.

Concepts were swirling in the back of my head before the end of that first meeting. My preconceived notions about their lives had been effectively squashed from the moment I stepped into their all-too-normal apartment, one that was not dissimilar to my own. I wanted to know why they lived like everyone else. Why hasn't the King accepted a raise, ever? Why does the entire family live in the same building, and why don't they have something more regal? There are no servants in the royal house. No housekeepers, no cooks, no nannies.

I began to climb a mental pedestal, one from which I would inform the world that our King deserves more. He'd already told me: *There's nothing wrong with living like the man down the street. There's everything wrong with thinking you're better than he is.* But still, my affection for my fifth-grade teacher and an admitted fascination with the family made me want to champion for more.

There was more to crafting a news story than wishes, however, and more to presenting it than sitting at a keyboard and pouring out my thoughts. King Jackson was willing to do more than speak with me; a teacher at heart, he wanted me to learn, and he wanted my classmates to benefit as well. He invited us to participate in a reception for Florida's new Prime Minister and to conduct an interview on site. While I spoke with him, my classmates would record everything. We were expected to cover the entire reception as if we were a working news team.

I was in over my head, and he knew it. With a hundred people swirling around and providing ample distraction, he guided me through the interview, prompting the questions I should ask, making me believe I was the one in control. We pumped the audio through the speakers placed around the room, and teenaged camera operators were getting in everyone's way. No one complained.

The interview was going well, I thought, and my notions of the article I would write seemed clearer than ever. This wouldn't be a fluff piece meant only to get me a better grade, it would be deep and thoughtful, and would be picked up by media outlets across the country.

But then he suddenly stood, said he would be right back, and rushed across the room to rescue his three-year-old nephew from some basic biology, and everything I'd intended flipped over on itself. Aside from being mortified because I hadn't flipped a switch to turn his microphone off, he added to an idea that was hiding behind all the others in my head. His nephew needed him; the rest of us were just there when it happened. But it was a glimpse into who he really is.

I was ready to write the article that night. I'd seen politics in action at the reception. What was, on the surface, a party to introduce new leaders to one another, was, deeper down, an exchange of power plays. Conversations were carefully crafted to be polite and friendly while also offering warnings. Skepticism about Florida's ability to assimilate into the rest of the world was offered as praise for the strides already made. I had opinions about the whole thing and was ready to tell everyone all about it. But more than that, I was beginning to see a side to everything that few ever see, and it had changed the things I wanted to say.

King Jackson was willing to continue humoring me.

What I wanted most was a glimpse of his family life. The world knows the public image, and he's never been coy about his politics. Under his rule, Pacifica has tripled in size and may grow more over the next few years. He was willing to go to war to defend Midlam and again when Florida posed a direct threat to the continent. Publicly, he's been steady-handed and firm; he's known for his decisiveness and unwillingness to back down when he knows he's right. He makes the tough decisions and does the hard work.

Yet, he is not a hard man.

None of the royal family are.

This is what drew me to them, I think. They do the work we expect of them, even when they don't particularly want to. Like everyone else, they have days when they just don't want to go to work. They'd rather lounge around the house and do nothing. They want time off as much as anyone else.

But there is no real time off for the King. His job is seven days a week, and he's basically on call for every minute of those days.

He never asked for it.

If he takes an afternoon off, he's still on the job. And rather than sitting in his chair watching sports, he's caring for his family. There is no divide in the Blackshear household; he doesn't get a break from those responsibilities just because he's the leader of the free world. At home, King Jackson is liable to be bathing his grandkids or changing diapers. He might be wrangling his nephews and niece or sitting on the floor building things with blocks. He'll get down on his hands and knees to clean, he'll scoop the cat's litterbox, and he does the dishes when he can.

He offers hugs and kisses to the tiny people in his care and doesn't flinch at sticky hands grabbing his face or cookie-crumb-covered lips. He cuddles on the sofa with his brother-in-law and

reads stories with him and readily admits—he lights up, even—
that his life became so much better when Hyrum decided to live
with them.

While he's an effective and admired leader in the world,
home is where he finds his purpose. His door is always open
to those he loves—literally because there is no actual door to
the main royal residence—and when he's surrounded by them,
that's when he's happiest.

I started this whole thing to get a good grade, then aspired
to write an amazing article about our King, but along the way, I
realized that none of us are owed that kind of personal access to
him. He allowed me in because there was a lesson to be taught
because I am not a reporter; I'm a student.

I did learn from him. I learned that I will never be a reporter
because I don't like the intrusion into the lives of people who
don't really owe anyone else that time. I learned what was
more important to me; I don't care about the grade, I don't care
whether I pass or fail this class. I don't care if this is more about
me than it is about him. I care that I walk away from this with
the bigger things, the lessons King Jackson and Queen Aubrey
wanted me to pay attention to.

So, this is all you get. Nothing salacious, no royal gossip.
Just a little bit about the family living in the building near Union
Square, the one with guards to keep the ill-intended from getting
inside. It's pretty much all you need to know. It's all I will ever
tell, so don't ask me for more. You only need to know two things.

1—There's a lot of love in that building.

2—King Jackson is a family man.

Oh, and the cat is pretty cool, too. Just don't tell him he's a
good boy. He hates that.

43

Eli the third came screaming into the world ten days before Will's forty-ninth birthday. He was only six pounds, but he was twenty inches long, something that would follow him for the rest of his life. He was tall and thin, with jet black hair and deep blue eyes that Drew swore were violet. He was born at home—in the same spot where Rhys had come into the world—because Oz refused to admit she was in labor, and by the time she agreed, the baby was coming, he was pushing his way out, unwilling to wait any longer.

Aubrey was the first to hold him because she was the one who delivered him. Once he was cleaned up and Drew had baptized him with a dozen kisses on his wet head, the first person to hold him was Eli the second. The old king stared at him with wonder, cooing at his new status as the most beautiful baby in the world, while promising to teach him inventive ways to get into trouble without his parents ever knowing.

"Wonderful," Drew said with a sigh. "Great Grandpa will introduce him to his first kegger."

"Go with," Oz said. "It would be your first, too."

"I've had beer on tap with your dad. That counts."

Finn waited in the living room with Jo and Zed and the rest of the family. I heard Jo tell him to sit down, twice, and the third time she warned him he was going to wear a path on the floor he blurted, "My father is being born *right now*. How can I sit still? That's my *dad*."

He was again ordered to sit before being allowed to hold

newborn Eli. Will carried him from the bedroom, wrapped in a purple baby blanket, and sat next to Finn on the sofa.

"Dad," he said, softly, dropping a kiss on Eli's forehead before gently handing him over, "meet my grandfather."

Will could count on one hand the number of times he'd seen his father cry. Once, when Will confessed he'd been portal hopping and had plucked Jax from the bridge; at that moment he realized Will was the Emperor and knew everything that went with it. The next time, they were walking down Market Street, heading for the portal where he would say goodbye for twenty-five years.

This time, the tears fell softly, without guilt-racked sobs, and he whispered to the baby, "I'm coming to see you tomorrow, and I'm not leaving until you've forgiven me. God, I miss you, but I can't wait to see you grow up."

Drew sat on Finn's other side. "Give it a few days, a week or two maybe, and I'll go with you. Maybe he'll listen to his old man. Whatever happened, maybe I can help fix it."

Will wanted to go, too. Four generations of Blackshear men and a good bottle of scotch—by the time they polished it off, they'd be so in love with each other that someone would surely throw up.

There was no way I wouldn't be there.

As had been done with Oz and Zed, the baby was introduced to the kingdom two days later, on the steps of Union Square, held by his father and surrounded by his family. Drew cuddled him close, kissed his tiny forehead, and then handed him to Jax, who proudly pulled the blanket away from his face so the people waiting could see, and said, "Your future King, Eli Nicholas Blackshear the third."

There were hundreds of people lining the street and sidewalk, and everyone close enough raised their arms and waved their hands back and forth, while a low buzz rode in the air, people speaking in whispers.

"Why are they doing that?" Hyrum asked Will.

"Tradition," Will said. "It began with the birth of Prince Maxwell, who would become King when he was only fourteen years old. His mother was deaf, and this is the customary applause given in the deaf community. Maxwell was the first royal infant presented who didn't begin screaming when the people cheered and then became tradition. I find it rather elegant and considerate."

Rhys and Marco raised their arms and began waving back to everyone, causing a hum of amusement to buzz through the crowd.

"Dat's my new cousin!" Marco shouted. "Say hi!"

They did not say hi. They smiled, and those up front mouthed "hello," but remained respectfully quiet until the guard began clearing the sidewalk and creating a path for the family to walk home. When we were inside, and the door closed behind us, the cheering started. It was a pocket of short-lived joy, and it was enough to make Marco happy.

"Dey sayin' hi!"

"Daddy, why are they so happy?" Rhys asked. "He's just a baby."

"Because they got to see the person who will be their king someday."

"What's that mean?"

"It means," Drew said, snatching Rhys up into a hug, "that someday he'll be the boss of you."

"Do I get to be the boss someday?"

"You my boss!" Charlie squealed.

Alex grunted, "Nuh-uh. He's Weezie."

"Rhys," Will corrected.

"Uh-huh. Weeze."

"One day," Drew said, heading up the stairs with Rhys, "you and your brother and sister and cousins will run Ozoo together. Since Eli will have more royal duties than you, if you like the job, you'll probably be his boss there."

"When?"

"When your dad and I retire. We'll probably be really old by then."

"Daddy's old now."

"I know! At the end of next week, he turns forty-nine! And next year he'll be *fifty!*"

"That's almost a hundred," Rhys said as if the idea were secret.

"Stop goading him," Will said.

"I'm not," Drew swore.

"I'm talking to Rhys. He's the one in control here, and you know it. Besides, he thinks you're old, too."

"Am I?" he asked Rhys.

"Little bit, yeah."

"That's my boy," Will chuckled.

The rest of the afternoon was loud, Christmas-morning-loud. Toys were dumped onto the living room floor, along with drawing paper and crayons and a sippy cup that Charlie declared he was too old for, but no one was allowed to throw it away because Jonathan or baby Eli might want it. Oz and Drew sat on the sofa, so close they looked like one giant blob of exhausted parent, cuddling Eli as he slept through the noise. Zed and Sophia sat across the room, arguing under the hum of children laughing as Hyrum ran a toy car through their multi-colored block building—I only caught one thing, Sophia hissing at him, "Just stay off me for ten minutes so I can enjoy a week or two without some parasite growing in me!—and when Jax and Aubrey slipped out of the room, I followed.

They went to the balcony, where no one was shouting or screeching or belching as loud as humanly possible, where farts were still funny, but no one would intentionally cut loose. A few minutes later, Will and Aisha followed, bringing glasses of iced tea instead of scotch and a promise that Jay and Navi were keeping an eye on the madness.

"Oz and Drew are barely awake," Aisha added.

"When are Jay and Navi finally getting married?" Jax asked. "I have paperwork waiting to register her as an official member of the family. It's got a layer of dust on it."

"Paperwork," Will snorted. "You have a standard form that you'll fill out on the computer, which you will then forward to the office of records, and ten days later someone will send her a new ID card."

"Shut up. Paperwork sounds better."

"They're talking about late fall," Aisha said. "Something simple and small, family and a few friends only. Well, family, friends, and George."

That made Will laugh. "Introduce him like that. This is our family, these are our friends, and this...this is George. He's not ours."

You like him now. Admit it.

"I tolerate him," Will said.

You helped him pick out two cats for Isaac. And then convinced him to get a third one for James.

"That was because he hates cats, and it was funny."

"Wick is right," Aisha said. "You like George. Maybe not enough to go out for a drink, but you like him."

They went out for a drink. After we picked out the cats.

"Stop talking, Wick," Will said.

"Well, then," Jax said. "I'm glad I didn't have the son of a bitch executed when I could have."

"The perks of being you," Aubrey said. "You get to be the better man, even in the face of the law."

"Eh. I'm not sure that's a perk. But if I have to be the damned king, I'll take it."

"Sweetheart, you don't *have* to be the king," Aubrey said.

"I promised you, a long time ago, I wouldn't step down in order to protect Oz."

"That was when my father was alive and leading Florida, and I didn't want him near our daughter. The promised ended when he did, Jackson. Step down if you need to. Oz is capable, and you'll still be here to advise her."

"I've made other promises since, Aubrey."

"Let go of them, then. No one wants you to be so miserable that you end up hating your life."

"My life—" He turned at the sound of the door opening. Rhys pushed it open with both hands, grunting under the weight, and he jumped out of the way as it creaked closed.

"It's loud in there," he said. "Can I come out here for a minute?"

Jax patted his lap. "Come sit with me, slugger."

Rhys wiggled onto his lap, straddling Jax's legs, and he looked at Aisha. "Mommy, Charlie just used the potty. Jay told him he was a big boy and Alex clapped for him. But he wouldn't put his pants back on."

"Of course not," she sighed.

"It's fine," Will said. "We agreed, our children can be nudists at home if they choose. If Aubrey and Jax want rules regarding attire in their home, they're free to do so."

"Our home is their home," Aubrey said. "I'll be far less concerned once they're potty trained, but we're not offended by Charlie's clear joy of his own skin."

"We'll revisit that in ten years," Will mused.

Rhys touched the tip of Jax's nose. "Uncle Jax, you look sad. Are you sad?"

"I'm not sad. I was just thinking, and thinking is hard."

"Hyrum says that thinking is the hardest part of the day but you gotta do it so no one else does it for you."

"Sometimes Hyrum is very wise."

"I still think you're sad."

"It's been a long few weeks, kiddo. I'm fine."

"You're upset. Let me kiss your forehead."

Jax leaned toward him. Rhys grabbed his uncle's face with tiny, sticky hands, and place a slow, gentle kiss on his forehead. Before he pulled back, Jax's eyes widened, and he sucked in a deep breath. "I love you, too, Rhys," he whispered.

"You don't hate your life, Uncle Jax. Do you?"

"No, I don't. I have a wonderful life."

What just happened?

"We can play school if you want to be a teacher."

"Thank you." Jax returned Rhys's kiss, planting one on his forehead. "I think I would enjoy that."

"Rhys." Aubrey reached over to pat his back. "Go inside and tell Jay that there are fresh cookies in the kitchen and that I said everyone could have one. Maybe if they're eating, the little ones will quiet down."

When the door closed, Jax said, "Will...that boy was inside my head, probing, and I could feel him looking for something very specific. He wasn't listening, he was searching. And when he found it?"

"You felt better," Aubrey guessed.

Aisha's eyes went wide. "I thought—"

"You wanted to know what else he can do," Jax said. "I think he just told me. He can do everything Hyrum can. Everything Will can. What Aubrey can. He sees what Oz and I see. And so much more."

"We suspected," Will said.

"It's Rhys," Jax whispered. "Oh, my god. That little boy just told me..."

"Sweetheart?" Aubrey prompted.

"He's the reason. He's the promise." Jax's voice cracked as he spoke. "He's why I won't step down. I can protect him. Who knows what else he can do? What he'll become?"

A wizard.

"Wick," Will sighed.

He wanted to do magic. It's all magic in a way. Maybe Rhys is the first real wizard. Your job is to make sure he's more like Hagar and not like Tobias.

"Tobias redeemed himself," Will reminded me.

After a lot of horrible things. And you don't know what might happen in Saint Francis. He might turn again.

"Rhys is not a wizard," Will said. "He's a little boy with a wonderful brain, and gifts we will teach him to control."

"How old were you, Will?" Aubrey asked. "When your parents realized what you could do?"

"Roughly his age, I believe. They suspected earlier."

"All those kids playing inside," Jax murmured. "What if they all have gifts? What the hell will we do?"

You should tell Jax about the school.

"He knows about the school," Will said.

No, I mean about the island, and what the school is really for.

Will had visited his parents in the other When, and while he was there, he spoke to Zed about the castle and asked when he'd purchased the land.

"It was given to me," old Zed told him. "Shortly before my

twenty-fourth birthday. A gift, with instructions to use interest from my trust fund to build the castle, and then the school."

"From?" Will prompted.

Zed grinned. "You know. Give him the island, Emperor. You already know what it's really for."

"But the Emperor who gave it to you—"

"Might not have been the Emperor who died."

Spaghetti, I'm telling you.

"You bought Treasure Island for my son," Jax uttered, unsure if that's what Will meant.

"Ozoo Enterprises bought Treasure Island," Will said. "Zed will be required to purchase it from Ozoo for a small sum to satisfy any tax liabilities, but yes, the island is now his, contingent upon the construction of the castle and the foundation of his school. It's more than an educational outlet for those who wish to learn to speak for the dead."

It's hiding in plain sight.

A place for all the people like you and like Rhys.

Will explained, briefly. Others with gifts would notice Rhys's abilities and find both a haven and compassion in the royal family. The school was a place for them to learn control, away from prying eyes and people who would be frightened by what they could do.

"Does his success depend on the government?" Jax asked. "Oz was Queen when Zed's alternate built it. The monarchy ended."

"Speak with him," Will urged. "The other Zed. I'm no longer concerned with preserving as much of the timeline as possible. Meet yourself, and meet your daughter, the queen. Find out what they did, and what they would do differently. Then create the laws you need to help Zed make that school a success."

Jax's chair creaked as he shifted.

He's excited.

"Come on," Jax said as he stood, "Let's have cookies with the monsters, and then you and I are jumping forward and having drinks with my kids and me, and—" he kissed Aubrey when she stood "—don't hold it against me if I plant one of those on your ninety-year-old self."

"Yes, I'll be terribly jealous if you kiss someone's great, great, great grandmother."

"Come with us. You can kiss old man Jax. Meet your middle-aged kids."

She hesitated. "Are you sure it's a good idea?"

"Angel, we're the King and Queen of Saint Francis. We can do anything we want. In any When we want. And what I want is to have a couple of cookies, kiss my grandkids, then go start whatever needs to happen to protect Rhys and everyone like him. In that order."

"And then build a castle," she sighed.

"The mother of all castles," he said. "For once? Damn, it's good to be King."

Also by Max Thompson

The Emperor of San Francisco: The Wick Chronicles, Book One
Ozoo: The Wick Chronicles, Book Two
Forked: The Wick Chronicles, Book Three
The Space Between Whens: Wick After Dark, Book One
The Blessings of Saint Wick: Wick After Dark, Book Two
The Whens of Wick: Return of the Wick Chronicles, Book One
The Book of Hyrum:Retrun of the Wick Chronicles, Book Two
JUMP: Return of the Wick Chronicles Book Three

The Psychokitty Speaks Out: Diary of a Mad Housecat
The Psychokitty Speaks Out: Something of Yours Will Meet A Toothy Death
The Rules: A Guide For People Owned By Cats
Bite Me: A Memoir (Of Sorts)
Epistle: A Love Letter
There Once Was a Cat From Nantucket

Visit Max online at his blog, The Psychokitty Speaks Out
http://psychokitty.blogspot.com
or on Facebook
http://facebook.com/thepsychokittyspeaksout

Books one of his people (K.A. Thompson) wrote

The Charybdis Novels:
Charybdis
As Simple As That
Finding Father Rabbit

The King and Queen of Perfect Normal
The Flipside of Here

It's Not About the Cookies
Rock the Pink

Visit K.A. Thompson online at her blog,
Thumper Thinks Out Loud
http://kathompson.blogspot.com

www.ingramcontent.com/pod-product-compliance
Lightning Source LLC
Chambersburg PA
CBHW070902260626
47162CB00007B/2528

* 9 7 8 1 9 3 2 4 6 1 6 7 1 *